3/10 = 3
11/10 = 3

THE DRAGONS OF ORDINARY FARM

by Tad Williams and Deborah Beale

pictures by Greg Swearingen

HARPER

An Imprint of HarperCollinsPublishers

For Hazel Beale, Tracie Phillips, Lisa Storer and Joanne Clare
Mothers and sisters all
And for David Beale
He's gone upstairs
But he knows, you know

The Dragons of Ordinary Farm
Text copyright © 2009 by The Beale-Williams Enterprise
Illustrations copyright © 2009 by Greg Swearingen

www.harpercollinschildrens.com

Library of Congress Cataloging-in-Publication Data
Williams, Tad.
  The dragons of Ordinary Farm / by Tad Williams & Deborah Beale ;
pictures by Greg Swearingen — 1st ed.
    p. cm.
  Summary: When their great-uncle Gideon invites Tyler and Lucinda to
his farm for the summer, they discover his animals are extremely unusual.
  ISBN 978-0-06-154345-6 (trade bdg.)
  [1. Farms—Fiction. 2. Animals, Mythical—Fiction. 3. Supernatural—
Fiction. 4. Uncles—Fiction. 5. Brothers and sisters—Fiction.] I. Beale,
Deborah. II. Title.
PZ7.W66826Dr 2009   2008035298
[Fic]—dc22   CIP
                                                                             AC

Typography by Joel Tippie
09 10 11 12 13 LP/RRDB 10 9 8 7 6 5 4 3 2 1
❖
First Edition

PROLOGUE

A HANDFUL OF SMALL BONES

Colin tested the parlor door. It was, as he expected, firmly closed and locked, but he hadn't planned on going in anyway. He got down on his knees and looked through the keyhole.

His mother, Gideon, and Mr. Walkwell were meeting in the parlor, where the old stained-glass window showed Eve in the Garden of Eden with the apple and the tree and the snake. Gideon had once said that whoever made the window obviously cared little for anything but the snake, and he was right: the creature traveled along the top, down the left-hand side, and then all the way along the bottom, and compared to Eve and the tree, it glowed and sparkled like the showroom window of a fancy jewelry store. The room was hardly ever used—the last time he'd been in there the dust had made Colin's nose itch something fierce. He immediately wished he had not thought about that, because now his nose was tickling as if the dust was all around him. If he sneezed—well, he didn't want to think about that. He could not afford even one more mistake. His mother was many things. *Forgiving* was not one of them.

Colin clamped his nose in his fingers and held his breath, killing the sneeze by sheer force of will. His mother's punishments were meant to "teach him to behave properly," as she always reminded him. He had never understood what that meant. The only thing they taught him was how terrible it was to get caught.

He stifled the sneeze at last—no small victory. He let go of his nose and placed his ear against the keyhole.

". . . I've invited two people to come to the farm for the summer," Gideon was saying. "They're distant relatives—a niece and nephew, two or three times removed, or however these things are calculated. Children, too, so perhaps that will be good for Colin."

"Outsiders," said Mr. Walkwell gruffly. "That is never good, Gideon."

"Interlopers." Colin's mother said it calmly, but her voice was harder than usual.

"Not interlopers," snapped Gideon with his usual high

impatience. "Relatives of mine, if you please."

Mr. Walkwell, the farm's chief overseer, spoke quietly as ever, his up-and-down accent as enigmatic as windblown patterns in dust. Colin had to strain to pick out his next words. "But why these outsiders, Gideon, even if they are family? Why now?"

"It is my decision," said Gideon crossly. "Are you going to fight me?"

"Of course not!" Colin heard his mother push back her chair and cross the room. Her approaching steps made him flinch—he almost turned and ran—but she stopped long before she reached the door. She had only got up to rub Gideon's shoulders, something she often did when the master of the farm was upset about something.

"We know you must have thought long and hard about this, Gideon," she told him kindly. "But the rest of us don't understand, that's all, and we all care about this place almost as much as you do."

"I'm out of options." Gideon's voice sounded raw. "I'm running out of money. I've been getting . . . letters from a lawyer. Threatening me. There are pressures you do not know about."

"Then tell us," Colin's mother said. "We are more than simply your employees, Gideon. You know that."

"No, I can't. And stop prying into my business!"

Which seemed to be all the explanation Gideon was going to give. That was how things usually went with the old man, Colin knew. Yes, that's what he was—an old man full of stupid, selfish secrets.

But his secrets control our lives! the boy thought angrily. *It's not just his farm—we live here too!*

The great front door of the house rattled and swung open. Colin jumped away from the keyhole and scuttled over to the grand staircase, praying that whoever was coming in would not see him in the shadows there. His heart hammered so hard inside his chest he thought it might break a rib. Then he heard the voice singing softly in German, and he stopped trembling quite so hard. It was only Sarah, the cook, carrying something through the lobby on her way to the kitchen. Another door opened and closed, then all was quiet again.

Colin got back to the keyhole in time to hear Gideon talking again. "... Are children. I'm glad of it! It will make them easier to control."

Mr. Walkwell said, "Or put them in greater danger."

"None of you understand," said Gideon. "I am being *hounded*, and it is not for the first time, either. But I will protect this farm with my life—my life!"

Silence returned. Colin watched the motes dance in the beams of light spilling across the lobby.

It was his mother who spoke at last. "Are you fearful that someone will take the farm away from you? It is difficult, I know, but perhaps ..." Even Colin's mother, brave as a lioness, was clearly worried about saying anything more.

"Perhaps you should think—just think, mind you—of marrying again . . . ?"

"Are you mad?" Gideon roared. "You forget your place, madam!" Suddenly there was a great scraping of chair legs and Colin, caught by surprise, had to throw himself back from the door and dive toward the shadows beside the staircase again.

The parlor door swung open and Gideon burst out barefoot, robe flapping, his face red with anger. Mr. Walkwell followed, his emotions as hidden as Gideon's were obvious. A few moments after they had both left the parlor, Gideon stomping through the door that led to his rooms and Mr. Walkwell out the front, returning to the farm, Colin's mother appeared, shutting the parlor door behind her as carefully as if she was leaving an invalid's bedchamber. She walked past Colin without looking at the shadows where he stood, then stopped just in front of the door that led toward the kitchen.

"Colin," she said without turning, "don't you have better things to be doing than spying on your elders?"

For long moments after she had gone through the door he could do nothing but crouch, breathing hard, feeling as though she had just punched him in the belly. At last he got to his feet and ran after her, despising himself as he did so but quite unable to stop himself. He would explain, he would tell her it was only an accident. Surely she wouldn't punish him for an accident?

But of course she would. He knew that. And she would know it wasn't an accident no matter how well he lied. She always did.

He would tell her he had just been trying to find her. That was mostly true, after all. He had hardly spoken to her or even seen her for several days. Sometimes it seemed like she didn't even remember she had a child.

The kitchen was empty—not even Sarah was there. Colin ran out the door that led to the vegetable garden. The light outside nearly blinded him and the heat was ferocious. Spring had not even ended, but the California weather had turned perversely, sickeningly hot. He spotted his mother on the far side of the garden, gliding swiftly and gracefully across it despite the blazing sun. Her strength amazed him, as always, and the longing for her suddenly overwhelmed everything else.

"Mother!" he cried. "Please, Mother!"

She had to be able to hear him—she was only a few yards away. Tears came into his eyes and the chasm of nothingness opened inside Colin's chest, an old and all-too-familiar acquaintance. She hurried on ahead of him across the open yard between the buildings, a mirage in the dust. Where was she going? Into the oak woods that began back there? She was always going off there by herself, or into the ancient greenhouse, or Grace's old sewing room. Why couldn't she just stop for once and talk to him instead?

"Mother!"

His strangled cry, it seemed, disturbed some of the animals in the Sick Barn just around the corner. Hoots and cries and screams rose into the gritty air, filling Colin's skull so painfully that everything echoed and throbbed. Something made an unearthly fluting, some other creature chattered and howled, and something else made a wet, barking sound, like a dog underwater. Colin gasped and covered his ears, trying to protect his poor pounding brain. "Stop it," he moaned. *"Stop it!"* But it did not stop—not for long moments more. Alarmed birds rose from nearby trees, shooting up into the sky.

The noises faded at last. His mother had come to a halt a short way into the oak grove, her back to him. As he stumbled up, she turned and silenced him with one look from her gray eyes. Then she turned back to the oak tree she seemed to have chosen, its pale, dry branches as shocked and contorted as bolts of lightning. Most of the green leaves had already withered in the unseasonable heat, which made it harder to see the bird's nest in the crook of one of the high branches.

Staring up at the nest, his mother began to sing, a swoop of wordless melody. Colin fell under the spell of it instantly, just as he always did, as he had since infancy. Her voice was as sweet and slow as warm honey. Colin's legs grew weak. Sometimes when he heard his beautiful, terrible mother sing, he thought he might be hearing the sounds the very first women in all the human race had used to lull their babies and soothe the sick. Her voice was so powerful, so loving, that when she raised it in song like this he could forgive her anything.

The melody went on, sparkling like sound made gold. A bird with black and white shoulders and a lovely red head crept out of the nest and moved cautiously down the bark of the oak tree, her tail flicking this way and that. For a moment she huddled in her own feathers like someone warming herself in a thick coat, then she fluttered down onto his mother's outstretched finger and squatted, as if making a curtsey, presenting her glorious wings and neck feathers to be ruffled, bobbing and wobbling comically on the slender finger like a puppy begging to be petted.

"Let me hold the bird," said Colin, charmed by the power of his beautiful mother. "Please . . ."

The singing stopped. His mother's fingers snapped closed like a trap. In the abrupt silence the handful of small bones breaking seemed loud as a drumroll. His mother opened her fingers and let the crushed bundle drop to the ground, one wing still fluttering feebly.

Colin clamped his hands over his mouth. He should have known. He should have known!

"Do you feel better now?" he shouted at her. He wanted to run but he couldn't. He looked from her to the dying bird. "Does that make you feel better?" He actually wanted to know, that was the terrible thing. As if maybe there actually was a reason for these things, and when he knew it he could forgive her again.

Patience Needle turned her clear gray eyes on her son. "Better?" she said. "A little, I suppose." She turned and began to walk briskly back toward the house. "Come along, Colin, and don't dawdle. We still have to decide on an appropriate punishment for a sneaking little spy, don't we?"

CHAPTER 1

AN INVITATION FOR THE KING
AND QUEEN OF ROMANIA

"You really want to ruin my life, don't you?" said Mom.

Tyler was playing his GameBoss and so far had managed to stay out of the fight, but his big sister never had the sense to keep her mouth shut. She jumped for any argument like a trout going after a baited hook.

"Oh, right, Mom," Lucinda said. "Ruin your life—as if! Just because we don't want you to go away all summer and leave us with some lady who smells like fish and whose kids eat their own boogers?"

"See, that's what you always do, sweetie," their mother replied. "You always exaggerate. First off, it's not going away all summer, it's a four-week singles retreat. Second,

Mrs. Peirho doesn't smell like fish all the time. That one day she was cooking something, that's all—some Portuguese thing." Mom waved her hand, trying to get her nails to dry. "And I don't know what you have against those kids. They both do really well in school. Martin goes to computer camp and everything. You could learn something from them."

Lucinda rolled her eyes. "Martin Peirho needs to go to camp for the rest his life—that's the one place you're allowed to have your name written on your underpants."

Tyler turned *SkullKill* up louder, but he knew it wouldn't do any good. When Mom and Lucinda argued and he tried to drown them out by cranking the volume, they just got louder too. It was hard enough to deal with fast-moving vampire gnomes and flying batbots without all that yelling in the background.

"Good Lord, Tyler, turn that thing down!" Mom shouted. "No, turn it off. We're going to have a family talk. Right now."

Tyler groaned. "Can't you just beat us instead?"

For a moment Mom got really angry. "Like I *ever* hit you. You better not say things like that in front of Mrs. Peirho and her family—they'll think I'm some kind of negligent mother." She stomped to the door. "I'm going to get the mail. When I come back, I want you both sitting on the couch and ready to listen."

Tyler sighed. He considered leaving—just walking out

and going to Todd's house. What was there to stop him? Mom *didn't* hit, and Tyler figured he could live through just about any yelling she could come up with. After all, he was pretty sure he'd already heard every kind there was.

He glanced at his older sister. She was sitting on the edge of the sofa, her arms wrapped around herself, leaning forward like her stomach hurt. Her expression was despairing. "*You* don't want to go stay with the Peirhos any more than I do, Tyler," she said to him. "Why don't you say something?"

"Because it never does any good."

Mom came back in wearing her "I'm calm now" face, her hands full of catalogs and bills. She sat down in her chair with the mail in her lap. "Now, let's start over, shall we? Instead of yelling about what you don't want to do, maybe we can talk about the good things that could come from this situation."

"Since when," said Lucinda, "have there been any good things for this family coming out of any situation?"

Mom's face clouded, her eyes shut tight. Tyler braced himself, wondering if she was going to yell, wondering if he was going to regret sticking around. But, to his surprise, Mom opened her eyes and even tried to smile. "Look, I know it's been tough for you since your father and I got divorced. Of course it has. . . ."

Tyler blew out air. What was the use of talking about

it? Talking wasn't going to bring Dad back or make Mom happier, whatever she thought. Talking wasn't going to turn Lucinda back into the older sister who used to make him dinner when Dad first left, who would cook macaroni and cheese and eat it with him on the nights when Mom couldn't do anything but watch television and cry.

". . . and of course it's difficult for kids when their mother wants a little time on her own," their mother said.

All the way across the room, Tyler could feel Lucinda struggling not to start yelling again.

"It's a singles retreat," their mother continued. "It isn't anything sleazy. It's safe and it's a perfectly nice place to meet people."

Lucinda lost the battle with herself. "God, don't be so desperate, Mom, it's pathetic."

Tyler watched Mom's face go all loose and miserable and his stomach clenched. Sometimes these days he felt like he hated his sister. Lucinda saw Mom's expression, too, and her face filled with shame, but it was too late—the words had been spoken.

Mom picked up the mail and began shuffling through it, but it was like she had suddenly gotten old and exhausted. Tyler felt sick. She might not be the greatest parent in the world but she did her best—she just sort of lost focus sometimes.

"Bills," said Mom, sighing. "That's all we get."

"Why can't we stay with Dad?" Tyler asked suddenly.

"Because your father is in a very important place right now with his new family—or at least that's what he says." She frowned. "Personally I think it's because that woman has him completely wrapped around her finger."

"He doesn't want us and you don't want us," said Lucinda miserably. "Two parents alive but we're still orphans."

Tyler watched, almost impressed, as Mom calmed herself once more—she must have started reading those parenting magazines again. "Of course I want you," she said. "And I understand that you guys are angry. But since your father left it's been hard. I can't be both parents all by myself. How can I find someone else if I spend all my time sitting home in my bathrobe, doing nothing but arguing with my kids?"

"But why do you *have* to find someone?" asked Lucinda. "Why?"

"Because it's a tough world out there. And because I get lonely, you know?" Mom gave them both her most sincere, brave-but-about-to-cry look. "Can't you two just help me out for once?"

"By disappearing?" demanded Lucinda, losing it all over again. "By moving into Castle Stinkfoot and spending the whole summer watching Martin and Anthony play *Star Wars* and take turns bubbling milk out their noses?"

"Jeez!" Mom rolled her eyes. "Who are you two, the king and queen of Romania? Can't you ever do anything that isn't exactly what your highnesses want?" She paused, staring at the open letter in her lap. "Gideon? I don't remember any Uncle Gideon."

Lucinda had picked up the family cat and was holding him on her lap, even though he didn't really seem to want to be there. When Lucinda was upset she petted the cat so much that Tyler figured someday she'd just rub the fur right off him. "Isn't there anyone else we can stay with?" she asked. "Why can't I stay with Caitlin? Her family said it's okay."

"Because they don't have room to take Tyler, too, and I'm not going to have him go stay at the neighbors' by himself," said Mom, but she was reading the letter and not paying much attention. She lifted the envelope and looked at it, then went back to the letter again.

Tyler scowled. "I'd rather watch Martin Peirho eat boogers than have to sit around listening to you and Caitlin talk about boys all summer." His sister and her friends spent all their time talking about the guys on television, musicians and actors, as if they knew them personally, and about boys in school as if they were the guys on television— *"Oh, I think Barton isn't ready to have a real relationship yet, he's still getting over Marlee."* Tyler hated it. He wished there was a game where you could chase stupid, fakey celebrity boys like that and shoot them all into little pieces. That would *rock*.

"Well, maybe you won't have to do either." Mom was looking strange, the way she looked when someone was giving her good news she didn't quite believe, like the time Tyler's teacher had told her how much she liked having Tyler in her class, how hard he worked in math and how good he was on the computer. Tyler had been proud, but at the same time his mom's surprise made him wonder if she'd actually thought he was stupid or something. "Apparently you have a great-uncle Gideon. Gideon Goldring. Some relative of my dad's, I guess. I sort of remember him and Aunt Grace, now that I think about it. But he's dead, isn't he?" She obviously realized this sounded pretty silly. "I mean, I thought he was dead. It's been years . . . He's a farmer, it says here, and he has a big place out in the middle of the state and he wants you to come visit. Standard Valley, it's called. I'm not sure where that is, exactly. . . ." She trailed off.

"What valley?" his sister asked. "Who's this Gideon? Some crazy old family member, and you're going to send us to stay with him now?"

"No, he's not crazy."

"But you don't know that—"

"*Stop it*, Lucinda—just give me a moment to read this carefully! You obviously learned how to be patient from your father." Mom squinted at the letter. "It says that he's been meaning for a while to get in touch with me since we're almost the last of the family. He says he's sorry he hasn't contacted me sooner. And he says he understands that I have two lovely children. Ha!" Mom did her best

18

sarcastic laugh. "That's what it says here—I wonder who told him *that* whopper? And he wants to know if they— that's you two—could come and spend some time with him on his farm this summer." She looked up. "Well? That solves all our problems, doesn't it?"

Lucinda looked at her in horror. "A *farm*? We'll be slaves, Mom! You don't even know this man, you said so—he might not really be your uncle. Maybe he just wants kids so he can work them to death milking cows and pigs and everything."

"I'm pretty sure he's related to your grandfather. And you can't milk pigs." Mom returned her attention to the letter. "I don't think so, anyway."

"So now you're going to send us away to some . . . death ranch," Lucinda said, almost to herself, and then she dropped her hair over her face and clutched her arms around her middle again.

Tyler didn't like arguing, but he wasn't any happier about this idea than his sister. "Not a ranch. A farm." He had a sudden memory of a picture he'd seen in his American history book, a decaying shack in the middle of a huge field of dust, a place as empty as the moon's surface. "Uh-uh. No way." He didn't think they had the internet on farms. He was even more sure they didn't have GameBoss and *SkullKill.* "I'm *definitely* not going to any boring farm all summer." He crossed his arms over his chest.

"Don't be so closed-minded," said Mom, as though they

were talking about whether or not he should try a bite of something gross like fried squid instead of ruining an entire summer that they'd never get back for the rest of their lives. "Who knows, you might really enjoy yourselves. You could . . . go on hayrides. You might even *learn* something."

"Yeah," said Lucinda. "Learn how to be pecked to death by chickens. Learn how people break child labor laws."

Tyler leaned forward and snatched the envelope from Mom's hand and examined the strange, squinchy handwriting. On the back of the envelope was a little drawing of two old-fashioned letters tangled together—they looked like an *O* and an *F*—and a return address that explained those two letters and confirmed all his worst fears.

"Mom, look at this!" he said, holding it out. "Oh my God, look at the name of this place! *Ordinary Farm!*"

"Yes, it does sound nice, doesn't it?" she said.

CHAPTER 2

FLAMING COWS AND
WINDOW MONKEYS

Mom was in such a hurry to get them to the station that Lucinda forgot her hair dryer. She couldn't imagine how she was going to get through the summer without a hair dryer, and she was pretty sure that they wouldn't have something that modern and useful on some stinky old farm in the middle of nowhere.

"Don't worry about it too much," Tyler told her as they walked across the train station parking lot. "They probably won't have electricity, either."

Mom looked at her watch three times between the parking lot and the platform where the big board said the train to Willowside would leave. "Come on!" Lucinda told her.

"Would it really kill you to be a little late to this singles thing? This is probably the last time you'll ever see your children before we get mangled to death by some kind of farm machinery."

"I'm not even leaving for that until tomorrow morning, as it happens," said Mom. "I'm just worried about you getting on your train." She grabbed one of Tyler's backpack straps to get him to move faster, but Tyler yanked it away again. "It's the only one for days that stops in Standard Valley—I don't think it's a very big town. Oh, good, there it is. Come on, children! Give me a kiss. Don't forget to write and tell me all about it. I'll find out the address of the retreat and have Mrs. Fleener next door forward your mail to me."

"Which means that when we write to tell you we're prisoners of a satanic cult and they're about to sacrifice us, you'll find out, what, two or three weeks later?" Lucinda asked, only half joking. It was like they were Hansel and Gretel abandoned in the woods or something.

"You kids, you're so funny." Mom shook her head. "You know, if you stopped complaining you just might enjoy yourselves. Now, give me that kiss."

Lucinda kissed her mother on the cheek even though she was angry, just in case it *was* the last time they ever saw each other. She didn't really think they were going to get chewed up by a haymower or something, but she couldn't help feeling frightened and sad, and the fact that she was tall enough now that Mom didn't have to bend over to be kissed just made her feel even more of both.

"Hurry, kids. Oh, and here's something that came in the mail for you from your uncle Gideon—I almost forgot!" Mom handed the parcel wrapped in brown paper to Tyler, since he was nearest, then blew them both a kiss and stood smiling brightly as they climbed onto the train. When they got into the compartment Lucinda went to the window. Mom waved to her as the train began to pull away. Lucinda waved back, but it made her feel like a dumb kid, like standing in line for Santa at the mall when you were too old.

We don't even have any bread crumbs to leave a trail, she thought sadly as the station disappeared behind them. *And no one's coming to look for us, anyway.*

The train was old, with paint chipped off the walls of the coaches and the seats sunken and wrinkled by what had to be a hundred years of other people's bottoms. It made Lucinda want to stand up all the way, but Mom had said it would take them at least five hours to get to Standard Valley so she led her brother to the least gross-looking of the available seats. The compartment was fairly full, mostly with people in clothes that didn't quite fit or who looked like English was their second or even third language. Many of them looked pretty miserable. Or maybe that was because that was how *she* felt.

Sometimes Lucinda really wished she knew how to stop being sad and angry.

23

They were a long way into their journey before either of them remembered the package Mom had given them. Tyler had been plugged into his GameBoss Portable—he loved the thing and could play it for hours at a stretch, deaf and blind to the outside world. Lucinda, eyes closed, had been thinking mournfully about the summers her friends were going to have—Caitlin and her family going to Tyner Lake to water-ski and swim and hike, and Trina and Delia, who, even though they were staying home, were still going to the city *and* taking guitar lessons. The two of them would probably learn to be musicians and wind up on television someday, hanging around with all the other famous people and appearing on commercials while Lucinda spent the rest of her life shearing sheep.

"This is pretty weird," Tyler said. He had found and unwrapped the package.

"What?"

"There's a note in it. It says, 'Lucinda and Tyler, please read this and pay close attention. It could save your lives.' What does *that* mean?"

"A note in what?"

"This book Uncle What's-his-name sent."

"Gideon."

"Huh?" Tyler was turning the pages of the book now.

"Never mind." She looked over, almost interested, but it didn't look like a real book. It had a kind of paper cover, for one thing, like someone had made it at a copier place.

Lucinda watched the tail end of a town going past the train windows. *Everything looks gross from a train window,* she thought. You could see into everybody's backyard and they always had their laundry hanging out and some pathetic, rusty old swing set for the kids.

Something flicked past the window so quickly that Lucinda jumped, startled. She thought it had actually brushed the glass—a bird, probably.

"Do cows have fire breath?" Tyler asked.

It took a second for her to understand what he'd said. "What are you talking about?" she said finally.

"Just answer the question."

"In real life?" She frowned, thinking. She didn't actually know much about cows. Milk. Gross-looking things hanging down underneath them that the milk came out of. Saying "Moo." Standing around in fields. Eating grass. None of those things had anything to do with fire. "No," she said. "Of course they don't."

"Man, this is a really weird book." Lucinda tried to take it from him to look at it, but he pulled it away from her. "Back off. I had it first."

She was too depressed to argue. There would be plenty of time for arguing later, anyway—all summer long, in fact. She put her feet on top of her suitcase and picked up the brown paper wrapping that he had discarded. The neat handwriting was different from the cramped scrawl in the original letter, which both she and Tyler had read several times, trying to decide if this farm visit was actually going to be as bad as they thought, or maybe even worse. The package was addressed to "*Master Tyler Jenkins and Miss Lucinda Jenkins,*" which was so silly it almost made her laugh. Along the bottom, in big letters, it said, "*DO NOT OPEN UNTIL YOU ARE ON THE TRAIN TO STANDARD VALLEY.*" The back had the same "*OF*" stamp as had been on the letter.

Different handwriting. What did that mean? That their surprise great-uncle wasn't the only crazy person they were going to have to deal with?

"Hey, listen," Tyler said. "This is so bizarre. 'It should never be forgotten, even in the most routine tasks of care and feeding, that these animals are large and dangerous. Even a belch from a contented . . . cow . . . can throw out a six-foot flame. Many . . . cow . . . keepers have remembered this only after being badly burned. Flame-retardant suits and other special equipment are recommended for all tasks. . . .'" He turned to her. "That means they can burp fire!"

"What are you talking about? Does the book really say that—that they are flaming cows?" Now she was beginning to feel seriously nervous. "This guy *is* crazy. We need to get off this train."

"What's asbestos? Because you're supposed to wear some kind of gloves made of it when you feed the cows."

Lucinda shook her head. "I don't know. Let me see that."

"Forget it."

"Give it to me or you won't get any of the money Mom gave me for lunch."

"That's not your money!"

"That's not just your book, either. It's addressed to both of us." He only glared back at her. "Come on, Tyler. Let me look at it. This is scaring me."

He stared for a moment longer, then handed it over. It was floppy and heavy and up close it really did look like someone had gone to Kinko's or somewhere like that to make it themselves. The cover, which was on even cheaper paper than the rest of it, said "Care and Feeding of Cows by Gideon Goldring." She opened it up. The very first page said:

Some may wonder why I would write this book when so few people will ever have so much as the glimpse of a cow , let alone take care of one. But the sort of information contained herein is hard-won and should not be lost. I am no longer a young man and it could be that I will not be around to share all my knowledge with whoever shall follow me. Therefore, I commit it to writing, in hopes that those who are to come will see their cows not only survive but thrive and fly high.

"*Fly high?*" Lucinda looked at Tyler. "He *is* crazy! He's really crazy!"

"You're telling me. Wait until you get to the part about catching them—it's all about putting nets in the tops of trees and stuff."

Lucinda peered at the page. "Hold on. This didn't use to say 'cow,' I don't think." She stared, then rubbed at the paper with her finger. "Before they copied it somebody went through this and put 'cow' in over some other word. See, it's shorter than the original word. There's a lot of white on either side."

"Yeah, you're right—here and here too. And here." Tyler leafed forward a couple of pages. "All the places that say 'cow' used to say something else." He looked at his sister. "What's that all about?"

"I don't know. I'm just wondering if we have enough money to get home if we get off in the next town." She took the money out of her purse and counted it. "Twenty dollars. Do you think that's enough? It's not enough."

"It's enough to get us lunch and a couple of Cokes."

Something slid past the window again outside, a little swipe of shadow, but when Lucinda looked up she saw nothing but the endless, dry California valley slipping past. "I can't believe Mom!" she said. "Sending us off to some crazy man who thinks cows breathe fire, and she doesn't even give us enough money to get home again if he tries to kill us or something! As soon as we get to the next stop I'm going to call her to come get us."

Tyler laughed, but he wasn't happy. "Then you better

work on your *Star Wars* trivia, because she'll take us straight to the Peirhos' house. Martin and Anthony are going to spend all summer quizzing you about what kind of underpants Boba Fett wears."

Lucinda shuddered. People always said she was too negative—her teachers even asked her why she never tried to see the good side of things—but this was proof, right here, that no matter how bad you thought things were going to be, they turned out *even worse.*

For once, Tyler was right. Arguing wouldn't help. There was no escape. "Well," she said, "I guess being killed by an exploding cow fireball will be less horrible than having to watch the Peirho twins and their battling action figures."

Tyler laughed. Lucinda almost felt better. Then something brushed her window again, and this time she looked up just in time to see a tiny furry head no bigger than a kiwi fruit looking in at her from the top of the window. For a moment it seemed even more bizarre than it was, its mouth at the top and its eyes at the bottom, until she realized the creature must be hanging upside down on the side of the train like a bat, watching her. She even thought she could see the tip of a leathery wing pressed on the glass. But it wasn't a bat.

"Tyler—" She stared right at it, certain that if she looked away it would disappear. "Tyler, there's a *monkey* on the train." It disappeared anyway, flipping away like a leaf blown from a car windshield.

"Yeah, and it's you," he said, not really paying attention. "Whoa, do you really think we'll get to see some cows explode? Like in *FarmFrag*?" He grinned, then put in his earbuds and said, *way* too loud, "*Maybe it will be an okay summer after all. I've never seen a real cow blow up!*"

The monkey face was gone from her window, but now everyone else in the compartment was staring at Lucinda and her brother. She shrank down in her seat and held the strange book in front of her face. Had she only imagined what she'd seen? Because outside of movies she was pretty darn sure there weren't any such things as flying monkeys.

Of course, there weren't any such things as fire-breathing cows, either. Lucinda tried to focus on the words on the page, but that wasn't working. She couldn't help wondering whether the summer ahead was going to be as boring as she'd first thought, terrifyingly weird, or somehow both at the same time.

CHAPTER 3

THE MAN WITH
THE WRONG NAME

The station sign for their stop was old and beat-up, missing a couple letters. WELCOME TO TANDARD ALLEY.

Tyler wiped sweat off his forehead, then pulled his baseball cap back down over his messy brown hair. It had been so hot on the train that he had drunk three whole soft drinks, but it was even hotter here.

Now that the train had gone, the platform was empty. Tyler felt like the two of them were the only people in the whole tiny town.

"So where's Uncle Gideon?" said Lucinda. They wandered through the empty station and looked out into the empty narrow street that ran in front of it. A few houses were in view but nobody seemed to be outside—not that Tyler blamed them. "Or are we supposed to walk to his crazy farm and die in the heat?" Lucinda continued.

"Someone's going to meet us," Tyler said, looking around. The station had nothing more than a ticket booth and a couple of vending machines, but it was cooler than the platform. "That's what Mom said, anyway."

"Like she was even paying attention." Lucinda pushed damp hair out of her eyes. "All she wanted was to go off to her singles thing."

Tyler just shrugged. A lot of what Lucinda complained about was true, but what could you do about it? Life was rotten if you were a kid. Grown-ups just did what they wanted, then said it was for your own good. You could go nuts worrying about it or you could concentrate on something more interesting. He reached into his pocket for his GameBoss, then stopped.

He had been hearing the strange sound for a few moments, a clop-clop-clopping that reminded him of something on television. Westerns, old Westerns, the kind his father forced him to watch on their weekend visits, thinking that Tyler liked them too. He didn't, but there was no purpose in saying anything, because if he said he didn't want to watch the movies Dad would just take him to the park or something, and stand around smoking and watching Tyler pretend to play on the jungle gym like he was still a little kid. Worse, they might go out to have a meal and Dad would pretend to be really interested in who Tyler's friends were and make him answer questions about what he was learning in school.

As if.

Clop, clop, clop.

"There's a horse out there," Tyler said.

"What?" Lucinda was looking around furiously as if Uncle Gideon, the flaming-cow man, was suddenly going to appear in the middle of the tiny station.

"A horse. Out there in the street, I guess. I can hear a horse."

"You're crazy." But she followed him out to the little street outside and its few rundown houses with their fences leaning every way but straight up and down.

There was indeed a horse—a big brown horse, standing in the street outside the station, and it was attached to some kind of huge wagon piled high with sacks. A very strange-looking man sat on a bench at the front of the wagon, holding the horse's reins and looking out at them from under the brim of an ancient straw hat. He had very tanned skin, a thin, hooked nose, and a puff of gray beard on his chin. His eyes were mostly hidden in the shade of his wide-brimmed hat.

"You are Tyler and Lucinda?" His accent made the words bump in the wrong places, like someone pretending to be a funny foreigner on television. "Get up on the cart, please."

"Are you . . . are you Uncle Gideon?" Tyler asked at last.

The man shook his head slowly. "No, no. Not me. I am Mr. Walkwell. I work for him." He climbed down and tossed the kids' heavy suitcases into the wagon and onto the sacks piled there as if they were pillows. Tyler couldn't help noticing that this Mr. Walkwell guy had very small feet. He wore little old-fashioned boots that laced up and looked like they should belong to a child, not a tall man. He also walked with an awkward two-footed limp, as though he were treading barefoot over broken glass. Just to make things stranger still, his boots made a weird crunching noise with each step. Tyler looked at Lucinda. She looked back. "Somebody has the wrong name," she whispered.

Mr. Walkwell swung himself back up onto the seat and gave them a sour look, as though he knew what they were thinking. "Get in." He had strange eyes, too, very red around the edges, as though he had been swimming. Also, the centers seemed more yellow than brown.

"Do we sit on the bench next to you?" Tyler asked.

"Better, I think, than if you sit on top of the feed bags," said Mr. Walkwell, his voice dry as the air. "They slide."

Tyler clambered up. Halfway he began to lose his balance, but the bearded man reached down and wrapped his thin, strong brown fingers around Tyler's wrist and lifted him up to the seat as easily as if Tyler was a loaf of bread. When Lucinda had climbed up too, Mr. Walkwell clucked once to the horse and the cart moved off. That was the last sound the man made until they were well outside of town.

Not only was this guy talkative and charming, Tyler thought, he smelled too. It wasn't a rancid smell, though, just . . . strong. He smelled like sweat and dry grass and . . . and animals, Tyler decided, among other things. Well, that made sense for someone who worked on a farm, didn't it?

After something like a quarter-hour of rolling slowly along past yellow fields, they turned off the main road onto a wide dirt track. This new road wound up through golden hills spotted with trees until the last bends disappeared in rocky high ground that kept rising beyond them.

"Where's the farm?" he asked.

"In the valley on the other side of the hills," said Mr. Walkwell.

"It's a long way. Why didn't you bring a car?"

He turned and gave Tyler a look that was downright unfriendly. "No. I do not like those noisy machines. They are unnatural."

Lucinda groaned. Tyler almost did the same. The farm was beginning to look like a very bad bet for television and other modern conveniences. He tried not to think about the horror of being unable to recharge his Game-Boss Portable for an entire summer.

As they crossed the crest of the hill they came out of the trees and saw Standard Valley stretched before them, carpeted with golden meadows, walled here and in the far distance with tree-covered hills that were surprisingly high, just a little short of being mountains. Below them wound a stripe that flashed silver in the afternoon sunlight—a river. In the very far distance, like a wall at the edge of the world, loomed some true mountains, the Sierras. The valley looked like something out of an oil painting. A nice one.

"Wow," said Tyler. "It's . . ."

"It's beautiful." Lucinda sounded surprised. Mr. Walkwell smiled for the first time, which brought a whole different look to the old man's weathered brown face, something charming and wild, the grin of a rascally pirate. He flapped the reins against the horse's back and they started down.

Soon they could hear the sound of the river, a gentle rush like wind in the treetops. The meadows they passed looked like there should be cows in them, but there were none to be seen anywhere, or pigs, or, in fact, anything farmlike at all.

"Where are the animals?" asked Tyler. For a moment

he wondered if it was the kind of farm that only grew cauliflower or something, but Uncle Gideon had definitely sent them a book about cows—about *some* kind of cows, anyway—and besides, they weren't seeing any asparagus fields, either.

"You can't see them from here," the old man said, then looked up at the empty sky. "But perhaps some of them are watching you."

Tyler and Lucinda exchanged another worried look.

As they neared the bottom of the hills, the road turned away from the river and mounted a low prominence. From the top they could see what had lain hidden near the base of the high ridge.

"It's . . . it's huge!" Lucinda said quietly.

Tyler had never seen anything like it. A cluster of wooden buildings stretched below them, connected by walkways and gardens, all wrapped around a gigantic wooden mansion several stories high in places, a sprawling pile of roofs and walls, with balconies and oddly shaped windows and even a tower on one side of it that looked a little like a wooden lighthouse. The hodgepodge of buildings was painted way too many colors to make sense, mostly reds and yellows and light brown and white, and it all looked like someone had created a gigantic space station out of really old buildings, then set it down carefully here in the middle of nowhere. Tyler could only stare. "What *is* it?" he said at last.

"That?" said Mr. Walkwell. "That is the house. That is Ordinary Farm."

"It's like something on television!" Lucinda whispered to Tyler as Mr. Walkwell drove the cart toward the huge, ramshackle farmhouse. "Like *Survivor: Transylvania.*"

"Or a game," he said. "*Castle Gorefest,* with ghouls in the towers and dungeons full of canker-monsters."

Whatever it looked like, it certainly wasn't what Lucinda had expected. Instead of a boring old farmhouse with a red barn or something, this place looked like someone had started with a normal farmhouse a long time ago, but just decided for some reason to keep on going, adding bits and pieces like a hyperactive kid who had been given several extra sets of Lego and was intent on using them all.

"Who built this weird house?" Tyler asked.

"Octavio Tinker," said Mr. Walkwell. He frowned, which brought something scary into his face. "You will keep respect in your voice for Ordinary Farm, and for those who have crossed the river. In his day Octavio Tinker was a very famous man—and a very, very wise man as well."

Crossed the river? He decided it must be the strange-old-farm-guy way of saying "dead." As far as the famous part went, however, he was impressed. But besides being famous, this Tinker guy must have been seriously weird—the house sure was. The pattern of it almost had the look of something natural, like a spiderweb or the coral in his science class aquarium, a spiraling of outbuildings, sheds, and odd square towers that swirled out from what was clearly the main house at the front and center of the property.

They rolled down and around the long half circle of driveway. The farm buildings and the different parts of the house seemed to face in a dozen separate directions, as if they had been set in place almost at random. The afternoon sun bounced back from the windows in unexpected ways that made Tyler feel dazzled and a little sick. Nearly at the center of the ring of odd structures, almost a hundred yards away from the sprawling front of the house, stood something that looked like it belonged in a psycho-killer movie, a gray wooden building several stories high with a big pipe slanting down from near the top, and no windows.

"Check out the haunted house," he whispered to Lucinda from behind his hand. "Who do you think lives there, Freddy Krueger?"

"Or maybe the *Friday the 13th* guy," Lucinda whispered back.

"It is a grain silo, but it is not being used," Mr. Walkwell informed him. "I do not know the names you say. No one lives there. And it is a dangerous place for children. Mr. Goldring will be very angry if you try to go there."

They were so daunted by his sharp ears that they both stopped talking.

The wagon rumbled to a halt beside a long porch that ran along the front of the house but just . . . *stopped* at both ends, as though it had once connected two other parts of the main building that weren't there anymore. The huge front door was surrounded by panels of stained glass.

"Get off, now," said Mr. Walkwell, as if he had been waiting patiently for quite long enough.

The children jumped down, still looking around. As they climbed up onto the porch, some distance away a tractor towing a huge empty trailer appeared from around one corner of the house, putt-putting along not much faster than a person could walk as it headed out across the open space. The big bearded man driving it swung around in his seat when he saw them and waved to Mr. Walkwell. "I took her to the Sick Barn!" he shouted.

Mr. Walkwell raised his hand to show the man he'd heard. "That is Ragnar," he told them. "You will come to know him well."

"Ragnar? Wow," said Tyler. "Sounds like some barbarian hero out of *RuneQuest*. And put who in the Sick Barn? Was it one of the animals? One of the cows?" He felt like he'd been holding in the questions for days. "And what's up with the cows here, anyway—do they catch on fire all the time or something?"

Mr. Walkwell stared at him for a moment, then pointed a brown finger toward the front door. "Mrs. Needle waits for you there. She will take you to Mr. Goldring, your uncle. Save your questions for him."

Tyler was feeling a little better—the tractor showed that there was *some* technology on the farm, whether Mr. Walkwell liked the stuff or not. All Tyler really needed was enough electricity to recharge the GameBoss. And this Mrs. Needle—he could tell she would be a plump, kindly little old lady like Mrs. Santa Claus from some children's Christmas special. She'd greet them with cookies and lemonade and say "My goodness!" a lot.

The front door swung open before they could knock, revealing a young man with a thin pale face. He wore a white short-sleeved shirt and gray slacks, as though his parents had just forced him to dress up for church. His thick black hair had been combed down with water at some point, but was beginning to pull loose into funny crooked tufts.

"Ah," he said. "You must be the children."

Tyler didn't like his superior expression, and he sure didn't like being called a child, either. "Yeah? Who are *you*?"

The young man's eyebrow rose, as though questions were rude. "My name is Colin." He couldn't be much more than Lucinda's age, Tyler guessed, but he seemed older because he was tall and because of his weird grown-up clothes and the stiff way he stood.

"We're supposed to talk to Mrs. Needle."

"That's my mother. She's very busy right now, but I

41

suppose I can take you to her." He stepped aside, beckoning them in as though he too was very busy and was just making some time for them out of kindness. He didn't offer to help with the suitcases.

Tyler was taken aback by the size of the entrance hall—it seemed more like the lobby of some old hotel. A big black iron chandelier with dozens of bulbs hung from the high ceiling—so there was electricity, at least—and the walls were covered with striped pale green wallpaper and old museumy paintings of people and landscapes. Padded benches and overstuffed sofas with flowery upholstery stood against every wall, framing close to a dozen doors leading off this huge front room. The center of the hall was dominated by a long staircase that forked upward to the left and right.

"*Sound of Music*," Lucinda said softly.

"What?"

"You remember, the kids singing? It was on a staircase like that."

Tyler rolled his eyes. That had been his sister's favorite movie, not his. Still, he couldn't help being impressed by the staircase, not because it looked like it was waiting for the Von Trapp kids, but because he now saw that each set of stairs ended flat against the wall—no hallways, no landings, no doors. The grand staircase led precisely nowhere.

"This way," Colin told them.

Tyler leaned toward his sister. "Scooby-Doo, where are you?" he whispered, grinning, but Lucinda was looking a little sickly and didn't seem to enjoy his joke.

Colin led them all the way to the back of the hall and opened a door. The room beyond was a kitchen three or four times the size of their living room at home. The noises of pans clanking and water running rolled out. Several people seemed to be working there, but Tyler couldn't quite see any of them past Colin.

"Mother," he announced, "the children are here."

A moment later a woman in a rather old-fashioned cotton dress walked out, letting the door fall shut behind her so that the lively kitchen scene suddenly vanished. Her black hair was as long and straight as a girl's, her skin even paler than her son's, both of which made it hard to guess her age. She was pretty in a thin, sharp-boned way, but it was her gray-blue eyes that made her extraordinary, Tyler realized—eyes so intense they almost glittered.

For a long moment the woman examined the children as they examined her. At last she smiled. It wasn't the most cheerful smile Tyler had ever seen, more like the kind teachers gave you when you made a joke about why your homework was late.

"Welcome to Ordinary Farm, children," she said. "I am Patience Needle, Mr. Goldring's assistant and the housekeeper at Ordinary Farm. I will be in charge of you whilst you are staying with us."

"Cool. So when do we see some animals?" Tyler asked.

Her smile went away for a second, but when it returned it seemed entirely friendly and natural. Mrs. Needle's English accent made her sound like one of those classy television actresses on public television. "Those details are up to Mr. Goldring, of course," she said. "But I am sure he will want to show you the farm soon enough."

"Where is he?" said Lucinda. "Our uncle, I mean. Great-uncle."

"I'm afraid he's not feeling well today, otherwise he would have been down to meet you. He asked me to send his apologies. Colin will show you up to your rooms."

"*Mother,*" Colin said, as though he'd been asked to carry them on his shoulders. "I have things to do."

"Then you can do them after you show Lucinda and Tyler to their rooms. I'm very busy, Colin, with Gideon ill. Run along."

Mother and son looked at each other. Colin turned away first. "Fine. Follow me." He stalked through a door on the other side of the room and let it bang shut behind him.

When they followed, Lucinda and Tyler found a steep staircase looming behind the door. At the top was a hallway covered with sweet-smelling wood panels. Tyler climbed the stairs and asked, "So, what kind of animals *do* you have here, besides cows? Horses? Chickens?"

"I don't work with the animals," said Colin as the corridor turned first one way, then another, closed doors standing on either side like sentries. "I'm modernizing the systems." His superior tone had returned.

Yeah, thought Tyler. *Horse and wagon picking up the guests. Nice job so far.*

They came to a new corridor, dark despite the dim electric lights every few yards that filled the hall with long, jittering shadows. The bulbs were so ancient and flickery that they looked like they had been in place here since Edison invented them.

"This house really is crazy," muttered Tyler.

"It was built by a genius." Colin actually sounded angry, like Tyler had called *him* crazy. "Octavio Tinker was one of the greatest scientific minds of all time. Very few people can even begin to understand his work. He was your mother's great-uncle. She's a Tinker, right? And if you're lucky enough—" He stopped suddenly, two angry spots of red high on his cheeks. Tyler thought how weird it was that this gangly, dark-haired kid knew more about their family relations than they did. Tyler opened his mouth to ask about this, but Colin cut him off like a slammed door. He turned right suddenly and led them into a final, very short hallway that ended in a wall with a window in it.

Two doors faced each other across the hall. Lucinda dropped her suitcase and went to look out the window. There was a flowering cherry tree at one side—the prettiest of a number of trees in front of their windows—and a gigantic white concrete building in the far distance.

The strange building looked like a tube half-sunk in the ground. Tyler, gazing out too, wondered what it was—a hangar or a bomb shelter of some sort? It was like something that had dropped from the sky, landing with a titanic crash and kicking up earth all around.

Colin Needle pushed open the doors on either side of the corridor. The rooms were small and neat, each with an old wooden-framed bed covered with a crazy quilt, a desk, and bare white walls. The room on the left had a bigger window and a good view of the cherry tree.

"This one's mine," Lucinda announced.

"Fine," said Tyler, and slung his bag into the other room.

"I have work to do," said Colin. "Dinner is at five. Don't go out of the house unless someone goes with you."

Tyler snorted. "Why not?"

"Because Mr. Goldring doesn't want you to. In fact, you should just stay in your rooms until someone is free to show you around."

"Why? Carnivorous cows or something?"

Colin Needle was clearly angry again. "It's a *farm*." He said it like a teacher talking to the dumbest student in class. "There are open wells and ditches, sharp tools, and very few lights. And animals, yes, who shouldn't be startled. So just stay in your rooms." He turned and walked down the hall, stiff and straight as a wooden soldier.

"What a creep," said Tyler when Colin was gone.

"He's not that bad. Kind of a nerd." Lucinda struggled to get her suitcases onto her bed. She was feeling more than a little overwhelmed by all the strange new sights. "Yuck. Could I feel more sweaty and gross? Me first in the bathroom."

Tyler laughed. "This is a farm, Miss Barbie Doll. You'll probably be using the outhouse in the back forty."

"Shut up, Tyler," said Lucinda. "You may belong on a farm, but I don't."

"Well, surprise—you're on one anyway."

Suddenly a bellowing, booming roar rattled everything in the room, including the window in its frame. Lucinda shrieked and jumped. The rumbling sound came from somewhere outside the house, but it was so deep and powerful Tyler could feel it through his feet even as it died away. It was an animal noise like a lion with a turbo upgrade, but there was something else in it, too, a kind of hissing crackle that made it more frightening than any lion because it was somehow *alien*.

"Whoa! What was that?" he said. "Man, what made that noise?"

His sister didn't say a word. She just stared at her hands as if she couldn't believe how strange they looked, shaking like that.

CHAPTER 4

THE SICK BARN

Tyler stared out his sister's window. His bones felt like they were still rattling from the force of that crazy sound. "Lucinda, are you unconscious or something? What made that noise?"

"Just one of the animals, I guess," she said in a pale voice, and then actually began to unpack her suitcase.

Tyler gave her a look of utter disbelief, then crossed the hall so he could look out his own window. "Luce," he called, "*Luce*, come look at this. There are farm guys running here from all over." Six or seven men were hurrying toward the place that looked like a vast white tube sunk into the ground. He thought one of them, bigger than the rest, might be the one Mr. Walkwell had called Ragnar.

Lucinda had stopped in his doorway as though she didn't want to see. "Maybe—maybe a cow got hurt . . . or . . ."

Tyler laughed harshly and dropped down to sit on his bed. "You're kidding, right? A cow. Well, it sure was one loud cow. It sounded like a *T. rex!*"

Something about the way she flinched tugged at him in some deep place where there were only feelings, not words, but he couldn't help it. He was angry. "I'm definitely going to find out what's going on," he said. "You have to come with me, Luce."

"No. I'm tired. I'm going to take a nap." She turned away from him, letting her hair fall forward in front of her face like a curtain, like a mask. Oh, but Tyler hated the way she did that—hiding from things she didn't want to see. Okay, maybe it was because she was scared, but you wouldn't catch *him* doing that, just praying for someone else to make the bad things go away.

"Luce, listen to me. There's something out there, something really weird. You heard it too. I know you did, Luce, so just admit it. I *know.*"

She still wouldn't say anything, but she didn't go back to her room, either. "Lucinda. Luce, come on!" He reached out his foot to push at her but he pushed too hard, with too much anger.

She finally looked up, her expression ice cold. "You *kicked* me."

"I'm trying to get you to pay attention!"

"I hate you, Tyler Jenkins."

"Luce, I'm sorry, but—"

"I hate you!" she shouted, then turned and ran into her room, slamming the door behind her. "I hope that cow really *is* a monster," she yelled from inside. "I hope it *eats* you!"

Tyler stared at her closed door. He almost knocked—he really wanted her to come with him—but he didn't, because he knew that asking her again wouldn't change a thing. Some things *never* changed.

As he stomped along the corridors and staircases of Ordinary Farm looking for a way outside, Tyler found his anger toward Lucinda easing up a little. She just wasn't good at stuff like this. She yelled about the smallest, most unimportant things until he wanted to slug her, but when she gave up, she really gave up.

When Dad first left, things had been bad—really *really* bad. It was Lucinda who had kept Tyler fed—Lucinda, trying to be the big responsible one. That was a time when she had definitely come through for her kid brother. . . .

And after a while, things got better. Mom had started work and was home most nights to make them dinner, though it was usually a bit late because she worked so hard. She would need an hour to kick off her shoes and pour herself a glass or two of wine—"decompression time," as she called it. After that she'd usually throw something together—nothing fancy, of course, just hot dogs and a can of baked beans or her two-minute quesadillas. Sometimes after the wine kicked in she could be quite amusing, doing imitations of the impossible people she had to deal with every day or making jokes about Lucinda's bad moods. Even Tyler had to admit his mother could be funny—in a grown-up, mom-ish kind of way—and okay-looking too. Inside Tyler, the alternating states of nothingness and anxiety had eased because things were no longer terrifyingly out of control. . . .

But about that time, Tyler began catching Lucinda staring at their mom, and what was on her face was a look of the most intense longing. All his sister wanted was a little normal stuff in her life, just a bit of what those perfect families on television had so much of, and Tyler knew it. And not long after that, the really dark stuff came for Lucinda. Recalling it now made it hard for Tyler to stay angry at her, even when Lucinda was acting like a total—

Tyler suddenly stopped, realizing that he had been walking for a while now without thinking much about it. "Wow," he breathed, looking around at the unfamiliar surroundings. He was completely, absolutely lost.

He was on a landing at the bottom of a staircase. In front of him lay a weird little parlor room with a glass door, and on the far side of the room he could just see a second door. He walked across the echoing wooden floor, wondering if he was somewhere he shouldn't be. Considering that Colin had told him they were supposed to stay in their rooms, that seemed pretty certain.

The glass door was unlocked. There was no furniture in the small parlor except a single overstuffed chair and a table with a vase and a dirty plastic flower so old that it might have been the very first plastic flower ever made. He crossed to the far door and found another staircase outside, this one leading somewhere else entirely. Tyler climbed the stairs and stepped into a corridor with windows along one side. He took a few steps, then something rattled against the window, startling him so badly that he gasped and jumped in the air. He had only the quickest glimpse of the thing that had bumped against the window from the outside, a round little head and a blur of greenish-gray body, but that glimpse had made no sense. Why were there *monkeys* here? Did colonies of wild monkeys live out here in the hills of California? Or was Great-uncle Gideon running some kind of crazy *monkey farm*?

He was lost, stalked by monkeys, and meanwhile, whatever had made that noise was out there and he was stuck in here. It made him want to hit something. He hurried back down the stairs and began searching even more strenuously, but every hall seemed to lead nowhere, every window to look out on puzzling, confusing sights, and nothing seemed to get him closer to finding his way outside.

Another hallway, another window, another rattle that caught him by surprise, but this time the perpetrator didn't hurry away. Yes, it really *was* a monkey crouched on the outside window frame, its little fingers splayed on the glass as it peered in at him. It was a small one, with big eyes and short fur, but it was definitely, unquestionably, a monkey. He had only a moment to stare back at the little animal, wondering nervously if it was rabid or something, wondering if it could get through the window and bite him, before it sort of flipped away and was gone.

Tyler ran in the direction the monkey had gone, opened a door, and found—glory Hallelujah!—stairs that led down and down and down. He didn't bother to count floors, he just ran down flight after flight until there weren't any more, then found a door and burst into the outside world, laughing hysterically.

He stepped onto a gravelly path. Some early evening cool had begun spilling into the heat of the afternoon, and the air was filled with the scents of dried grass and baked yellow earth. There was an animal tang too—Tyler suddenly remembered visiting the zoo when he was small, how the lion cages had stunk of big-animal urine.

Then something leaped, rattling along the edge of the porch roof.

Tyler jumped with surprise. The monkey moved in an awkward, bouncing way along the roof guttering, as if it was injured somehow. Tyler followed it along the edge of the house as it led him around a corner and into a place that was a sort of courtyard, with an archway opening at the far end.

And then the creature dropped from the roof and into a patch of light angling into the courtyard. It stood exposed, staring at him. If Lucinda was here, she'd be saying, "Ooohh, look!" or something like that, because it was kind of cute. The monkey spread its arms, as though waving at him to hurry. Bizarrely it was wearing a cape. No, Tyler realized an instant later, his heart suddenly speeding, that was no cape.

The monkey had wings.

Even as he watched, astonished, the little creature jumped and flew to the far end of the courtyard, disappearing into a patch of thick, high grass. Tyler started toward it, then froze as he realized he was about to run in front of a large window and that Mrs. Needle was on the other side of it, talking to someone he couldn't quite see.

The grass rustled. The monkey was going to get away. Tyler took a breath, waited until Mrs. Needle turned her back to the window for a moment, then leaped out of the shadows and dashed past the window as fast as he could. He threw himself down into the grass and lay breathing and listening. There was no sound of pursuit—but no sound of the creature he'd been following, either. Only crickets.

He sat up. Through the archway he could see the huge cement building they'd noticed from their windows, the bomb shelter or whatever it was. The concrete seemed to glow a little in the light of the late-afternoon sun, but it also had lights of its own strung along the side of it, as if for security, and at the moment it looked as mysteriously fascinating as a UFO. Tyler dashed across the grass, out of the courtyard. Up close, the tube-shaped building was even bigger than he'd guessed, more than a hundred feet long. Narrow, high windows started halfway up its side, their bottoms a dozen feet or more above the ground. Tyler really wanted to look through one of them, but knew he wouldn't be able to climb the sloping concrete wall to reach them, so he crept silently along the edge of the building looking for a door. He found something better at the far end—a metal platform that ran beneath the last three windows. He stared at it for a long moment, listening to the crickets.

"Don't go out of the house," Colin Needle had told them. *"Just stay in your rooms."*

Yeah. Right.

Tyler ran toward the platform and began climbing. The ladder was really rusty—it shed flakes when he put his weight on the first rung and it creaked alarmingly. He froze at the top, holding his breath, but the crickets seemed to think all was well and were still making noise. He slid off the ladder and crawled along the platform to the first window, then peered in.

What a disappointment—something really big was blocking most of the window. It gleamed a little like plastic in the uneven light, and was patterned like a quilt or a honeycomb. Tyler's mind tried to make sense of it. He was probably looking at sacks, he decided at last, sacks of animal feed piled high and then secured with a net.

Tyler crept to the next window. The pile of sacks sloped off a bit here, enough to give him more of a view of the building's interior. Bright lights were burning inside—the place looked more like something industrial than part of a farm, like an auto repair garage at night—and in their glare Tyler could make out some of the farmhands slicing open more feed-sacks with knives as big as machetes, then emptying them into a huge trough. Nothing very interesting, he decided.

The pile of sacks, just beside him on the other side of the window, heaved.

Tyler's breath caught so sharply that for a moment he thought he would choke on it. He stared, trying to make sense of the weird motion just a few feet from where he crouched.

The massive pile heaved again and Tyler felt himself go cold all over. They weren't sacks at all but something alive, something as big as an elephant—no, a dinosaur! Whatever it was groaned, a sound so deep and loud that the window and the platform both vibrated as if a hurricane had hit them. Tyler staggered to his feet in sudden terror and slipped on the slick metal platform, then he was sliding under the railing, scrabbling for a hold. . . .

A strong hand reached down and grabbed his collar. For one second Tyler's legs thrashed over empty air. Then a second hand curled itself into his hair and Tyler, yelling with pain, was yanked back onto the platform so hard that he hit the wall beneath the window and made it rattle. The thing on the other side of the glass made a groaning, rumbling noise, and the whole platform shuddered again.

"You stupid boy!" somebody shouted next to his ear. "You *stupid* boy!"

Lights came on suddenly all around the concrete building—*fwam fwam fwam!*—burning lights, bright as the sun. For a moment Tyler couldn't see anything. When the spots in front of his eyes finally faded, he was looking up into the very angry face of Mr. Walkwell.

CHAPTER 5

MESERET

"Go away, Tyler," Lucinda said, but the person at the door only knocked again, louder. "I already told you, leave me alone."

"Lucinda Jenkins? Open up please."

It wasn't Tyler but a deep-voiced man. She jumped out of bed and pulled on her jeans. She worried for a moment about opening the door to a stranger, but he didn't ask again and somehow that reassured her.

The stranger was a big, bearded, fair-haired man in overalls. He looked fit and very muscular, but his whiskers and long hair were both streaked with gray, and the deep wrinkles around his eyes and on his forehead suggested he was at least her father's age, if not older.

"You'd better come down," he said. "Your brother is in trouble."

Because of his accent, it took her a moment to understand, then panic exploded through her. "Oh! Is he hurt?"

The bearded man shook his head slowly. She couldn't figure out his expression—was he hiding a smile or something less pleasant? He had a couple of old, pale scars on his cheeks, which made her nervous. "Not hurt. But I think you must come down."

She didn't know what to do. She didn't know this man at all. Their first night in the middle of nowhere, and what had her dumb brother gotten into? "I'm . . . I'm not supposed to go anywhere with strangers."

He looked at her hard for a moment, then he really did smile—the scars disappeared into the crinkly lines around his eyes and it changed his whole face into something much, much nicer. "Fairly spoken, Lucinda Jenkins. Ragnar Lodbrok is my name. Now we are not strangers."

"But . . . I still don't know you."

He laughed. "And I do not know you, but I will trust you not to harm me. Still, we go downstairs only to the kitchen, and perhaps then one of the women there will speak for me, yes?"

She felt a little better, although she kept some distance between them as she followed him out the door. "What happened? What did Tyler do?"

"What boys do." Ragnar didn't seem too put out about it. "But it was not yet time."

"Time for what?"

He shrugged his broad shoulders. The bearded man reminded her a little of the scarecrow in the old *Wizard of Oz* movie—he had an almost boneless way of moving—but the scarecrow hadn't been anywhere near so broad across the back.

Scarecrow probably didn't have tattoos like that, either, she thought. She'd just noticed spikes of blue-black ink sticking up past Ragnar's shirt collar.

Mrs. Needle was waiting at the bottom of the stairs, pulling a sweater on over her thin shoulders. "You found her, I see," she said to Ragnar. "I'll say it again—I don't think you should bring her. This will be difficult enough."

Ragnar nodded, but under his polite reply his voice was hard. There was some sort of power struggle between these two, Lucinda guessed—an old one. "Yes. But this secret is broken. She may as well learn now."

His words frightened Lucinda so much that her knees went weak. Had that grumpy joke she shared with Tyler been right after all? Was this some kind of weird cult like she'd seen on so many TV shows? Were she and Tyler about to be given the chance to join or be killed?

They left by the front door and walked down the driveway, then cut back, skirting what looked like kitchen gardens, until in the distance they saw the big white tube-shaped building she had seen earlier, lit up now like an airport at night. Fearful, she slowed down, but Ragnar's strong hand closed on her arm, gently but unbreakably firm, and kept her moving.

Long before they reached the building she could see two figures standing and waiting for them, one big, one small. Her flutter of relief lasted only a moment. The way Mr. Walkwell's hand sat on her brother's shoulder made it look like he was a prison guard and Tyler was a criminal. At least, she *thought* the small shape was Tyler: it looked just like him except for one thing—the expression on his face. Her brother was pale as a piece of printer paper and looked absolutely terrified. She'd never seen him that way.

Lucinda was getting more frightened by the second.

Mr. Walkwell let go of Tyler and walked forward to meet Ragnar and Mrs. Needle. Lucinda hurried over to Tyler. "What did you do?" she whispered.

"There's a *monster* in there," he told her, eyes wide, lower lip trembling. "I'm not lying, Luce—a real, honest-to-God monster!"

"Well, here you two are," said a man's voice from behind them, dry and sour. "Tyler and Lucinda Jenkins. Welcome to the farm . . . I suppose. I hadn't planned our first meeting to be quite so dramatic."

Lucinda whirled around, startled. Hobbling up the

61

path toward them from the other end of the house was a strange-looking old man in a red-and-white-striped bathrobe. He was tall and thin, with a crest of white hair that stuck up as though he'd just got out of bed, and even under the spotlights he looked as tan and wrinkled as the leather of Tyler's old baseball glove.

"Are you . . . are you our uncle Gideon?" she asked.

"Your great-uncle, to be technical. But I think 'Uncle Gideon' will do." He narrowed his eyes. "And despite the more relaxed attitude these days about choosing names for children, I'm going to assume that you, girl, are Lucinda, and that this young ne'er-do-well is Tyler."

"There's a monster in there," Tyler said. "In that Sick Barn place. A *dinosaur*!"

Gideon Goldring stared at them in silence for a long moment. "I'm not happy about this," he said at last, and made a noise in the back of his throat. "I don't like Nosy Parkers prying into my business." He gave Tyler a fierce look—actually glared at him. Despite being frightened, Lucinda felt a moment of anger. *If you don't want people nosing around,* she thought, *you shouldn't invite them somewhere and then get all mysterious!* She didn't dare say it out loud, of course.

"But here we are," the fierce old man said, "so I suppose I don't have much choice. No, it's not a dinosaur, boy— it's something *much* more interesting. And her name is Meseret." Uncle Gideon pulled a pair of glasses that were little more than two lenses out of the pocket of his bathrobe and inspected Tyler's face like a doctor examining a particularly interesting wart. "Yes, you look a bit shocked—no surprise there, but no less than you deserve. I shouldn't reward you for being a troublemaker, but if I send you two back to the house now we'll just have to do this some other time." He snorted. "Children—*pfah!*" Gideon turned his attention to Lucinda, then back to Tyler again, as if he was making some huge decision. "Well? Do you want to see her properly? Do you want to meet Meseret?"

Tyler stared at back him and then slowly nodded his head. "That thing in there? Yeah. Yeah, sure."

"What is going *on* here?" Lucinda almost screamed. "Will someone please explain it to me?"

"We're right here, child," said Mrs. Needle with more than a touch of impatience. "There's no need to shout."

"Oh, there probably is," said Uncle Gideon, and he laughed, a sort of cracked hiss that didn't make Lucinda feel much better at all. "Come along, then, all of you—follow Simos, if you would be so kind."

"Simos" was apparently Mr. Walkwell. Tyler and Lucinda followed him as he scrunch-scrunch-scrunched his way around the front of the Sick Barn to a heavy metal door. As before, he sounded like he was walking on packing material, but he was on the same soft dirt as the rest of them and he was the only one making a noise. When they reached the door, Mr. Walkwell opened a little cabinet beside it and punched numbers into a keypad inside, as though this was some kind of top-secret missile base out of a spy show.

The door swung open silently and Mr. Walkwell stepped into bright fluorescent light. Tyler stared in, his pale face suddenly reluctant. Lucinda felt a sudden urge to take his hand as she used to when he was still her little brother instead of the irritating kid with the headphones who lived across the hall. She stepped forward, but as soon as she touched his hand he pulled away and walked into the Sick Barn. Lucinda followed a little more slowly.

She would never forget how the place looked in those first moments—a long room that seemed to stretch for a city block, with a dozen banks of lights hanging from a grid of pipes beneath the curved ceiling. Stainless steel tables stretched along one side of it, and the walls and shelves and open spaces were cluttered with bags of supplies and gasoline cans and cabinets full of tools, so that the place almost looked more like a garage than anything to do with animals. Lucinda would never forget how it smelled, either—that weird mixture of a doctor's office and a zoo on the hottest day of summer. It made her eyes water.

But as impressive as it all was, she would never be able to remember exactly how it *felt* to see Meseret for the first time. Some things were so powerful that as soon as they came into your life they changed you completely—changed everything, so that the *you* who was trying to remember was just too different from the *you* who hadn't known.

It felt like she was in a movie, one of those special-effects epics that she had to go see when it was Tyler's turn to pick. Lucinda was looking at a stretched-out shape that almost entirely filled the massive steel pen running down the far side of the room, a scaly shape the size of a small jet plane. Even though she had been expecting something to fit Tyler's word, *monster*, her brain couldn't make sense of the immense thing in front of her. It was a giant robot, maybe, some kind of theme-park attraction, but it couldn't be *real.*

It lifted its huge head on its huge neck and looked back at her with snaky yellow eyes almost as big as hubcaps. Nothing else, Lucinda found out, was as convincing as actual eye contact.

Her shrieks didn't seem to bother the creature much. Its yellow eyes followed her, but without much obvious interest, as she stumbled backward toward the door and slammed into Colin Needle, who had just walked into the Sick Barn.

She fell down at Colin's feet, still staring helplessly at the monster and trying to remember how to breathe. He didn't bother to help her up, but the big farmhand Ragnar did.

"Don't fear," Ragnar said. "She will not harm you."

"It's a monster!" Lucinda shouted.

"See? I told you!" Tyler had stopped a good dozen feet from the pen to stare, which was clear evidence of how frightened he still was. But he was shaking with excitement too. "See! It *is* a real dinosaur. I wasn't lying!"

"Don't be stupid," Colin said. "That's not a dinosaur."

"Have you children forgotten all the stories?" Ragnar sounded almost sad.

The monster in the pen stirred and the immense leathery flaps folded against her long front legs scraped along her scales. Wings.

"Oh my God," said Lucinda, almost in a whisper, not talking to anyone but herself. "It's a *dragon*. It's a real, true dragon."

Colin pushed past her. "Why are you showing them the Sick Barn?" he demanded of Ragnar. "Why didn't anyone tell me you were all coming here? I'm going to tell Gideon."

"He's here," said Mrs. Needle, pointing to the corner of the room where the old man in the striped bathrobe was talking quietly with Mr. Walkwell. "And we didn't tell you because I thought you needed your rest."

Colin scowled like a three-year-old about to throw a tantrum, but turned away instead. Uncle Gideon was coming back toward them, but Lucinda didn't think that was the only reason Colin wasn't arguing with his mother.

Gideon's voice rose sharply and suddenly. "Here now, boy! What's-your-name—Tyler! Don't get too close to her.

She hasn't been feeling well."

Tyler had been moving steadily forward, drawn toward the huge creature as though hypnotized. He looked like he was over his fear and into his I-wonder-how-it-works phase, something that usually spelled trouble for anything that interested him. Lucinda felt a clutch of fear. If he got eaten, how would she explain it to Mom?

It really was a dragon. There was no avoiding the fact, no arguing with it. Lucinda couldn't see every detail because much of the creature's body was hidden by the metal rails of the pen, but unless there was some normal kind of animal longer than a school bus that had scales and fangs and wings, then she, Lucinda Anne Jenkins, was standing in the same room as . . .

"A dragon," she said again, loud this time, finally starting to feel the wonder of it all.

"She certainly is," Uncle Gideon said. "I will introduce you to her—and I do mean introduce. This is a *dragon*, not just some kind of giant lizard or crocodile. You must treat her with respect. Her name is Meseret."

"Un-be-lievable!" Tyler was bouncing up and down again. "This is *so awesome*! Where did she come from?"

Uncle Gideon scowled. "*That*, at least, you're going to have to wait for until *I'm* ready, boy." He was still frowning as he said, "Now step forward carefully. That's right. Just stand and let her smell you."

Tyler and Lucinda had moved up to within a couple of

feet of the bars. The dragon's nostrils twitched like little volcanoes getting ready to erupt. It was all Lucinda could do not to run away. The smell, the size—she was terrified.

"Move slowly and quietly, will you?" said Gideon. "She has very little experience of human children. In fact, as far as we know, before today she hasn't met any except Colin."

"Poor dragon," said Tyler, too quietly for anyone but Lucinda to hear.

The dragon fixed Lucinda with an emotionless stare. The huge eye glowed with red-gold light like the coals of a fire, and for a moment it seemed something Lucinda could fall into, fall forever, twisting helplessly downward. . . . She backed away, knowing that if she didn't she'd scream again. "This is too weird," she said. "Everybody here's acting like . . . like this is all *normal*! Like it's . . ."

"Ordinary?" asked Uncle Gideon, the light winking off his spectacles. He looked amused and angry at the same time, a strange combination. "Yes, I'm afraid the name of the farm is a trifle deceptive."

"Oh, man—flaming cows!" Tyler said, laughing a little wildly. "Flaming cows! Now I get it!"

Uncle Gideon nodded. "Ah, you did receive the book, then. I was worrying I'd missed getting it in the mail in time. Good. Obviously it's not really about cows. And I do want you to memorize it. They're not at all like ordinary animals, dragons."

Lucinda felt like her head was going to blow up. "But this can't be real! If this was really true, it would be in the news . . . people would know . . . it would be *on television!*"

Without warning something grabbed her arm, and a second later she and Tyler were both being dragged across the Sick Barn by Uncle Gideon. He was holding her wrist so tightly her bones ached, and his face had gone red with anger. When they got out into the glare of the outside spotlights he abruptly let go. They both staggered. From the corner of her eye Lucinda registered the others coming out of the Sick Barn, too, but no one said anything.

Gideon stood in front of them, and he didn't just look like an eccentric old man in a bathrobe anymore. He looked really mad and really scary. "Now you listen to me," he said in a voice that trembled with fury. "You have no idea—*no idea, I tell you*—of the great privilege you have received in being invited to this place. And yet I find that the first thing you two do when you get here is abuse my hospitality. You, boy, do exactly what you are told not to do. You were told not to leave the house, weren't you?"

"I warned him, sir," said Colin. He sounded pleased.

"And then you, girl, start telling me this place should be on television." Gideon made a sputtering noise, like a snake about to bite. "You have been here five minutes and you would give away our hard-won secrets to a society of idiots and thieves, would you?"

69

"No, I didn't . . ." she began, but there was no stopping Gideon Goldring.

"I cannot tell you how deeply disappointed I am in my first impressions of you both. Moreover, you just confirm my worst fears. Once people have been allowed into Ordinary Farm, there's no control—no control at all! Yes, children, if you haven't guessed, I am very, very angry."

Tears sprang into Lucinda's eyes and her heart hammered. She looked to Tyler, but he had his head down, avoiding Uncle Gideon's eyes. Her little brother wouldn't argue, but he wouldn't give in, either. He was too stubborn for that.

"Give me your hands," Gideon said, suddenly and loudly. "Right now! You are going to swear me an oath."

Lucinda saw the mouths of some of the others fall open in shock. She looked at Tyler.

"*Now!*" roared Gideon.

They did so. Somehow there seemed nothing else they could do. Lucinda heard distant birds in the trees, a breeze ruffling leaves, the ragged breathing of this terrible man, their great-uncle.

"Promise me," said Gideon, "swear on everything you hold sacred, that you will never, *never* betray the secrets of Ordinary Farm to the outside world!"

The old man's grip was so tight that she could feel him trembling, and she suddenly had the feeling that he was more than just angry—Gideon Goldring was frightened.

Really, seriously frightened that they might tell people about the farm. An odd calm came over her. "Yes," she said, "I promise."

Tyler didn't say anything for a moment. "As long as you don't try to hurt me or my sister," he said. "Remember, you asked *us* to come here."

Gideon let go of their hands. He sounded surprised. "Hurt you? You are my relatives—you are family!"

"Okay, then, I promise."

Another silence fell. When Lucinda looked up at Gideon to see if he was getting over his anger, the heels of his hands were pressing his eyes. "God," he cried suddenly, "oh, God, my head!" Suddenly he swayed and almost fell.

Mrs. Needle, black hair streaming, ran to his side. "Gideon, enough! You are still unwell. You must come away now and lie down." And she began to lead him to the house. Gideon leaned into her, hobbling and wiping at his eyes.

"Just like Mom told us," Tyler said quietly. "Right, Lucinda? A nice, old-fashioned summer on the farm."

CHAPTER 6

FREE-RANGE MUFFINS

By the time they reached the grand lobby and its blind staircase, Colin could just barely hide his anger. Only a few hours on the farm and these two interlopers were already getting special treatment! The boy—what was his name? Tyler—had immediately broken the rules, but instead of being sent home they had both been rewarded. Already they had been shown the second biggest secret on the farm!

Of course, Colin had known that having strangers on the farm would cause trouble, but who could have guessed it would have begun so quickly? Now he understood and could even sympathize with his mother's dark, cold rage when Gideon had announced it.

His mother had taken Gideon upstairs, the old man stumbling like a sleepwalker. No matter how much medicine she gave him, Gideon didn't seem to get any better. That was strange: it wasn't like Patience Needle to come up short, although she hadn't had much luck with the female dragon, either. It gave Colin a strange, slippery feeling—half joyful, half terrified—to think of his mother failing at something.

At Colin's mother's order, Caesar came down from Gideon's rooms to lead the two Jenkins children back to their beds. Colin avoided the bent old black man. He had made the mistake once of referring to Caesar as a servant—what else would you call someone who took trays to Gideon, turned down his bed each night, and ran his bath and folded his clothes?—but Caesar had turned on him. When the man straightened up, Colin had discovered, Caesar was actually quite tall and more than a little frightening.

"Don't you ever call me that," Caesar had said, his weary, wrinkled face twisting into something quite different. "I work for Mr. Goldring because work is all I know how to do and because I owe him a big old favor, but I am no man's servant. Not ever again. Do you hear me, child? *Do you hear me?*"

All Colin had been able to do at the time was squeak a yes. He had done his best to avoid the fellow ever since.

"Come, children," Caesar now said as he led Tyler and

Lucinda away. "Must be tired, you two. Quite a day, quite a day. Ordinary Farm ain't like other places, and now you know it. Enough to tire anyone out. Come along to bed."

When they had gone, Colin stood in the silent lobby, too disturbed for bed, too full of irritated thoughts and anger. Gideon had actually had the nerve to suggest that Colin would enjoy having "people his own age" on the farm this summer. As if these two children were anything like him! As if he himself were a child instead of an adult in all but the official sense. Which is what any kid had to be if they were like Colin, a boy without a father, but also with a mother who never spoke about her previous life and treated Colin more like an assistant than a child. All in all, he hoped Gideon had learned a lesson about who he could trust and who he clearly *couldn't*. . . .

Colin Needle's attention was suddenly drawn to a rectangle of white sitting on a silver tray. It was the tray that Caesar used to carry upstairs the mail and other papers that Gideon needed to see. The old fellow had obviously been distracted by the afternoon's events and had left the tray with a small pile of undelivered mail out on a table near the door leading to the kitchen. Colin sidled over to look through the envelopes.

Feed bills. Equipment bills. A postcard for the brats from their mother, and a couple of letters from a lawyer—Colin didn't recognize the name, although this was by no means the first time he'd snooped in Gideon's correspondence. More bills. Assessor's office—that would be taxes. Lots of money going out as usual, but nothing coming in. No wonder Gideon was always half crazy with stress and worry. Ah, but what was this? Colin's heart beat faster as he recognized the gray envelope. He had been waiting, hoping, for one of these.

He cocked his head and listened to make sure nobody was coming, then lifted up the letter. The return address in the corner confirmed what he'd suspected: *Jude Modesto Antiquities, Santa Barbara, California.* It was from the antiques dealer, the one Gideon was always so secretive about, although Colin had figured out their arrangement long ago. But far more important to him was the information inside—including the man's email address.

Colin's mother and Caesar were still upstairs. The cook, Sarah, and her helpers would be here very soon to begin preparing dinner. At best, he had mere minutes. Colin slipped the gray envelope inside his sweater and hurried into the empty kitchen and straight toward the kettle.

Steam coaxed the sealed envelope to open as neatly as one of the pale flowers in Colin's mother's garden spreading its petals to the spring sunshine. He slipped out the letter and read it quickly:

> *Dear Gideon,*
> *Of course I'd be delighted to meet with you—I always*

*enjoy your company and sharing in the miracle of your
wonderful collection. In fact, I have a new buyer who
is very interested in just the sort of items with which
you've favored my little enterprise in the past. He will
be thrilled if I am able to offer him more "genuine Gold-
rings." Of course, I call them that only to myself—I have
kept your injunction to secrecy quite faithfully, I assure
you. . . .*

The letter went on like that for a few more paragraphs,
full of all the slimy politeness that grown-ups used when
they were pretending they wanted something other than
simply to make money. When Colin grew up he wasn't going
to be such a hypocrite. When he wanted something he'd say
so. When he didn't like someone—the way he already didn't
like Tyler Jenkins—he wouldn't bother to hide it.

Of course, he would have to be in charge. You only got
to make the rules and do what you wanted when you were
in charge. His mother had taught him that from the first
moments he could remember.

Colin memorized the email address in Jude Modesto's
personalized letterhead and sealed the letter back up,
then made his stealthy way back out to the lobby. He had
dropped the letter back onto the tray only a few moments
before his mother reappeared, brushing straight black hair
away from her pale forehead.

"This foolish plan of Gideon's is going to cause us all a

great deal of grief," she said, then suddenly seemed to see her son properly for the first time since she had walked into the room. "What are you doing, Colin? Are you loitering?"

"I'm going to our rooms, Mother." He was desperate to get to the computer before he forgot the email address. "I just need to make a note for later on. But I'll be right down after that, if you need any help at dinner."

She looked hard at him for a moment. "Very well. But don't dillydally. I'm not in the mood to be crossed this evening."

A little shiver ran up his back. "I'll be right back."

Suddenly she smiled broadly, so that if Colin hadn't been able to see the rest of her distracted, chilly face, he would have felt quite warm and loved. "That's my good boy. That's a boy who knows how to behave toward his mother." She leaned forward as if to kiss his cheek, but stopped half a foot short, her dark lips smacking the air, then she turned and walked out of the lobby, pulling out her keychain so she could begin locking up.

Colin scuttled to the office in their rooms, and his own computer there—the one with all the security software, so that neither his mother, Gideon, nor anyone else at all could find out what he did. He quickly composed a letter to Modesto.

Please forgive my contacting you this way. I am a business associate of Gideon Goldring and I have certain things that will interest you, both information and an actual rare object. I know you are very interested in Mr. Goldring's collection. If you would like to learn much more than you have so far been told, I require only two things: a meeting with you and absolute secrecy.

When you make your next appointment with Gideon, send me a message at this address to let me know where and when it will be, and I will arrange to meet you there beforehand so we can discuss things of great mutual interest. However, if you breathe a word to Mr. Goldring or anyone else about our arrangement, you will never hear from me again.

Signed,

X

Colin knew the note was probably a little melodramatic, but he still thought it sounded grown-up and serious enough to keep the man interested. He already had what he thought of as the "bait"—an object that would surely provoke Modesto's interest. He had been saving it specially. . . . Now all he had to figure out was how to deliver the actual prize. He had been thinking about the problem for weeks, but this next bit could be more than disastrous if it went wrong—it could be fatal.

The best way, of course, would be to get someone *else* to do it. . . .

Weighing different strategies, Colin sent the email and made his way back to the kitchen. To his pleasure, his mother told him she had confined those brats to their rooms for the rest of the night, and had sent Caesar up with a tray of food and to stand over them till early morning, doing guard duty. Colin grinned to himself—that punished all three of them. For the rest of the evening, he meekly did everything she asked, and afterward she even patted him on the shoulder. Colin didn't like that. Only a little kid neded to be patted and reassured by his mother. He was stronger than that. That's why he was going places in this world.

Still, it took him a while to get to sleep that night, and he was troubled by dreams of angry, vengeful monsters.

Morning, and his mother's rap on the door sounded like a gunshot.

"Get up, Colin, it's almost six already. Go and get those children and bring them down to breakfast. Now, please."

"But I want to have a shower—"

"Now."

He got up, already in a bad mood. Barely dawn and the unwanted strangers were causing trouble for him already. He hated to start the day, especially what was going to be a hot summer day, without a shower. By the middle of the afternoon he would feel like things were growing on his sticky skin, like the clinging plants that had filled and choked off the farm's unused greenhouse.

He pounded hard on Tyler Jenkins's door to wake him up. When the boy had gone grumbling off to the bathroom, his eyes half shut, Colin knocked a little less roughly on Lucinda's. She opened it wearing only a long T-shirt, the skin of her legs almost as pale as his mother's. That wouldn't last long, not in Ordinary Farm's relentless summer sun.

"It's time to come down to breakfast," he told her. "It's going to be a long day so you need a good start." He felt stupid saying it, like one of those commercials for breakfast cereal, but he couldn't help feeling bad about dragging her out of bed. She looked tired and fretful.

Of course, she had just met Meseret only a few hours before. He couldn't guess what that must be like for an outsider.

"Oh, thanks, Colin," she said. "I'll be out in just a minute."

She closed the door. She'd actually thanked him. Quite different from her brother, who emerged from the bathroom at that moment, the toilet still gurgling. "What are *you* staring at?" Tyler demanded.

"Not you, I promise."

"Can we see the dragon again?"

"It's not for me to say."

"Look, just tell me how it got here, then."

"I told you, it's not for me to say." Colin sighed. *Children.*

"When you're both ready I'll meet you at the top of the stairs down the hall and take you down to the dining room." He walked away, keeping his back as straight as he could. He'd show these urchins how to look dignified. If there was one thing his mother had made sure of, it was that Colin had good posture. He ignored the snorting noise Tyler made behind him. The boy was almost a savage, after all.

Ten minutes later, still ignoring Tyler's endless questions, Colin led the Jenkins children into the kitchen, where he introduced them to the women preparing breakfast—red-cheeked Sarah, blonde, round, and bustlingly warm; tall, superior Azinza from West Africa; and the little, solemn-faced Tibetan girl, Pema. None of the young women liked him very much, Colin knew, but they all feared his mother, which kept them polite. Once names had been exchanged, he pulled the Jenkins children out of the kitchen and led them onward into the dining room with its long tables. Most of the farmhands were there already, and they turned to gaze with curiosity at the new arrivals.

Colin led Lucinda and Tyler to the serving table. The spread was a good one this morning: eggs of every kind, bacon, sausages, ham, hash brown potatoes, a platter of fried mushrooms and tomatoes (which Tyler Jenkins was careful to avoid, although he seemed to have taken more than a little of everything else), waffles, pancakes, and at least five or six different kinds of muffins. When they had loaded their plates, Colin looked around. The only empty space big enough for all three of them was next to Ragnar, so he reluctantly led them over.

The big blond-bearded man grinned and reached out to shake hands with the children. Their hands disappeared into his massive grasp like pink baby mice being swallowed whole by a python. "Greetings to you both." Ragnar turned a less friendly look on Colin. "And to you, young Needle."

"Where did that dragon come from?" Tyler demanded.

"That is Gideon's story to tell, not mine," Ragnar said.

"Do you all live here on the farm?" Lucinda asked. More farmhands were coming in now, although all but the kitchen workers were men.

"Gideon has generously given us homes, all us refugees," Ragnar explained. Colin tensed, afraid the man might say too much—Ragnar was far too full of himself— but the Scandinavian giant only turned to Mr. Walkwell, sitting at a nearby table. "Isn't that right, Simos?"

The farm's overseer looked sour. "You children, get on with the eating" was all he said. "It is a long day ahead."

"Ick, Tyler—you've got enough syrup on your plate to float an ocean liner," Lucinda complained. Her brother ignored her and began to eat. Colin Needle realized that he was hungry too. Then, just as he bent to his plate, a cool hand closed on his shoulder.

"Ah, there you all are," his mother said.

It was always the same feeling Colin's mother brought to him, part excitement, part worry. Had he made a mistake of some kind? He had done just what she'd asked, hadn't he?

"Do you mind if I join you?" she asked the two guests. "I'm look forward to getting to know you both." She turned her smile on her son. "Have you been showing our guests around?"

"Yes, Mother."

"He's been very helpful, Mrs. Needle," said Lucinda.

Colin suddenly decided that for an unwanted guest, the Jenkins girl was not so bad. "Can I get you anything, Mother?"

"Just some fruit and yogurt, dear, thank you."

By the time Colin came back she was doing her best to charm the Jenkins children, and her best could be quite impressive. Tyler did not look entirely convinced, but Lucinda seemed taken with his mother's accent, her careful, clever way of talking, and her occasional bright smiles. Colin found himself proud of his mother, proud that he was her son—that *she* had chosen to have *him*. Who needed a father, or even to know who his father had been? His mother could be difficult, it was true, but that was because she was special. A sort of genius. That was one of the reasons Colin felt so drawn to Octavio Tinker, the founder of Ordinary Farm. Genius had its own rules. Genius had to get its own way.

"You know, Lucinda," his mother was saying, "you have such a charming face. . . ." She reached out her long fingers toward the girl. "You should cut your hair shorter to show it off."

A little startled, Lucinda leaned back suddenly and lifted her arm, knocking over a basket full of muffins that had been set down on the table beside her. The basket bounced and the muffins leaped out, rolling across the floor. The little dark-haired farmhand, Haneb, who had been passing behind her, danced back with a cry of surprise and almost dropped his breakfast plate. Even as he did so, though, Haneb struggled to keep the left side of his face turned away, and tried to shield it with a free hand, but this only ensured that some of the food slid from his plate and fell to the floor amid the now free-ranging muffins.

"Oh! Oh, I'm *so sorry*," said Lucinda as she jumped up. She began gathering muffins into the basket, and as she did so stuck out a hand toward Haneb. "I'm really sorry. Hi, I'm Lucinda and I'm a clumsy idiot, *obviously*. . . ." Suddenly she gave a horrified gasp and straightened up, stumbling back from the dark-haired man as though she had been struck.

Haneb stared at her for a moment, both eyes wide and the good one blinking. The left half of his face was a mass of scars, the skin melted like candle wax, the eye pulled half shut. Colin had often thought that if the man had any concern for the feelings of others, he would wear a mask like the Phantom of the Opera. Especially when people were eating.

Haneb ducked his head and, without picking up any more of his breakfast, scuttled away toward Mr. Walkwell's table. Once seated, he began to eat quickly without looking up.

Tyler hissed at her. "Jeez, Lucinda, treat that guy like Frankenstein much?"

She stared at him, embarrassed but also angry. "It surprised me, that's all." She turned to Colin. "Poor guy! What happened to him?"

"Burned." Were these children going to blunder and crash through every little private matter on the farm? If so, it was going to be a very long summer.

"Whoa," said Tyler, interested for the first time. "Really? What burned him?"

A shadow fell over them—a large shadow. "Come along, you young ones," Ragnar said. "The sun is almost at noon!"

Tyler looked at his watch. "It isn't even six thirty yet!"

"On a farm that is the middle of the day," Ragnar said cheerfully.

"Has anyone decided what chores these children are going to do?" Colin asked. He had a sudden horror that Gideon was going to expect him to entertain these barbarians, to *play* with them or some other impossibly childish idea.

"Work?" Tyler blinked. "Can't we see the dragon again? What was her name?"

Ragnar grinned. "Meseret. You like dragons, do you? Then you have never met one on a windy mountainside with nothing but an ax in your hand." He laughed. "I do not think you will see more of the great she-worm today— she has been ill. But there are other things worth doing . . . and seeing. I have good news for you, young Master Tyler. There shall be no work for you today."

"What?" said Colin. "But everyone has to work!"

"Not today," said Ragnar firmly. "Gideon has decided that the safest thing is for the children to be taken on a tour of the farm, the better to stop any more unfortunate explorations."

Colin's mouth fell open. Could anything be more unfair? "But . . ."

"As for you, young Master Needle, Mr. Walkwell asks me to remind you he needs his feed budget, and will you please work with your mother to get it to him by the end of the day."

So the children would get a tour of the farm while he was stuck with bookkeeping? "Really?" Colin asked miserably. "Today?"

"Today." Ragnar laid a big hand on Colin's shoulder, squeezing hard enough to make his point. "You know Mr. Walkwell does not joke." He turned to Lucinda and Tyler. "No more wasting time," he said. "Let us go."

"Bye, Colin," said Lucinda.

Her brother grinned at Colin. "Yeah. Enjoy yourself."

The three of them walked away. Simos Walkwell and the farmhands filed out to their various jobs. His mother went off with the kitchen workers to supervise the making of the week's shopping list. Colin Needle was left alone with his oatmeal.

It had gone cold.

CHAPTER 7

A Cloud of Horns

Mr. Walkwell sat waiting for them in front of the house. He had hitched two horses to the ancient wagon this time, the brown mare that had brought them back from the train station and a spotted gray, perhaps to help with the extra weight of a rusty old two-wheeled trailer piled with feed sacks that had been attached to the back of the wagon. The whole thing had the look of a small and not very exciting parade.

Haneb, the slender man with the scarred face, sat in the wagon, staring down at his feet. Three other farmhands sat with him among the feed sacks, short, squat, tan-skinned men who looked as if they might be Asian.

They touched the brims of their odd hats and smiled shyly at the children.

"It's the Three Amigos," Tyler said quietly to Lucinda, but she either didn't remember the movie or didn't think it was funny enough to laugh.

Mr. Walkwell didn't say a word as the children and Ragnar climbed on. When they were settled atop the feed sacks he clicked his tongue and the horses started around the driveway, wagon wheels scrunching through the hard-packed gravel. He was no more talkative when Tyler asked questions about the previous night, the dragon, or the day's itinerary.

"Simos could beat standing stones in a staring contest," said Ragnar, smiling. "You're wasting your time, boy!"

They drove for almost a quarter of an hour across the farm to their first stop, which surprised Tyler: he would have guessed all the animals would be close to the house. When they had reached the base of the hills and the house was almost out of sight behind them, they came to a halt at a chained gate. On the gate's far side a trail led away down the straw-colored hill.

Mr. Walkwell unlocked the gate. "You two children stay with us," he said, suddenly and sharply. "If you disobey or anger me you will go back to the cart to wait."

The Three Amigos (whom Ragnar had introduced as Kiwa, Jeg, and Hoka) got down and began to pile feed sacks on their shoulders until each was carrying three.

Mr. Walkwell took four (Tyler felt secretly certain by the ease with which he lifted them he could have carried more) and massive Ragnar took three on each shoulder. Without being asked, Tyler helped Haneb lift a sack onto his shoulders. The scarred man did not meet his eye, but mumbled a thank-you in accented, liquid-sounding English.

"More dragons?" Tyler asked Lucinda quietly as they fell in line behind the Amigos. "Do you think this is where they live?"

Lucinda pulled up, horrified. "You're joking, right? We're not . . . I'm not going near a bunch of . . . *wild* dragons!"

Mr. Walkwell growled as he almost ran into them from behind. "Keep walking, you children. If you trip me and I drop these sacks on you, you will not thank me."

But Lucinda was not moving. "Are we going to see a bunch of wild dragons? A herd or whatever? Because I don't want to do that."

The wiry old man made a snorting noise. "Do you think the world is so full of these most ancient ones that they roam about in flocks, like pigeons?" He shook his head. "No—they are special and rare. We have two dragons here on the farm. You saw one in the Sick Barn—Meseret, the female. Her mate is named Alamu. We will not see him today." He made a strange noise in his throat. "If we are lucky."

"I don't understand," Lucinda said.

"No, you do not," Mr. Walkwell agreed. "Walk faster, please."

Tyler said, "You let the male dragon, like, roam wild? Is that safe?"

"He would kill himself trying to get out of a cage or barn, but if he is well fed Alamu is perfectly content to stay near Meseret, hiding in the high rocky places. Naturally we keep him very well fed."

When they reached the bottom of the hill they found themselves in a woodland of madrone and oak trees, so that instead of the hot sun they walked through ragged patches of shade. The farmhands stopped and began dropping the sacks in a little clearing where a long-dry pond had become a shallow bowl of green weeds and yellow grass. Metal troughs stood at the base of several of the trees. The men began cutting open the bags and pouring dark green pellets that looked like giant rabbit food into the troughs. Tyler stepped forward to have a closer look.

A long brown hand descended on Tyler's shoulder, stopping him as if he'd run into a wall. "Stay here, boy," Mr. Walkwell said. "They are easily startled."

Ragnar, standing at the center of the clearing, lifted his fingers to his mouth and whistled three loud, shrill notes. They all waited, Haneb and the other farmhands standing close to Ragnar, as if a rainstorm was coming and the blond man was a tall, sheltering tree.

"What are we waiting for?" Tyler said at last. "And why isn't it coming?"

"Not one but many," Mr. Walkwell said. "And they *are* coming, child. Likely they were far away. Listen!"

For a few moments Tyler had no idea what he meant— he could hear nothing but the rumble of a distant storm. Then he realized it was June in the California valley and there wasn't a cloud anywhere in the sky. The drumming noise grew louder until the ground itself began to quiver. Tyler had a sudden feeling that the entire grove of trees was being lifted up by gigantic engines and was just about to take off into the sky like a rocket ship.

Then the unicorns came.

They flooded into the clearing like a storm, with so much power and such a swirl of reddish dust, muscled flanks all white and gray and dappled, that they seemed like clouds hurrying along the ground, struggling to fly as far as possible before they burst and released their burdens of rain. But there was no mistaking the bright sharp horns, or the flashing of their eyes, or the glint of their pearly hooves when some young ones excitedly reared in the air at the center of the clearing, jabbing at the air.

"Oh!" said Lucinda beside him, and for the second time in two days Tyler realized that his sister was holding his hand. Strange as that was, he didn't pull away. As he watched the tall creatures thundering back and forth across the clearing, snorting and bucking, ivory horns shimmering like flickers of lightning, he felt he was watching some kind of magic river, that if he lost contact with the ground it might just carry him away and he would never be heard of again.

"*Oh!*" his sister said again. There really wasn't much more to say.

The unicorns crowded into the clearing, bumping and rearing so that it was hard even to guess how many there were—two dozen? three? They seemed at least as big as ordinary horses (Tyler didn't have a lot of experience with real horses), but more slender and long-legged, with great tangled banners of mane at their necks and tufts on their chests and ankles. But it was the horns that made something amazing into something truly unbelievable, the pointed spirals that grew, not from the tops of their heads as in the sappy posters Lucinda still had in her room, but farther down, just below the line of the eyes, like the horn of a rhinoceros.

The herd formed into groups around the troughs and fed, horns clacking together gently, almost silently, ranged according to some hierarchy that Tyler couldn't make out, since it didn't seem to have much to do with age or size or color or anything else. At some troughs the young unicorns fed first, while at others the small ones stood patiently while an adult with a mane like store-window Christmas snow took the lead.

"They're so beautiful," Lucinda kept saying, over and over.

"Where do they come from?" Tyler asked Ragnar, who seemed more likely to answer questions than Mr. Walkwell. "What are they eating? Do you have to feed them every day?"

"They come from China," Ragnar answered him. "Or they did once. Now they are gone. *Ki-lin*, they called them. And they eat grass and other things, but we give them every day a . . . what is the word, Simos?"

"Vitamin supplement," growled Mr. Walkwell, who was squatting beside a gray adult unicorn. It watched him nervously from the corner of its eye while it ate, and he in turn examined it for any signs of ill health.

"Yes, vitamins," said Ragnar. "Because the grass alone is not enough to keep them healthy, I think. And there are other medicines in the food too. These are the only unicorns still living in the world, so we must take good care of them."

"Yeah," said Tyler. "Awesome." He was certainly interested in the unicorns, but more interested in going back to see the dragon again.

Lucinda, who didn't seem to have listened to anything said, was walking slowly toward the nearest trough, her eyes wide as though she was hypnotized. Tyler hoped she wouldn't do anything embarrassing, like start crying with joy or some other girl-and-unicorn thing. She stopped only yards away from one of the young unicorns, which examined her with large gray eyes. It didn't look frightened, but Tyler thought it didn't look happy, either. When Lucinda did not move any closer it put its head down again and nosed in the trough.

Mr. Walkwell and Ragnar were together off to the side, looking over other members of the herd. The young unicorn's pearly horn moved back and forth in front of Lucinda as it fed.

Tyler watched his sister, who was staring at the creature as if she had just opened her front door to find her number-one boy-band heartthrob waiting there to take her on a surprise date. She slowly reached out her hand to touch the horn. Tyler watched, wondering if he should say something—the unicorns were wild animals, so they were dangerous, weren't they? Or were they? It was hard to know in such a crazy place.

A lot of things suddenly happened all at the same time.

Haneb saw what Lucinda was doing and ran toward her, crying, "No! No!" The unicorn reared up and made a startled noise, something blaring and utterly strange. As it came down it shook its head violently from side to side. The horn whipped past Lucinda's face so fast she didn't even flinch until after it was gone.

Haneb reached her and pulled her away, but now all the unicorns were milling and snorting, prancing nervously, making little tornados of dust spin up. Mr. Walkwell whistled a single shrill burst and they began to calm, but still would not come close to the troughs again.

"You scared me!" Lucinda shouted at the scarred man, yanking herself free of his protective grasp. She burst into tears, then turned and retreated toward the wagon.

"Wow, are you nuts?" Tyler said to her as she hurried past. He was stunned and impressed that his boring sister would do something so . . . Tyler-like. "They said not to touch anything. That thing almost stabbed you!"

Haneb, who looked as though what had happened was somehow his fault, shuffled off to gather up feed bags.

"Everyone back to the truck," Ragnar said. He bent to pick something off the ground, then went to talk to Lucinda at the edge of the clearing, where she stood wiping her tears away. "You could not know," he told her kindly, "but the *ki-lin* do not like their horns to be touched. Very sensitive."

"I . . . I didn't mean . . ." Lucinda swallowed. "It was just so beautiful."

"Yes, they are," said Ragnar gently. "But it is no ordinary thing, like a bull's horn or a deer's antler. It is a sort of tooth that grows up through the skull, like the tusk of the white corpse whales—two teeth, actually, growing together. The *enhjorning*—as my people call it—uses it to test the air, the water—to smell, almost, as a cat uses its whiskers or a snake its tongue."

"A *tooth*?" said Tyler. "*That's* weird."

"Shut up," Lucinda said, and gave him a dig with her

elbow. Her eyes were red and puffy. "Just . . . don't say anything." She abruptly veered away from the two of them and walked over to Haneb, who was watching with a worried expression, but whatever she said seemed to put him at ease: he nodded his head vigorously as they walked and talked, still keeping his face turned away from her as much as possible.

"I am glad she thanks Haneb," said Ragnar. "The little man may have saved her life."

"Saved her *life*?" Tyler made a face. "You're joking, right?"

Ragnar held out his large hand. Lying across the palm was a hank of Lucinda's golden-brown hair, cut as neatly as if by a pair of scissors. "The horn did this. It came that close. It is not wise to startle a unicorn. They are lovely to see, but they are not pets and they are not even friends."

A cold tingle went right up Tyler's backbone. He wasn't always crazy about his sister, but he didn't want her shredded by some razor-horned horse, either.

"Are we done?" he asked as they climbed back onto the wagon and waited for Mr. Walkwell, who was still crunching toward them. "Where do we go next?"

Ragnar gave him a serious look. "It depends on whether you two learn to do as you are told. Because now we are going to show you some of the *dangerous* animals."

CHAPTER 8

REPTILES, MORE OR LESS

"But I still don't get it—where did the unicorns come from?" Lucinda asked as the wagon bumped along. "And the dragon?"

Ragnar smiled and shook his head. "I have said many times: that is not for me to answer. But look there and you will see something."

Lucinda didn't want to look at anything else. She wanted to keep the amazing sight of the unicorns in her memory and not let anything else push it out—that cloud of manes and tails and flashing eyes and horns.

And horns, yes. Poor Haneb. The farmhand had only been trying to protect her. She still felt bad about how she had reacted.

"What is it?" Tyler asked. "It's . . . huge!"

Lucinda looked up, suddenly fearful that they were being taken to something even more terrifying than the dragon—a chained ogre out of a story, or some monstrous, girl-grabbing gorilla. Instead she saw only a pale, white-washed building stretched along the valley floor below them. But what a building it was, sunk half into the hill-side, a single low wooden structure like a dozen oversized shoeboxes placed end to end, its roof covered in solar panels. It seemed as long as the immense playing field at her school. "It's . . . a giant barn," she said.

Ragnar nodded. "It is, child. That is the dragon barn. No dragons in it now, since Meseret is in the Sick Barn, but you will see what else is there."

"Was it built just for the dragon?" Tyler asked as the wagon crunched to a stop.

"No, this was made for an earlier owner of the land who kept cattle. We tore out many of the stalls to make space for Meseret. You will see."

"There are train tracks going right into it," Lucinda said as they walked through the low, dry grass toward the high doors.

"Of a sort," Ragnar said. "They are for a rolling flatcar, to bring feed. And to move Meseret when it must be done."

"Why would you even do that?" Tyler asked. "That dragon must weigh as much as a whale!"

"A small one, yes. But these creatures are delicate, and what makes one animal sick can sweep through them all. So we move the sick ones to the special barn. But you are right—it is not easy to move Meseret, even with the lifting-thing."

Lucinda was too startled by the smell and the heat that hit her as they went through the big doors to wonder what a "lifting-thing" might be. The ceiling of this barn was dauntingly high, twice as high as the Sick Barn's, spider-webbed with metal girders and dozens of bright hanging lights. The odor of the place made her nose prickle and her eyes water. It smelled like the dragon, but more so—more musky, more sour, more . . . strange.

Stranger than a dragon? she couldn't help thinking. A day ago she couldn't even have imagined meeting a dragon at all. She heard a sound behind her and turned to see Colin Needle coming in after them.

"Hello, Lucinda," he said. "Looks like I caught up with you."

"Are you not supposed to be working on the feed budget, Master Needle?" asked Ragnar sternly.

For a moment, as the pale boy stared angrily at the big yellow-haired man, Colin didn't look very nice at all. "As it happens, my mother sent me here to ask Gideon something."

Ragnar was still frowning. "Mr. Goldring is here? I thought he was ill this morning and was going to stay in bed."

Colin shrugged. "He changed his mind. My mother wasn't very happy about it, but you know how Gideon is—"

Just then something screeched, a noise like failing car brakes. Lucinda jumped. "What was that?" she demanded. "You said the dragon was gone!"

"Don't be such a baby," Tyler growled.

She wanted to slug him. Like he wasn't ever scared of anything! How about when Mom tried to get him to eat sushi?

Ragnar patted her shoulder. "I said no dragon. But the other serpents—this is their home too."

"And not just reptiles," Colin said helpfully. "Almost all of our cold-blooded animals live here. There are amphibians and some . . . well, not fish, exactly."

"Their water must boil," she said. "It's so hot in here!"

"We turn up the heating lights while Meseret is gone," Ragnar explained.

"Why?" asked Tyler.

Colin was happy to show what he knew. "Most of the time, she contributes a lot of the warming of this place all by herself."

Tyler scowled. "What, she breathes fire on everything?"

"No, Tyler." Colin said "Tyler" like he was an elementary school teacher. "Just with body heat. She's extremely large and she's warm-blooded."

They crossed the open area inside the doors and trooped

up the stairs behind Ragnar, who didn't look quite so big in this building. The second floor ran like a giant balcony all the way around the interior of the massive barn, leaving the middle open. From up there Lucinda could see the huge, empty expanse of straw-covered concrete where the dragon usually lay.

"Gideon is probably in the cockatrice pen," said Colin.

"Well, perhaps, then, we show those to you, if Gideon is there," Ragnar told Lucinda and Tyler. "But everyone must wear the eye shields."

"Goggles," Colin translated.

A large wire enclosure took up much of this side of the second floor, and someone was moving around inside it. The figure straightened up when it saw them and gave a jerky wave with a garden-gloved hand. Lucinda could tell it was Gideon only by his skinny shape and his bathrobe, since his head was covered by something like a bee-keeper's hood, which made him look like a very badly dressed space alien. It came to her suddenly that she didn't know what frightened her more—the animals or this stranger, this supposed relative, who, out of the blue, seemed to have claimed their lives.

Scattered on a table near the beginning of the wire mesh lay thick plastic goggles, each with its own elastic strap, and the kind of paper masks people wore in hospitals. Ragnar passed Lucinda and Tyler one of each, but Lucinda only stared at hers with dismay. "Do these cockywhatsits have diseases? I don't want to catch some snake disease." She heard Tyler snort but ignored it. *Someone* had to be practical.

"Not for disease." Ragnar pulled on the goggles and tugged the mask into place—the elastic barely stretched around his big head and bushy beard. "For spit."

"What?"

"You'll see," said Colin. "Don't worry, Lucinda, we're not going inside the pen. They're too nasty—and they bite, also. But it's the spitting you really want to avoid."

"Gross!" she said.

"Excellent!" said Tyler.

Uncle Gideon came out of the pen, being careful to latch the door behind him. Lucinda could see movement inside, but the enclosure was full of boxes and boards piled haphazardly and it was hard to make out what was actually in there. Gideon pulled off his hood and gave them an uncertain look. Lucinda, though she quaked inside, determinedly met his gaze. Gideon said, "What did you think of the unicorns?"

"It was amazing," Lucinda said. "They're beautiful!"

A broad grin spread across Gideon's face. "Aren't they?" he said. "Aren't they?"

"Where do they come from?" asked Tyler.

"Yes, when I see them running, I believe that what we're doing here is worth every dollar and every drop of sweat." Gideon mopped his brow with his sleeve. He was wearing ordinary pants under his bathrobe, but had bedroom slippers on his feet instead of regular shoes. "And in here we have the cockatrices and the basilisks. Don't take those goggles off until we tell you it's all right."

"What are they?" she asked. "Ragnar said they spit."

"Yes, yes. But it's perfectly all right." He frowned. "Haven't you even heard of these creatures before? Devil me, what happened to teaching children the classics? Basilisks go clear back to Pliny the Elder in ancient Rome—although old Pliny could have learned a thing or two from taking a tour of our little zoo." He wiped his forehead again. "For one thing, he'd find out that the cockatrice and the basilisk are actually the same creature."

"I don't know what either of those are," said Lucinda, trying to peer more closely through the wire without actually touching it. She was very nervous something might jump out at her. Considering the brightness of the lights overhead, the pen was quite dark and it was hard to make out anything. "Cockastripe?"

"Cock-a-trice," said Gideon. "A medieval monster, or at least it was in the eleventh and twelfth centuries when it started to show up in bestiaries. Head of a rooster, tail of a serpent. And basilisks were supposed to be dragons that could kill with their eyes—just by looking at someone!"

Lucinda took a step back. "But that's not true, is it?"

Gideon laughed. He seemed stronger than he had the night before. Maybe Mrs. Needle's medicine was helping him. "There's a grain of truth in most mythology, children. Ah, look there." He pointed to the corner of the cage where a quite remarkably ugly creature the size of a turkey had scrambled up onto a pile of wood to stand looking at them. From neck to long, draggled tail, it was covered with scales, between which poked straggly feathers, but its head was bare. At first Lucinda thought it was some kind of vulture, but the beaked face wasn't quite right. Then she saw that the beak was actually a snout full of little needle-sharp teeth. It lifted up a huge, bony claw and nipped at it for a moment, then put it down and tipped its head to stare at them again, yellow eyes unblinking.

"It's horrible!" said Lucinda.

"I daresay it thinks the same about *you*," Gideon pointed out in a grumpy voice. "But no animal is horrible, girl. Not one. They are all as they are made by Nature."

"Why does it have feathers?" Tyler asked. "It doesn't look like a bird."

"No, it's not. As best I can tell, it's something closer to a late dinosaur—feathered, like an archaeopteryx. But one thing about it *is* rather horrible. Ragnar?"

Ragnar shook his head as though he didn't approve, but he walked to a part of the pen nearer the cockatrice and banged on the wire with the flat of his hand before pulling back quickly. As the creature turned its hairless head toward him he stepped away. It kinked its neck and then jabbed its head as though trying to cough out something stuck in its throat. A stream of clear liquid splashed on the wire where Ragnar's hand had struck.

"Poison," Gideon said cheerfully. "And not a nice one. Isn't that fascinating? Won't do much more than irritate your skin, but if it got in your eyes you'd be blind—hence the goggles. And if you swallowed it you would be very sick, if not dead, which is why we have the surgical masks. Now come on and I'll show you the earlier stage of the life cycle—the fearful basilisk!" The skinny old man strutted along past the end of the wire enclosure, bathrobe flapping like the robe of some tatterered king. He seemed different today—happier, calmer, almost like a normal old man. Lucinda stepped wide around the spot where the poison had splashed on the fence.

The group stopped in a little bay between pens. Metal trays, each with its own lights—as if it needed to be any hotter in here!—had been set up side by side, perhaps a dozen in all. The bottoms of the trays were covered with straw, and each tray held from one to a half-dozen eggs. Lucinda could see they weren't chicken eggs. They were too round, and slightly saggy, like Ping-Pong balls someone had baked in an oven.

"The cockatrices tend to eat their own eggs in captivity, we've found," Gideon said. "And the young are vulnerable while they're small, so we keep them out of the main pen for the first few months." He indicated a row of glass tanks against the back wall of the barn, beyond the egg trays. "Come and see."

The tanks were like miniature versions of the wire pen, with sand on the bottom and piles of rocks. The creatures inside didn't seem as interested in hiding as those in the bigger pen. A half-dozen of them, each the size of a pet rat, crowded up against the glass; and when their long, hairless tails writhed they had the look of nestling snakes, although their lumpy little bodies were covered with fine, pale down. The creatures also had claws on their bony front feet, but no back legs that Lucinda could see. She shuddered as the blunt little snouts banged against the glass.

"They don't use their poison to kill prey when they're this small, but mostly for self-defense," Gideon said. "And they're so small it's not a stream of it they shoot but a mist—you might not even know you'd inhaled it until paralysis started to set in. Hence, I'm guessing, the idea that a basilisk can turn a man to stone with a mere look." He nodded vigorously. "Hungry. Do you want to see me feed them?"

Suddenly it was too much for Lucinda. She stumbled back, retreating as far from the scuttling creatures as possible until she had the second-floor railing at her back. She felt like she might faint or throw up.

"Hey, you okay?" Tyler asked. He actually sounded like he meant it.

"Yes, I'm just . . ." She took a deep breath.

"Come and see something else," said Colin kindly. "The flying snakes are in the next pen. They're rather pretty."

He was right. A tree stood in a generous, wide tub, and the red and black and gold snakes hung from its branches. Every now and then one of them would snap open pale wings like a Japanese lady's fans and glide to the ground. The largest wasn't much longer than Lucinda's forearm, and their enclosure didn't stink like the cockatrice cages.

"That's a spice tree," said Uncle Gideon. He had finished feeding the basilisks and come to join them. "Frankincense, to be specific, the resin that we are told the three wise men brought as a gift for the baby Jesus." He smiled a hard little smile. "It's harder to keep the tree alive than the winged snakes."

"Whoa," said Tyler suddenly. "Flying snakes. Are there flying monkeys here too?"

"Only one on the whole farm," Uncle Gideon said. "She's a real rarity."

"I saw her! The night I saw the dragon!"

"You did, did you?" Gideon shook his head. "I'm surprised. Zaza is usually shy of everyone, even us. That's why we let her have her freedom. Actually sometimes we don't see her for weeks."

"Her name is Zaza?" Tyler said it like he was memorizing something important—like a cheat code for a game he was playing, Lucinda thought. She just wanted to get out in the open air again, to somewhere that didn't smell like reptiles.

Farther along the second floor there was another pen, this one just a flimsy chicken-wire fence. The floor was covered with shallow pans of water. A number of slow, docile-looking creatures sat in the water or crawled stiff-legged across the floor. It was only when Lucinda looked at one that stood unmoving that she realized what made them so unusual.

"They have heads at both ends!"

"Awesome!" Tyler leaned over the rail, which made the light material buckle a little and earned him a poke from Uncle Gideon.

"Don't break my cage, boy, we'll have amphisbaenae all over the place. Yes, they do seem to have two heads, don't they? An amphisbaena's back is a decoy, it turns out—a tail with scales that look just like the creature's eyes, mouth, and nostrils on the other end. A myth put to rest, this one. Still, they don't exist anymore on earth—except right here."

"Why is that, Uncle Gideon?" Tyler asked.

"Well, well, well," said Uncle Gideon with a hard smile. "That inconvenient curiosity of yours just won't let up for a minute, now will it?"

Lucinda could see the look in Tyler's eye. "What do you expect?" he said. "We're surrounded by magical animals, but you won't even—"

"Stop right there!" cried Uncle Gideon, causing strange sounds to rise from cages all around. "Magical—what utter garbage! All of these animals, boy—*all of them*—have at some time been alive in Earth's history. Apart from our work here they are all now completely extinct, as far as we know. These are real animals, as created by Nature, and if I hear any more fairy-tale nonsense from you," Gideon spluttered, "why, I'll . . ."

Tyler said, "Well, it's DNA, then, isn't it? Making monsters by, like, gene splicing . . ."

Uncle Gideon actually started to turn purple. "You, boy," he said, "have clearly been watching too much so-called 'reality' TV. Or reading trash magazines, I don't know what. We will hear no more of that rubbish, if you please!" He took a breath; his color eased. "Now," he said, as if trying to be jolly again, "enough arguing. We have many more things to see and a limited amount of time. Come along. Sadly the hippocampus is in the Sick Barn—I think it may be dying. It was one of our finest specimens."

"Some animals are not meant to be kept captive," Ragnar said—a touch darkly, Lucinda thought.

"Yes, well." Gideon clapped his hands together as though he'd finished a difficult, messy job. "I don't think we'll take the time to show you all the birds upstairs. The roc is only small, and to be honest I doubt our phoenix is actually a phoenix. Now come along. We may still have time to see Eliot—he likes to come out in the morning, but morning is almost over!"

His eyes, in his wrinkled face, were bright—too bright. Lucinda could not meet them. She dropped her own, looking at her feet and wondering what might be coming next, and what kind of creature Eliot could possibly be.

Uncle Gideon took them to the pond in his small truck, an electric vehicle not much bigger than a golf cart. The others followed in Mr. Walkwell's wagon. Unlike Mr. Walkwell, Uncle Gideon clearly had no dislike of motorized transport, and did, in fact, seem to go to the opposite extreme—he drove like he was auditioning for NASCAR. Nor had he even bothered with a seat belt. "We'll get there much faster this way," he shouted at Lucinda and Tyler as they crashed down into a dip in the road, then actually lifted off the ground as they bounded up again. "And Eliot doesn't show himself much after noon."

"Who's Eliot?" asked Lucinda as she clung to the frame of Gideon's little truck. Death by dragon, death by golf cart—one way or the other, they were clearly doomed.

"You'll see, if we're lucky. If anyone knew he was here, Eliot alone would bring in tourists by the hundreds of thousands!"

"You're going to bring in tourists?" said Tyler.

"What? No, never!" Uncle Gideon took his eyes off the bumpy road long enough to give Tyler a very stern glance. The truck promptly jounced so hard that Lucinda's head and ears began to ache. "That's the most important rule of Ordinary Farm—everything here is a secret. Secret, secret, *secret*!"

"We know," said Tyler pointedly.

"Just remember, even a breath of what's here getting out to the world at large will ruin everything. Everything!" He shouted the words, then fell silent, looking as sour as if he had caught Tyler and Lucinda making a video of the place to post on the internet. He said nothing for the next several minutes as they careened along the bumpy road, then emerged at last out of a little forest of oak and red-barked manzanita.

"Wow! That's not a pond." Lucinda stared out at the vast, flat expanse of water that filled the bottom of a medium-sized valley. "That's a lake!"

"'The Pond' is what old Octavio used to call it. He had a rather . . . dry sense of humor," said Gideon. "Why do you think he called this place Ordinary Farm?"

"What's in there?" Tyler asked. "A whale?"

"Nothing so ordinary." Gideon giggled to himself. He seemed to be in a better mood again. Lucinda had thought he was going to shove them out of the truck when he had been yelling about secrecy. "No, let's park and walk over to the rocks and sit quietly. Then maybe we'll see him."

"The sun feels good," said Uncle Gideon. "I should get out more often, no matter what Mrs. Needle says."

They had been sitting on a high place above the water for some minutes. Suddenly Lucinda spotted something long and silvery moving just beneath the surface of the water. "There!" she said. "I see something!"

"Ssshhh," cautioned Uncle Gideon. "Not too loud. Eliot is one of the shyest of the animals we have."

"Eliot? That's a weird name for . . ." Tyler abruptly fell silent, watching with his mouth open as the creature broke the water about a hundred feet away from where they sat, its silvery expanse of neck kicking up a curl of wake below. "For . . . for a sea serpent," he finished. The shiny, snakelike head swayed from side to side, then darted back down into the water. The curling neck remained visible above the surface for a moment, a shining loop, then it, too, disappeared like a knot being undone.

Lucinda's heart beat fast as she watched the graceful monster slide down and then back up to the surface again, but this time more from excitement than fear.

"I'm afraid the name *Eliot* is a bit of a joke," said Gideon. "Ness, like Loch Ness, do you see? *Eliot Ness*?"

"I've heard of Loch Ness," said Lucinda quietly, staring. "But I still don't understand the Eliot part."

"Never mind. He was a famous man, but long before your time. In any case, our Eliot goes after fish like the old Eliot used to catch bootleggers. Watch."

They sat watching the lake monster feed, all silvery swiftness, until the sun was high in the sky and Gideon, weirdly calm now after a morning of watching his creatures, decided it was time they headed back for lunch.

CHAPTER 9

TEA WITH THE
EMPRESS OF LILIES

Lucinda woke up late in the afternoon, feeling the way she had once in fifth grade when she'd come down with a really bad fever and had to stay home from school for almost two weeks. Time had seemed to pass in strange pieces when the fever was strong, and sometimes it had been hard to remember whether something she was recalling had been real or just a dream.

Like now.

She had only meant to take a little nap, but she had dropped unconscious like someone had hit her with a club. Now she lay on her mattress, breathing the too-warm air and remembering every little bit of the events of the morning. It was hard to believe it had all happened, the unicorns and dragons and sea serpents, but there couldn't be any such thing as a dream this complicated and realistic.

Not unless you went crazy.

That was a disturbing thought. Lucinda sat up. It was breathlessly hot in her room. She struggled out of bed to get a drink of water from the bathroom.

She knocked on Tyler's door for at least a minute. He didn't answer, so she wandered down the stairs with the idea of finding something better to drink than warm tap water. Within moments she realized she had taken yet another wrong turn and was in a dusty hallway covered with dark red wallpaper, the walls full of empty picture frames.

What's with this crazy place? she wondered. *Why do I keep getting lost?* It was almost like the house itself kept turning *away* from her, like when the other girls at school had secrets and were freezing her out. Lucinda hated being on the outside—it took all her strength away, left her feeling too weak to do anything except say sour, nasty things.

But right now there was no one to say anything *to* —only the house and its long, dark, many-angled corridors full of stiflingly warm air.

None of it made any sense—not the house, not the farm. Where did someone get actual, honest-to-goodness *dragons*? Was Tyler right about Uncle Gideon being the mastermind of some weird genetic project like in a science-fiction movie? What else could it be? The animals weren't robots or any kind of special effects, that was for sure. Meseret had looked her right in the eyes. Lucinda had no question that dragon was real.

She looked down at the threadbare carpet and its design of green roses. She'd never been in this hall before, she was sure. She sighed and started off again. She spent at least ten minutes wandering up and down hallways and staircases without coming across an outside window or anything else she recognized.

Finally she opened a heavy paneled door and found herself in another unfamiliar place, a sitting room of some kind—a parlor, with dusty sofas and shelves full of photographs. The carpet, with its black and gray patches and green roses, was mirrored more or less in reverse by the wallpaper, where the background was a pale green and the twining roses were black. Lucinda hesitated before backing out. The pictures had caught her attention. She let the door fall shut behind her and walked deeper into the room. There were dozens of photographs, and they all seemed to be of the same dark-haired woman.

Lucinda sat down on one of the sofas, the better to examine the pictures on the coffee table, but the cushions were thick with cobwebs and dust. She jumped up, brushing herself off with little squeals of disgust, and decided she could look at things just as well standing up.

In some of the photos the woman was with other people—one looked like a picnic beside a lake, where she sat smiling on a blanket with half a dozen other people in old-fashioned clothes—but in most she was alone, smiling or laughing or sometimes just looking at the camera with calm attention. Some were black-and-white, some were in color, although none of the color photos looked quite realistic. The woman was very pretty, with a long-legged figure and the kind of long, dark brown curls Lucinda had only seen before on women in old paintings.

At last, Lucinda turned to examine the rest of the room. It felt like a place no one had visited for years—faintly creepy, maybe even haunted, she thought—but strangely she wasn't at all frightened; in fact, she almost felt like she was dreaming. In one corner a tailor's dummy stood like a headless scarecrow. Lucinda walked over to the shadows where it stood and put her hands on the dummy's waist. It was slender, but the hips and breasts were full. Their mother's friend Mrs. Peirho made clothes sometimes, and she had a tailor's dummy too. She had told Lucinda that they could be adjusted to your own exact size. Had this one belonged to the woman in the pictures? Whoever she was, Lucinda thought, she must have been very small. . . .

"Wasn't she lovely?" said a voice. "Her name ,was Grace."

Lucinda let out a little scream and whirled around. Patience Needle was standing right behind her, as if she had suddenly risen up from the floor. Lucinda stumbled and put out a hand to steady herself on the tabletop. One of the framed pictures teetered and then fell. Lucinda did her best to catch it, but it tumbled to the floor and the glass broke, making a noise almost as loud as her scream. When Lucinda picked it up, feeling both ashamed and angry, she cut her fingers on a jagged edge.

"I'm sorry I startled you, dear," said Mrs. Needle, and held out a hand to Lucinda, who shrank from her. "And I'm sorry things have been so strange for you children since you've arrived. You're lost, aren't you? Oh, look, you've hurt your hand. Really, you must let me help you."

Lucinda's fingers were really starting to ache now. The blood was making a little pool in her palm, and looking at it suddenly made her feel dizzy.

"Poor you!" said Mrs. Needle. "That's a nasty gash there. Don't worry about the broken glass, I'll clean it up later." Mrs. Needle took a clean white handkerchief out of the pocket of her skirt and wrapped it around Lucinda's injured fingers. "You must let me help you—I *insist.*"

Standing this close to Mrs. Needle, Lucinda could smell the faint but lovely scent of lilies, rich and sweet. "Who is that woman in all the pictures?"

"Her name was Grace Tinker—well, Grace Goldring after her marriage. She was Gideon's wife. He lost her many years ago but he loved her very, very much. I don't think you should mention her in front of him." Mrs. Needle put a hand on Lucinda's shoulder. "Look at this place! I'm ashamed to see how long it's been since we've dusted in here—what must you think of us? Now come and let me take care of you."

Relief that she was no longer lost suddenly flooded through her. Lucinda let herself be steered out of the old parlor and taken down some stairs, then gently coaxed this way and that, as if she was a boat drifting down a river. "Here," said Mrs. Needle at last, ushering Lucinda into a room unlike anything she had yet seen in this strange, strange house.

It was very large, but at Ordinary Farm that wasn't unusual. One wall was a giant filing cabinet with what seemed like hundreds of little drawers in rows reaching up to the ceiling, like the cells of a wooden beehive, each perhaps the width of a hand. A rolling ladder stood to one side and a long desk stretched along another wall. Part of the desk was covered with stacks of books, but it also held a microscope and a computer, although the latter seemed weirdly out of place in the otherwise old-fashioned room.

At the far end of the room stood several open doors, and Lucinda caught glimpses of two bedrooms and a bathroom as Mrs. Needle led her to one of the chairs. She made Lucinda sit down, then vanished into yet another room. "I'll just make some tea!" she called.

Lucinda heard a kettle moan, then whistle, then shriek

as she stared around the room, still feeling groggy. High windows rose along the wall across from the desk, but although the light of late afternoon was still in the sky there didn't seem to be much to see outside but another section of the house's crazy-colored outside walls. Below these windows stood dozens of potted plants that filled the room with the smell of live greenery and damp soil and something else less pleasant—something that was like meat, or blood.

Mrs. Needle came back bearing a steaming mug in one hand and a small bottle in the other. She set down the mug, then unwound the handkerchief from Lucinda's fingers.

Something cold splashed on Lucinda's cuts, something that stung like Mrs. Needle had dabbed them with acid. Lucinda gasped, but the pain dissolved swiftly, leaving her trembling. A moment later a delicious coolness had settled over her hand and the throbbing had melted away.

"Oh! What was *that*?"

"Now drink this," commanded Mrs. Needle, handing her the cup of tea.

Lucinda stared at the creamy brown liquid inside the china mug. The smell of the tea—a fragrant, black-leaf smell—washed over her. She lifted it to her lips. She had not known tea could be anything as intense as this, as dizzying and delightful.

"There," said Mrs. Needle, taking the mug away from

her, "you'll feel much better now."

The room wavered like a mirage. Lucinda's heart was pounding, she suddenly realized. There was a vase over-filled with white lilies nearby, and their scent was carried to Lucinda by a breeze from the window. She was drown-ing in it. Her throat felt squeezed, and she saw her own hand like a claw pulling on the neckband of her T-shirt. Mrs. Needle was very pretty, but she seemed to be a long distance away, like an empress on a high throne. An empress of lilies . . .

"Hush, dear, hush," said Mrs. Needle, patting Lucinda's hand.

Lucinda blinked. She hadn't been saying anything, had she?

"Are you feeling better, Lucinda? How are your cuts?"

"Much better, thank you."

"Good." Mrs. Needle held out her hand, revealing the bloodstained handkerchief she had taken off Lucinda's wounded fingers. "Do you see this?" she said. "People in this modern age of machines and invisible electricity talk so much about their new ideas, but really nothing is new."

Lucinda stared. How beautiful Mrs. Needle's mouth was as it formed the words she spoke—and how beautiful the words, pronounced in that perfect English accent.

"Take blood, for instance," Mrs. Needle continued. "Long before there was any talk of . . . genes or the DNA, people knew that blood and hair and spittle contained the magical essences of things." She nodded her head slowly, then looked up at Lucinda and smiled. "Would you like to see a little trick?"

Lucinda could only nod. She had suddenly noticed that at some point Mrs. Needle had let down her black hair. It was much longer than Lucinda had guessed—halfway down her back or more. *Letting your hair down.* She understood the expression now. It meant being friends, feeling comfortable. Right now, she felt very comfortable.

"Watch, then." Mrs. Needle folded the bloodied handkerchief into a ball so that only the white was visible, then closed her fingers around it entirely, making a fist. "Look closely!" She opened her hand and the wadded handkerchief slowly unwound until the bloodstain was again visible—but it had changed shape. Now it looked like the silhouette of a girl. With its long, straight hair it could almost be Lucinda herself. Then the red silhouette began to move. It might only have been Mrs. Needle gently flexing her hand, but it looked like the little blood-Lucinda was . . . dancing.

"Oh." Lucinda let out her breath. "Oh, wow! How do you *do* that?"

Mrs. Needle closed her fingers on the handkerchief once more. "Just a little trick. An amusement. You enjoyed it?"

Lucinda felt as if her head was as big and round and

light as a helium balloon. "Can you do it again?"

Mrs. Needle's shook her head sadly. "It only works once, I'm sad to say." She brightened. "But if you could bring me something of your brother's, I could show you another charming trick. Would you like that?"

"Something of . . . ?"

"Blood, like this. Or maybe just some hair . . ."

"But I don't know where he is. He went out somewhere."

"Did he now? Well, why don't you have a look in his room? Perhaps he's left a comb there." When Mrs. Needle smiled she looked like a beautiful queen from a fairy tale. "Why don't you go see?"

"I'll get lost again," Lucinda told her sadly.

"No, you won't. Just go out that door. Oh, do hurry—I'm having such a good time with you, I don't want to waste any of it."

Lucinda walked to the door, dizzy and uncertain. It felt like the most popular girl in school had suddenly decided she wanted Lucinda for a best friend, and that was thrilling—wasn't it?

Mrs. Needle had been absolutely right. Once out the door, Lucinda climbed a single staircase and found herself in the hallway she shared with Tyler. He still wasn't back, but she pushed his unlatched door open and went in. It was already a typical Tyler mess, which was pretty impressive considering he'd only had a day or so to get it started. She found his hairbrush where he'd dropped it on the floor near the bed, its bristles snarled with his light brown hair. Normally she wouldn't have touched any of Tyler's personal items without putting on a hazmat suit, but at this moment she was feeling dreamy, and distant, and the prospect of not doing this thing seemed so hard, like swimming against incoming waves. . . . It wouldn't matter so much anyway—not really.

She found her way back to Mrs. Needle's room with the same weird ease—one moment she was in the hall, the next sitting at the table again.

"Oh, well done." Mrs. Needle clapped her hands. There was something so charmingly open, the way she did that. "Here, let me have it." The Englishwoman peeled one of Tyler's long hairs out of the knot wrapped around the bristles and put the single hair in a little dish, then passed her hand over it once and struck a match. The hair burned blue for a moment and made a puff of smoke that seemed far too large for the size of the flame, then the smoke swirled into a shape—Tyler's face, as unmistakable as a photograph. Her brother was brushing his hair and his features were contorted in a grimace of pain because the hairbrush had caught in a tangle. Lucinda and Mrs. Needle both laughed. A moment later the smoke-Tyler fell apart.

"That's *amazing!*"

"I'm so glad you enjoyed it." Mrs. Needle handed her

back the hairbrush. The entire tangle of hair was gone from the bristles, although she had only burned one. "I do love to make children happy. Now, have some more tea, dear, and let's talk. I want you to tell me *everything*. You see, I'm really very interested in you and Tyler, but I know so little about you." Mrs. Needle laughed again and patted Lucinda's arm. "Did your mother give you good advice for your trip in the days after she received Gideon's letter?"

Lucinda giggled in sour amusement.

"She must have had some wise things to say, your mother."

When Lucinda's giggles became outright laughter, Mrs. Needle frowned kindly and put her cold hand over Lucinda's. "I'm so sorry—I don't mean to pry if it's difficult to talk about her. Is she hard to get along with?"

"Yeah, sometimes," said Lucinda. "She doesn't really listen to me." She frowned, trying to remember. "What did she say? God, she's always talking, but she never really says anything. Oh yeah. She said she hadn't known we had a rich relative and would we please not scare him off. Ooh," she said, full of a pleasurable sense of naughtiness. "I feel like I want to tell you just everything."

"Then do so, dear," Mrs. Needle said, smiling. "We'll be such good friends! I promise you won't find a better listener than me."

Lucinda talked and talked, and out came more than she had ever told anyone in her life. She didn't know why she wanted to talk so much today, but it seemed so natural to share all kinds of secrets as the sky went from dark purple to black beyond the windows, as the two of them sat like old friends in the room reeking of white lilies and the faint tang of blood.

Chapter 10

Old Banana Breath

When he first got back from meeting Eliot the sea monster, Tyler had been exhausted, but after a few minutes of lying on his bed and feeling the afternoon get hotter, he knew it would be harder to fall asleep than it used to be on Christmas Eve when he was a kid. How could he just lie there? He was in the middle of the biggest adventure a kid had ever had—like something out of the most spectacular special-effects movie of the year. It made a top-of-the-line video game like *Deep End* seem like *Pong* or some other ancient history. Dragons! Unicorns! Sea serpents!

What if there were real dinosaurs here too? Or outer-space creatures? And where had they all *come* from?

A scratching at the window distracted him. Something was sitting on the sill, a bundle of gray and white with a pink face and two huge eyes.

The monkey! The *flying* monkey!

Tyler went slowly toward the window, careful not to frighten the little animal. He stared. The monkey stared back, seemingly undisturbed by his nearness. It wasn't very big—less than a foot tall, greenish gray on the back and pale on the belly, with a spiky green-gray cap of fur atop its round little head like a hairstyle out of some hilariously ancient 1980s music video. What was most amazing, of course, were the wings, although they were folded and hard to see. It didn't have a separate pair of wings on its back like an angel (or like the only other flying monkeys he knew about, the ones in *The Wizard of Oz*), but instead they were more like a bat's, stretching between its arms and its knees.

What had Uncle Gideon called it?

"Zaza?" he said quietly. The monkey tipped its head and stared at him as though Tyler, of the two of them, was the more unlikely creature. Tyler lifted his hand to touch the glass. "Zaza?"

The monkey tilted over backward and dropped off the windowsill so unexpectedly that Tyler felt his heart stumble for a moment, as though he had broken an expensive ornament, but the monkey only spread her wings and sailed in a lazy circle down to the cherry tree below Lucinda's window. She stopped there, clinging upside down to a branch, still watching him with her shiny, dark little eyes as if she was waiting for something.

She seemed to want Tyler to follow her.

He wasn't quite sure how he found his way down through the confusing maze of stairs and hallways, and down to the ground floor and then outside—he seemed to do better with this house when he didn't think about it too much—but a few minutes later he was standing beneath the bough of the cherry tree looking up at the winged monkey. The dry grass crackled under his feet and the hot air was full of little buzzing things.

"So is that really your name, huh? Zaza? That's a funny name."

The monkey yawned as though Tyler was a fine one to talk but she wasn't going to be rude enough to say anything about it. Then, without warning, she dropped down from the tree onto his shoulder. Tyler jumped and said, "Hey!" but she only settled in and began to scratch herself. He was surprised by how light she was. For her size he'd expected her to be something like a small cat, but instead she didn't seem to weigh much more than his long-gone hamster, Fang, although she was a great deal bigger.

He took a few steps away from the house and the monkey leaped up from his shoulder, then drifted back down toward him in a long, shallow glide and went once around his head before she flapped again and circled away. She sure *seemed* like she wanted him to follow her someplace.

Well, it beat lying in bed.

Zaza led Tyler around the outskirts of the house, through an orderly vegetable patch the size of a small baseball field where she plucked and ate a succession of different greens growing close to the ground, then through a tangled, deserted-seeming garden and past a greenhouse at its center that looked like it had been abandoned for a long time. Tyler could see strange shapes through the dirty glass, and in some places huge leaves pressed up against the panes from the inside, as though whatever had once been cultivated in there had been allowed to run riot. It was a little creepy, all that oversized green life just on the other side of cracked glass. He was glad that the little monkey didn't linger.

She led him around the corner of another building, which was connected back to the house by a long covered pathway. Tyler found himself looking across a big open space with a view of the immense cement half-cylinder of the Sick Barn. He could see the high windows where he had peered in the night before—had it really been less than a day since then? Amazing. But as much as he wanted to see the dragon again, he didn't want anyone to notice he was out of his room just when Gideon seemed to have forgiven him, so he forced himself to turn away and focus on where the monkey was leading him. Still, he couldn't help saying to himself, "There's a dragon in there, and I saw it. A real . . . live . . . *dragon!*"

How many other kids could say that?

This house and its buildings and grounds really *did* go on forever! Tyler's own room was a quarter of an hour behind him now and the main farmhouse—the part of the house that everyone used most—was completely out of sight. The monkey had led him past more neglected gardens and past several more outbuildings until finally they reached a long, low structure two stories high except for a domed turret looming above the middle of it. Another overgrown garden stretched beside it, full of old, tangled rosebushes and sprawling hedges that had not been trimmed for years.

Tyler trotted down a covered passage lined with wooden pillars that ran the length of the long building, like a covered walkway in a Greek temple—something Tyler had seen in a schoolbook, or more likely, some game design. But instead of being marble, everything was made of wood and painted in shades of brown and gray and green and white. Well, except the parts that were glass, and there were plenty of those. Tall windows lined the ground level as well as the floor above.

Zaza, gliding along in front of him, suddenly halted and crawled through a broken window, disappearing into the building. Dismayed, Tyler wondered, *Does she want me to climb in through a twelve-inch hole eight feet off the ground?* He had passed at least two doors, though, so he walked back and tried the nearest.

Bingo! The door swung open. Nobody locked anything around here.

Tyler stepped into a small room, a sort of antechamber with dark wood paneling, lots of coat hooks, and a stand with several dusty umbrellas. This wing of the house had the smell of a place nobody had disturbed for a long time, like an underground tomb.

Or a palace, he thought a moment later as he stepped through into a library. *More like a palace.*

It really was like some fabulous scene in a movie: Tyler grew dizzy just looking up and around. The walls were covered with bookshelves, from the dusty carpets almost to the roof. There was no second floor, just a high ceiling and all those big windows letting the afternoon sunlight stream in. Plenty of daylight still remained, but the old-fashioned electrical lights he'd seen everywhere around the farm hung all around the big room as well, high in the rafters and also on long wires over clusters of over-stuffed chairs and sofas. Tyler had the thrilling sense that the farmhouse really *was* a palace, or even an entire lost ancient city—everywhere you went you found something crazy and wonderful. He had never imagined that there could be so many books in one place—this was a palace of books, an *empire* of books.

It's too bad they wasted all this space on 'em, Tyler thought. *It could have been a totally sweet game room.*

Books, after all, were pretty boring, and he usually did his best to avoid them. It was because his mother was always going on about how kids who read were better than the ones who didn't—better than game-playing idiots like her own son, she meant. But Tyler knew better. GameBoss and TV were so much more interesting than almost any book—especially this kind, the old kind that surrounded him now, most of which didn't even have pictures.

But still, he had to admit the place itself was pretty cool.

He walked a little way down the broad central aisle until he was beneath the spot where the roof bulged up into a dome. The dome had little windows of its own, and it was painted on the inside with all kinds of weird things—animals and trees and strange letters he couldn't read. He walked back and forth beneath, calling out and listening to his voice echo back from the high ceiling and the dome.

Outside, the sun went behind a cloud. The room darkened and Tyler suddenly didn't like the place quite as much. He began turning on lights, climbing onto chairs to reach some of the big switches on the walls, sneezing as dust puffed up from the chair cushions. Not all of the switches worked, but golden light blossomed from enough of the lamps that the library began to look cozy and welcoming again. Tyler began brushing dust off the sofas. He felt a bit like Goldilocks as he tried them out. When he found one he liked, he lay down completely and put his dirty sneakers up onto the upholstery, then put his hands behind his head and looked around, master of an entire building.

A guy could get used to this, he thought. Then he found himself face-to-face with a pair of staring eyes.

Tyler yelled and leaped to his feet. A moment later he laughed at himself, although his heart was still beating fast. "You dork!" he said out loud. What had spooked him was only a stupid old painting looking down at him from the wall, lit now by one of the electric bulbs so that the man's glaring eyes seemed almost alive.

It wasn't Gideon—the man in the picture was about the same age but his clothes were really, really old-fashioned, a long coat with a high white collar, and his face was a different shape from Gideon's too. What about the guy who'd built the farmhouse? What had they said his name was—Octavio something? Yes, that was it, Octavio Tinker. This must be him, Tyler decided. The person responsible for this whole crazy place.

The man in the picture did look a bit like a mad scientist. His dark gray hair stuck out over his ears like little wings, and his mustache curled up at the ends like something out of a cartoon. Tyler could imagine him twirling them between his fingertips and saying, "And now—tremble before my death ray!"

But he didn't look completely like a villain. A dog sat comfortably at his feet, some small black and white breed that Tyler didn't recognize, and Octavio held an object in his hand that looked mysterious but not particularly ominous—a striking concoction of golden metal, brown wood, and glass lenses.

Tyler stood up and walked toward the picture, squinting at the thing in the man's hand, but he couldn't make much of it—it looked like something out of a kid's story, some kind of magic seeing-device.

Probably just an old-fashioned microscope, Tyler decided at last. *Back in the past they probably thought that was the coolest invention ever. Man, they would have freaked out if they saw a GameBoss!*

What was interesting, though, was the way that the man in the picture stared out so intently, not at the viewer, as Tyler had first thought, but at something . . . *beyond.* Tyler turned, wondering if some other portrait might be staring back from that wall behind him, but instead he saw only a very simple dark door set in the wall between two sets of tall bookshelves.

As Tyler walked toward the door he felt a little tingle on his neck, as though old Octavio might be climbing down out of the frame behind him. He knew that was totally silly, but he looked anyway. The mustached scientist was still in his painting, staring out with solemn amusement.

An old brass key with a loop of yarn dangling from it was already in the keyhole, as though someone had unlocked the door only moments earlier. Tyler opened the door slowly, half expecting to find a dead body (or a half-dead murderous zombie or something else that would be in a scary movie). Instead he found himself in a fairly ordinary old bedroom—a retiring room off of the library—with a four-poster bed and a large washstand. He took a few steps inside and stopped. There was very little dust in here, and the air seemed different from in the library just a few feet away—close and tight in his throat.

The washstand had an old marble sink and a jug for water. Behind the basin, mahogany columns framed a huge mirror. Tyler moved to the front of the sink, drawn by something he could not at first put his finger on—then he saw it: the room reflected in the mirror was not exactly the same as the one he was standing in. Here, where Tyler stood, the light had disappeared from the window high on one wall, across from the bed. But in the mirror of the washstand the light of the reflected room was stronger, and he could see that the sky outside the window was still early-afternoon blue.

A chill went up and down his back, and his scalp tingled.

He moved closer to the mirror, but was distracted suddenly by something on the floor, peeking out from underneath the washstand. Tyler reached down and picked it up. It was a tattered old piece of paper, its edges shredded and stained. What remained was covered with somebody's skinny, old-fashioned handwriting. It was too dark in the bedroom to read it. He clutched it tightly, then looked up again. The light in the mirror still seemed different. He reached out his hand to touch the mirror and his reflection reached out too.

The Tyler reflected in the mirror was wearing a watch—the diver's watch his father had given him for his twelfth birthday, with all the dials and things he'd never figured out how to use.

But he had left the watch on the table in his room—there was nothing on his own wrist but freckles.

His blood roaring in his ears, Tyler lifted his other arm. The mirror Tyler did the same, perfectly synchronized. Tyler here and now held the scrap of paper in that hand; the hand of the reflection was empty.

He stared openmouthed at the mirror, and as he did so he saw something else. Someone in a dark, hooded cloak was standing in the reflected doorway behind him, watching him.

This time Tyler shouted aloud with surprise and terror, a ragged noise that echoed flatly in the small room. When he whirled around no one was there. He dashed out of the haunted room into the library aisle and stopped, listening for footsteps, listening for any evidence that whatever he had seen through that washstand mirror was, in fact, here with him now, pursuing him. Something with clawed fingers grabbed at the back of his neck.

When his shrieks finally died down and no werewolf or vampire had seized him, Tyler climbed back onto his feet—he had been lying on the floor with his hands over his head—and discovered a very frightened Zaza clinging to the nearest bookcase, staring at him with eyes so wide it seemed certain she'd never seen a boy having a total wuss-out fit before.

"So that was *you*, huh?" Tyler tried to laugh, for the monkey's benefit if no one else's. "Old Banana Breath. Should have known. Land on a guy's neck . . ."

But, of course, unless the winged monkey also had a hooded cloak she liked to wear, it still didn't explain the person he'd seen in the reflection.

Tyler was shivering now. He'd had quite enough of the library. He turned off the lights as quickly as he could and hurried outside.

Zaza followed him, although none of her fluttering circles brought her too close, and she kept looking at him worriedly, as if he might start screaming and thrashing again at any moment.

The flying monkey left him outside the doorway leading to the kitchen. Tyler could hear people talking in the dining room, but he didn't go in. He hurried through the kitchen, pocketing a few bits of fruit for the monkey in case she came back to his window again, then made his way upstairs. He found their hallway so quickly and easily this time he didn't even realize he was there until he saw the familiar carpet. He left the fruit in his room and knocked on Lucinda's door, but she didn't answer. He certainly wasn't going to wait. His sister was probably downstairs already and Tyler was getting hungrier by the second.

He almost ran directly into Colin Needle downstairs, who stepped without warning into the dining room doorway like he was trying to block Tyler's entrance.

"What are you doing?" Tyler demanded. "I nearly knocked you over."

"Oh, sorry." Colin didn't sound like he meant it. "I see you're finding your way around."

"Yeah," said Tyler, trying to push past him, but Colin moved back into his path.

"By the way, I noticed that you were in the library."

Suspicion made Tyler's skin prickle. "How do you know *that*?"

"Because you turned on most of the lights, stupid. Even in daytime I could see that from my window. Nobody's been in there for years so I knew it must be you. We've all seen how the famously daring Master Jenkins likes to go out and stick his nose into things."

"Just get out of my way," Tyler told him, pushing him,

but Colin wasn't ready to move yet.

"And I saw you making friends with the monkey," the older boy observed. "How sweet."

"What if I did? She's not your monkey, is she?"

"Lord, no!" Colin sounded like a little old man instead of a teenager. "My mother *hates* that animal. I was just going to warn you not to bring it around her." He gave Tyler an odd, sudden smirk—he looked like he had a secret he was itching to tell. "Well, toodle-oo!"

Tyler watched him go, nettled. That had been a deliberate attempt to get under his skin. But why? Why should Colin care what Tyler did?

As he pushed through into the dining room, he suddenly recalled something he'd forgotten in the last hour's excitement and confusion. That weird trick mirror above the washstand had startled him so badly that he'd left behind the ancient piece of paper he'd found there—the one with the scratchy writing.

Well, it would just have to stay there, Tyler decided. He was hungry now—no, *starving*. And besides, he couldn't see himself going back into the haunted library any time soon.

CHAPTER 11

STANDARD ISSUE

Tyler seemed very revved up, bouncing on the edge of the bed. "Lucinda, get up. We're going into town!"

Lucinda's head felt as heavy as a balloon full of wet sand. The morning sun was streaming through the window, and she could hear a jay squawking somewhere outside. She vaguely remembered finding the Grace Parlor, as she thought of it, then Mrs. Needle giving her a cup of tea, but not much else that had happened after that. She realized she must have slept all evening and all night.

"Luce, *wake up now*! We're going into town."

"Huh?" Her tongue felt like it was coated in peanut butter gone bad.

"Come on, you've been sleeping since yesterday afternoon. Hours and hours—you missed dinner. So, c'mon, Luce, *get up!*"

He had the grace to look a little shame-faced.

Lucinda tried to sit up, which was no easy thing with her brother going *boing, boing, boing* on the edge of the bed. She had a clean bandage on her hand, and the cuts beneath didn't hurt too badly at all. "Okay," she mumbled, pushing herself out of bed. "Just let me put my shoes on." She frowned at herself in the mirror. "And comb my hair."

Tyler rolled his eyes but got out of her way. "Just don't take forever. Man, you should see all the awesome stuff there is on this farm, Luce. I spent a few hours doing the rounds with Ragnar—you know, the guy with the beard?"

"Stop bouncing or wait outside, will you?"

"I like Ragnar. But, man, I hate that Colin guy."

"Would you quit obsessing about Colin? What did he ever do to you?"

"Why? Do you like him or something?" Tyler stopped in the doorway and stared at her with horror. "Oh, perfect— my sister has a crush on the evil henchman."

"Tyler! He's not an evil anything. Just shut up. My head hurts."

"Come on, Luce!" Now he was jumping up and down in the hall.

"Okay! I'll be right there!" She slammed the bedroom door shut on him, which punished no one but herself.

Normally that would have been enough for them to stay silent with each other for hours, but Tyler kept trying to talk to her as they sat on the wagon in the hot sun. At first it just made her more irritated, but after a while it occurred to her that for once Tyler was actually trying to *communicate*. It was like someone had stolen her little brother and substituted some kind of pod boy.

"There's been so much stuff going on!" he said. "I tried to wake you up before we went out this morning, but you were totally snoring. It was so cool! Ragnar let me feed the griffins. They're little. There isn't a mom or dad. They're, like, birds—they have eagle beaks, but they have bodies like something else. Ragnar said people used to say they were part lion, but really it's just that they're kind of yellow like a lion and they have this kind of weird fluffy fur on the back end where the feathers stop—"

"So why won't anyone tell us where they come from? What's the big secret?"

Mr. Walkwell half turned in his seat, as though he was going to say something, but instead he just flicked the reins and muttered to the horse.

"I know," Tyler said quietly. "I asked Ragnar that. He just says it's up to Uncle Gideon. But it has to be some kind of DNA thing, because otherwise why would they have baby griffins but no mother?"

"How should I know?"

"And there's other stuff I found out too." He was whispering now. "I'll tell you later. The house is *haunted*."

Which was just what Lucinda and her headache didn't really want to hear.

Standard Valley was not a town in the sense Lucinda thought of the word. It only had a couple of main roads and one main shopping district—if you could call a gas station, a feed and hardware store, a bank, a grocery store, and a coffee shop, all in a row across from the train station, by any name as fancy as "shopping district." Lucinda found it depressing, but at least the sun had gone behind a swirl of dark clouds, making the day much darker. It was still unpleasantly hot but the glare was gone, and she thought she could even smell something like rain in the air.

As the horse-drawn wagon clopped into the center of town, a few men standing around a truck parked next to the gas station looked up. One of them—a gray-haired man with a big belly and a baseball cap pushed far back on his head—grinned and gave a kind of salute, then shouted, "I see you're still driving last year's model!"

To Lucinda's surprise, Mr. Walkwell shouted back, "At least when this one backfires all I am smelling is hay!" And then he actually smiled. It took her a few seconds to figure out that not only had secretive, grumpy Mr. Walkwell acted like he knew the man, he had even made a joke.

"Who's that guy?" she asked.

"Hartman," said Mr. Walkwell. "He owns the gas station. I have met worse men in this world than him." Which meant he sort of liked him, as far as Lucinda could tell.

"Look!" said Tyler as they rolled to a stop in front of the feed and hardware store. "A hitching post! Just like in a cowboy movie!"

Lucinda, sipping the last from a bottle of water, was more interested in the idea of getting hold of some lip gloss and maybe some sunblock. Her lips were already dry and cracked after only a couple of days, and she could just see surviving the summer and returning to school only to have the other girls make fun of her because of her farmer tan and ruined lips.

They spent a boring half hour in the general store. Lucinda found her skin-care products and Tyler, for some reason, bought a flashlight and a ton of batteries. Mr. Walkwell put in an order for some supplies—apparently the feed and hardware store and grocery store were run by the same people. As he limped around looking at things, the few other customers nodded at Mr. Walkwell as if they knew him. The heavyset woman behind the counter smiled at the children and asked them their names as they paid for their goods.

"You staying for the summer?" she asked. "Oh, you'll have fun. It's nice for city kids to spend some time on a farm. See how things really work!" Lucinda wanted to laugh, but of course she didn't. If this woman only knew! "Are you having a good time so far?" The stout woman was really looking at them, Lucinda realized. "They don't get many visitors on that Tinker farm. . . ."

Suddenly Mr. Walkwell was there, hands resting heavily on the children's shoulders. "We must go now," he said. "Much work to do."

Lucinda could tell the woman would have liked to ask more questions. In fact, she noticed most of the other customers in the store had been listening too.

"You must not talk to strangers," Mr. Walkwell said as they stepped outside. "Time to go back."

"Ragnar said we could get a milkshake," Tyler protested. The sky was dark and the air was close—Lucinda could feel a few tiny drops of rain. "Because he said I did good work this morning."

Mr. Walkwell made a sour face, but turned them toward the diner. "Very well. But remember, many people here are curious about our farm and we must keep our secrets. Your great-uncle has shown great trust by bringing you here."

"If he's got so much trust," Tyler muttered, "why isn't he telling *us* any of the secrets?"

Mr. Walkwell only snorted.

Almost every store around here was called Standard something or other, so Lucinda was glad to see that the diner was called Rosie's, although someone hadn't been able to resist putting up a cutout wooden sign in the shape of a coffee cup, which stood on the roof next to a sign that said, OUR COFFEE IS WAY ABOVE STANDARD!

Half a dozen or more people were in the coffee shop, most of them men in farmer's caps, eating lunch, talking, or watching the television in the corner—some kind of local weather report. There was a long counter, as she expected, but instead of booths the rest of the place had a scatter of tables and chairs. Nothing much on the walls but a calendar and some hand-drawn posters for events at the local school. They didn't have a waitress, either—you just told your order to the grumpy-looking guy that everyone seemed to call Rosie, although Lucinda couldn't tell if that was a joke or not. He sure didn't look like a Rosie.

Tyler apparently decided he was much more than just milkshake hungry and ordered himself a cheeseburger and fries, but Lucinda still felt queasy. They found a table and Mr. Walkwell sat staring silently. Lucinda was happy just to hold a glass of ice water to her forehead, soaking in the wonderful cool.

The food came and Tyler went into Full Scarf Mode, shoveling everything in like it would vanish in two minutes if he didn't. He was just filling his mouth with the last chunk of his burger when Lucinda realized that three black-haired, brown-eyed kids, more or less her and Tyler's age, were standing beside the table watching them.

The boy, who looked like he enjoyed a good meal himself, asked Tyler, "Dude, you eat *fast*. Are you from Europe or something? Haven't you ever had a cheeseburger before?"

Tyler looked up, surprised. "I was hungry."

The older of the two girls, a young teenager like Lucinda, wore a shirt that said BOYS LIE. "Then do you come from a part of America where they don't have napkins?" she asked, grinning. Tyler stared at her for a moment, then dabbed away the ketchup smeared on his chin.

"Go away, you bad kids," Mr. Walkwell said, frowning. "Go away." The old man stared hard at them, but the trio didn't retreat. For a long moment nobody said anything. Lucinda was afraid there was going to be some kind of fight.

"So what did you bring us?" the boy said at last.

"Steve!" the older girl said. "You are so rude!"

"Bring you?" Mr. Walkwell scowled. "I don't bring you anything. I only bring things for good kids."

"I helped my dad fix the bulk tank," the boy called Steve said. "Alma washed the dishes. Carmen didn't do anything—she just talked on the phone."

"You are such a liar," the older girl said. "I made all the beds this morning—even yours, Steve."

Tyler looked at Lucinda. He was clearly just as mystified by this as she was.

"Okay, I look, I look," Mr. Walkwell said. "Whose turn is it?"

"Mine," said Steve.

Carmen shook her head. "Liar again. It's Alma's."

Mr. Walkwell reached into the pocket of his battered old jacket, which he seemed to wear no matter how hot it was outside, and pulled out a fluffy ball of Kleenex. Alma, who was small and wore red corduroy pants, shyly held out a cupped hand and Mr. Walkwell put the bundle in it. She unwrapped it carefully to reveal a knobby branch with several small blossoms on it, all carved out of a single piece of pale wood.

"Oh," said Alma, her eyes wide. "It's . . . *beautiful*."

"Nothing, it is nothing." Mr. Walkwell waved his hand as though he couldn't stand to look at such a poor thing any longer. "Almond blossoms. We had them in my old country so I like them. Take it."

"Thank you." Alma backed up a few steps but continued to stare at the carving in her hands.

"So you're the kids staying at Ordinary Farm," Steve said, leaning on the table. He squinted at Tyler's plate. "Hey, are you going to finish those french fries?"

"You are so *rude!*" his older sister said. "I'm Carmen Carrillo, this is my brother, Steve, Alma's the youngest. We live on the next farm over, Cresta Sol—our parents own it. We heard there might be some kids visiting Ordinary Farm this summer. You should come over to our place sometime."

Lucinda looked to Mr. Walkwell, certain that he would

want to end this conversation, but he was watching Alma instead, who held the carved almond blossoms up close to her face, peering intently. The old man was actually smiling a little. A joke, Lucinda thought, and now this—two Walkwell firsts in one day!

The door to the diner banged open loud enough to make Lucinda jump. The round man with the baseball cap from the gas station came inside, his clothes spotted with rain. "Hey, Walkwell," he called. "Your big friend's over at the store and I think he's looking for you."

Mr. Walkwell got to his feet and limped toward the door. "Ragnar? How did he come? In that machine of the inferno?"

"The truck, yes," said Hartman, the gas station man, winking at the kids.

"You children stay here," Mr. Walkwell told Tyler and Lucinda. "Don't go away anywhere." As he went out the door with Hartman, the round man was saying, "If you people at Ordinary Farm would just learn to carry *cell phones* . . ." The door banged shut. Rosie, the proprietor, glared at it for a moment, then turned back to his other customers, all of whom had watched this with much interest.

After a long moment's silence, Steve said, "Hey, you seen any ghosts?"

Tyler almost dropped his milkshake, and Lucinda suddenly remembered the strange remark her brother had made on the way into town. "Wh-what do you mean?" he asked.

"Steve," said Carmen, with a warning in her voice.

"I'm just asking!" The boy turned back to Tyler. "Our grandmother tells all these stories—she grew up here and she knows all these Indian legends. Crazy stuff, but kind of cool. Anyway, the Indians used to think the gateway to the underworld was on your land. Or something like that. The spirit world."

"Really? Uh, cool. What else does your grandmother say about—" Tyler began, then the door banged mightily once more at the front of the coffee shop.

Mr. Walkwell leaned in the door and called, "Tyler, Lucinda, you come with me now. We must go."

They left the café, the Carrillo kids trooping out behind them. Outside stood Ragnar, his long hair and beard stringy in the rain and his big face flushed. "The big . . . the big cow, she is about to give birth, I think. The young ones—they can drive back with me."

"As you wish," Mr. Walkwell said. "I am taking the wagon. If I am slow, I am slow. Anything that is meant to be . . . Heaven will make certain it happens when it should."

"Bye!" said Carmen. "Come see us—we're just over the ridge from you. Cresta Sol—there's a big sun on the front gate."

"Thank you, Mr. Walkwell!" Alma cried, still holding her carving as though it was a delicate living thing. "It's beautiful."

* * *

Ragnar might be built like some kind of football player, but he drove the ancient, rattling truck like somebody's little old grandfather, hunched forward, both hands clutching the wheel until his hairy knuckles were white. The rain had mostly stopped, but a few drops still splattered the windshield.

"I thought we were in a hurry," Tyler said as Ragnar maneuvered around a corner like the truck was loaded with explosives.

"Shut up, boy," the farmhand said, but not unkindly. "I have not been doing this driving long."

"Huh. I never would have guessed." Tyler scowled when Lucinda kicked him. "Ow! It was a joke!"

"Is the . . . the dragon really having a baby?" she asked. "Is that a problem?"

Ragnar shook his head. "She has had trouble with laying her eggs before—none of them have lived. Nobody knows about dragons. They are old and strange creatures."

They drove for a little while in silence. "Hey, those kids said that Ordinary Farm was, like, the gateway to the spirit world or something," Tyler said at last. It had obviously made a big impression on him.

The blond man snorted. "Those children say lots of things. Their grandmother is a tale-teller, so they are full of stories." Ragnar squinted at the road. "There is a saying in my old country: 'The man who stands at a strange threshold should be cautious before he crosses it, and he should glance this way and that, because who knows beforehand what foes may sit waiting for him?'"

Her brother leaned toward her. "Well, *that* couldn't make less sense, could it?" he whispered.

The farm seemed to be in an uproar as they pulled into the gravel driveway. Several farmhands were at the front door where Uncle Gideon was handing out orders. Their great-uncle was wearing a white lab coat, but he still had on his bedroom slippers and looked quite distracted.

"Thank goodness," he said as Ragnar and the kids got out. "Where's Simos?"

"You know he will not go in the truck," Ragnar told him. "He will be here soon. He told me what to do."

"Then come on. She's taking a long time to give birth. It's hard to tell from external temperature, but I think she might have a fever." From the distance came a noise like a broken foghorn—obviously the sound of an uncomfortable dragon. Gideon finally noticed Tyler and Lucinda. "You two run along. Mrs. Needle will give you something to do."

"Can't we come?" Tyler asked. "I want to see the dragon again."

"No, you can't. She's not used to you and she's in distress. Besides, she's making a lot of noise and it might draw Alamu."

"Draw a what?" Tyler asked.

"Alamu. Her mate." Gideon frowned and flapped his hands at the children. "Blast it, I don't have time to talk to you two right now. Go on inside."

"So much for being on a farm," Tyler grumbled to Lucinda as they went into the house.

"What's that supposed to mean?"

"We're supposed to see stuff like this, aren't we? The miracle of life and all that garbage?"

"You heard Uncle Gideon, didn't you? Hello-o! Angry male dragon roaming around!" She couldn't believe her brother sometimes.

Tyler shook his head. "They're never going to tell us anything. We're going to have to find things out ourselves."

"What are you talking about, Tyler?"

"Oh, never mind." He turned and stomped up the stairs.

Brothers! Lucinda thought. She'd begged her parents to get a dog instead, but nobody ever listened to her.

CHAPTER 12

FARM WORK

After several days of discomfort that kept the whole farm in a state of alert, Meseret finally laid an egg.

Lucinda snuck a quick peek at the dragon's egg from the door of the Sick Barn. It looked like a partially deflated beach ball, a pale leathery sack big as the beanbag chair her brother spent most of his time in back at home, headphones on, sneakered feet on the wall, GameBoss Portable held only squinting inches in front of his eyes.

They're sure making a lot of fuss over a big beanbag, she thought. It wasn't that she didn't care; there was just something about being around the dragon that upset her, something about the watchfulness in the creature's huge red-gold eyes. Lucinda often found herself making excuses to avoid being near the dragon very long—not that anyone was urging her to stay. The Sick Barn was a busy place now and it was easy to get in the way: Uncle Gideon and Mr. Walkwell hardly left Meseret's side for the first week. Apparently this was the third or fourth time Meseret had given birth and none of the other eggs had hatched, so everyone was worried.

The children spent most of their time that week with Mrs. Needle or Ragnar, doing chores and helping out, or trying to. Tyler hated doing the inside jobs, and he didn't like Mrs. Needle at all. Lucinda had more mixed feelings about the Englishwoman. She remembered very little of the conversation they had shared, but she remembered feeling very grown-up and privileged to be spending time with someone so interesting and special. When Lucinda came in to the farm office one morning to ask a question and found Mrs. Needle winding her long black hair into a French pleat, it felt like stumbling onto a fairy creature in a patch of forest moonlight. Patience Needle was so pale, so lovely—and yet somehow as fierce as a panther and more than a little frightening. Lucinda didn't really know what to think.

Being around Ragnar was entirely different. He was obviously fairly old, but he looked like a barbarian out of one of Tyler's games, or some long-haired professional wrestler. Ragnar didn't try to be tough or cool, although in his own weird way he really *was* cool.

"Where do you come from?" she asked him one morning, amused by his pronunciation of "jam jar" as "yam yar."

"Denmark, you would call it. But I have not been there in a long time. Everything is different now, they tell me." He shook his head, staring out past the field whose wire fence he was fixing, as though he could see Denmark just beyond. For all Lucinda knew, he could. (She had never been much good at geography.)

Tyler seemed glad of this opportunity to rest for a moment and wipe the sweat from his face. They had been working all afternoon restringing wire fences in the valley sun, and even though Ragnar did the lion's share of the chores—Lucinda suspected this whole thing was more about babysitting them than getting any actual labor out of them—it was still hot and tiring work. "Why did you come?" Tyler asked. "Here, I mean."

Ragnar laughed. "Things had gone sour for old Ragnar. I had little choice but to take Gideon's kind offer."

"I don't get it," Lucinda said.

"And I hope you do not 'get it,'" he told her, serious now. He bent and heaved up another bale of wire in one hand as if it was a roll of aluminum foil, and directed Tyler where to help steady it against the fence post. "But you are Gideon's kin, which is for the good. Others around him are sometimes forced to pay a very high price indeed." He laughed again but it almost sounded angry. After that he began banging huge metal staples into the post and it was too noisy for them to ask any other questions.

So many jobs! Feeding all the animals, doctoring them, repairing their cages and pens and tanks, as well as taking care of the farm's vegetable garden and house and kitchen. Not to mention the huge variety of creatures—not just unicorns and dragons, but skittish, snarling wampus cats, hoop snakes, and even something called a hodag, a truculent creature that looked like a badger covered with crocodile skin and smelled like old cheese. Lucinda couldn't begin to imagine how Uncle Gideon and his employees kept a place like this going with only a dozen or so employees, although Mr. Walkwell, for one, never actually seemed to stop working. Twice she had woken up in the middle of the night and gone out to the hall and the bathroom there only to spot him through the window, driving his wagon across to the Sick Barn or limping across the farm hauling bags of feed by moonlight. Didn't he ever sleep? And how could somebody who was so obviously crippled, or at least severely limited in his mobility, work so hard? She had no idea what was wrong with his legs—she had asked Ragnar, but he only shook his head and said, "Mr. Walkwell has his own stories. They are not mine to tell."

Some things Ragnar would talk about, though. He was

happy to tell her about the Carrillo kids they had met at the store.

"They come from the farm next door," he told them. "The family has owned that land for a very long time. Those children's great-grandfather loaned old Octavio workers to do repairs on the farmhouse, and helped him find people to do some of the other jobs on the place— Gideon did not bring me and the others until later, you see. So the Carrillo family does not know your uncle's secrets but he likes them and trusts them. Sometimes he even goes to their house for the Christian and American holy days."

Lucinda wasn't sure exactly what the last part meant— American holy days?—but she gathered that the Carrillo kids weren't considered Official Enemies of the Farm or anything, so it made a little more sense that Mr. Walkwell carved things for them. Still, that was the last thing she ever would have imagined such a strange, grumpy man doing.

Lucinda and Tyler quickly settled into a routine. Mondays, Wednesdays, and Fridays they went with Ragnar and did repairs and other small chores around the farm in the morning, then came back in the afternoon to help the people working mostly inside. Lucinda ran errands around the house, helped Pema take care of the bed linens and other things, or helped Sarah and Azinza put things away in the pantry. Azinza looked like nothing less than a supermodel and made Lucinda feel like a dwarf. The African girl was at least six feet tall, with cropped hair and a profile like the most exquisite sculpture Lucinda had ever seen. Her skin was so dark it had almost a blue sheen to it; beside the beauteous Azinza, Mrs. Needle actually appeared quite ordinary.

Tyler mostly wound up helping old Caesar as he made his rounds replacing lightbulbs and broken coat hooks and hammering in nails that had worked their way out of the house's ancient paneling.

"Caesar sings a lot," Tyler told Lucinda one evening as they went down to dinner. "And he can tell you anything you want to know about polishing silver, that's for sure. But when I ask him how he came to the farm, he just says, 'I was in a worse place before, the good Lord knows,' and he won't say anything else. Why won't any of them tell us anything? Did Uncle Gideon clone the people who live here too—is *that* the big secret?"

On the working-outside days they usually rode around with Ragnar, or Mr. Walkwell on the occasions he was free. Sometimes Haneb came with them too. Lucinda tried to thank him again for saving her from being hurt by the unicorn, but the slender man was so shy that even her gratitude seemed to pain him. She and Tyler usually helped feed the animals—hoop snakes and griffins both liked milk, Lucinda learned—and sometimes even groomed them. Once Lucinda got to currycomb a unicorn, which was one of the most exciting things she had ever done. Ragnar held its head (so that it wouldn't spear her with its horn like an olive on a toothpick, Tyler explained in a loud stage whisper) while Lucinda brushed burrs out of its shaggy pale coat. Up close it smelled a little like a horse, but also a little like flowers and a little like something else—something prickly and odd, like electricity.

Sometimes they fed the baby animals, which was Lucinda's favorite chore. Once, Mr. Walkwell let her put on a bird-headed glove to feed a baby griffin, which was about the size of a housecat. It had a four-legged body but a head like a bird, and was covered all over with golden down like a baby chick. Despite having fierce little claws the baby griffin was more nervous about her than she was about it. Lucinda had to be very patient until it would accept the bits of worms and ground tuna fish she held in the puppet's beak.

"If this is a baby, how big do they get?" she asked.

Mr. Walkwell gestured to one of the older siblings in the main pen a few yards away—the aiglet, as Uncle Gideon called the baby, had a small cage of its own. Tawny, feathered hind legs were tucked under its body as their owner napped, its tail occasionally lifting to slap away flies. It was big—about the size of a lion—and she was suddenly grateful that they didn't have to get the baby out of the adults' enclosure to feed it. The tail went *slap* again and the adult griffin sighed in its sleep, a strange noise that might have come from a trumpet made of bone.

As the first week passed, then the second and third, and June gave way to the first of July, Lucinda began to get a sense of how the farm truly worked, but it only made her more confused. First of all, she came to realize, it didn't seem to be a farm at all. Gideon and his workers didn't seem to be raising the animals for any purpose, and except for the acres of grass that would be hay for winter feed, and the orchard of fruit trees behind the house, the only normal thing the farm seemed to grow were the vegetables and spices and herbs in Mrs. Needle's kitchen garden. It was a good-sized garden, full of plants Lucinda had never seen before, and even had a mysterious greenhouse with lots of elaborate, Victorian-looking ironwork, but Mrs. Needle wasn't growing anything to sell. In fact, nothing on the farm seemed set up to make money or satisfy more than a few basic needs for the people who lived there.

No, Ordinary Farm was more a zoo than anything else— everything seemed to revolve around taking care of all the fantastic animals. But zoos made money by selling tickets to people, Lucinda knew, and that certainly wasn't going on here (although Gideon could make millions, she realized— maybe billions—if they ever did). So what was going on? If they weren't making anything, and they weren't show- ing anyone the dragons and unicorns, then how were they paying for all the food the animals and people ate, and the medicine, and the people's salaries, and . . . ?

She hated to admit Tyler was right, but the whole thing just didn't make sense.

And there were a lot of mouths to feed. The herders, Kiwa, Jeg, and Hoka—"the Three Amigos," as Tyler called them—spent most of their time in a hut out by the pastureland, but came into the house to eat. Besides them and Haneb and Ragnar and Mr. Walkwell, more than a half dozen other men of many colors and sizes worked on the property and lived in a bunkhouse near the reptile barn. Lucinda hadn't had a chance to learn their names yet. So what was that altogether—eighteen or nineteen people to be fed and housed, not including herself and Tyler? And if the animals had been *made*, somehow, as Tyler thought, then there had to be things she and her brother hadn't seen—a laboratory and people to staff it.

So how did it all work? Was Uncle Gideon rich? You'd sure never know it from his old striped bathrobe and his threadbare pajamas, which he seemed to be wearing most of the times she saw him, even in the middle of a hot afternoon. In fact, rich or not, Lucinda was pretty sure he was at least a little crazy, especially when she thought about the scary way he had forced that promise out of them.

Still, even if their great-uncle turned out to be the world's richest loony, it didn't explain the dragons.

It was a Friday, the third Friday since she and Tyler had come to Ordinary Farm, and Lucinda was in the huge front parlor. The room had a marvelous stained-glass window featuring a gorgeous snake—Lucinda found herself quite hypnotized by it—plus a large collection of mirrors and clocks, which she was giving an offhand dusting when she heard the bell summoning everyone to dinner. She was thinking with pleasurable anticipation about the apple brown betty Sarah was baking when Gideon walked in the front door.

Lucinda assumed that he was on his way to dinner as well, but he only walked by her on his way to the staircase, his face sagging and empty.

"Uncle Gideon?"

He didn't even speak or look back as he trudged through a door at the back of the stairs and off somewhere into the depths of the house, his bathrobe flapping like the cape of a defeated superhero who had just decided to retire from the crime-fighting business. Then Colin Needle came through the front door also, his bony face twisted with anger.

"What's wrong?" Lucinda asked him. "What's going on?"

Colin was so upset that flecks of spit flew from his mouth as he spoke. "I tried to tell him I was sorry. I tried to tell him how upset I am too. But he never listens to me! He just pushed me aside like I was *nothing*."

Lucinda had never seen the older boy show much emotion. She felt sorry for him, though—she'd been on the other end of Gideon's anger and knew what it felt like.

"Sorry about what? What's happened?"

Colin looked at her almost blankly. Then he said, "Meseret's egg isn't going to hatch. There's a baby inside but no heartbeat. Again. It's happened every time." His anger surged again. "But he blames my mother for it! In spite of everything she tried to do!" He was getting loud now and it made Lucinda a little nervous—Gideon couldn't have gone very far in such a short time. "Like she's supposed to fix the dragon, fix the money, fix everything that's wrong with this stupid farm! Fix all his stupid mistakes!"

"Colin, I'm really sorry . . ." she began, but the boy was so consumed with his feelings that he wasn't even looking at her. Instead Colin turned and half walked, half ran toward the kitchen.

Suddenly Lucinda was in no hurry to follow him. She wasn't very hungry anymore. In fact, the thought of apple brown betty made her stomach turn.

CHAPTER 13

CHEEKY MONKEY, SNEAKY SQUIRREL

Tyler woke up late on Saturday, the day after the bad news about Meseret's egg. Nobody was talking much at the breakfast table—even the farmhands seemed depressed.

"It has happened three times before," Ragnar said, shaking his head. "The eggs will not hatch. It begins to look like she will never give birth to a living wormlet."

For a moment Tyler thought the big man was making some weird joke about eggs. "Omelette?"

"Wormlet—a dragon child. *Worm*—that is the word for dragon where I come from." Ragnar smiled sadly. "Where I grew up, we were terrified of them. We would have thought the news that a *lindenwurm* egg had died was cause for celebration. Now we all fear that Meseret and her mate will be the last of their kind."

Ragnar grew up believing in dragons? Tyler wondered where that might have been—in Storybook Land? "What's her mate's name, again?"

"Alamu." Ragnar went back to the heavy work of shoveling in his breakfast, an immense pile of bread and fruit and sausage. It was a process that even Tyler, who could put food away faster than his mom could earn money to pay for it (as she always told him), could only watch with stunned respect.

After finishing breakfast, Tyler pocketed a nectarine for Zaza and headed back to his room. The little winged monkey came to his window at least once a day and happily took any scraps he gave her. He had begun to think of her almost as a pet.

He put the nectarine on a napkin on top of the dresser, then stretched out on the bed, wondering what he was going to do today while everyone else seemed to be mourning a bad egg. He hoped Mr. Walkwell didn't have more slave labor in mind for him. The old man could be a very hard taskmaster, and he didn't particularly like Tyler's habit of asking lots of questions. He was a good teacher about farm things, but about anything else—forget it.

Something was poking uncomfortably into the back of Tyler's neck. He reached under his pillow and his fingers found something crinkly and rough—paper. He sat up, unfolding it. Had someone left him a note?

No, he realized with astonishment, he'd seen this piece of paper before, yellowed with age and chewed into a fringe along the edges like a cowboy's chaps. It was the scrap of paper from the library, the one he had lost when the figure in the mirror startled him. But how had it wound up here?

The paper had been tattered to begin with and Tyler lying on it hadn't helped things, so he had to smooth it out very carefully. He squinted, trying to make out words. It was handwritten in ink that had turned mostly brown and the letters were funny, old-fashioned cursive with odd, stringy shapes. Some ancient grocery list or something, perhaps from one of the old newspaper boxes they used in the barns to make nesting material for the basilisks and some of the smaller birds. The only interesting thing about it was how it might have wound up in his bed.

Then, just before he dropped the paper into the waste-basket, the word *dragons* jumped out at him.

Tyler held the faded letters up to catch the morning light. There wasn't much left on the page that was read-able—most of it had been water smeared or shredded into confetti—but he could make out the sentence:

. . . if dragons are not strictly fabulous, then we shall find them before, not during, the spread of their tales into Europe. . . .

Fabulous? Wasn't that what people said on fashion shows or something—*"You look fabulous, dahling!"* How could a dragon be fabulous? He ought to ask somebody, but he suddenly felt jealous about sharing this little bit of paper with anyone—it was, after all, the first bit of the mystery that seemed to be his and his alone. But who had put it here, since he had definitely not had it when he came back from the library? Lucinda, and then forgot to tell him? One of the housekeepers?

Zaza. Of course, it had to be the monkey. Perhaps she had seen him drop it and thought she was returning something of his. Did monkeys think like that? Tyler went to the window to look for her, but nothing living was in sight except for a single, fat black squirrel watching him from the branch where Zaza often sat. The squirrel's staring eyes seemed an odd color, as if it were sick. Tyler didn't like the look of it. He ducked his head back inside and pulled the window closed.

When he turned again to the scrap of paper another clear fragment of writing caught his eye, a darker black swath of ink that had been protected by being folded in on itself:

. . . *and if, as I believe, this Breach or Fault shall prove to be a phenomenon of supernature, that is, NATURE THAT HAS NOT PREVIOUSLY BEEN DISCERNED OR DESCRIBED, then it could be*

I owe it to all humanity to make public what I have found. This likely will be the dilemma from whose solution my entire career will take direction.

Whatever the heck *that* meant. None of it made sense so far, although the words *Breach* and *Fault* stuck in his mind. What was the person writing talking about? And who had written it? Octavio, the guy in the painting?

The library, he decided. That was where it had come from, and even though he didn't like the place and its creepy washstand mirror, that was where he'd have to look for more pieces. Tyler sighed. If you had asked him a month ago what he'd do with his first free day of the summer, going to the library would not have been the activity he'd have bet any money on.

"Really?" Lucinda looked up from her diary, staring at Tyler like he was some stranger pretending to be her brother. "You want me to come with you? You're actually asking *me*?"

Tyler groaned, weighing the flashlight in his hand. Was this going to be just what he feared, another stupid argument with his sister? Why couldn't she just go along with things?

"I mean . . ." She shook her head. "I'll do it, yeah. I'm just surprised. You don't usually ask me to go with you."

"I do too." A nervous little something in Tyler was tapping its foot, but he was doing his best to ignore it. "Whatever. The reason we have to go there is because I think I found part of Octavio Tinker's diary."

"Really?" Her eyes got big. "Uncle Gideon's grandfather, or whatever he was?"

"Yeah." He took the folded page out of his pocket and held it out. "Here, look. Mice kind of got it. . . ."

She handed it back when she'd finished. "'Supernature'? I don't understand it."

"Neither do I, but I bet if we find more, we will."

"I don't want to get into any more trouble, Tyler."

He made a noise of frustration. "Come on! Uncle Gideon's practically *daring* us to find out what's going on here. Don't you want to know?"

She stared at him, then sighed. "Okay. When do you want to go?"

"Now, when no one's watching. Well—I'm not sure where Colin is."

"It's okay—he's off working on his computer."

"Good. Do you have to run any errands for the Wicked Witch of the West?"

"Oh, don't be so mean," she said, then shook her head. "Anyway, she's in the kitchen, helping Sarah and Azinza with something. She told me she wouldn't need me for an hour."

"Perfect." He resisted the urge to yank her onto her feet, but only barely. "Come on, then!"

Out in the hallway, when Zaza dropped down from nowhere onto Tyler's shoulder, Lucinda jumped. "Whoa!" she said. "Oh, it's the monkey. She scared me."

"She kind of likes to hang out with me." He couldn't help being a little proud of it.

Zaza seemed nervous, turning in circles on his shoulder as they walked around the house and through the garden and outbuildings toward the library hall. It seemed a longer trip this time, Tyler thought, but the house was always funny that way.

The monkey suddenly leaped up shrieking, wings flapping hard, nearly scaring Tyler and Lucinda to death. It took a long time before she settled on Tyler's shoulder once more and went back to tugging anxiously at his hair. He looked up but couldn't see anything in the trees or skies overhead that might have frightened her.

Lucinda was impressed by the library, all right—not so much by the picture of Uncle Octavio, who she thought looked very full of himself, but by the sheer number of books. "This is more than we have in our whole school library," she said. "More than in our whole *city* library!"

"Yeah, but most of 'em are, I don't know, crazy science and math books and stuff you wouldn't like—not a single copy of *Mallchickz Go to Malibu*."

"You're being a craphead again, Tyler. I haven't read those books since I was in fourth grade—when *you* were reading *Axel the Tow Truck Fixes a Flat*."

He laughed in spite of himself. How had she remembered that? He had really liked those stories—Axel had a best friend who was a girl motorcycle and all the characters were cars and trucks. "Come on," he said, and switched on his flashlight—this time he wasn't going to give away their presence by turning on the lights. "I'll show you the haunted room."

The room didn't look quite as creepy as it did before, but Lucinda didn't exactly look like she wanted to move in, either. "Why did you say 'haunted'?" she asked in a whisper.

He took her to the mirror at the washstand and swept the flashlight over it. At first it looked like nothing more than an ordinary mirror, reflecting Tyler and his light, Lucinda, and the room. After a while, though, it *still* looked like that.

"I don't get it," his sister said.

"It was different last time." Tyler was embarrassed. He could hear the upset in his own voice and didn't like it— too much like a little kid. "I could see me, but I was *different*—different clothes and stuff. It wasn't the *same* me. And the light in the room was different, too, like a different time of day. I'm not lying, Lucinda!"

"I believe you," she said, surprising him. "We've seen unicorns and a dragon, so why couldn't there be a haunted mirror?"

Tyler let out a breath. He hadn't expected to be believed. Suddenly he felt so much lighter he almost thought he could float up into the air like Zaza. "Good. Anyway, it's also where I found this piece of paper—on the floor here. We should look through the drawers."

Most of the washstand drawers were empty, but in the bottom right drawer they found an old-fashioned pen, the kind you dipped into a bottle of ink. Part of the length had been chewed off by something, and the bottom of the drawer was broken so that they could see down to the darkness under the dresser. Tyler was just pushing it closed again when Lucinda grabbed his arm and pointed. A shred of yellowed paper was caught in the jagged edge of the drawer's broken bottom. Tyler's heart began to beat more quickly. It was only a tatter the size of a fingernail clipping, but when he pulled it out and held it up next to the page with the writing, the paper was the exact same color.

They tried to move the washstand away from the wall, but it was either much heavier than it looked or had been bolted to the wall, perhaps to keep the heavy mirror on top from tipping the whole thing over. Tyler got down on his hands and knees and began probing the hole at the bottom of the drawer with the ruined pen. *Something* was still in there. He poked at it until sweat ran down into his eyes and dripped onto the dusty floor, then finally had the idea of poking it out toward the front where he could get a grip on it and gently ease the whole thing out.

Lucinda leaned in as he held it up. It was a leather-bound notebook, full of pages just like the one he'd found on his bed. The whole thing had been badly chewed by mice or some other scavengers, so that many of the pages were little more than tangled curls of paper. Still, a quick riffle through the pages showed lots of writing—the mice hadn't ruined it all.

"Look at the cover," he said. The chipped remnants of what had once been gold paint read:

. . . ty of O avi M. T nker, Esq.

He felt a ripple of excitement so strong he shivered. "It's really his—and we've got it. But we can't tell *anybody.*"

Lucinda nodded, her eyes wide.

Outside, Zaza was waiting, perched on the top of Great-great-great-whatever Octavio's picture, peering down at them as though not quite trusting that whatever came out of the retiring room was going to be the same as whatever went in. Lucinda stared at the painting.

"What's that thing in his hand?" she asked. "I've never seen one of those before. Is it some musical thing?"

"I don't know." Tyler really looked at the golden thing for the first time. Besides the long, trumpetlike tubes, it was made up of an overlapping series of jagged-edged circles and points, as if old Octavio had just taken out the workings of some large clock and screwed them together in some random order. Then Tyler noticed that in his other hand Octavio held a black velvet bag, and suddenly he realized that it was meant to hold the shiny device.

"Like the picture was about *that thing* as much as about him," he said quietly, but Lucinda heard him and nodded as if she had been thinking the same thought.

They were halfway back to the house when Zaza suddenly leaped off Tyler's shoulder and flapped into the air, making strange, shrill noises more like a bird than a monkey— like the sound the jays made at home when something got too close to their nests.

The big black squirrel again, or another just like it, crouched silently on the branch of a tree. Zaza darted upward and flew at the squirrel, but it didn't flinch, nor did the pale yellow eyes even blink. There was definitely something wrong about the creature, but except for its size and eye color Tyler couldn't have said what. It watched calmly, unmoving, as Zaza flew at it, chittering loudly, once, twice, three times. Then the winged monkey gave up and flitted away between the trees. Tyler and Lucinda began walking toward the house again.

"What was *that*?" His sister's voice was a harsh whisper.

"A squirrel," he said, trying to keep his voice calm. After all, only a baby would be afraid of a *squirrel.*

"Then why does it have eyes like a goat?" she demanded.

"Yellow, with that little sideways slot? Squirrels don't have eyes like that."

"*Tyler Jenkins!*" someone shouted.

He pulled up, looking around. "Who's that?"

"It's Mrs. Needle!"

"Maybe she needs you for something."

"She's calling *you*, Tyler!"

She was right, of course, but he wished she wasn't. "Shoot," he said. "Now what? Here, you take the book. Go. Hide it in your room."

"What are you talking about?"

"It's too big to go in my pocket, Lucinda, and I don't want her to know we found it!"

She looked at him, ready to argue, then Mrs. Needle called again from somewhere just ahead. For someone so soft-spoken, the woman could sure put some *edge* in her voice.

Lucinda abruptly grabbed the book, hid it inside her pants, and then doubled back around the corner of the building. She vanished just as Mrs. Needle appeared from the other direction, dressed in black as usual, a look of irritation on her pale face.

"Tyler Jenkins, I'm very disappointed in you," she said. "You should know better than to go exploring old buildings without permission. Some of them are dangerous."

He did his best to look calm and innocent. "What do you mean?"

"The library, Tyler. It hasn't been maintained for years."
Mrs. Needle took his wrist in her cold fingers and began
to lead him back toward the house. "You should not be
in there by yourself. Something could . . . fall on you. You
could be badly hurt." She didn't sound like she'd regret it
very much.

Tyler let himself be marched across a patch of open
ground, relieved that at least his sister had gotten away
with the book. But how had Mrs. Needle known they
were in the library? He and Lucinda hadn't turned on any
lights!

He looked up. The black squirrel was perched on the
edge of the roof, squat and black as a loaf of burned bread.
Only the pale eyes had color, the unblinking stare that
Lucinda had described so well.

Eyes like a goat.

CHAPTER 14

THE MOTHER OF ALL MOTHERS

From her window Lucinda saw Tyler walking past below, on his way to the henhouse with a bucket of soapy water, a brush, and an expression of extreme annoyance. Mrs. Needle had obviously put him to work and it didn't look like he would be back any time soon. She felt that she ought to lock the door and start looking through the old mouse-chewed notebook they'd found, but it was too hot and stuffy—just the thought of it made her feel sleepy.

She knew Tyler would be furious with her if she didn't at least hide the notebook, though, so she lifted her mattress and slid it in on top of the lumpy boxspring, then went downstairs.

She peered into the kitchen. Sarah and Pema were cleaning the counters.

"Come in," the cook said when she saw Lucinda. "Have some lemonade." Sarah took a pitcher out of the refrigerator while Lucinda got herself a glass. "I hear you are going to *eine Feier*!" she said as Lucinda drank.

"What's that? A fire?"

"*Eine Feier*—a celebration. Tomorrow. You have invited been. It is a Fourth of July celebration at the other farm, with the children."

Which sounded okay if it was the kids they'd met in the diner, the Carrillos. At least they were more or less the same age as Tyler and her.

Lucinda rinsed out her glass and put the lemonade back, then wandered out to the front of the house. The porch was empty, the gravel-covered drive spreading in front of her. What she really wanted to do was go see some animals—the unicorns, maybe, although they frightened her more than a little. She couldn't forget that horn flashing past her face like the breathless swish of a sword blade. And they were so wild! She could imagine them leaping over any fence they wanted to, no matter how high, as free and uncaged as clouds.

Lucinda ambled over to the henhouse. Tyler was in a foul mood.

"Did you hide the . . . the thing?" He opened his hands like he was playing charades. *Book.*

She rolled her eyes. "Of course." She looked at him for a moment, pushing soapy water back and forth across the disgusting floor of the henhouse. The smell of the place was revolting. To her astonishment, though, she heard herself ask, "Do you want some help?"

He stopped scrubbing long enough to stare, as if some alien being had taken his sister's place. "Nah, I can't. I have to do it myself—the Wicked Witch told me. She's mad at me for exploring." He smiled. "But thanks."

She was on her way back from the henhouse when she saw Colin Needle in the distance, crouching by the door of the Sick Barn, examining the door latch.

"Hello, Colin," she said. He jumped up like he'd been burned.

"Oh! Hello, Lucinda. Nice to see you." He waved his hands—at nothing, as far as she could tell. "Can't stop to chat just now—loads to do. Sorry!" He hurried past her, back toward the house, his stiff strides much more rapid than usual, like a man on stilts hurrying to find a bathroom.

Lucinda reached out. The door to the Sick Barn was open. She wondered why he'd been examining it so carefully. She cautiously stuck her head in. "Hello?" When she heard no answer, she stepped inside.

At first she thought there was no one else in the great high-ceilinged barn except her and the vast, unmoving bulk of the dragon, stretched in its long pen like a ship docked for repairs. The idea of being alone with such a monster was enough to make her back toward the door.

"Miss?" The farmhand Haneb was coming toward her from the other end of the barn, bulky from the neck down in a baggy gray safety suit. His lanky black hair hung in his face and he held his head at an odd angle to hide his scars.

"Do you come for the boy Colin, miss?" he asked her. "He has gone. Or for the master Walkwell or the master Ragnar? They are both gone also, to fetch more medicine."

"Medicine?" She let the door fall shut behind her. As it banged closed a deep rumble came up from the pen in response, a sound that made Lucinda's insides vibrate beneath her ribs. "Is she still sick? I thought she was all right."

"Meseret?" He shook his head sadly, still carefully keeping the scarred side away from her. "We do not know. Perhaps it is just the sadness of her egg . . . that it dies. . . ." He shrugged, struggling to find words. "To learn more, next week we give her . . . give her . . ." He frowned. "Sleeping medicine. Then we take away egg, so Mr. Walkwell and Mr. Gideon can study it."

It was by far the most she had ever heard Haneb say.

Lucinda stared at the pen, trying to look braver than she felt. Just the size of the dragon, its back corrugated with scales like an alligator's but wide as a bus, made it hard for Lucinda to get her breath. Being this near to something so big and alive was terrifying beyond explanation. If Meseret made a sudden movement, Lucinda knew, she would turn and run out of the barn, no matter how embarrassed she would be about it later.

The dragon lay with her egg between her forelegs like an exhausted puppy with a favorite toy. The rest of her immense body was stretched, belly down, to the far end of the pen, her great hind legs all but invisible under the swell of her pale, shiny belly. The egg was startlingly small, no bigger around at its base than a basketball, although its narrow, oblong shape made it almost twice that big. It was bizarre to think something so big as Meseret could start out smaller than a sleeping bag. Then, as Lucinda saw the mother dragon's sagging, yellowed eye, she remembered again that this egg wouldn't be growing up to be anything.

"Poor thing," she said, almost to herself, stepping closer. Haneb carefully moved to Lucinda's left side as they stood at the railing. "She seems so exhausted. Like she's just given up." She looked at Meseret's eye, mostly closed but still fascinating, inescapable. "Is everyone sure the egg isn't alive?"

"Yes," said Haneb, then hesitated. "If you want, I show you Mr. Gideon's magic, same I showed Master Colin."

When she nodded, he pulled a fireproof hood with a plastic face shield over his head, then shyly took Lucinda's arm with his thickly gloved hand and led her along the edge of the dragon pen to an old metal desk and a laptop computer. The dragon didn't move, but her huge, half-lidded eye shifted slightly to watch Lucinda—yes, to watch *her*, not Haneb, she felt oddly sure. Was it just because she was unfamiliar? Lucinda stood on her tiptoes and leaned over the rail. The fire-colored eye widened, just a little, but it was enough for Lucinda to feel quite boneless in her legs. She let herself back down again—slowly.

Meseret's head was the size of a small sports car, a great wedge of bone and scale and teeth with backswept fins growing from just behind the orbits around her eyes. Her neck was long and muscular, but quickly spread out into the shoulders and the huge, folded membranes of her wings, which grew in a batlike flare (as far as Lucinda could tell—it was hard to make out many details with the dragon lying down) between the uppermost toes of her forelegs and the top of her hips. The bottom two toes on each side, scarcely thicker than Lucinda's arms but long as tree branches, provided the struts on which the wing skin stretched, like paper over the balsa-wood bones of a kite. For a moment Lucinda longed to touch the near wing—it seemed so delicate, a translucent banner of flesh next to the castle of craggy hide.

Haneb clumped past her in his strange suit. With his hood on he looked like a robot out of an ancient science-fiction movie. He held some kind of plastic wand in one hand, attached by a curly cord to a plastic box about the size and shape of a briefcase. He looked so strange and moved so slowly, she almost expected him to vault over the walls of the pen like an astronaut in reduced gravity, but instead he fumbled open the gate with his free hand and trudged inside.

Meseret rumbled again. Lucinda felt the sound from the soles of her feet upward, but when it finished a curious vibration remained in her skull, as though her brain was still bouncing from the dragon's low growl. She realized after a few moments that the hair on her neck and arms was standing up, her skin tingling.

She couldn't believe how small Haneb was compared to the bulk of the dragon—Meseret had raised her head a little and the top of his hood barely reached the bottom of her rolling eye! "Oh, be careful!" she said, but she doubted he could hear her.

Haneb knelt beside the egg. The dragon's rumble went up in pitch, but Haneb did not slow or stop. He extended the wand toward the egg until it was only a few inches away, then moved it even more slowly forward until it touched the waxy shell.

Lucinda suddenly realized what he was doing—it was one of those ultrasound things, like they used on pregnant women—and turned toward the desk and the computer screen. The black-and-white image was moving and changing, a murky, confusing mess that only gradually resolved itself into something like a huge wad of chewed gum wrapped in cellophane—the baby with its wings folded around it, she guessed. The picture was completely still. When Haneb stopped moving the wand there was no other movement: the thing in the egg might have been stone.

"Oh!" she said, and suddenly there were tears in her eyes. *How terrible!* The tiny baby dragon, dead in its egg that way, never to see light or feel the air. "Oh, no. The poor little thing!"

Meseret's vast eye turned to Lucinda again, a red-gold ball with a thin black slit that went all the way from the top to the bottom. The buzzing in Lucinda's head intensified, as though whatever was stuck in there had just discovered there was no way out and was beginning to get angry. Lucinda tried to look away, but the eye seemed to glow in the dark room so that even the great bulk of the dragon itself began to fade into shadow and the glowing golden orb was all she could see, burning like a coal, like a tiny sun.

Something pushed at her thoughts again, a feeling of anger and despair so powerful and so alien that it seemed like an electrical storm inside her—Lucinda could almost feel lightning crackling and sputtering in her skull. Everything went swimmy behind her eyes—red, black, red, black, whirling and whirling . . .

Why was the ceiling suddenly sideways? Why was she standing pressed against a wall, held by some kind of flesh magnetism? Why was Haneb floating on his side before her, his face full of alarm?

"Miss, miss, you okay? Have you hurt?"

She groaned and closed her eyes. She couldn't push herself off the wall, but with her eyes closed, it felt less like a wall and more like the ground. She opened her eyes again. Now it made sense. She was lying on her back. Haneb was bending over her.

"What happened?"

"You fell. Have you ill, miss?"

"Oh, God, do I have what the dragon has? Am I going to die?"

Haneb actually smiled. The flash of white, extending to both sides of his ruined face and creasing the scarred side in a surprising way, allowed her for the first time to see him without seeing his wounds first. "No, miss. You not going to die. Not from dragon illness—people don't get it. I think just it is very hot for you today."

Before Lucinda could reply, Meseret let out another deep, grumbling noise. For some reason this one seemed less despairing, more like . . . a warning.

"Oh," Lucinda said, staring at the dragon. "Look!"

Meseret was up, swaying unevenly as if she had not stood in a while, but still up on her stout legs. The crest of her back, which had only stretched a yard or two above Lucinda's head when the beast was lying down, now arched high above like a suspension bridge. Meseret lifted her head, her huge nostrils sucking air. The dragon bumped hard against the bars of the pen, making them rattle and creak, then opened her mouth and *growled*. Lucinda stumbled back with her hands over her ears, doing her best not to scream. *It's just like King Kong,* she thought, terrified. "She's trying to get out!"

Haneb clutched her arm. "She doesn't get out. She is tied and the pen keeps her wings close. And she is not angry at *us*." He tugged Lucinda toward the door.

"So why are we running away?"

"We are not running from her." Haneb's smile was long gone, but his teeth were still showing like the snarl of a frightened dog. "Alamu comes. Her mate."

Meseret threw back her head and belched out an immense, rolling cloud of flame and black smoke that rippled through the metal struts on the ceiling. Even from two or three dozen yards away, Lucinda could feel the heat like an oven door suddenly swung open.

"But why is she angry?" Lucinda squealed. It was true— she could *feel* the dragon's fury coiling like a hot wire in her thoughts.

"Because he will take the egg if he can," said Haneb, fumbling at the door. "He will eat it. Hurry now."

"But he can't get in, can he?"

"Look up." He pointed toward the ceiling with his padded glove. There were two huge skylight windows among the struts. "Alamu is smaller than her. If he gets onto the roof he will come through easy."

Lucinda helped Haneb wrestle open the heavy door. It felt like a nightmare, one of those dreams where you run but can't escape. "We must quickly let Mr. Gideon know," Haneb said as they stumbled outside. He yanked off his hood. His black hair was damp and his scarred face shiny with sweat. The two of them began to run away from the Sick Barn, headed back toward the main house. The air outside the barn had a strange smell—acidic and prickly.

"What can Gideon . . ." she began, then fell silent as a nightmarish shape came around the nearest corner of the house.

Alamu was not even half Meseret's size, but terrifyingly faster in his movements than the female dragon. He was covered with copper and black scales that gleamed like a rattlesnake's back in the clear morning light, and as he reared up to more than twice Lucinda's height, the dragon flashed curving claws like bunches of ivory bananas. He turned his wedge-shaped head sideways, examining them, then dropped back down suddenly and stretched his head forward, squinting in exactly their direction. Haneb jerked Lucinda to a halt. "Quiet," he hissed. "*And do not move!*"

She couldn't have moved at that moment if she'd wanted to.

The dragon's wings unfurled, slow and beautiful like a butterfly's emerging from a cocoon. Then, his thin body suddenly whipping into the air, the monster came flying straight at them.

He was on them before they could even duck. For a moment Lucinda could hear nothing but her breathing and the rush of her blood, then something cracked past them like a snapped towel—a towel big as a missile. Alamu flew over their heads, his sand-colored wings rippling along their edges, then folded those wings so swiftly that he plummeted to the ground and landed with a thump that Lucinda felt in her bones. Now that he was between them and the greater safety of the barn, Alamu began walking toward them, his head held low.

Haneb, holding Lucinda's hand in a painful grip, shoved her behind him and said, "Back! Go back into that canning shed!"

"What?" She looked over her shoulder and saw a small wooden shed a dozen yards away, built next to one of the farm's many wells. The door was off. She couldn't imagine it keeping the dragon off her for more than a few seconds.

"Go!" he cried. "Please, miss, but go slow!" And then he stepped forward and away from her, clapping his gloved hands with a muffled thump and calling out, "*Ha! Ha! Ha!*" to the dragon, over and over. Little shudders ran down the length of its neck. Now Alamu was watching only Haneb, a snake watching a hopelessly trapped mouse.

Lucinda backed into the doorway of the shed, but couldn't bear to step inside where she wouldn't be able to see what was happening. Haneb had stopped again and was standing utterly still as the dragon stalked toward him on its hind legs, head extended on a line with Haneb's own. As Alamu breathed in and out, little flames danced around his nostrils.

The creature paused and sniffed delicately at the air all around the unmoving Haneb, who had dropped his hood somewhere in the excitement. Lucinda was terrified the monster would engulf the small man's poor disfigured face in fire. Was this what had happened to him before? Were those dragon-scars?

Alamu's long head moved closer on the supple neck, a yard of bone and teeth and muscle, the air in front of the nostrils rippling in the heat. The copper and black scales caught the light, glittering. The mouth opened, showing the curving fangs and a snaky black tongue.

From somewhere far away came a deep, flat ringing—a bell, but not quite like anything Lucinda had ever heard.

The dragon stopped, alert and listening A moment later it snorted and turned away, then began to run across the open space beside the Sick Barn, each step as heavy as the pounding of a sledgehammer, until suddenly it leaped into the air and sailed away from them again, tail lashing, a serpent wriggling across the sky.

Lucinda heard herself breathing out. Haneb had dropped down to sit on the ground and was staring at his hands as though he was astounded to discover he owned a pair. Lucinda ran from the shed, shading her eyes as she looked up. Alamu flew fast but the sky was big and clear: as he headed away over the house toward the reptile barn and the far pastures, she had a last view of the dragon, sunlight glowing through his translucent wings.

"Wow," she breathed, then suddenly began to cry.

CHAPTER 15

BEATING THE BIG CRAB

"Oh, Tyler, you really should have seen him!" Lucinda said as she climbed up next to him in the wagon. "It was the most . . . I was so scared! But he was beautiful too! Like a snake or a lizard—no, like a bat—I don't know. And he was all shiny and he breathed fire and I was so scared I thought he was going to kill us—I was sure I'd die!"

It was the day after Lucinda's dangerous adventure and she still hadn't stopped talking about it. Tyler was getting a little tired of hearing the story over and over, and glad that she wouldn't be able to talk about it at the Carrillos' house. He was also grumpy because with the upset last night and all the attention given to Lucinda, he hadn't found time to have a proper look at Octavio Tinker's journal, or what remained of it.

Still, Tyler supposed, he'd feel a whole lot worse if his sister had been turned into dragon barbecue.

"And Haneb, he was *sooo* brave—did I tell you?"

"Yeah, you told me. . . ."

"He stepped right out in front of it and he told me to go in the shed and hide. I thought he was going to get burned to bits! If it wasn't for Mr. Walkwell ringing that bell, the dragon would probably have killed us both. *Alamu,* right, it's Alamu!" Lucinda added breathlessly. "That's the dragon's name. Alamu." She said it more like the name of some new boy in school than of something that had almost turned her into fried chicken. "He's really scary—Alamu, I mean—and beautiful. But *amazingly* scary!"

"You were lucky, girl," said Ragnar as he finished adjusting the horse's harness. The yellow-haired man had carried her back to the house wrapped in a blanket after the dragon had flown away. Lucinda had been shivering so much her teeth clicked together. "Yes, Haneb was brave, but if Mr. Walkwell had not rung the feeding bell over at the reptile barn you still might have been killed."

"But I wanted to ask you last night—how did Mr. Walkwell even know what was happening to us?"

"We have a tracking device on the male dragon," announced Colin Needle. He had come out silently and stood in the doorway, listening. "I found it at a scientific supply company on the internet. We always have to know where he is, just because of things like what happened last night."

"Aren't you coming to the party, Colin?" Lucinda asked.

"No, I have a lot of important things to do."

Tyler wondered what could be so important that it was worth skipping a party, especially when you lived on an isolated farm.

"It's really too bad you can't go," Lucinda said. "It sounds like it's going to be fun."

For a moment Colin Needle showed something like genuine regret—he actually looked human. "It's all right. The Carrillos . . . well, they don't like me much."

"Gee," said Tyler. "I wonder why."

"Be quiet!" Lucinda elbowed her brother hard. "Nobody likes *you*, Tyler Jenkins."

Colin stood and watched as Ragnar flipped the reins and the horse started around the long gravel driveway. "Have a good time," he said, then turned and walked back into the house.

"We can't leave yet," Ragnar said. "We are still waiting for Simos."

"Mr. Walkwell's going with us?" asked Tyler.

"He likes the Carrillo clan." Ragnar grinned. "Ha, I will tell you one thing from yesterday that would make even the gods laugh. When the dragon came, Simos himself drove the truck to the reptile barn! I did not know he even knew how!" He turned to Tyler. "He did not waste time looking for me or Gideon—when he learned your sister was at the Sick Barn with Alamu he knew he had to go quickly."

"Cool!" said Tyler. He wished he'd seen it—Mr. Walkwell forced to deal with the modern world.

"I hope it didn't hurt his poor feet," Lucinda said dreamily.

"Then when he came walking back," Ragnar went on, chortling, "all he said was, 'Someone go and get that stinking machine. Now I must bathe.' Poor fellow!"

Mr. Walkwell appeared at last and they set off. Tyler made a few driving jokes, but the wiry old man only glared at him, maintaining a dignified silence. The wagon rolled along through the valley and over the dry hills on the far side until they finally reached the road to the Carrillos' farm. Ragnar hopped down to unlatch the front gate, which was made of white-painted iron bars and had a smiling sun beneath the letters: CRESTA SOL DAIRY FARM. It seemed like the kind of thing you would see in simple colors stamped on a carton of milk. After a moment Tyler realized that it probably was just that—the logo for the Carrillo family's dairy.

"What's 'Cresta Sol' mean, anyway?" he asked. "It sounds like a toothpaste."

"Maybe it's Spanish for 'My brother is very ignorant,'" Lucinda suggested.

The long driveway was gravel, the huge front yard mostly dirt except for an old swing set. Two figures Tyler recognized from the diner ran toward them, the boy, Steve, and his older sister Carmen, laughing and shoving each other.

"Come on," Steve said when they reached the wagon. "Alma's making something so she's being all artistic and she won't come out, but we put the Ping-Pong table up in the backyard and I've already beaten Carmen like a hundred times straight."

"Liar," his sister said. "You only won the last time because I stepped on one of your dolls and almost broke my leg."

"It's not a doll," Steve replied with dignity. "It's a collectible action figure of Helldiver from *Deep End*."

"*Deep End*? You play that?" Tyler was more than interested.

"Play it? I totally own that puppy. Well, except the last level. Can't get past the Grand Central Crustacean."

"Oh, man, that was so hard. Took me forever."

Steve's eyes bugged out. "You did it? You beat the crab?"

"Once, yeah. But I was playing it on Easy."

"Oh, man, I don't care, you have got to come show me."

Steve grabbed Tyler by the arm and dragged him toward the house just as a woman in jeans and a top that looked like a painter's smock stepped out the door, so they all nearly collided. She was about the same age as Tyler and Lucinda's mom, but she had long black hair pulled back in a ponytail and was a little shorter and a little more rounded.

"You two must be Tyler and Lucinda," she said. "Steven, quit yanking on the guest's arm."

"The crab, Mom! He totally knows how to beat the crab in *Deep End*."

"I only did it once," Tyler protested.

"That does sound impressive." She smiled. "However, Steven, no disappearing to play games right now. Stay outside and show our guests around—you can all play something together." She turned to the new arrivals. "Hi, I'm Silvia Carrillo. Happy Fourth of July."

"Thanks for inviting us," Lucinda said.

"You want to play Ping-Pong? Or come in and get something to drink?" Carmen spread her hands out. She was wearing a grown-up-looking bracelet full of jingling silver charms. Tyler had to admit she was kind of pretty for a girl his sister's age.

"Yes, everyone come in," said Silvia Carrillo. "Simos, Ragnar, can I get you men a beer?"

"To take with me, please," Ragnar said. He looked genuinely regretful. "I have work to do back at the farm, helping Gideon. I will come back tonight for everyone."

"Working? On the Fourth?" Silvia laughed. "You are *way* too dedicated."

Steve and Carmen took them on a quick tour of the house. They looked into Steve's impressively neat room as they went by and both boys gazed longingly at the game station. The youngest girl, Alma, waved shyly from the room she shared with Carmen. "I'll be out in a minute," she called. "Hi, Lucinda, hi, Tyler. Happy Fourth of July."

The Carrillos had more room than Tyler and Lucinda had at home with Mom, but their furniture was old and the television was small and the kids' clothes looked like hand-me-downs. Still, they seemed pretty cheerful. Tyler wasn't quite used to a family who joked without being mean and who seemed to have as much fun with each other as the Carrillos did.

At last they all trooped out to the covered patio in the backyard. At the edge of the patio a man in a bright white shirt, jeans, and sandals was tending a brick barbecue. He turned as the children arrived, smiled just enough to make his mustache twitch, then returned his attention to the coals.

"My dad's not really as *unsocial and rude* as he looks," Carmen said loudly. "He's just more interested in his barbecue than in people. Right, Dad?"

"Wait just a few minutes too long and the coals cool off," said Mr. Carrillo with his back to them. "Then the meat doesn't cook right. That's *science*."

"Our father, Hector Carrillo," said Steve. "Props for the mad barbecue genius."

They drank lemonade and played Ping-Pong, and it was so normal and pleasant that for a while Tyler almost forgot about the mysteries of Ordinary Farm. Mr. Walkwell hobbled out to discuss the fine points of barbecue with Mr. Carrillo. The old man had said yes to red wine, and now he seemed to be enjoying himself. More Carrillo relatives arrived, aunts and uncles and cousins, everybody putting food on the picnic table until it seemed there wasn't enough room left for people to sit and eat. Casserole dishes and salad bowls started to fill the Ping-Pong table too.

"Oh my *God*," said Lucinda. "There's enough food here for an army!"

"Yep," Tyler said happily. "There sure is."

A little old lady so short and round she might have been a Munchkin from the land of Oz, with hair the shade of red Lucinda was used to seeing on lead singers in punk bands, smiled and said, "I hope you brought your appetites, children."

"This is Lucinda and Tyler, Grandma," Carmen said. "From next door. This is my Grandma Paz."

"Ah." The tiny old lady now looked at them more carefully—maybe even a little suspiciously, Tyler thought. "You are the ones from the Tinker farm, yes?"

They both nodded.

She sighed. "So young! Well . . . enjoy yourselves." She smiled sadly and headed back to the kitchen.

"Is it my imagination," said Tyler quietly to his sister as they got into line to fill their dinner plates, "or was she acting like we were going on some kind of suicide mission?"

By the time Tyler had emptied his third plate he was seriously considering finding some place to lie down and die, but he knew he'd be dying happy.

What had been most surprising about the day was how comfortable Mr. Walkwell seemed. He drank his wine, teased the Carrillo children, and talked at least a little bit with almost everybody—it seemed like an entirely different person had come to the party in a Mr. Walkwell costume. Tyler even saw him flirt a little with Grandma Paz, which made the old lady whoop with laughter and cover her mouth with a chubby hand.

Little Alma had been standing near Mr. Walkwell for a long time, her hands behind her back. When he had finished talking to one of the Carrillo uncles, she stepped up and handed him a long something the size of a pencil case, wrapped in yellow tissue paper. Mr. Walkwell opened it up, but in such a way that Tyler couldn't see what was in it. Mr. Walkwell looked at it for a moment, then looked at Alma, who was stepping from one foot to the other as though she wanted to run away. He said something quietly to her, laid his big brown hand on top of her head, then put the package into the pocket of his overalls. She blushed furiously but looked very happy.

"What's that all about?" Tyler asked.

"She's trying to learn now to carve wood like Mr. Walkwell," Carmen said, "so she probably made him a present."

"She's getting pretty good," Steve said. "She made me a T. rex out of soap, but I left it in the shower and now it's kind of a half rex."

"You must be very, very careful," said Grandma Paz.

Tyler and Lucinda put down the dirty dishes they had carried into the kitchen.

"They're doing fine, Mama," Silvia Carrillo said.

"I don't mean that." The old woman shook her head. "I mean where they stay. That Tinker farm. It is a dangerous place—*tierra peligrosa.*"

"Don't start with the stories, Mama, please," begged Mrs. Carrillo.

"Everybody knows! My own *abuela*, my grandma, she was Yaudanchi—an Indian. She told me the stories. Back then, when the Indians lived here, a man went to find his wife who died. He followed her track all the way to that place, that valley. He found a big hole in the ground that led to the underworld, the Place of the Spirits. When he got there he found all the ghosts of all the people that ever were."

"Mama, quit trying to scare these poor children."

"Not scare! Warn!" the old woman said stubbornly. "My *abuela*, she said that one day the ground would open up and all the world would fall into the Place of the Spirits! That the ghosts would come out, ghosts and monsters!"

"Oh, cool, Grandma's telling a story," Steve said, walking into the kitchen with a stack of salad bowls. "Carmen, come on!"

"Monsters?" asked Tyler. Lucinda looked really worried, but whether it was about the story or Tyler's questions, he couldn't tell. "What kind of monsters, exactly?"

But before the old lady could answer him, Mr. Carrillo popped his head through the door. "It's just about dark," he said. "Anybody want to see some fireworks?"

"You kids go," said Mrs. Carrillo. "My mother and I are going to finish the dishes—and have a discussion about how to treat guests."

Mr. Carrillo had a big family-sized box of fireworks— the kind that Lucinda and Tyler had always been told were too dangerous to use. As he and the other men set them up on the wide expanse of dirt in front of the house, Mrs. Carrillo emerged. She uncoiled the garden hose and handed it to Steve. "If any sparks go up, then you put them out," she told him.

"But I want to do some of the fireworks!"

"Honey, there's no wind and the things are fifty feet from the house," protested Mr. Carrillo, but Silvia Carrillo was unmoved.

"Yes, that all sounds good until the house catches on fire," she said. "Steve, you stand there with that hose."

It was half an hour after the last True Volcano Blossom had sputtered out. Everyone had run out of things to do except sit around the back patio, stuffed and content, listening to the returning noise of the crickets and Mr. Walkwell blowing quiet tunes on a simple wooden flute— the gift, Tyler realized, that Alma had carved for him. He could tell because of the enraptured way Alma sat at his feet watching the old man play. The tune was so strange and the evening so warmly magical that he didn't even notice the large approaching shape until Ragnar stepped from the driveway into the soft light of the back porch.

"Sorry I am so late come," he said. "A lot to do."

"Do you want anything to eat?" said Mrs. Carrillo. "There's plenty left."

"I thank you, but no," he said, smiling. "I think I will carry this group back. Tomorrow is not a holy day like today, so we will be early to work."

"Let me send some back with you, then," she said. "We

have plenty of leftovers."

While she dragged Ragnar into the kitchen to load him down with chicken, potato salad, and black beans, Steve sidled up to Tyler. "Quick, dude," he whispered. "Just show me how to do the Bubble Cave."

They hurried into Steve's room and fired up Deep End, and Tyler gave him a quick tutorial on how to pick out the nonexploding bubble to ride through the cave and onto the next level, then left the other boy struggling with the Grotto of Ghouls and went looking for the bathroom. Through the open bathroom window he could hear Mr. Carrillo and Mr. Walkwell talking. The word *trouble* caught his attention, and instead of turning on the water to wash his hands he moved closer to the screen.

". . . That's all. I know he likes to keep his business to himself, but he needs to know about this."

"What kind of men?" Mr. Walkwell asked. "They did not come to the house."

"Men in suits. They said they were with the agriculture bureau, but Hartman said they were in town the day before and bought gas with a Mission Software credit card. That's that guy Stillman's company, you know, the guy who's in the news all the time. Do you think they're trying to find a place around here to open a factory or something?"

"Who knows?" Mr. Walkwell was doing his best to sound like he didn't care, but Tyler could hear something strange in his voice—was he a little drunk? "But if they come spying around the farm, *I* will teach them a lesson."

"Don't get yourself in trouble, Simos," said Mr. Carrillo. The two of them wandered away from the vicinity of the window still talking. Tyler washed his hands and went out, his head full of confusing information. Men in suits asking about the farm? Old Indian ghost stories? He had thought things were already as strange as they could get. Apparently he had been wrong.

On the way back to the farm, with the stars spread overhead and the horse clop-clopping along, nobody spoke for a long time. At last Lucinda asked, "Ragnar, why do the Carrillos keep talking about ghosts at Ordinary Farm? I don't think they know about the dragons or anything, but their grand-mother was telling this story about . . . about . . ."

"The Place of the Spirits," said Tyler. "She said there were ghosts under the house, or something like that."

Ragnar nodded, but as if he was thinking rather than agreeing. "I do not think there are ghosts under the house," he said at last. "I think that is fair to say."

Lucinda had grown dreamy again. Her voice soft, she said, "When is Uncle Gideon going to tell us what's really going on at Ordinary Farm?" Tyler was glad she doing the asking for once, but he knew they weren't going to learn anything that way.

Ragnar shook his head. "I have nothing to do with that, child."

"I hope it's not dead people," Lucinda said drowsily. "I hope Grandma Paz was wrong about that. I don't want to have to meet any dead people."

Ragnar breathed in sharply but said nothing. Mr. Walkwell, sitting beside him, made a sound that Tyler at first thought was a laugh. He only realized when he heard it a second time that the old man had quietly begun to snore.

CHAPTER 16

HUMPTY DUMPTY'S HANKY

"It isn't like you to go into town, young fellow," said Gideon. "Are you courting someone? The young woman at the Dairy Duchess stand, perhaps?"

Colin tried to smile at the old man's heavy-handed humor. "No, sir, I just wanted to do some shopping. Look at some computer magazines."

"Well, well, it's a pleasure to have you, of course. I won't be able to spend any time with you—I have a very important meeting—but you'll find plenty to do, I'm sure, a young fellow like you." He said it, as most old people did, as though Colin was somehow being unfair just by being young.

"I'll find things to do, sir."

"Yes, certainly. I see you've got your briefcase with you—very businesslike!" Gideon had brought along a case of his own—or, rather, a large box that Ragnar had stashed in the trunk while Colin watched from an upstairs window. Colin knew what was in the box, too. But he had not, of course, bothered to mention any of this.

"Where should we drop you off?" Ragnar asked. The big man wanted it clear that Colin was getting out first, so that he wouldn't be seeing where Gideon was having his "important meeting." They thought they were so crafty! Colin almost laughed. "Just at the store. Where should I meet you—and when?"

"I can't imagine what I'm doing will take more than an hour," said Gideon. "Why don't you meet us at the café and we'll have a sundae before we head back. Even your mother couldn't disapprove of that, could she? It's the day after the Fourth, after all—we deserve a little celebration!"

"Oh, yes, Gideon," said Colin, carefully suppressing any trace of sarcasm in his voice, "that would be *super.*"

Colin knew exactly where Gideon was going because the antiques dealer, Jude Modesto, had taken the bait of Colin's email and told him where they would be meeting—at Gideon's "secret office."

Gideon Goldring was not the kind of man to transact

his business in front of every curious soul in Standard Valley, and there were obvious reasons he didn't want to have Modesto (or anyone else) visit Ordinary Farm, so he had taken the precaution of leasing a tiny office in a small, half-built business park several blocks away from Standard Valley's main street. Luckily for Colin it was still twenty minutes until Gideon's meeting, so the old man and Ragnar were going to get a cup of coffee first. They invited Colin to join them at the café but he declined politely. When they headed toward Rosie's, Colin walked into the general store, then straight through and out the back door. Once he was out of sight, he tucked his briefcase under his arm and began to sprint toward the business park.

The building was small, and except for a chiropractor's office and a secondhand store that was apparently closed today there were no other businesses yet in place: Gideon's office was on the second floor above one of several empty storefronts. Colin paused at the bottom of the stairs long enough to slow his breathing and wipe the sweat from his forehead, then walked up and pushed the door open.

As Colin had hoped, Jude Modesto had let himself into Gideon's sparsely furnished office and was waiting. The antiques dealer was plump and pink, his bulk overflowing the inexpensive office chair, and he had a little tuft of a mustache, which did not make him look as young and fashionable as he probably thought it did. Modesto's glasses slid halfway down his nose as he mopped sweat from his face with a handkerchief. "You kept me waiting long enough," he said crossly, staring Colin up and down. "Look at you—you're just a kid! What do you want from me?"

Colin was very conscious that Gideon Goldring would be coming through the door in less than a quarter of an hour, but he did his best not to look hurried. He settled into the big chair that he supposed must usually be Gideon's, unlatched his briefcase, then paused and gave the antiques dealer his sternest look. "Just one question, Modesto. Are you rich enough?"

"What nonsense is this?" Modesto wiped his forehead furiously, as if to scrub away even the memory of being talked to that way by a mere boy. "I'm a very important man. . . ."

"Yes, I'm sure you are, but we're not talking about *important*, we're talking about *rich*. I'm asking whether or not you would like to be really, really rich. Are you happy dealing in trinkets, Modesto? Setting things up for the people who have the real money? Or would you like to get in on a truly big score"—Colin hoped he wasn't overdoing the tough-guy lingo: he'd written the whole speech out and memorized it the night before—"a score that will set you up for life?"

"Are you some kind of crazy person?" Modesto struggled to get up out of the low chair. He looked like Humpty

Dumpty about to fall off the wall. "Look, kid, I got your email and I said I'd meet you. Fine. I've met you, and now you'd better get going. Just because you live in Tinker's house doesn't mean you have anything I'm going to—"

"I have *everything*," Colin said harshly. Time was getting short now and he had to hurry. "You'll never get into Ordinary Farm on your own—Gideon Goldring will never let you. But if you help me you'll get access to things you've never even dreamed of, things that make those antiques you've been selling for him—those vases and obsidian knives—look like cheap souvenirs. You'll be rich beyond your dreams. Are you really *that* sure you're not interested?"

Jude Modesto stared at him. Humpty Dumpty's handkerchief came out, went back and forth across the wide, pink face. The chin, with its little sandy beard, twitched. "What are you offering? To get me onto the property?"

"That's not going to happen. Now, as for what I *do* have—do you want to find out? Yes or no?"

Modesto glowered. "You have five minutes, kid," the fat man said at last. "Start talking."

"I won't need that much time," Colin said. "Now listen. I'm going to give you something today and you're going to take it with you and get it tested. When you do, you're going to be desperate to talk to me—you're going to want to come and camp out by the gates of the farm. But you're not going to do that. Instead, you're going to send me an email, and it's going to say one word—'Yes.' And then I'll let you know where we go from there. Got it?"

Jude Modesto was clearly wrestling with the still-strong impulse to heave himself up out of the chair and storm out of the room, but he was also impressed by Colin's certainty. "You know, you're a very rude young man."

"No, I just don't like to waste time. Here." Colin reached into his briefcase and pulled out a pill bottle. Inside the bottle a small, pale chip sat on a folded piece of dark cloth.

"That little white thing?" Modesto squinted as he took the bottle. "What is it?"

"That's for you to find out. Remember, you're not testing me—I'm testing *you*. I already know what it is. But I'd suggest you give it to someone discreet—someone you really trust. Because you're not going to want this to be general knowledge."

For the first time, Jude Modesto looked less than certain of himself, even a bit worried, as though Humpty Dumpty had just heard that all the king's horses and men might not honor their putting-him-together contract after all. "Tested?"

"Yes. Oh, and I'd recommend you have it done by someone with training in biology."

Modesto was about to ask another question when they were both distracted by noise outside the office: a car door slamming downstairs in the parking lot. If it was Gideon, he was ten minutes early! Colin felt like he was going to be sick.

"I have to hide," he said, looking around in terror. *Why couldn't Gideon show up on time like he was supposed to?* "Where can I hide?"

"Don't look at me," snapped Modesto, although he seemed nervous too. "I didn't ask you to come."

Colin wanted to hit the fat man. "But if he finds me here, that's the end of a multimillion-dollar deal for you."

Now they could clearly hear footsteps on the concrete steps outside. Colin was thinking of trying to force the window open, despite the air conditioner built into the frame, when Modesto pointed at a couple of fabric partitions with metal frames standing against the wall. "Hide behind those," he suggested, wiping at his sweating face again. "But you better do it fast, kid."

Colin set the two screens side by side, close to the wall, leaving room to hide behind them, but then realized that his feet would show at the bottom. He had just dragged a box behind one of the screens when the door of the office began to open. Colin jumped up on the box and held his breath.

"Modesto? Ah, I see you let yourself in." It was Gideon's voice, all right.

"Mr. Goldring. A pleasure to see you, sir."

"Yes, I'm sure." Gideon's chair squeaked as he sat down.

"You know Ragnar, I think."

"Mr. Lodbrok, nice to see you again," said Modesto.

Colin inched forward a little, doing his best not to bump the fabric, and put his eye to the crack between the two screens. If he hunched a little he could just make out the area around the desk. Gideon looked wilted by the heat, his rooster comb of white hair a bit bedraggled. His eyes, though, were still bright and fierce. "So, Modesto, I'm sure you'd like to know what we have in the box."

"Of course," the dealer said. "Always the highlight of my day—no, my entire month. What have you brought me this time?"

Gideon carefully lifted something out of the box. Colin couldn't quite see it, but Jude Modesto obviously could. "Goodness!" he said. "I mean . . . goodness! Is that a red-figured amphora I see? Oh, my, that's one of the most astonishing Greek vases I've ever seen—might even be the Berlin painter!"

"Might indeed," said Gideon with a tone of deep satisfaction. "But I'll leave that to the experts. I've a couple more pieces for you. Some Phoenician glass and a Meso-american obsidian knife. Should be worth a few dollars." He chuckled.

"Oh, yes, they're lovely, lovely. Oh, I'll have no problems selling these, Mr. Goldring. What a treasure trove old Mr. Tinker must have left you! I would dearly love to have a look at it all someday—surely you should have the collection reappraised, just to make sure the insurance is adequate!"

"No, I'm afraid not, Mr. Modesto. I have my ways, as you know, and I don't hold much with visitors."

"But you wouldn't even have to see me!"

"I said no. Now, what do you think these might be worth?"

How much things were worth was a subject that interested Colin very much, and he listened carefully as Jude Modesto made an estimate and wrote out a check as an advance.

It's still small change compared to what we could get, Colin thought. *You think too small, Gideon—too small!*

"Thank you, sir," said Gideon, tucking the check into his wallet. "A pleasure doing business with you. Let me know when you've finished the appraisals and are putting the items up for—"

"Gideon," said Ragnar suddenly. "Someone is coming up the stairs!"

And now Colin could hear it too—the thumping of what sounded like several pairs of heavy feet.

"No one would be . . ." Gideon began lightly, then suddenly his tone changed as the door opened. Colin couldn't see it, but he could see the look on Gideon's and Ragnar's faces—like a wolf had suddenly strolled out of the dark and into the middle of camp.

"What the hell is going on?" Gideon demanded.

"S-sorry to catch you by surprise," said Jude Modesto, suddenly so nervous he was stuttering a little, "but I'd like to introduce you to my best client, Edward Stillman."

"*Stillman!*" Gideon said it like the world's worst curse word. "What the hell are you doing here? Modesto, you traitor!"

Ragnar turned on the antiques dealer. "I should break your neck for this."

Modesto squealed and tipped over his chair trying to get away. In the excitement Colin changed position so that he could get a better view. Three men stood in the doorway. Two of them were extremely tall, muscular, and bald, so that they looked like twins even though one was black and one white. It wasn't hard to guess that they were bodyguards. Between them stood someone Colin had never seen before, a small, fit man with white hair—Edward Stillman, apparently.

Jude Modesto had taken refuge behind Stillman and his guards. Ragnar looked like he didn't care how many men he'd have to wade through to get his hands on the fat little antiques dealer. One of the bodyguards reached menacingly into his coat, but Stillman raised a tanned, well-manicured hand. "Now, now, no violence, please. Let's keep the guns holstered. Mr. Modesto didn't sell you out, Gideon. I have been his main buyer for your collection for some time. I just insisted he let me meet with you in person. He didn't know anything about our previous acquaintance."

"Previous acquaintance? You call trying to steal my wife, my farm, and my life's work a 'previous acquaintance'? You really have a way with words, Stillman." Gideon got up from his chair. "Come on, Ragnar."

"Not so fast." Stillman gestured and one of the burly men moved forward. He and Ragnar stood chin to chin, staring at each other. They were about the same size, but Stillman's guard looked about thirty years younger. Colin pulled back. *Some bodyguards*, he thought, and felt a hysterical giggle rising inside him. *I could be waiting back here to kill this Stillman guy and they didn't even search the place.*

Colin suddenly realized what was really at stake. These were bodyguards—*armed* bodyguards. If he made a suspicious noise they would probably shoot him first and ask questions later. The urge to giggle suddenly felt much more like an urge to throw up. Colin clenched his teeth together violently—he didn't want to do either.

"Now, if everyone has finished demonstrating their toughness," Stillman said, "perhaps we can talk business. Mr. Modesto, you are no longer needed—wait in my car, please. The driver is running the engine and the air-conditioning is on."

"I won't forget this!" Gideon shouted as Modesto scuttled out like a crab trying to get back to its tide pool.

Colin had another, even more disturbing thought. *This*

guy Stillman is Modesto's main buyer—he said so! He's some kind of enemy of Gideon's. And Modesto's going to give the piece of eggshell to Stillman. His insides felt cold and heavy. What had he done? And more important, what would happen if Gideon found out? At the very least, Colin and his mother would be thrown off the farm forever. The only thing he really cared about would be taken away from him.

"You can't keep me here, Stillman," Gideon snarled. "You're scum and I don't have anything to say to you. We're going to walk out now and your hired thugs can't stop us."

Stillman smiled and shook his head. "Please, Gideon. If you won't talk to me, I can have police and FBI agents swarming all over your farm by nightfall. You really don't want that to happen, do you?"

"Police? That's nonsense!"

"Try me and find out."

A hard silence filled the room. When Gideon finally spoke, he sounded like he had been punched in the stomach. "What . . . what are you talking about?"

"Oh, good, I have your attention," Stillman said. "Sit down." Gideon sat. Ragnar returned. "Gideon, my life has changed a great deal since I saw you last. I'm sure you've heard that my company, Mission Software, has now gone public?"

Gideon glared at him and did not answer.

"It made me a pretty penny. More than a few pretty pennies, in fact."

Mission Software—Ed Stillman! Colin had heard of him—the man was a billionaire. But why on earth would someone like that know anything about their farm?

"If you just wanted to brag, Stillman," said Gideon sourly, "you could have sent a press release instead of holding us at gunpoint."

Edward Stillman laughed. "You're just as charming as ever. I don't see any guns out, do you? Now, listen carefully. You and I both know that by all rights the farm should belong to me. It belongs to *my* family, not yours. If Octavio had been in his right mind he would have made that clear before he died."

Colin almost fell off his box again. This was crazy! Stillman and Gideon—related?

"You're full of crap," spat Gideon, his face an angry red.

"You aren't even a Tinker," said Stillman. "You just married one. Stole one, to be more accurate. Because Grace should have been mine."

"Don't you dare talk about her!" Gideon's eyes were almost popping out of his head. Ragnar put a big hand on his shoulder, to calm him or perhaps to restrain him. "Don't you dare say a word about my wife!"

Stillman shook his head. "I'd hoped you would be more reasonable than this. You won't make a good impression in court, you know, with spit flying out of

220

your mouth like that." He sighed. "Well, it doesn't matter. I have no urge to make friends with you, Goldring. I just wanted to tell you that I'm going to get that farm. I know there's more going on there than simply Octavio's collection of antiques. My uncle Octavio was a brilliant, brilliant man—the world underestimated him, but I haven't. He would have wanted me to have that farm and have access to his research."

Gideon thrashed beneath Ragnar's restraining grip. "Liar! You already tried to steal it from me with your blasted lawyers—*but you lost!* The farm is mine! You'll never get it!"

Stillman shook his head again, like a father watching a child throw a tantrum. "Gideon, Gideon, the only reason I'm warning you is that I would prefer to keep the police and FBI out of this. I don't want the authorities running loose on that farm any more than you do. I don't know what's there, but I do know I'd rather not share it with the federal government. But if I can't get the farm any other way, I'll let them have it before I'll let *you* have it, you little thief." And now it was Stillman who was starting to turn red beneath his deep tan. "Do you understand me? One way or another, you're as good as gone."

"You can't do anything," Gideon said. "You already lost once."

"Oh, but I can," said Stillman. "Because I discovered a letter that we didn't have the last time we went to trial—a letter from Grace." He grinned. He didn't look quite so much like a refined billionaire now. "That's right. You only kept that farm because the law decided Grace disappeared after old Octavio died. But now I have a letter that makes it a lot clearer what really happened."

Gideon suddenly looked very old. "What . . . what are you talking about? What letter?"

"Oh, I brought you a copy." He gestured to one of the bodyguards, who produced a manila envelope and handed it to Gideon. "She wrote to my mother a few days before she so conveniently vanished. You can see what she says, can't you? 'Gideon is getting more angry and desperate all the time,' I believe she says. Also, 'I worry that there may be violence. It frightens me. Gideon frightens me.' Dear me, that doesn't sound good, does it?"

"She didn't mean violent toward her," said Gideon weakly. "She was worried that I might lose my temper with that old . . . with Octavio."

"Yes, yes, you will explain it to a jury, I'm sure. And we will all be fascinated to hear again how my sweet little cousin Grace—beautiful, kind Grace—just happened to run away on the night her grandfather died, leaving you the sole master of Octavio Tinker's property. How touching! How dramatic! How . . . *convenient*!"

Gideon shoved the copy of the letter back into its envelope. "I'll never give you a square inch of Ordinary Farm. Nothing—not even a spoonful of dirt!"

Stillman shrugged. "I'm bored with you now, Gideon. You're just as petty as you ever were. Don't you realize *you can't win?*" He tipped his head toward his bodyguards. "Come on, gentlemen. We have work to do—lawsuits to file, murder investigations to reopen."

"You're bluffing," Gideon said. "You want the farm too much yourself to risk getting the police involved again."

"Yes, you tell yourself that." Stillman stopped in the doorway. "Oh, and remember this—you've only been surviving so far because I've been buying your antiques. I know your finances better than you do, and so far it's suited me to keep the farm in business. But if I decide not to buy any more of what is clearly my own family's legacy, and I pass the word among my collector friends, for good measure, that I caught you selling fakes, where are you going to find the money to run that place, let alone hire enough lawyers to keep me from getting it?" He laughed and walked out.

"That scum." Colin could see Gideon's face through the crack. He looked as though he'd been beaten up. For a moment, despite years of dislike, Colin almost felt sorry for him.

"Is he really your wife's clansman?" asked Ragnar. He didn't seem very sympathetic to Gideon's position, although Colin always had trouble reading the Norseman. "You did not tell me that."

"Why should I? What difference does it make? He's

a liar. I had nothing to do with Grace disappearing." He looked at Ragnar and his expression hardened. "You're not questioning that, are you? You don't think I'd murder my wife, do you?"

"I judge no man," Ragnar said.

"Thanks for that vote of support," Gideon said bitterly. "Come on. We have to pick up the boy and go home."

"We promised him ice cream."

"I don't give a damn," said Gideon.

Colin crouched silently until he heard them leaving, then went to the window and watched them get into the truck, Gideon moving like a very, very old man. It was only as he watched them drive away that he realized they would probably beat him back to the coffee shop, and that Gideon's bad mood would get worse if they had to wait for him.

They did and it did. Colin didn't get any ice cream. Gideon and Ragnar looked like they'd just come from a funeral. The drive home was a very quiet one.

CHAPTER 17

AIN'T GOING TO TARRY

After dinner Tyler knocked on his sister's door and actually waited until she said, "Come in," before bursting in. He ran to the window and drew the curtains while Lucinda watched, puzzled.

"What's that about?"

Tyler waved away the question. "So where's the book?"

Lucinda pulled it out from under her mattress. She was curious, but not quite as worked up as her brother. While they had been taking care of the baby griffins with Ragnar, Tyler had just kept hopping from foot to foot as if he had to use the bathroom. Badly.

"Let me look," he said now. "Come on, I found it!"

"Booger. We both found it. Besides, it's hard to find anything left to read." She leafed through a few pages. Chewed-page confetti rolled out in little showers. "The mice have chewed almost all of it."

"Here, let me see." But instead of snatching it, he waited until she put it in his hands, then carefully pushed the shredded pages apart. "Look, here's some bits in the middle they didn't get. Really weird old handwriting." He spread a page as flat as he could and began to read out loud.

"But here is my question: Why must we think of it as simply a fourth dimension? Perhaps it would be more instructive to consider it as akin to earth's terramagnetic field—as something that surrounds and permeates the dimensions we perceive rather than being simply one more dimension. At the places of intersection, the lines of force would cohere, much as the lines of an electromagnetic pole cohere, albeit invisibly, and influence physics in our three known dimensions, and perhaps beyond them. If so, then the structure of the Breach itself might be something familiar to most scientists, a Fibonacci spiral.

"This Breach, as I named it in the first of these journals, or Fault Line, as I have begun to call it since setting my sights on California as the most

propitious spot for prospecting, has now become my central obsession. ('Fault' is by way of a small jest, since the earth of America's western coast is rotten with faults of the seismic variety, coupled with the fact that several people have suggested my fascination with this line of study is a bit of a 'fault.')

"Man, it just goes on like this," Tyler grumbled. "Old Octavio has a totally bad case of can't-talk-normal-English."

"Do you want me to read it instead?"

"No."

"If it does take the form of a Fibonacci spiral, there would not only be a point of intersection with physical space, but at that intersection would be found areas of greater concentration of what is currently thought to be a single medium of unchanging density—the fourth dimension expressed as a cohered monopole at the center of a fifth-dimensional rolling vortex. That is to say, at the heart of the infolding there would be a place where a near infinite expression of that medium would be located in a very small part of our four-dimensional matrix. Would that not be a very merry thing to find?

"In any case, Father and Mother are both quite put out with these kinds of 'maunderings,' as Father puts it, and forbid me from such research until at least the

time when I have received a doctorate and may pur-
sue knowledge without the shame of being perceived a
'crackpot'...

"Man, this guy is the mayor of Mad Scientist Town!"
said Tyler, laughing.

"But what does it all mean?" she asked. "What's a fourth
dimension?"

"How should I know? In my science class we learned
how to make a rocket out of a plastic soda bottle." Tyler
riffled through the pages of the ruined notebook. "That's
about all there is left to read—just a few words and sen-
tences here and there and some math stuff. The only thing
for certain is that he's saying there's an earlier diary, and
if old Octavio's the kind of guy who keeps diaries there
might be a whole bunch of them stashed away somewhere
and *not* eaten by mice." Tyler handed her back the notebook. "Hide it again. If there're more I'm going to find
them. If anybody's going to tell us what's going on with
this place, it's the guy who built it."

Something fell against the window.

Both Tyler and Lucinda jumped. Suddenly frightened,
Lucinda shoved the diary under her pillow.

Tyler went to the window and pulled back the curtain. "I
knew I was right," he said. "I knew it! Look outside, Luce."

Lucinda stood up and stared out the window. The
cherry tree filled much of her view, its blossoms gone and

the leaves turning purple-brown.

"What do you see?" he asked.

"Just the usual stuff."

"Okay. Stand there and watch for a minute." Tyler clattered out of the room and down the stairs.

Lucinda shook her head. What was it now—more ghosts? Tree ghosts? Midafternoon tree ghosts?

Tyler appeared a few moments later in the overgrown patch of dry grass under the window. He stood there for a moment, then started walking, in the direction of the library and the rest of the unused wing without even looking back. Lucinda reached up to tap on the glass to get his attention, but before she could do it something dark hopped onto a branch high above Tyler's head. It squatted for a moment, fat as a toad and just as still, then jumped effortlessly to the next tree.

It was following him.

Tyler turned around suddenly, heading back again toward the kitchen and dining room. The black squirrel followed, changing direction itself a few moments after he did. Lucinda felt a sudden surge of panic, although it seemed ridiculous—what could a squirrel, even a big one, do to a boy Tyler's size? Still, she couldn't help pulling up the window to warn him.

"Tyler!"

He didn't turn, but the squirrel did, fixing her with the queasy yellow of its stare. For a moment she felt sure the animal was truly looking at her—as if marking her for future attention. She swallowed hard and rattled the window back down. Her brother and his hopping pursuer vanished from sight.

Tyler came back into the room a short while later. "Did you see?"

"That creepy squirrel again—and it was following you!"

"Yeah—duh. It's been doing it for days. Everywhere I go, unless I'm out with the farm people. Even then I keep thinking I see it, hiding up in the trees, watching. And it keeps Zaza away—I hardly ever see her now."

"What's going on? Why would it do that?" She felt suddenly chilly, as if she had a fever. Those eyes!

"I don't know. It started when I found the library. I think Mrs. . . . . I think somebody's using it to keep an eye on me."

"You were going to say Mrs. Needle."

"Yeah, well, she creeps me out. I think she's a witch or something."

"Tyler Jenkins! Do you *hear* yourself? A witch? This isn't one of your video games."

"And it isn't one of your 'We're all friends, everybody learns a lesson, then we all hug' TV shows, either. There's some creepy stuff going on around here, and I'm not just talking about dragons and . . . and hoop snakes."

Lucinda sat down on the bed, too tired to argue. She didn't want Mrs. Needle to be bad. She didn't care if everybody hugged, but she did need friends. She was lonely with only her brother for a friend. She wasn't used to it.

"Look, just do me a favor," he said. "I want you to go to that library and see if you can find any more of Octavio's notebook. If I go that thing is going to follow me and *somebody* is going to know about it."

The library? Where Tyler said he'd seen a ghost? She absolutely did not want to do that. "How do you know it won't just follow *me?*"

"Because I'm going to take Secret Squirrel for a little walk around the property."

Lucinda never really said yes, but she didn't say no forcefully enough to stop him, either. She watched from her window as Tyler wandered past, looking around like a little kid playing army spy—trying to convince the squirrel he was doing something secret and important, she guessed. She was too nervous to be disgusted—and maybe, just maybe, Tyler was right, because within a few seconds the black squirrel reappeared, then waited until Tyler had rounded the corner and headed out toward the front of the house before it hopped after him, its weight making even some of the bigger branches bounce and sway.

Lucinda forced herself to follow her brother out of the house, but headed in the opposite direction. She didn't look up for fear of what she might see, but once she heard a rattling noise above her head that froze her in her tracks. She stayed that way for long seconds, heart beating, breathless, until a blue jay squawked loudly and flew away past her and the trees were silent again.

Silence and dust greeted her inside the library. In the fading evening light slanting in through the big windows she could see the footprints she and Tyler had left during their last visit—or at least she *hoped* that's who had left them. The place was half in shadows and extremely creepy, but Lucinda was afraid to turn the lights on in case someone at the house should notice.

Why didn't I bring a flashlight? She had to admit it—Tyler was better at this ninja spy-stuff than she was.

Her footsteps made little smacking noises as she crossed the library to the picture of Octavio Tinker. What was that thing in his hand, that weird brass tangle of curves and wheels? Why was it the brightest thing in the picture? The old man's eyes seemed to sparkle with self-regard—*I know and you don't!* He must have been as hard to put up with as Uncle Gideon.

Lucinda knew she should investigate the little room with the mirror—after all, that was where the other piece of journal had been found—but she honestly didn't know whether or not she could walk into a place that Tyler said was haunted. Instead she stalled by exploring the rows and rows of books. A lot of the library was shelved in alphabetical order by subject. She found nothing under

"Ordinary Farm," although that seemed a little too obvious anyway, but she looked under "Tinker" and actually found a book about Octavio, titled *Octavio Tinker, the Crystal Prophet*. Her excitement faded a little when she saw that it was some sort of biography written for kids, a book at least sixty years old with corny-looking black-and-white photos and lots of weird diagrams. Still, she took it off the shelf. It might not be old Octavio's journal but it was something.

She wandered up and down the aisles, scanning the shelves of books and trailing her fingers across their dusty spines. None of the volumes seemed to be newer than decades old, and none of them looked obviously like a journal, although it would take years to open them all and make sure. She was about to give up when something caught her eye.

Standard Valley.

There were at least a half dozen books in a row with those words on the cover. She pulled them from the shelf, tried to swipe the dust from the floor so she could sit, then realized it was hopeless and took them back to the chairs near the front of the building. Three of them were stapled piles of paper—Yokut County phone books ("containing Canning, Standard Valley, Tentpole, and Harper's Creek"). There were no listings for Tinker or Ordinary Farm in any of them, so she put them aside. Another was a hard-bound book from some organization called the California

Grange titled *Yokut County Grange*, followed by a list of nearby towns, each one with a number, one of which was "Standard Valley #723." She leafed through it, but it was just some kind of farming thing with information about water rights and who to contact in Sacramento or Washington, D.C., about various farming problems. She flipped it onto the pile with the phone books.

The last one didn't look any more interesting than the others—something titled *Building Allotments and Land Surveys of Standard Valley, 1963*—but it fell open right to a page titled "Property: O. Tinker," a sort of blueprint drawing of buildings and other things. Even as she stared at it, something like a cool breeze whispered down the stacks, ruffling her hair and making her gasp. She looked around in surprise but the library was empty and all the windows she could see were closed.

Lucinda hurriedly shelved the other books, but held on to the land surveys. Then she took a deep breath as she walked back across the library to the door between the shelves—Tyler's haunted mirror room. The key was still in the lock.

After the chilly visitation she had just experienced her brother's talk of ghosts seemed even more meaningful than before. She really, *really* didn't want to go in. Still, as she turned and saw old Octavio's painted, half-amused eyes on her, she knew she didn't want to just walk out, either. This was a mystery. This was an *adventure*. She reminded herself of all the brave heroines in the books she'd read, took one more breath, and walked in, the book clutched to her chest like armor.

It doesn't feel any more haunted than the rest of the library, she told herself. It was just old, and dusty, and probably— ick—spidery.

She forced herself forward. Like it or not, she'd have to pull out all the dresser drawers and see if anything had fallen down behind them. She should probably look under the bed as well, the horrible, cobwebby bed. . . .

She stopped, staring into the mirror. No one looked back but herself, so for a moment she didn't even understand why she felt so alarmed. Then she saw that on the wall in the mirror room somebody had written a word in the dust: OLIS. She turned, hoping that the strange word would be there too, in the real room, that it was just some stupid thing her brother had traced on the wall . . . but it wasn't. The strange word only existed in the mirror.

Lucinda didn't stop running until she was back in the overgrown garden. The sun was going down and a little wind had sprung up, but this time the cooling breezes of the outside world were welcome.

She was walking along toward the kitchen door in the growing dark when a tall figure stepped out of the shadows, startling her so that she almost dropped the book clutched to her chest.

"What you doing, missy?" It was Caesar, the man who brought Gideon his trays and who helped out around the house. He looked at her with concern. "You look like you seen a haunt."

She actually laughed—he didn't know how right he was! Or maybe he did. She didn't know and she didn't care. She was sick of mysteries and just wanted to get into her room and pull the blankets over her. "I'm okay."

"Didn't mean to scare you. Just taking the old vegetables and such out to the compost heap." He showed her the bag in his hand. "What you doing running around in the nearly dark?"

"Just . . . exploring."

He shook his head. "This not the best place to go exploring after dark. 'Spose they already told you that."

"Everybody told us that. But they won't tell us why."

He gave her a strange look. "And you and your brother all bound and determined to find out, huh?" He shook his head again, slowly, as though he couldn't quite bring himself to believe it. He bent down until his dark, broad face was at the same level as her own. His breath smelled like cinnamon. "Look here," he whispered. "I'll tell you this for free. You seen the best part. You seen the animals, them unicorns and all. Now go on home. There's other things happened here ain't so nice. Not so pretty. You and your brother too young to get tangled up in this kind of nonsense—that old man and his crazy notions—and we've

236

had some bad people here too. You go on home."

"What?" she asked as he straightened up. "What do you mean?"

"You heard me," he said quietly as he walked past her, headed for the vegetable garden. When he spoke again, it was in a normal tone—a little loud, even, as though someone else might be listening. "You have a nice evening, now, missy."

As he vanished into the gloom, he was singing a slow song Lucinda didn't recognize.

> *"The big bell's tolling in Galilee*
> *Ain't going to tarry here*
> *Ohhhh Lordy*
> *Ain't going to tarry here. . . ."*

CHAPTER 18

A HOLE IN THE WORLD

Ragnar appeared at breakfast and announced to everyone in the kitchen, "I have news, but it is not very good, I'm afraid. Alamu found his way into the Sick Barn and took the unhatched egg. Now we will not be able to study it to learn what went wrong."

"Oh, no." Lucinda looked really upset. Tyler usually teased her about her obsession with cute little baby animals—she loved any nature program with tiger or bear or lion cubs—but he felt the sadness too. These were the only dragons in the world, after all: if they couldn't reproduce, they would also be the last. "When did it happen?" he asked Ragnar.

"In the dawn. He fooled us, for he usually sleeps until the sun is high. Haneb saw him flying away with it in his mouth."

Colin Needle had just walked into the room. "That's terrible news!" he said, then began filling his plate.

The rest of July was hurrying past in a round of daily chores and other even less satisfying activities. Tyler felt more frustrated than ever. Mysteries bloomed around every corner but answers were a lot less common.

Uncle Gideon was barely to be seen. The people in the kitchen (who seemed to know pretty much most of what went on at Ordinary Farm) said he stayed locked up in his study day and night, performing experiments of some kind with Mrs. Needle. It meant a lot of extra work for Ragnar and Mr. Walkwell.

One evening Tyler ran into his great-uncle wandering alone in Mrs. Needle's vegetable garden, distracted and apparently confused. When Tyler said hello the old man looked at him as if he didn't know who Tyler was.

Was he ill? Crazy? Whatever the case, it made Tyler nervous.

Worst of all, though, every time Tyler went outside the house on his own the black squirrel followed him, ignoring both his shouts of protest and his attempts to shake it out of the trees. Even when he threw rocks at it, the squirrel scarcely reacted: if a stone came too close it moved just far enough to avoid being hit, but other than that it seemed completely unafraid. Tyler knew he was being watched—but by whom exactly, and why? Who could make a squirrel do something like that, anyway?

Prevented from exploring, Tyler devoted his afternoons and evenings to studying the few fragments about Ordinary Farm he had collected—Octavio Tinker's mouse-gnawed journal, the children's book, and the book of surveys Lucinda had brought back from the library and passed to him with shaking hands. Lucinda's ghost message, OLIS, wasn't in the dictionary, and Tyler had combed the shredded pages of Octavio's diary for any mention of OLIS there, but with no luck. Another mystery.

The children's book told him a little about Octavio Tinker's early life. Born at the end of the nineteenth century in upstate New York, Octavio was a brilliant man who had been a pioneer in the science of crystals and had become famous—famous enough for a children's book to be published, anyway!—for growing, at very high speeds, huge crystals that looked like diamonds and other jewels. He had demonstrated this technique all over the world—there was even a picture of him growing some crystals for President Franklin Roosevelt. But the picture that really got Tyler's attention was one labeled "Professor Tinker and His Continuum-Scope." The device he was holding in the photo looked very much like the one in the painting, except bigger—Octavio, sporting a very impressive mustache, looked like he was about to play a solo on the French horn.

So it was a real thing, after all, something he'd actually invented. After skimming the rest of the kids' book, Tyler put it down and went back to the journal.

An hour later he had puzzled out a few more smeared or torn words and phrases, including scientific-looking terms like "crystallometry," "Fulcanelli's Cross," "flux growth," "covalent bonding," and "node of pure Grailite," but none of them meant anything to him at all. (After checking the dictionary, he suspected some of them might not even mean anything to his science teachers.) But he also pried apart two stuck pages and found a comparatively unchewed section of Octavio's writings that he read with growing excitement:

> *The Chinese philosopher says, "The adept must . . . learn the method directly from those skilled in the art. . . . What is written in books is only enough for beginners. The rest is kept secret and is given only in oral teaching. . . . Above all, belief is necessary. Disbelief brings failure."*

Under this, Octavio had added,

> *But as a general rule, believers are not scientists and scientists are not believers. Where can I find someone to help me create the perfect Continuascope?*

There it was, although spelled a little differently—a Continuascope! And when he was thinking about moving to California, Octavio was still thinking about improving the device. Tyler wasn't certain about the rest of the passage—the dictionary said an "adept" was just someone who had secret knowledge. Octavio had wanted secret knowledge and he had also wanted help building a scientific instrument. So it was interesting, but it still told Tyler precisely nothing. OLIS hadn't led to anything, either. A whole afternoon's work, and he really didn't know any more than when he'd begun.

Studying, he thought sourly. *Grown-ups act like it's so great, like you can do anything in life if you just study enough. Okay, I'm studying! And in my own free time! And what do I get for it?*

Nothing but nothing, was the obvious answer.

"And Colin said he really wished he could go to school like we do—you know, a real school with other kids and teachers and everything. He's homeschooled. His mom has always taught him here. Isn't that sad? No wonder he doesn't always know how to behave. . . ."

Lucinda was babbling away, but Tyler was still doggedly going through the Octavio Tinker material and hardly paying attention—especially since she was babbling about Colin Needle, who Tyler thought was about as interesting as a pimple on someone's butt. He had the survey book in front of him open to the Ordinary Farm pages as he made notes on a piece of binder paper.

". . . So maybe you should try being nicer to him," Lucinda finished. "Maybe he could help us find out some of this stuff you're so interested in."

"Colin?" Tyler couldn't believe what he was hearing. "You want me to make friends with Junior Doctor Evil?"

"He really seems like he needs friends, Tyler."

"So does a skunk. That doesn't mean I'm stupid enough to pet one."

"You are so mean!"

"Hold on." He waved his hand at her. Something had finally clicked. "Come here, Luce. Look at this."

She scowled, but wandered over. "What?"

"Okay, this is what the farm looked like in 1963. Most of the buildings are pretty much the same, but there's also a bunch of stuff that isn't here anymore. See these buildings?" He pointed to a cluster of shapes on the survey map that looked as though they should be between the house and the library. "There's nothing there now. Just a garden."

"Maybe that's the stuff that burned down in the fire."

"What fire?"

"Ragnar said there was a fire—it was a long time ago. Uncle Gideon had a laboratory with all kinds of stuff in it. And he lost it all because the lab burned down."

"Wow, really?" Tyler stared at the plans. "Okay, that probably explains some of the missing buildings. But that's not what I wanted to show you. Look at this map. Really look at it."

Lucinda squinted, wrinkling her forehead. "What am I looking at?"

"That's just it. What *are* you looking at? Don't you notice anything?" He put his finger on the survey and traced the shape.

"Oh. Oh yeah! It . . . it all kind of makes a big spiral. Like a shell, or something. When you look at the farm buildings and the house buildings."

It was true. Although they weren't all connected, the buildings marked on the plan seemed to spin off from a single empty point at the center of the property. The shapes of the actual buildings were already strange and off-kilter, and the hole left by the burned-down buildings obscured it even more, so that Tyler had never noticed the shape while walking around the real farm, but here on paper you could see it clearly.

"But why?" Lucinda asked. "Why build it like that?"

"Because Octavio Tinker was a major nutcase, probably." Something else was still puzzling him, but he couldn't figure it out—something missing, like a noise he hadn't even noticed until it had stopped. "That stuff in his diary sounds like it comes right out of the Ultimate Scroll II strategy guide. . . ."

"Where's the haunted house thing?" Lucinda chewed her lip. "If that's the reptile barn over there, and that's the front of the house, then the haunted house thing ought to be right . . . there." She put her finger in the center of the open space, the empty hub around which the buildings seemed to spin.

Tyler stared. "Whoa! You're right. Lucinda, you're right!" The "haunted house thing," as his sister called it, was the big, empty, windowless building they had passed when they first arrived at the farm, a weird structure that looked kind of like a scary mansion out of a movie, with ancient gray boards and a big tub that stretched down from it, like a mosquito's stinging snout. "But that barn or whatever it is *looks* like it's been around since a lot farther back than 1963 . . . so why isn't it on this map?"

"It's not a barn," Lucinda said, leaning on him to examine the picture. "Don't you remember? They told us." She chewed her lip. "It's a . . . what is it? Oh yeah, a grain silo. But since most of the animals here don't eat grain, Uncle Gideon doesn't use it."

"So has it been here all along?" He looked at the empty spot on the survey. "Then it should be here on this map. But it isn't, so maybe they built it since then—well, that's just weird. No one would build a silo just to keep it empty. . . ." He trailed off. "Oh, *man*. Lucinda—silo! S-I-L-O!"

"So? What's so . . ." It sank in. "Oh my God. But the message in the mirror said 'OLIS.'"

"Yeah! That's SILO backward!"

Tyler laughed, still amazed how it had all come out. "I'd

bet all my allowance for the rest of my life that something in that mirror is trying to send us a message—and the message is 'Check the silo.'"

It was all Lucinda could do to keep him from going at once to explore the place. He felt like a child being sent to bed early when she reminded him about the black squirrel, but he had to admit she had put her finger on a problem. For a moment he considered sending Lucinda to explore the mystery in his place, but she refused before he could even suggest it.

"Forget it—I'm not going in some crazy haunted silo," she said very firmly. "If you want to get killed by ghosts or collapsing farm machinery or . . . or something, then *you* do it."

That night Tyler lay awake for hours, unable to fall asleep, trying to imagine a way to thwart the spy squirrel. It came to him in the long, quiet hour just after midnight—something he had seen in a shed at the back of the house. He fell asleep at last and dreamed of buildings and people made of paper, all threatened by a spreading fire.

All the next day Tyler could hardly concentrate on anything, his mind so full of what he was going to do that Ragnar and even shy Haneb wound up shouting at him to be careful. He thought he would go crazy waiting for it to get dark enough for him to get started, but after finishing the day's chores he came back to his room and collapsed on the bed. The room was stuffy with afternoon heat and he promptly fell asleep. He woke up to Lucinda's knock on the door.

"Did you change your mind?" she asked when he stumbled over to let her in.

"No," he said, suddenly panicked that he might have missed his chance. "What time is it?" The light coming through his window was tinged with the shadows of approaching evening. "Shoot!"

He grabbed his sweatshirt, then went through the pockets to make sure he had not only his flashlight but extra batteries.

"Did you put that thing out for me?" he asked.

Lucinda was watching him with arms crossed. "Yes, I did."

"Right where I said?"

"The oak tree at the edge of the garden right where you said, yes." She shook her head. "Tyler, I don't think this is a good idea. . . ."

"You never think anything is a good idea unless it includes watching television or talking on the phone," he said.

"That's really mean, Tyler. And it's not true, either. Who went into the library for you and saw the message and found you that map?"

"Okay, I'm sorry. You're right. But we have, like, two or three weeks left before we go home. What if Uncle Gideon never tells us anything? What if he never asks us back? In, like, another year we'll be wondering whether this even happened."

"That doesn't seem very likely."

"Whatever. I'm going. If you still want to help me, go downstairs and make sure nobody comes looking for me." He shouldered his backpack and let himself out, hoping he looked at least a bit more like Indiana Jones than like some snot-nosed little kid running away from home to go live under the picnic table.

The dark shape made the branches tremble as it hopped along above his head. Tyler did his best not to look at it—not that he wanted to, anyway. The squirrel was just plain creepy at the best of times. But now he had a bigger reason to look away.

That's right, you ugly old devil squirrel. You just keep following me.

He stopped beneath the oak tree, dropped his backpack on the ground, and pretended to be tying his shoes while he felt along the trunk for the long handle of the fruit-picker. Perfect—there it was. Lucinda had left it leaning just where he wanted. He crouched, whistling tunelessly, and waited.

After a few moments he heard the scuttle and spring of the squirrel leaping from a nearby tree to the oak. Tyler kept tying and retying his shoe, waiting until the squirrel, as it usually did, moved to a lower branch. The thing was practically fearless. Well, this time he'd give it something to think about.

The leaves rustled just above him and he looked up slowly. There it was, two limbs up, about four or five feet out of Tyler's reach even if he jumped. But he wasn't going to jump. Instead he wrapped his hand around the fruit-picker's handle and got onto his knees as though he was about to stand up. The squirrel stopped moving, waiting to see if he was going to throw a rock as he had on so many other occasions.

He heaved up the fruit-picker like a giant butterfly net and whacked the basket over the squirrel just as it was about to leap to a higher branch. It *squealed*, the first time he'd ever heard it make a sound, a ghastly, high-pitched rasp like something being burned alive. It was so horrible that Tyler almost let go of the handle. The thing struggled hard, scrabbling against the thick, strong fabric of the basket. It was all he could do to find the wooden peg bouncing around on the end of the rope, but at last he grabbed it and it pulled the basket shut. The squirrel was still struggling like a mad thing inside it, but for the moment it was caught, snorting and screeching in muffled rage. Tyler considered just bashing the basket against the tree over and over until he killed the thing, but had a sudden fear that he might only release it instead. Judging by the noises it was making, if it got out now it would want to do a lot more than just follow him.

He left the fruit-picker propped against the branch, the rope tied as tightly around the handle as he could manage, to keep the basket closed. Tyler ran off toward the front of the house and the rest of the farm.

I did it! He felt like he could jump over the tall, turreted farmhouse. *So what do you think of that, Squirrely?*

Not much, judging by the furious sounds from the tree behind him. Not much at all.

It was only a few hundred yards from the house to the silo, if that was what the building really was, but as the lights of the windows faded behind him he felt like he was scuttling across the dead surface of the moon. When he thought he was out of sight of the most likely observers— people tended to cluster at the kitchen end of the house— Tyler switched on his flashlight. The ground was bumpy and uneven, covered with dry grass, and he made as much noise as he dared. He'd seen a rattlesnake once up by the unicorn pasture. He didn't want to step on one of those in the dark.

The moon was behind the silo so he didn't even see it until he was close enough to realize that a big black some-thing was blocking the stars. Staring up at the weird shape of it—it really did look like a haunted house—Tyler had some serious second thoughts about the whole thing.

Come on, stupid, he told himself. *Don't be such a wuss.*

He knew he'd never manage to trap the squirrel again the same way—in fact, he was wondering if he'd ever be able to go outside the house at all with an angry devil squirrel after him. This was probably his one chance.

He had walked past the tall old building enough times to know it had a door on the side perpendicular to the house. He crept around the silo, shining his flashlight and shuffling his feet loudly to warn away any snakes (or extra-large spiders). He found the door and began to look for a handle, but instead the weathered wood just dropped away under his hand with a quiet squeak as it swung open. Not even latched. Tyler swallowed and took a step into the silo, his flashlight held before him like a laser pistol.

It was *big* inside—that was the first thing he noticed—a big, empty space with a ceiling so far above his head the flashlight beam couldn't reach it. It was also absolutely and completely empty.

Tyler was standing on a little platform at the top of a flight of wooden steps that led down to the floor, which was about twenty feet below ground level. He swept the flashlight around and down to the floor. Nothing. Not even rats, which he had been thinking about in a slightly worried way. He made his way down the creaking stairs and onto the bottom of the silo. Not just empty, but extremely clean—if anyone had ever stored grain here, they had vacuumed the place out afterward. He shined his light in every corner but saw nothing. The place was empty. If there had been a secret here it must be long gone.

Then a glimmer on the floor caught his eye. He turned the light on it as he approached. Metal—the bolt on a trapdoor in the floor near one edge of the room. The bolt had a brand-new lock through it.

He rattled it in frustration. New and very strong. He had brought a pocketknife, but using a knife on that metal would be like trying to tunnel through a stone with a plastic teaspoon. Something was definitely weird, though. Why leave the front door unlocked but put some monster big lock on *this* door? What was down there? How could he get through the lock without making so much noise it would bring everyone out of the house? And even if he cut the bolt somehow, how could he replace it so no one would know? The whole thing seemed almost impossible, and certainly wasn't going to happen tonight—probably his last moment of freedom before he suffered death-by-monster-squirrel.

When he emerged from the dark silo Tyler was amazed to see how much brighter things looked in the light of the moon. He walked around the silo on the far side from the house, shining his flashlight beam along the walls in the unlikely chance there was another door he'd never seen in all the times he'd gone past the odd building.

There was no other door. There was, however, a gap that had opened up between the walls of the silo and the ground itself, like a narrow moat around a medieval castle.

Tyler got down on his knees and looked into the space between the silo and the earth. The walls of the silo extended far down, almost certainly farther than the floor inside, which meant that if he went down far enough and found a way in, he would be on the underside of that tempting, frustratingly locked trapdoor. The boards were thick, but they were also old and had buckled in places, warped by years of moist soil. He hesitated before climbing down into the narrow space beside the foundations of the silo—if there were going to be snakes or giant spiders anywhere, this would be the spot—but his frustration at the idea of never finding out what was in here was stronger.

It wasn't easy holding the flashlight in his mouth. Tyler was sure he was going to chip a tooth, but he needed both hands to make it down the crumbling earthen wall and into the soft dirt that had collected at the bottom, up against the silo's wooden boards. He crawled along, pushing on them one after another.

There. That one was loose.

He braced himself with his feet against the wood on either side and began to pull at it. The nails gave a little. After a while he realized he could use the flashlight handle as a crowbar; soon he began to feel the wood loosen. When the board finally came out he tossed it aside and stuck his hand through, swinging the flashlight around in the gap beyond. Nothing. Still dark. He couldn't even see the floor or the far wall, but if he turned the flashlight up he could see wood close above him. That must be the floor with the hatch door, he realized. If he could get through, he would indeed be under it!

He managed to work loose the board next to the gap, and after what seemed like another half hour of hard, sweaty work, it came free as well. The last nail pulled out with a screech that did not echo. The gap was just big enough now for him to get his shoulders through sideways.

Tyler had maneuvered his shoulders and arms through the space between the boards when the flashlight fell out of his mouth. He grabbed at it in panic, overbalanced, and tumbled through into suddenly freezing blackness.

Nothing stopped him. Seconds went by and still he plunged downward, as though he was tumbling through the utter emptiness of space. He tried to scream, but no sound came out of his mouth.

Lucinda! His thought was like a leaf whipped in an icy wind. *You were right. I'm so stupid . . . !*

Falling. He fell forever. And forever was *cold.*

CHAPTER 19

THE SECRET GUARDIAN

Lucinda had a bad feeling. Actually she had several.

Instead of all of the farm folk being clustered in the kitchen and dining room as they usually were—where she could keep an eye on them, as Tyler had asked—most of them appeared to have chosen this night, of all nights, to be somewhere else. Mr. Walkwell and Ragnar had gone out after dinner on some mysterious special task, the kitchen workers told her, Uncle Gideon was simply absent again, and Haneb was at the Sick Barn looking in on Meseret, who had been acting strangely since she had lost her egg—so much so that everyone was afraid she was sick with some unknown dragon illness. Even the Three

Amigos had vanished, perhaps gone with Mr. Walkwell and Ragnar, perhaps just back to their cabin on the far side of the farm or off to the dormitory to play cards with the other farmhands—no one could say. Only old Caesar, Sarah, the cook, and her two helpers, little Pema and tall Azinza, were in the kitchen, the women washing dishes while Caesar prepared to take a tray with tea and sandwiches up to Gideon.

Which meant, Lucinda thought miserably, that Tyler could stumble into any number of people out there and get both of them in serious trouble.

She picked up a dish towel and started drying.

"So where's Mrs. Needle?" she asked after a while.

Azinza frowned at her. "Child, why do you ask so many questions tonight? Mrs. Needle, she does not like us talking about her."

Sarah made a snorting noise. "That is the truth. She is secret like a wall with no window, that one."

Caesar paused in the kitchen doorway, the tray balanced on one hand. "You womenfolk do know that the devil finds work for idle hands, don't you? And idle tongues too." Shaking his head, he went out.

"I think Mrs. Needle have tea with Mr. Gideon," Pema offered suddenly, breaking the silence that followed. She had the habit of looking down and speaking very quietly, so that sometimes you could only hear the soft murmur of a voice, but no words at all. She was pretty, too, like a doll, and although she looked older than Lucinda, she was half a head shorter. Being around Pema made Lucinda feel like a horse or something even clumsier.

"Oh, she's probably having tea, all right," said Sarah, her mouth tight and her pale skin flushed with some emotion Lucinda couldn't quite read. "With her little friend."

"Colin?" asked Lucinda.

"He wishes that were true," Sarah said with a snort. "If she paid half as much mind to her fatherless child as she does to that animal, the boy wouldn't be up to such strange mischief. . . ."

Pema took an audible breath. Even tall Azinza straightened up as though Sarah had said something dangerous. "You shouldn't talk so," Azinza hissed. "She hears things."

It felt like something cold had clutched the back of Lucinda's neck. "Animal? What do you mean?"

"That . . . thing," Sarah said, ignoring Azinza's warning shake of the head. The usually cheerful cook folded her arms across her bosom. "No, I won't be quiet. I am a Christian woman, whatever has happened to me. She talks to that creature as if it were her own pet, and what is godly in that? Sits and talks, and I swear that it listens."

Pema laid a small hand on the German cook's broad arm. "Please, Miss Sarah. Do not say any more. Azinza is right—it is foolishness to speak ill of—"

"A witch?" Sarah scowled. "There, I said it. Don't these children have a right to know? She talks with a black squirrel and it chatters back at her, for all to see! And only our good Lord knows what she has done to Mr. Gideon to make him so foolish, so . . . so . . ."

Even as Sarah suddenly, startlingly began to weep, Lucinda ran out of the kitchen in terror.

Tyler was right! Lucinda could hardly breathe. A witch! Mrs. Needle really was a witch!

She ran out into the yard, disoriented in the dark after the lights of the kitchen. She was sickened to think of Tyler out there alone, being watched by who knew what. She stumbled toward the middle of the open space, wishing the moon would hurry out from behind the clouds. She thought she saw the bulk of the silo now, but something was moving, something that caught the faintest sheen of moonlight. Tyler? She wanted to call out but didn't know who might hear. The farm, which only a short while before had seemed strange but mostly safe, now seemed to be a nest of fearsome strangers.

If that was Tyler, he was moving away from the farm-house—not toward the silo, but out toward the pastures and the reptile barn. Perhaps he had already tried the silo and now meant to explore some other parts of the farm. He didn't know how much danger he was in! She felt like a fool. Her brother had been right, she had been wrong. She had wanted everything to be okay, just like she always did, and she had kept her eyes closed to the things that seemed to suggest otherwise.

A shudder went through her at the memory of Mrs. Needle's cold, bright eyes, the woman's pale hand on hers. When had that been? She remembered drinking tea with her, but not being touched—Mrs. Needle hardly ever touched anyone, even her own son. But now the memory of that cool white hand lying across her own seemed as strong and painful as a memory of being burned.

The dark figure ahead of her was moving faster than she had thought. If it was Tyler, he was running. Had something happened to him? In any case, she could not simply let him roam the farm property without being warned. Too many of the farm folk were out tonight, and he needed to hear what Sarah and the others had said about Mrs. Needle.

Something came to her—a noise? No, it was a feeling, a distinct sadness floating into her thoughts like the wail of a ghost, raising the hair on the back of her neck.

Lost.

Gone.

Lost.

The feeling swept over Lucinda and made her stop where she was, quivering, as though a freezing wind had struck her. It was like a voice in her head, a voice without words that still spoke clearly of terrible grief and an equally terrible, deeply buried anger. Lucinda felt as though she couldn't hold so much sadness inside her—that she would burst like a balloon that had been inflated too far.

Then the feeling was gone, although a sensation of powerful unhappiness lingered for several moments after. Lucinda's cheeks felt cold. She touched them with her fingers and found that they were wet with tears.

What was going *on* here? Was it the ghost she'd seen in the mirror? What else could fill her with such a sensation of misery? Was the whole farm haunted?

While Lucinda had been distracted the dark shape, moving with surprising speed, had almost disappeared from her sight. She pushed herself away from the sheltering darkness of the buildings nearest the house and out into the clouded moonlight, one shadow following another.

Whatever or whoever she had been trailing was long gone, and Lucinda was stumbling through a dark wood at the far end of the pasturelands, just at the base of the hills that marked the edge of the property. The moonlight seemed to have weakened, and she had turned around so many times in the shadow-spotted trees that she wasn't even quite sure which direction the house was in. She was crying a little despite herself, frustrated and frightened, and was just about to sit down and wait until people came in the morning to find her when she saw a light a short way up the hill.

Was it Tyler with his flashlight? No, it wasn't a flashlight at all, but the uneven, flickering light of a fire. It must be the herders—Kiwa, Jeg, and Hoka—who liked to sit beside their campfire late into the night, singing mournful, deep-throated songs that seemed to vibrate like plucked strings. Still, even in the dark she didn't think she could have stumbled that far out of her way. Also, although she could now hear a single gruff voice raised in song, it didn't sound anything like the music of the Three Amigos.

Lucinda moved closer, worry and hope fighting each other inside her chest. She could see the fire moving and sparking in the gentle night breeze in a clearing just ahead, but there was no sign of the singer. She paused at the edge of the clearing, alarmed by the strangeness of the hoarse yet plaintive song, like the howling of some lonely animal set to slow, rhythmic music.

Something was lying on the ground just at her feet. She bent and picked it up. A boot, small as a child's shoe, still warm from the leg and foot that had been in it. As if in a dream, she reached her hand into it, then yanked it out, startled. It was stuffed with shredded paper, which rustled beneath her fingers.

Something squeezed her arms against her sides with the strength of a giant snake. A huge hand folded over her mouth.

Lucinda screamed but no sound came out except a muffled murmur. She was lifted clean off the ground, feet kicking. Her heels beat against the legs of her captor, but seemed to make no more impression than kicking the trunk of an oak tree.

"Sssshh," a voice whispered in her ear, the hot breath making her squirm in terror. "He will hear you. He has little enough freedom—do not take this from him."

Then she recognized the voice. She was still frightened, but at least she knew who held her.

"I'm going to put you down," Ragnar whispered. "Do not run—it will startle him, which might be dangerous. Do not speak, either. He will be off soon, to look to the fences."

She had no idea who "he" was, but she nodded her head. The big man set her down as if she weighed no more than a coffee cup. For a moment, overwhelmed by the strangeness of the night, the succession of shocks and surprises, she almost ran away despite her promise, but something inside held her back.

No one's hurt me. Ragnar wouldn't do anything to me. Strongest of all, though, to her surprise, was that she wanted to *know*. For once she wanted nothing more than to get answers to the questions that were swarming in her head like startled bees.

A moment later a shape came springing down the hillside. There was just enough firelight to show its odd, jerky movements. It was *dancing*, she realized, leaping and capering with arms stretched high as if to clutch at the stars. From the waist up it had the shape of a naked man, slender and muscled, but below that were the haunches

262

and narrow, hooved feet of a deer or goat.

The head dipped down for an instant into the firelight and Lucinda almost screamed. The face was Mr. Walkwell's.

The animal-man leaped up again, then whirled around and was gone, bounding up the slope with tremendous speed and agility, disappearing over the crest of the hill. Lucinda, her knees suddenly too weak to hold her weight, sank down to the ground beside the discarded boots, the paper that had spilled from them crunching beneath her.

"He's a . . . Mr. Walkwell's a . . ." She shook her head, shocked. "What is he?"

Ragnar laughed. "He is one of the Old Ones, child. I do not know the right name for his kind, but the *Graekers* worshipped them as little short of gods. The Greeks, I mean. Sometimes I still do say the wrong words, despite all my years here."

Lucinda picked up Mr. Walkwell's boot. The whole night felt like a dream, but she knew it wasn't. "The poor man. He has to walk in these—no wonder he goes so slow. Always having to hide what he is."

"Not always." Ragnar helped her up and led her across the clearing toward the stone circle in which the fire burned. When she knelt to warm her hands he crouched beside her. "The nights are his—like this one."

"Is he from . . . does Mr. Walkwell come from the same place as the dragons and the unicorns?"

Ragnar poked the fire with a long branch. A few sparks drifted up and winked out. "I do not know all of Simos's story, because he was here long before the rest of us came . . . but in a way that is true. He *is* from the same place as the dragons. We all are. But *place* is not the right word. It is hard to explain."

"Maybe somebody should try," she said, but without anger. She had lost it back in the trees. "No one ever tells me or Tyler anything until we find it out for ourselves." A sudden thought made her heart race. "Tyler! He's out exploring—I have to find him!"

"He will be well," the bearded man said. "Nobody will come onto the farm and hurt him when Simos is on guard."

It wasn't people getting in from outside she was worried about, but people who were already here—one person, anyway. "Sarah and the others—they said that Mrs. Needle is a witch."

Ragnar frowned and took a moment before answering. "It is true that where she came from that is what they called her. They would have killed her for it too. But your great-uncle trusts her, and she has helped him, there is no doubt of that. After the fire took his laboratory and all his things I thought he would waste away in sorrow, but since then she has helped him find new life—new purpose."

Lucinda's mind was still whirling with questions, but before she could ask anything else Ragnar stiffened and rose. A knife that she had not even seen was suddenly in his hand, glinting in the firelight. A moment later a bizarre, lumpy shape came swinging down the hillside, sometimes upright, sometimes going on all fours. Before she could do more than take a frightened breath, the weird thing came to a sudden halt at the edge of the clearing and split into two pieces, one of which fell to the ground.

Mr. Walkwell straightened and prodded with his hoof at the bundle he had just dumped. He rolled it over, revealing a pale face and slack, open mouth. He looked up from the motionless man at his feet and cocked an eyebrow at Lucinda, who had shrunk back into Ragnar's shadow.

"What is the child doing here?" He seemed more irritated than embarrassed to be standing in front of her naked, although he was so shaggy he might as well have been wearing trousers. Lucinda could not help staring. Even trousers would not have hidden the fact he had hooves instead of feet, and it was almost stranger to see him without his hat than without pants. Where his hair had blown back from his forehead in matted, sweaty curls she could see pale, circular marks—the place where his goat horns grew, she realized, although he had cut them off or filed them down. With his scraggly beard and the fire reflecting red in his eyes, he looked like the devil himself. Lucinda should have been terrified, but the face was still Mr. Walkwell's, the man who hated cars and carved wooden toys for children.

"Don't blame Ragnar. It's . . . it's my fault," she said. "I was out looking for Tyler. I got lost, and then . . . I saw the fire . . ."

Ragnar crouched beside the man Mr. Walkwell had dumped on the ground. The stranger was wearing dark clothes and a dark stocking cap. "Where did you find him?" Ragnar asked.

"Beside the Junction Road fence," said Mr. Walkwell. "He only got a few steps past it. I came down on him from behind. He did not have time to see me."

The old man had just run out to Junction Road, then run back carrying a large man on his back, all in a quarter of an hour or less, Lucinda realized. Here was another thing Tyler had been right about all along—Mr. Walkwell wasn't just inhumanly strong, he wasn't human at all.

"Is . . . is he dead?" Lucinda asked.

Ragnar shook his head. "Simos has only stunned him. We want these people to know they are not welcome, and for that they must live to tell those who have hired them." He had finished going through the man's pockets. "Empty, of course. But I will wager that if you find his car, you may also find a telephone with the number for that greedy man, Stillman." Ragnar sighed heavily. "He is digging to see what he can find, or perhaps just reminding us he is out there. This is a problem that is not going away."

"I don't understand," Lucinda asked. "Who is Stillman?"

"A bad man. A rich man too. He is a descendant of

the Tinker family and he wants this farm. Anything else, Gideon will have to tell you himself."

"If I find the telephone, I will bring it back. I do not understand those things and I do not want to," Mr. Walk-well said. He looked sternly at Lucinda, as though she might have been about to peddle him a cell phone herself. "It makes my head itch even listening to people talking into one."

"They hardly work here, anyhow," Ragnar said. He had pulled off the unconscious man's clothes, leaving him in only his underpants, socks, and undershirt. He didn't look very dangerous now. "He is ready, Simos."

Mr. Walkwell leaned down and scooped the man up like a bag of groceries, then slung him across his shoulder. "I will take him back. He and his master will have something to think about when he wakes up."

A moment later he had bounded off, so quickly that Lucinda had completely missed the point between *going* and *gone*. She could smell him, though, a tang that was not unpleasant, but still made her nostrils twitch.

"As for you, we take you back to the house," Ragnar said. "You have had enough questions answered for one night, yes?"

Lucinda nodded. Tyler would be safe. How could anything bad happen to him with a magical creature like Mr. Walkwell guarding the farm?

CHAPTER 20

LAST ONE

Tyler wasn't falling anymore. Now he seemed to be floating in darkness, but *floating* didn't come close to describing how uncomfortable he was. He was so dizzy that ordinarily he would have felt sick to his stomach—but he couldn't *find* his stomach. It didn't even seem like he had a body. It seemed as though he was only a brain floating in some jar of dark liquid, eyeless, voiceless, helpless.

But he was still cold—shockingly, shiveringly cold. No body, but still freezing—how unfair could things get?

Tyler tried to move and found he *could* feel his body a little, but it seemed impossibly distant, as though his head was a kite and the rest of him was a mile below him holding the string. He began to wonder if something really bad had happened to him. Was he unconscious? Crippled? Worse, was he dead?

A kind of angry strength surged through him at the thought. Whatever was going on, he wasn't just going to accept it. Tyler Jenkins didn't just let things happen to him—he *made* things happen. He exerted all the strength of his thoughts to push the darkness away, to go some-where, to wake up, to do *something*.

Nothing happened.

He tried again and again. He thought of heroic things. He thought of terrible things and then told himself only he could stop them from happening. He thought of the people he loved—his mom, his dad, even Lucinda (yes, he supposed he really did love her, as much of a pain as she was sometimes)—but none of these thoughts did anything to change the terrible facts. There was nothing to push against. There was nothing to get away from. He was lost in complete emptiness, floating in unending black like a bubble in a tar pit.

Tyler cried, then, or at least he thought he did. It was hard to tell.

He didn't know how long he'd been drifting helplessly when he realized for the first time that although he still could not tell up from down or left from right, the black-ness no longer seemed like a single uniform thing. He could feel little differences that, if he had been in water, would have been changes in pressure, or colder or warmer currents. Some bits of the darkness seemed to be flowing over him, others to be flowing away. Some seemed more inviting, some less. But did it mean anything?

When he felt that warmer current again (he could just as accurately have called it "clearer" or "gentler" or even just "safer") he first tried to follow it, but after considering for a moment he changed his direction, doing his best to reach out in the direction from which this new feeling came—better to be moving toward whatever caused that feeling of greater safety, he thought, than away from it. To his relief, he thought he could actually feel himself beginning to move, although not in any normal way.

Things *were* changing. He felt it—he was certain. As the currents of black washed over and through him, the different sensations began to seem so strong that he almost felt he could name them, although the words that floated up in his thoughts were obviously nonsense, things like *greenward* and *whenwise*, and once he even heard a voice in his head saying, "A half-turn toward yes, but on the nextward-facing side." Still, he didn't have to understand how it worked to use it—it was a bit like typing class. After you got the hang of how to do it, you didn't even have to look down at your fingers on the keyboard anymore, you just watched the words appear on the screen in front of you. He was learning—that was what he was doing. He just didn't know what exactly was being learned.

After a timeless time, Tyler began to see the changes he had at first only felt. Light was growing around him—not a single glow, but streaks and sparks, as though reality itself was starting up again, like a video game that had been stuck. Something drew him toward one of the smears of light, then a moment later the glare was all around him—and then he fell through.

Cold, was his first thought. He could feel ground under his feet, hear wind in his ears. *But it's still so cold!*

His second thought was, *Christmas.* Because everything around him was white, white, white—the whole world was covered in snow. Trees, rocks, the side of a hill, all banked and drowned in white. A winter wilderness. The bitter wind even brought snow swirling up from the drifts on the ground, like puffs of smoke. Tyler wasn't wearing anything but his ordinary clothes, nothing warmer than a sweatshirt to keep out this icy chill. His lost flashlight was lying in the snow beside him, as out of place as he was. He bent and picked it up. Already he was trembling so hard he could barely stand.

Where am I? How'd I get here? Oh, man—I'm gonna freeze to death!

A moment later two brown shapes tumbled out of the hill in front of him. One of them was huge, but both of them were covered in fur. A cave, Tyler abruptly realized— they had come out of a cave, the big one attacking and the small one falling backward. Now the big shape was up on its hind legs, claws and teeth flashing. It was some kind of bear, and the small, huddled, doomed creature on the ground was a person in fur clothing, lying unmoving in the icy flakes.

Whoever the poor guy was, he was going to die, that was obvious. The bear was bigger than anything Tyler had ever seen, taller than a polar bear but dark. It had dropped down onto four legs now and was closing the distance between itself and the still figure. The bear had started out cautiously but had clearly decided its downed enemy posed no danger.

Freezing, shivering, a hundred yards away, Tyler suddenly realized he was about to watch a human being die. He scrabbled in the snow with numb hands, trying to find a rock, but the snow was too deep. He began taking hopping steps down the deep snow of the hillside, waving his arms and shouting.

"H-Hey! No! L-L-Leave him alone! H-H-Hey!"

The bear stopped. Tyler took another couple of awkward steps before he realized what he'd just done.

"Oh, c-crap," he said.

With a fresh new meal in sight, this one with its fur already removed, the bear reared up and waved its claws. It ducked its head, opened its huge, fanged muzzle, and roared, a sound so loud and deep that it shook snow from some of the trees. It was at least twice Tyler's height and looked as impossibly large and deadly as a T. rex.

I'm gonna die, he thought. *And I don't even know how this happened. . . .*

There was a flurry of movement at the bear's feet as the small shape there rolled over and bent, then for a moment actually seemed to be trying to tackle the monstrous animal. The bear took a step back and doubled over, its growl rising to a bizarre coughing snarl as it nipped at its own belly where the long handle of a spear was now wagging, the head sunk deep in the bear's guts. The monster took a step toward the fur-covered figure in front of it, still snarling, and swiped with its massive paws, but the human threw himself to the side and the strike narrowly missed. The bear hesitated for a moment but blood was already spattering the snow beneath it. It dropped to all fours and lurched away unsteadily down the hillside toward the trees, staining the snow with its blood as it went. As soon as it disappeared from sight, the fur-clad warrior got to his feet again and looked to Tyler, who was standing knee-deep in the snow, dumbfounded, shivering even harder as he realized how close he had come to getting eaten.

"The Great One would have killed me," the spear wielder said in a tone of dull wonder, his voice surprisingly high-pitched, as if he was no more than Tyler's own age. What showed of his face in the crude fur hood was bloody. "Where do you come from?"

Tyler tried to say something, although he had a feeling

that the words *California* and *Standard Valley* wouldn't mean much here, but his teeth were chattering so hard he couldn't talk. He wasn't cold any longer, though, he suddenly realized. In fact, he felt surprisingly warm. He took a step forward and then decided that he must have walked into a sudden blizzard, because suddenly everything was white and his mouth was full of snow.

He only dimly felt it as the hooded stranger pulled his face out of the snow and began to drag him back toward the cave.

Tyler was lying on the floor beside the tiniest, most pathetic fire he had ever seen, three skinny sticks and a wad of damp grass. He was cold again, miserably so, his body racked by shivers so strong he thought they might break his bones. The man he had saved was crouched nearby, wiping blood from his face with a handful of snow. The features that began to appear from beneath the smears of red were smaller and younger than Tyler had expected, although it was still hard to tell because of the remaining mud and blood.

The stranger looked at him with a mixture of mistrust and pity. "Who are you? Why did you risk your life for me? Why do you wear such strange skins? Are you from the Ghost Lands?"

That sounded vaguely familiar, but Tyler was too busy shaking himself to pieces to try to answer any of it. The caveman, if that was what he was, watched him for a moment, then pulled Tyler into a sitting position, tugged him back against his own chest, then untied the rawhide laces of the rough jacket or poncho he was wearing. When he had it undone and opened, he cradled Tyler against his body like a child and then closed the thick hide garment around them both.

After a few moments Tyler began to warm up, just enough so that he could feel the sting of returning feeling down his spine. He pulled his hands up and tucked them into his armpits to get warm. They began to tingle and smart too. After a few more moments Tyler realized from contours of the bare skin he could feel pressing against his back that it was not a caveman in whose lifesaving embrace he was being warmed and who had just stabbed a stone-headed spear into the biggest bear Tyler could ever imagine. It was a cave*woman*. A girl, even.

"Do you have a name?" Tyler asked her. Now that he didn't feel quite so much like he was going to die, the weirdness of the whole adventure had begun to overwhelm him. How had he ended up here? Where was he, anyway? Somewhere on present-day Earth, or back in time, like in a movie? And why could he understand this girl's speech? He could hear the harsh, unfamiliar words she spoke even as the meaning of what she said bloomed in his head.

"Nothing as strange as 'Ty-ler,'" she told him. "They

called me Last One because I was the youngest, but they are all dead now. I suppose I am Last One for real." From the sadness of what she said he would have expected at least a tear, but although claw marks on her forehead and cheeks still dribbled blood, she had the hard, secretive face Tyler had seen on some of the men waiting at the Veteran's Hospital bus stop back home, the mark of a difficult and frightening life.

Back home. How was he going to get home?

"You saved me," Last One said. "The Great One would have killed me for trying to take his cave. I was only looking for someplace to get warm and I was careless. I should have smelled his fresh stink."

"I have to go," Tyler said, struggling to his feet. "My family . . . my sister." He shook his head. "I have to go back." But how would he get there? He had stepped out of thin air, it seemed.

"You will die if you go outside," she told him. "It will be dark soon and the bear is not dead. If he lives, he will be back. One like him took all my family. I do not know what we did to anger the Great Ones so." Her matted hair fell in her face as she looked at Tyler's thin clothes, his soaked athletic shoes. "He is not the only hunter, either. And your skins will not keep you warm out there, I think."

"But I have to go." He didn't doubt anything she said, but with returning feeling in his hands and feet he was also swept by a tremendous, aching loneliness. Whether he had actually somehow traveled back in time to the ice age or this was some even stranger place, he couldn't stand to think he might be stuck here. If he waited through the night he might not be able to find the spot where he had arrived. "I have to go," he said again.

She sighed. It was weird to hear such a modern sound of frustration here in this place. "Then I will come with you, because otherwise you will be dead before morning."

"You don't need to do that."

"My life is yours now." She said it as simply as if she was talking about the weather. "The Great One would have taken me, otherwise."

He had been right, Tyler decided as he tottered out into the cold wind with the girl beside him. Although he was already starting to shiver badly, he could still see traces of his deep footprints coming down the hill, traces that would be gone by morning. Not that it helped him much—the prints simply stopped at a point halfway up the slope—but even that was something.

He halted where the footprints began. There was nothing here but cold air and snow, but he closed his eyes tightly and tried to ignore the wind, his own trembling body, and the idea that the wounded, angry bear might be back at any moment. What had led him to this cold world? A feeling, a trace of something he couldn't explain. What could take him back? Something similar, he hoped.

For a long moment he couldn't see or feel anything except the beginnings of what it was going to be like to freeze to death here on the hillside. Then the girl took his hand in her own and the trace of warmth, instead of distracting him, reminded him of what he was looking for—home.

Something like a faint light in the distance almost startled him into opening his eyes, but it was not a light from the world around him, it was a light inside his thoughts. Tyler moved toward it, or it moved toward him. It wasn't easy—other currents pushed and pulled at him, trying to tug him off the track, but he did his best to ignore them and to keep moving forward. The light became stronger, but whatever resisted him became stronger, too, until Tyler felt that he was trying to shove his way through water that was hardening into ice all around him.

Lucinda, he thought. *She'll get hurt if I'm not around. I have to get back. She needs me to help her be brave.*

And he needed her, too, he realized, to remind him there were other ways to do things besides charging straight ahead.

The thought gave him an idea: Tyler changed his angle and found he could move toward the light not by fighting his way, but by slipping ahead through the areas of least resistance while remembering always what his final destination was. The light came closer—a light he could feel in his bones, so that he wondered if he was glowing from the inside out like an X-ray. He reached for it. He found it and stepped through.

It was only as the warmth rose all around him that he realized the girl from the winter world was still holding on to his hand.

Tyler opened his eyes. For a moment disappointment washed over him like a drowning tide. It was too dark to see anything, but he could feel rough stone under his hands. It was another cave, more rock and dirt. He wasn't home—he hadn't managed to do anything!

He crawled forward, pulling his flashlight out of his sweatshirt pocket and shining it over the rock walls. It seemed to be something like the bear cave. Then he saw a flat roof above him that looked too solid and smooth to be natural stone.

The girl had scrambled away from him, cowering from the light, obviously terrified.

"It's okay," he told her. "It's just a flashlight. See?"

"*Uhawa ganu dut?*" she asked, eyes wide with alarm.

"Huh? Can't you understand me?" He shook his head. Why should things suddenly be any less weird on this farm?

The flashlight beam revealed the trapdoor in the flat ceiling above them, and Tyler finally realized where they were—in the silo, under the floor. He swept the light back across the cavern and saw that the silo had been built on top of a crevice in the ground, a great mouth of rock and dirt. He and the girl named Last One had just crawled out of it.

The Fault Line, he thought. *Octavio Tinker's Fault Line! This is it!*

He clambered up the ladder bolted to the cavern wall next to the trapdoor, but the door was locked, and all his rattling and shaking couldn't open it. They were trapped in a deserted building.

Oh well, he thought, then began to shout. "Hello! Help! Somebody help us!" He pounded on the trapdoor. "Ragnar? Mr. Walkwell? Somebody? Help!"

He had been calling for about five minutes when the trapdoor above him rattled and he heard the snap of the lock opening. The door lifted and fell back with an echoing *thunk,* then a bright beam of light came through the opening in the ceiling and swept the cavernous room, blinding Tyler for a moment. The cavegirl growled in fear. Tyler swung up his own light as if in self-defense and the light moved off him. A dark shape clambered down the ladder and dropped to the floor.

"Oh, Jenkins, you idiot," said Colin Needle, shaking his head in gleeful disgust as he looked from Tyler to the cavegirl. "You just couldn't mind your own business, could you? And now you've *really* messed up. You might as well go pack your bags."

CHAPTER 21

A BLOW TO THE BRAIN

One thing Colin really liked about those Jenkins kids: they were their own worst enemies. It never seemed to have occurred to them that he might be keeping track of where they were. Both of their rooms empty after night-fall? Something had to be up. Noises in the silo, a building that was kept empty at all times? Who else would it be?

But it wasn't just Tyler Jenkins he had discovered in the Fault Line cavern. There was a girl, too, a stranger—Paleolithic, from the looks of her. It happened occasionally with the Fault Line, these spontaneous manifestations. Like stuff washed up on a beach, he supposed, or left behind on a riverbank, tossed out of the flow of time. It wasn't the first time and it wouldn't be the last. But Jenkins screwing up so badly—*that* was something Colin had been waiting for.

"I'm serious," he said. "Go pack your suitcase. You're as good as gone."

"You creep!" Tyler stomped toward him, pointing a finger. "What are you doing, following me everywhere I go?"

"Gideon should never have brought you to the farm." Colin turned his back and went quickly up the ladder and through the trapdoor, into the empty silo. "But now he's going to realize his mistake, because I'm going to tell him what you've been doing—messing with his biggest, most important secret." He shoved open the door and went out into the warm night.

"Oh yeah?" said Tyler. He ran up the ladder and out the door after Colin, waving his flashlight like it was a *Star Wars* light saber. Colin laughed—did the kid really want to pick a fight? He was a full head shorter than Colin was. Still, the idiot kept coming at him, and the light got in Colin's eyes, blinding him. He had underestimated and did not get his hands up in time as Tyler Jenkins swung a fist and hit him in the neck. Colin stumbled back, choking, and the younger boy was on him with arms windmilling so fast Colin was driven farther backward.

"Tyler, stop!" someone shouted even as Colin slipped and fell.

The Jenkins kid seized the advantage and began pummeling the side of Colin's head. Colin swung his own right hand around and delivered a satisfyingly nasty blow to Tyler's face, then he was back in the game again, slapping and scratching and butting with his head until he could get off his back. Another flashlight was playing over them and someone was still shouting at them as they jumped at each other.

"Tyler, no, *no!* Let go of him!" It was Lucinda's voice.

They were rolling, struggling with each other like wild animals. Jenkins managed to get on top of him again and Colin was lashing out, hitting anything he could, when Tyler suddenly straightened up. Lucinda had grabbed the neck of her brother's sweatshirt and was pulling as hard as she could. She had caught him by surprise. Tyler fell back, allowing Colin to struggle free.

"What are you two *doing?*"

The words were barely out of her mouth when Colin jumped past her and tackled her brother again—he wasn't going to lose the advantage she'd given him. The two of them went down again, kicking and thrashing so that dust flew up in a cloud, obscuring the beam of Lucinda's flashlight. Then, suddenly, there was triumph: Colin was atop the wretched Jenkins boy, sitting on his chest. He put his forearm on Tyler's throat and heard the choking sounds begin. God, he was going to enjoy this!

Then a shadow moved over Colin and something smashed down on his head, turning his bones and muscles to water. After that, it all just went blank.

* * *

The next thing he felt was a throbbing in his head like the aftermath of an explosion, as if something had blown his skull into hot pieces that were barely holding together.

My brain, he thought. *Somebody knocked my bloody brain out.*

Colin tried to sit up, but just the tiny movement of bracing his hands against the ground made him feel dizzy and sick so he gave up. It was dark where he lay, which was just as well. Light in his eyes would have felt like a blowtorch.

"What's with this farm?" Lucinda was saying. "I mean, Tyler, who *are* all these people? What are they up to? Witches? Monsters? Magicians? You were *right,* Tyler, you were so right, and it just keeps getting crazier!"

"You think that's crazy," her brother answered, "but you haven't heard what happened to me yet."

The pain in Colin's head was so bad that he began to think he might throw up. He rolled over onto his hands and knees and crouched, his aching head against the cool dirt. The two Jenkins children fell silent.

When he could, Colin turned around and sat up, but even that careful movement made the world swim and he groaned loudly. At this new sound the stranger in the hooded cape moved toward him, growling quietly as if in reply and raising a menacing hand. The face in the hood was smeared with dirt so that Colin could see little more than staring eyes and bared teeth, but the large rock in the creature's dirty paw made things clear: *this* was the bastard who had smashed in his skull. And if this spawn of the Fault Line wanted to do it again, there wasn't much Colin could do to stop it. He raised trembling hands in front of his face.

"No! Don't hit him again!" cried Lucinda.

The crouching shape stopped and cocked its head like a dog when its name was called—hearing but not quite understanding. "*Na krut?*" it asked. It was a girl, or at least the voice sounded like it. "*Na krut?*"

"Nah, I guess not," Tyler said. "Don't *krut* him." He laughed a little, which only made Colin ache to hit him again. "Hey, I speak cave language!"

"Cave language?" Lucinda asked.

"Yeah, you'll never guess where I've just been, Luce. I think it was the ice age. It wasn't very easy getting back, either—I'm still not quite sure how I did it."

For a moment Colin forgot the throbbing misery of his head. Tyler's words rang in his thoughts like a sudden thunderclap. *The ice age?* Was that what the Jenkins kid had just said? That he'd *gone* somewhere, not just been around when this prehistoric murderess had washed up out of some backwater of time?

"Yeah, that's where the girl's from," Tyler went on excitedly. "Her name is Last One, or at least that's what she told me when she could still talk. Do you think she'll learn how again? She sure took care of Junior Doctor Evil." He turned toward Colin. "Hey, Needle, had enough? You step to me, you better step up *strong*."

"Spare me your trashy hip-hop video dialogue," Colin told him, but inside he was suddenly very frightened. Was it true? Could Tyler Jenkins navigate the Fault Line without an instrument? This could change everything. Even if Colin's grand scheme worked out, the one he had spent months planning, Gideon would probably still prefer these stupid, heedless kids. It was unfair beyond belief! They had to go—they'd ruin everything. "You've gone too far this time, Jenkins," Colin snarled. "Gideon is going to have you both out of here by tomorrow morning."

"Colin, please," said Lucinda. "Whatever we did wrong, we're sorry. Tyler, what are you talking about? Ice age? Where did she come from, really?"

"I told you, I went to the ice age . . . I think. Anyway, it was totally snowy, and there was this giant monster bear, and she killed it with a spear." He shook his head as though even he was having trouble believing it all. "First I was exploring the silo and I . . . I fell through. Through something. We were right, Lucinda—that's where the Breach is, or the Fault Line, or whatever Octavio Tinker called it. It's a cave underneath the silo. It's like a hole in time or something!"

Shock and fear washed over Colin. How had they found out all these things? Had someone spilled all the secrets to them? "Are you actually saying you traveled through the Fault Line?" He made his voice hard, wanting to test Tyler. "That you went into the past . . . and came back? That's impossible."

"You calling me a liar?" The boy looked like he was about to jump all over Colin again but Lucinda reached out a hand toward him. "I came back by . . . I don't know. I came back the same way I got there. I found the spot I came in and just . . . thought about going back. Sort of." He shrugged, at a loss for words.

So it was true. But Colin was only defeated, he realized, if Gideon found out. Otherwise they were just annoying kids. Maybe it wouldn't be such a good idea to tell Gideon Goldring, after all—who knew what information might come out of such an argument?

Lucinda was walking in circles. "Ice age? This is all so crazy! I didn't even get to tell you what happened to *me*. Mr. Walkwell—he isn't even human! He's some kind of part man, part animal. A faun, I think."

Tyler stared at her as if she had lost her mind. "What, like Bambi?"

"No, you know, like the guy in what's-it-called—Narnia."

"Mr. Walkwell is a lion?" Now Tyler sank down in the dirt beside the cavegirl, shaking his head. "I don't get it."

"I'll explain later, but he's a goat-man. I think it's called a faun."

Oh, they were a cute little comedy act, these two, Colin

287

thought. He would dance for joy when he was finally rid of them. "Not just a faun, but a tutelary spirit," he said, wiping some of the dirt and blood from his face with the sleeve of his sweater. "To be precise, Mr. Walkwell is the genius loci of Ordinary Farm." He was feeling his way back to control again. "How did you find out about Mr. Walkwell, Lucinda?"

She told him about the fire, the singing, and the man Mr. Walkwell had captured.

"Stillman?" said Colin. He tried to sound casual, but his heart was thundering. What had he gotten himself into? He had thought he was only manipulating that fat fool Modesto, but Stillman was a billionaire and he wanted the whole farm! Still, it was too late to turn back now. "I think I've heard the name, but I can't imagine what interest he'd have in some little farm like ours."

"Oh yeah," sneered Tyler. "Some little farm. Right. Some little farm with dragons and monsters and a hole that leads back a million years into the ice age."

"You'd better keep your mouth shut about that," Colin told him. "I won't be able to save you if you start babbling about visiting the past."

"What are you talking about? Why should I keep my mouth shut? And why would *you* want to save *me*? Especially after I kicked your butt."

Colin bit back his anger. "After your primitive friend hit me, you mean." He took a breath. *Calm*, he told himself.

Calm. "Because if you keep your mouth shut and do it my way, Gideon will think it was just an overflow from the Fault Line. It happens occasionally—that's where the griffin eggs came from, they just . . . *showed up* one day. Sometimes the Fault Line opens up enough that we could step into it if we dared. Other times it just sort of spits things out. We have to tell him it was one of those situations, because if you tell Gideon you went into the Fault Line on your own and came back, he'll know you were messing around with the silo and he'll go completely berserk. He really will kick you out in a heartbeat."

Lucinda looked upset, but her brother looked suspicious. "That still doesn't explain why you want to help us. You hate my guts, Needle. Admit it."

He hesitated. "I'll admit I don't like you much, Jenkins. But your sister has been nice to me, and I'd hate to see her punished for something you did." Which was just true enough that he could say it with convincing feeling: Lucinda *had* been kind to him. Colin wasn't used to it.

Lucinda Jenkins looked at her brother with an expression almost of triumph, an expression that said, *See? I told you!* She turned to Colin and smiled. "Thank you, Colin. That's generous of you."

He felt a little bad—but only a little. "Well, if you agree, we'd better figure out how we're going to explain that"— *thug,* he thought, looking at the creature who had hit him; but he didn't say the word, only gestured—"to Gideon."

"Hang on," said Tyler. "That's all fine, but how can Gideon afford to get rid of us, anyway? We know all about this place now. We could tell everyone what we've seen."

Colin laughed. "He wouldn't just let you go. He'd have my mother brew up one of her special medicines and adjust your memories. She's good at that—it's sort of like hypnotism. She's had to do it with a couple of government inspectors over the years." He couldn't help noticing that Lucinda's expression had completely changed. The girl was looking at him as though she had just remembered he was a space alien who wanted to eat her. "Lucinda? Did I say something that upset you?"

"N-no," she said, shaking her head rapidly. "No, Colin. Go on."

He had no idea what that was about, but he didn't have time to waste worrying about it. He was trying to get this whole disastrous night back under control. Colin couldn't afford anything that would upset his plans before he met with Modesto again; there could be no more excitement on the farm, no more upheavals, starting now.

Both Jenkins kids were watching him, waiting to hear what he said next. The cavegirl who had almost knocked his head in now crouched beside them, cowed and anxious. With nothing but his wits, Colin had taken control of a bad situation and was back in charge.

He was very proud of himself.

CHAPTER 22

AT LAST, SOME ANSWERS

Uncle Gideon was wearing his bathrobe and slippers, as usual. Several days' growth of gray beard furred his cheeks and he smelled more than a little stale, like clothes that had been hanging in a damp bathroom for a couple of days. Still, his wits seemed as sharp as ever: after Tyler finished telling his story (or at least the carefully crafted version Colin had prepared, in which Tyler was an innocent victim of the Fault Line instead of someone who had broken the rules to explore the silo), Gideon stared at him for several moments with open suspicion. It was all Tyler could do not to squirm under that disbelieving gaze.

He didn't like letting Colin Needle call the shots on

this, but he was glad he didn't have to tell anyone about Octavio Tinker's diary or any of the other things he and Lucinda had collected. And now that he was facing his great-uncle's mistrustful gaze, Tyler had to admit that the last thing he wanted to be telling Gideon Goldring was the actual truth.

"Well . . . that's quite some news," Gideon said at last, straightening in his chair. "So the Fault Line is active again—just conjured up an ice age for a few minutes and spewed out this young woman? How lucky for you, Tyler, that the manifestation barely touched you—how lucky for all of us! I don't know what I would have told your mother if we'd lost *you* instead of gaining a new farmhand." He looked entertained by the idea in a sour sort of way, then grinned at Tyler and Lucinda. "But now you two know our biggest secret! You should be honored."

Tyler was still shivering a little. *Honored! I could have been killed!* In all the excitement that fact had kind of escaped him until now. *Okay, maybe it was my own fault, but they ought to have warning signs up around that thing!*

Most of the farm folk had gathered in the kitchen. The cavegirl had already fallen into the gentle clutches of Sarah and the rest of the kitchen staff, who had taken her off to bathe her and dress her in something more suitable to a California summer than her heavy, greasy animal hides. Tyler wondered whether she would really become a farmhand—obviously, no one had asked the girl whether that was what she wanted.

As if sensing Tyler's thoughts, Gideon said, "Now, what shall we name our newest arrival?"

"She's got a name—she's called Last One."

"What sort of name is that for a modern young woman?" Gideon chuckled. "No, we'll call her . . . I know. We'll call her Ooola. That was the name of Alley Oop's girlfriend in the Sunday comics—quite appropriate for a young Paleolithic lady, don't you think?"

Tyler had no idea what the crazy old fellow was talking about, but he was too tired and too grateful not to be in trouble to argue about it. "Why can't she talk our language anymore?" he asked. "When I met her I could understand her and she could understand me too."

"Ah, but she never could speak *our* language," said Gideon. "While you're in the field of the Fault Line, there is a sort of, I don't know, instantaneous translation that goes on. Mind to mind, so that although both parties might be speaking completely different languages, their own languages, they can still understand each other. I think it's one of the ways in which the flow of time protects itself—that is, it lessens the potential for something catastrophic happening. Prevents paradoxes." Gideon warmed to his subject, as if he was beginning to enjoy himself a little. "If you were to sit on top of the Fault Line—always assuming that you actually *could*, and it was a day in which there was no, well, activity there—then you'd probably be able to understand each other again, because there's usually a leakage of energy in the immediate vicinity." He grew stern again. "Don't even think about trying that, young man."

"I won't," said Tyler. "I promise."

"That's also the reason cell phones and even regular telephones and other electronic things don't always work right around here. It's the Fault Line." He shook his head. "No, young Ooola will just have to learn English like Sarah and Ragnar and all the others did. Don't worry, we've done all this before."

"So *everyone* here's from the past?" Lucinda asked. Tyler looked at Ragnar and the herdsmen, the Three Amigos, who were talking in quiet voices at the table a few yards away. No sign of Mr. Walkwell yet, he couldn't help noticing. He wondered how he was supposed to treat the man now that he knew he had goat legs. It was all pretty weird.

"The past? More or less," said Gideon, but the old man suddenly looked a little cagey. "To be honest, not even my grandfather Octavio knew exactly how the Fault Line works, for all his research. He believed it might open not just on other times but on alternate versions of Earth as well." He chewed the inside of his cheek. "So far I've only observed time rifts, but who knows? We're at the leading edge of a science no one else has even dreamed of." Pride deepened his voice.

"Then why are you keeping it a secret?" Lucinda asked.

"Shouldn't there be people here, scientists from all over the world?"

"Good God, child, are you mad?" Gideon sat up in his chair as if someone had just tried to steal the bathrobe right off his skinny back. "It wouldn't be scientists, it would be the *government.* And they wouldn't just be studying it, they'd be trying to figure out how to use it—trying to change the past, who knows? Next thing, the entire fabric of time and space would collapse. Hand it over to the so-called authorities? Not bloody likely."

"But what are *you* doing with it, Uncle Gideon?" Lucinda asked. Tyler was impressed. He'd never seen his sister so serious about something that didn't have commercial breaks and well-known guest stars. "Why do you get to be in charge of something so . . . so *big,* so important?"

Gideon flushed red. "Because Octavio Tinker discovered it, all by himself! He tried to get the government's help when he was first searching for it and they laughed at him. Every university in America treated him like he was a crackpot! It belongs to the Tinkers—it belonged to me and my wife—and I'm going to hold on to it, thank you very much." He had gone from calm to quivering in a few moments. "And just because you know about it now, girl, don't think that you can tell me what to do with my own property. If someone called the government in here tomorrow, you know what they'd get? *Nothing!* Because I've got enough dynamite to blow the whole thing into a heap of dirt, and I'd do it gladly before I'd let anyone waltz in here and start telling me how the Fault Line should be used." He wasn't just trembling now, he was red in the face and breathing hard. For a moment Tyler felt certain that Gideon Goldring was going to reach out and grab his sister by the throat.

"Your tea, Gideon," said Mrs. Needle. She'd swept in without Tyler even noticing, appearing behind the old man's chair like a magic trick. "Don't shout at Lucinda. She's a good girl and she's just concerned about doing the right thing." She gave his sister one of her cold smiles, but for once Lucinda didn't respond, looking away as though she didn't want to meet the Englishwoman's eye.

"You're right, of course, Patience." Gideon looked at his tea but didn't touch it. "It's all a bit much, that's all."

"Of course. You have a tremendous responsibility, Gideon." Mrs. Needle laid a pale hand on his shoulder. "A real burden. You have decisions to make. There is a great weight on you right now." The hand looked like a white tarantula.

Gideon shook his head, suddenly calmer, even a bit weary-looking. "In any case, now you kids know the greatest of our secrets here at Ordinary Farm. I'm sorry you had to wait so long, but as Patience so aptly puts it, it's a tremendous responsibility. Now you really are part of the family."

Tyler nodded, but a part of him wondered what that

meant exactly. They had already *been* part of the family when they arrived, which was more than any of the rest of these people could say. He looked around at the group. The Three Amigos and Ragnar and the others seemed to be in a cheerful mood, as if the truth of the Fault Line was a secret none of them had much liked keeping. It was almost like a party, but there were other strange currents that Tyler couldn't understand.

"So that's it?" he asked. "There's just this big . . . hole in the universe? In time or whatever? And it just happens to be here?"

Gideon had been staring at his tea. "What? No, boy, it doesn't just happen to be here. Octavio Tinker went searching all over the world for a place like this. The only other spot that had the same likelihood turned out to be in the middle of the ocean about a thousand miles south of Madagascar—not a great location for an experimental site." He grinned. "Octavio found the Fault Line, he bought the land, he built the house. I think I will have a little of that cider, Sarah."

Mrs. Needle seemed about to say something disapproving but kept her mouth closed, though her lips thinned to a line. "Shouldn't these children be getting to bed, Gideon?" she asked instead. "After all, they've had a very busy day—especially Tyler."

"He had a bit of an adventure, Patience, that's all. Boys are sturdy! I know I was at that age."

"Oh yes, but before that Tyler did his chores, and then all that boyish larking around, messing about . . . *chasing squirrels*. He must be ready to sleep like the dead." She caught Tyler's gaze and something flashed in her eyes, a cold, poisonous glint that made his heart flutter.

She knows, he thought. *She knows exactly what I did.*

"But Uncle Gideon, what *is* the Fault Line, really?" Lucinda asked. "Did all the people here just pop out of it? I still don't understand."

Before their great-uncle could answer, Sarah, Azinza, and Pema emerged from the back with a young woman Tyler at first didn't recognize. Her eyes were wide, as though at any moment she might have to run for her life. Her wet reddish hair curled around her face, and she was draped in a colorful length of fabric far too long for her— one of Azinza's dresses. It was only when Tyler realized that the thin red lines on her face were doctored cuts that he realized it was the cavegirl, Last One.

"Ah, our newest guest!" said Gideon, with all the forced good fellowship of a department store Santa. "Ooola, welcome to the family. Someone get her some cider."

"Don't be mad, Gideon," said Mrs. Needle. "She's probably never had strong drink in her life. If you could bring her some water, Sarah, and something to eat. Not too much, though, or she'll likely make herself sick."

Tyler didn't like the way that Gideon had just taken away the girl's real name. He wanted to say again that she already *had* a name, a perfectly good one that meant something to her, but he knew he would simply be laughed into silence by the old man. He was dizzy with the warmth of the kitchen, and despite the nastiness of her intent, Mrs. Needle had been right—he was also extremely tired.

"To go back to your question, Lucinda," said Gideon, "Octavio Tinker was decades ahead of his time. He deduced the existence of what he called the 'fifth dimensional transit,' and then proved it when he found this place. I won't bother to try to explain it all—it's very complicated. But the simplest way to imagine it is that the first three dimensions are space, the fourth is time, and the fifth is probability." Gideon made a round shape with his hands, then indicated a straight line running through the middle of it. "The Earth has fifth-dimensional transit poles just like it has magnetic poles. That's the point where the fifth dimension transits our four-dimensional space."

He sat back with his cider, raised the glass, and took two large swallows. "So here's to old Octavio. He may have been a tightfisted, mean-spirited son of a gun, but he sure proved all those other eggheads wrong. Because we're sitting right on top of the fifth-dimensional transit. The place where our Earth comes into contact with all the other earths it has ever been—and we don't even know about all the *possible* earths. The Fault Line is a doorway into time." He sighed, suddenly looking as though the air had leaked out of him. "If only we knew how to navigate it—how to find our way back from inside it. You're lucky that ice age bit of it stayed open long enough to let you out, boy. You could have been lost in it forever." He looked down at his glass. Suddenly he looked very old. "Lost forever . . ."

"Now, Gideon, you'll scare the children." Mrs. Needle had resumed her "nice" voice—she sounded like Mary Poppins.

Only this Mary Poppins rides a broomstick, Tyler thought, *not an umbrella.*

He didn't really understand what Gideon was talking about—he had found his own way out easily enough. Well, maybe *easy* wasn't the right word, but . . . "You mean you can't go into it and come out again?"

Gideon shook his head sadly. "We used to be able to navigate it. Octavio and my . . ." He stopped and took a breath. "Octavio had an instrument that allowed him to move in and out of the Fault Line—to travel through it like an explorer with a compass or a sailor with a sextant. It was called the Continuascope. But it was lost several years back. . . ."

Suddenly Tyler was wide awake. "That thing in the painting," he said, unaware for a moment he'd said it out loud.

"Tyler!" Lucinda warned him, but it was too late.

"What are you talking about, child?" Gideon demanded, his voice suddenly harsh. "What painting?"

Tyler swallowed. It was too late to turn back. "There's a painting of ... of Octavio Tinker. In the library. He's holding something—it looks kind of like a weird musical instrument, right?—and I always wondered what it was."

Gideon stared at him with narrowed eyes. "And what were you doing in the library, boy?"

"Just ... exploring. After my chores were done."

For several heartbeats no one said anything. Then the dangerous moment—and it had felt quite dangerous—abruptly passed.

Gideon slumped back in his chair and took another gulp of cider. "That was it, all right. The Continuascope, the world's only fifth-dimensional navigation device. It worked by crystallometry—genius, pure, elegant genius. But it's lost now."

"But can't you make another one?" asked Lucinda.

"Hah!" Gideon's laugh was bitter. "How could I replicate *his* genius—*his* secrets? The records are lost too. Lost . . ." He shook his head in defeated anger. "You don't understand how old Tinker worked! Making sure that everyone around him knew only a little bit of what there was to know. Then when it went wrong, there was nothing that could be done—nothing!"

Something important had slipped past him in all the talk, Tyler realized, some crucial detail, but he couldn't figure out what it was. He looked around. Ragnar and Sarah and the others were listening to the conversation, and everyone looked horribly tense.

"I'm . . . I'm pretty tired," Tyler said at last. It was not a sentence he would ever have imagined himself using, especially when it seemed so many questions could at last be asked and answered, but he was very aware that he was no longer thinking very clearly. If he accidentally gave away that he had found Octavio's diary, or that he had gone to the Fault Line by choice and then navigated his way out of it on his own, who knew what Gideon would do?

Gideon looked into his emptying mug of cider. "You two go on up to your rooms—plenty of time to talk. We still have you for a while longer. But this is all top secret! You two made me a *promise*, remember. . . ." Gideon's eyes filled with dark emotions.

"Sure." Tyler nodded and got to his feet. "We made you a promise." He swayed a little, and Lucinda stepped forward and put a hand under his elbow.

"Come on," she said. "Good night, everybody."

Tyler couldn't help noticing that a number of new, quiet conversations had already started in the room before they even reached the door.

"Tyler!" Lucinda whispered as they climbed the stairs. "You were so totally right about Mrs. Needle being a witch!"

He tried to concentrate while she told him about the kitchen conversation, but it only confirmed what he had already known in his heart. "Bad," he said. "She's bad. But there's more than that going on. They still haven't told us . . ." He shook his head. "I can't think, Luce. Too tired. Tomorrow . . ."

"But there were people trying to get onto the property—Mr. Walkwell caught one. And . . . and I think I heard the ghost. I heard it in my head! I'm scared, Tyler. I want to go home."

"Are you kidding?" He was so exhausted he was slurring his words. "Things are just getting good."

Tyler left his sister in the hallway. He managed only to kick off his shoes before he fell on the bed and tumbled down into a deep sleep.

CHAPTER 23

THE LOST AND THE LEFT BEHIND

Lucinda still found it hard to believe that Ragnar had been born more than a thousand years ago. He looked like an ordinary man—somebody's motorcycle-riding dad, maybe. She leaned over the cart. "Are you really all from . . . from the past?"

"That question again?" He smiled, but only barely. "It is the past to you, child. To me this is the future, although I would never have dreamed it to be so."

"But how does it work?" asked Tyler. "How did Gideon find you?"

Ragnar shrugged. "He was not looking for me. He was hunting for worms—dragons, you would say—to bring back. He got me instead. As to how it all works, it is magic, whatever Gideon calls it, so I can tell you nothing about it." He gestured to the bags of feed stacked on the cart. "Now, are you going to help me?"

Lucinda took a bucket and filled it with the damp mash that the sea goats liked. She threw handfuls over the fence and watched them scramble out of their shallow tub of water after it, sliding over the wet floor of their pen, hissing and bobbing their heads. She would miss feeding them and the other animals when they went home. It was hard to believe their time at the farm was almost over.

"But . . . what was it *like?*" she asked Ragnar at last.

"I do not know what you mean."

"When you first came here. Were you scared?"

Now he did laugh, but it wasn't much happier than the smile. "What I left behind—that was my death, and *that* was fearful. Coming here I faced nothing worse than an unfamiliar place and a new tongue to learn. Of course, I did not understand that I had left my own time behind as well."

"You didn't know?"

"Of course not, child. Not at first." He heaved a broken cage up onto the cart. "What was I to think? It was strange enough that I had escaped the doom that was upon me. When I came to this place, I saw only a farm at first."

"Oh, tell me about it." Lucinda went back for another bucket of mash. "I really want to hear."

"How did Gideon find his way around?" Tyler asked. "Was it really that Continuascope thing? How did it work?"

"That craft is beyond me—and anyway, the device is gone." He shook his head. "Sometimes it seems that everything good in this place has been lost."

"What do you mean?" Lucinda asked. "This place is amazing!"

Ragnar lifted several of the heavy sacks off and dropped them to the ground with a dusty thump. "The friends I've met here tell me we Norsemen are a gloomy lot. Still, I cannot help thinking this house and perhaps *all* the magic of this place is cursed. Certainly it has seemed so since the night Gideon's wife disappeared."

"Disappeared?" Lucinda thought of the room so full of pictures of the dark-haired woman that it had seemed like a religious shrine. "I thought she died."

"Nothing so simple." He frowned. "She was swallowed by the Fault Line."

For a moment Lucinda couldn't speak—she felt cold all over. *"Swallowed?"*

"That is what I call it. I do not speak Gideon's tongue of science. She went in and she did not come out. It was the most ill-fated night of all."

"Where?" Tyler demanded. "Where was she when it happened?"

Ragnar gave him a strange look. "I do not know. Somewhere in the Fault Line. It is the family's gift—but it is also a curse, I sometimes think." He looked up suddenly, his face stricken. "I am sorry! Gods, I am a fool."

"Why are you sorry?" Lucinda asked.

"Because I have called your family cursed."

Lucinda had to think about it for a moment before she understood. "Oh, right. I keep forgetting that we're related to Gideon."

"Not to Gideon, in truth," Ragnar said. "To his wife. And through her to Octavio himself."

Now Tyler was the puzzled one. "What does that mean?"

"You are of the Tinker clan. Grace was a Tinker—Octavio's granddaughter. Gideon and Grace never had children. You are not related by blood to Gideon, but to Octavio."

"So is that why we're here?" said Tyler, slowly. "Me and Lucinda? Because we're old Octavio's blood relations?"

Ragnar heaved up another bunch of feed sacks. "I do not know why you are here, boy. Gideon has many thoughts he does not share with me. Still, I am glad you two came. It has brought some new life to this place—life that was needed." He looked almost wistful.

Lucinda felt as though she was suddenly seeing things clearly that she had only glimpsed before through a fog. "So Gideon married into the family."

"Yes. It was against Octavio's wishes, at least at first." Ragnar said. "Gideon came to work with the old man and help him build his device, but he also fell in love with

Octavio's granddaughter, who he had seen grow from a child to a woman. There was much anger, at least at first, when the two of them married."

"Octavio was angry?"

"So I am told, but he came to accept it at last. And for some years things were good. Then came the bad night when Grace vanished into the Fault Line and was lost. That same night, Octavio Tinker's heart failed and he died."

"Oh my God!" Lucinda said. "That's so terrible! How did it all happen?"

Ragnar shook his head. "I was not there. It is not my story to tell. Already I have talked and talked—talked too much. We have work to do. Besides, what more do you need to know? The whole sad story is in these words—Gideon lost his wife and his thane on the same night."

"His thane? What's that mean?" Tyler asked.

"Ah, it is not a word of your time, but mine. The one who held his oath—his lord, you might say."

"This is America," Tyler told him. "We don't have lords."

Ragnar's half smile returned. "Words change—men do not. In all ways Octavio was Gideon's lord. But it was the loss of Grace that crippled him. He searched years for her, until the Continuascope was lost too." He looked around, then lowered his head a little between his big shoulders and said quietly, "He was already a little mad, I think, when the Continuascope was lost in the laboratory fire and he could not even search for her anymore." He shook his head.

"So she just disappeared into the Fault Line," Tyler said slowly. Lucinda could not help noticing the strange expression on her brother's face—he was lost in thought, staring at nothing, as if he was on the last level of some game and completely absorbed. Why was he zoning out when they were finally getting some answers?

"Why did Gideon bring you and the others here?" she asked.

The big man snorted. "You would rather talk than work, I see. He brought us because he needed workers to keep the farm going . . . workers who will keep the secrets."

Tyler abruptly stood up. "I have to go back to the house!" He turned and headed off at a trot.

"What about your chores, boy?" Ragnar called.

"I'll be back, honest!"

Lucinda stared after him, wondering what was going on. She had a sinking feeling that she was going to wind up doing his share of the work as well as her own.

A hot, sweaty hour or so later Ragnar finally sent her back to the house to get lunch while he went to talk to Mr. Walkwell about some fencing.

Lucinda was rinsing the worst of the dust off her face and hands at the faucet outside the Sick Barn when she felt the hairs at the back of her neck begin to rise. She even looked around to see if someone was standing behind her, but no one was in sight: she was alone with the concrete bulk of the huge barn. Then the weird, powerful sense of someone else's feelings flooded into her again, bringing a sense of loss as sudden and shocking as being doused with a bucket of cold water.

Lost . . . lost . . . lost . . . !

Her first impulse was to run away—but how could she run away from thoughts in her own head?

Lucinda lifted her hands to her cheeks and found they were wet. The force of the misery—whoever's misery it was—had brought her to tears.

Go away, ghost, she thought desperately. *Leave me alone!*

But it would *not* go away, and she spun in helpless circles, holding her head. It was only then, as though she had turned toward the sun with eyes closed and felt its heat, that she realized she could tell where the painful, unhappy thoughts were coming from.

The Sick Barn.

Lucinda looked around but there was still no one in sight. She walked slowly to the front of the great concrete tube. The overwhelming sense of someone else's misery was growing a little less, but it still battered her mind like a strong wind.

The door to the Sick Barn was open, propped with a stone so it wouldn't latch shut. Lucinda poked her head in, heart beating fast and prepared for almost anything, but there was little to see. In fact, except for the huge bulk of Meseret sprawled in sleep, tethered to the floor with massive bands of canvas, and some movement in some of the smaller pens and cages, the place seemed empty. But who had left the door propped? And whose terrible, mournful thoughts had invaded her mind? Was it the ghost in the library mirror? Or something worse—some horror conjured up out of its natural time and place by Gideon's Fault Line?

And then Meseret's great, red-gold eye flicked open, as if a gypsy fortune-teller had lifted the cloth cover off a crystal ball. The long, narrow reptilian pupil widened a little and several ideas thundered in her brain at the same time.

NOT EGG THIEF.
WHAT WANT HERE?
SAD SAD SO SAD!

Lucinda didn't hear individual words, but instead felt the meanings with the suddenness that a splash of paint would shout "Red!" As the alien ideas cascaded over her, a sudden, clear understanding came with them: the voice she had been hearing in her head, the mournful thoughts that she had mistaken for ghosts, had come from Meseret.

The dragon was in her head.

Lucinda's first impulse was to turn and run, but the misery that she could feel as clearly as heat or cold held her. The immense reptile let out a floor-rumbling groan and tried to stand, but the heavy canvas restraining straps, each one as wide as a bedsheet, kept her belly against the floor and her winged forelegs pinned against her sides.

"Oh, you poor thing . . . ," Lucinda said, then trailed off in sudden fear as the dragon stopped struggling and turned her terrifying eye on Lucinda. "I'm . . . I'm sorry you're tied up," she said, her voice little more than a squeak. "I'm so sorry your egg . . . your baby . . . died."

Now, as if her idea had leaped between them in the same way the dragon's thoughts had jumped to Lucinda, the dragon shuddered and shook her massive head from side to side as if to shake it free of something. Lucinda guessed from the slowness of the great beast's movements that Meseret was drugged.

NO DEAD! Drugged or not, Meseret could still make the inside of Lucinda's head rattle like it was thunderstruck. *NO DEAD! TAKEN!*

It took Lucinda a moment to make sense of the thoughts.

"Taken? You mean . . . by Alamu?" It hadn't occurred to her until that moment that it might not be very smart to argue with a giant winged monster forty feet long—especially one that was clearly angry and upset. But instead of the burst of anger she feared—or even a scorching belch of fire, which could reach her even where she was standing,

312

she abruptly realized—what came to her was only a squall of misery, like cold wind and dark clouds.

NOT LITTLE WORM. NOT HIM!
LOST. TAKEN. EVERYTHING GONE.

And then there were images with the ideas, pictures in her head that Lucinda could not make sense of—a setting sun, a tangle of bones, a cliff wall of sheer red stone looming above drifts of sand.

NO QUICKENING. NO BABY.

Lucinda saw an image of something that was neither a dragon baby nor a human infant—more of a shining point of light, like a welcoming door opened into darkness.

GONE . . .

It was too much, the power of the dragon's thoughts, the strangeness of them. It felt like having a stranger pull on her arm and shout in her face in a foreign language, shrieking for help. Lucinda took a few stumbling steps backward. Something creaked behind her and she saw Haneb standing in the doorway, pulling his protective hood back on as he returned from somewhere outside, his scarred face wide-eyed with surprise to find Lucinda standing beside the dragon's pen.

A moment later she was rocked off her feet by Meseret's bellow of anger and pain, her ears popping with the pressure.

EGG THIEF! The thoughts crashed through Lucinda's head like an avalanche, almost knocking her down again even as she struggled to rise. *HIM. THIS ONE. EGG THIEF!*

Haneb hurried toward her, head down as though he crossed a battlefield beneath a hail of bullets. He grabbed her arm and pulled her to her feet, then yanked her toward the door.

"What you doing?" he shouted, his voice muffled by the hood, his eyes frantic behind the faceplate. He grabbed her arm and began pulling her. "No suit! Dangerous! Come away! Come away now!"

He can't hear what she said, Lucinda thought. *He can't hear her thoughts like I can.*

"It's you," she said wonderingly as they reached the door. Behind her the dragon groaned. "She's calling you a thief. She says *you* took it."

"What?" Haneb still had his hood on, but his startled look was easy to see even through the protective mask. "What you saying?"

"Meseret. The dragon. She says you stole her egg."

For a moment his eyes widened even farther, as though they might leap right out of his skull. Then Haneb turned on his heels and ran away from her across the farmyard.

CHAPTER 24

SQUIRREL MEETS WORLD

Tyler wasn't sure he understood everything she was saying—his sister was pretty worked up.

"So, hang on—the dragon *talked* to you?"

"Not talked, not exactly. But it totally *communicated* with me, Tyler. I'm not kidding! I could get most of what it meant. It kept saying—*she* kept saying—that Haneb stole her egg! And when I said it out loud Haneb got this super-guilty look and ran away!"

"But why would he steal an egg? It's not like they don't feed people around here."

"Tyler! I'm serious! This is the craziest thing yet!"

"I am being serious—and it may not be the craziest

thing happening around here . . . although talking dragons *is* pretty hard to beat."

For a moment Tyler thought she was going to go into her old hurt-feelings act, but instead she finally noticed the papers spread all over his bed. "What are you doing? And why did you just take off and disappear like that?"

"Oh yeah. Well, see . . ." He was about to launch into an explanation of everything he'd been thinking, but something about her face made him say instead, "You know, that's really amazingly weird, what happened with the dragon, Luce. Do you think you can do it again?"

She seemed surprised to be asked. "I don't know. Maybe. She was really upset and I think she's on some kind of drugs—tranquilized." She shook her head. "I still don't understand why Haneb would steal an egg from her."

"Maybe she got that wrong."

Lucinda frowned. "She seemed pretty certain. But he wouldn't do that, would he? He's so nice."

Tyler shrugged. "Who knows? We're leaving in a couple of days and we're not going to figure everything out by then." He saw her expression. "Yes, even I admit it. We're not going to solve all the riddles—not this time. These people are crazy and this place is totally nuts—it's like someone crashed a bunch of amusement park rides together. Whee! It's the Haunted Monster Time-Travel Train!"

Lucinda laughed. "Okay, now I'm asking again. What's

all the paper, and why did you take off and leave me to do all the work?"

"Sorry about that. I was just trying to find out more about the Continuascope. Because I have an idea."

"Another idea? How are we going to get almost killed this time?"

Now Tyler laughed. "Hey, you're the one who keeps messing with the dragons, not me."

"Just tell me your idea."

"Okay, but first I want to hide all this stuff. I already took notes on the parts I want to look up at the library, so I don't need to take it with me."

"Notes? Library?" Lucinda pretended to look around the room. "Where did my little brother go? Someone stole my little brother!"

"Very funny. But I'm not kidding, we have to hide it. Gideon'll freak out if he knows we found all this stuff and didn't tell him. Besides, you know the Wicked Witch is going to be going through these rooms after we're gone."

Lucinda shivered. "I don't know. Maybe we should hide it somewhere else on the farm—like the reptile barn or something?"

"When? And it might be hard to get to it when we come back next time."

"*If* we come back." Lucinda actually sounded like she wanted to, despite all the frightening, crazy things that had happened. Tyler was impressed. "How about our bathroom?" she asked. "Is there anywhere to hide it in there?"

They trooped in and began investigating. After a bit, Tyler stood on the toilet seat and began pushing at the boards of the ceiling until he found one that was loose. "I think I can get this off," he said as he began to wiggle it back and forth.

Lucinda hardly seemed to hear him. She was staring at Tyler's hairbrush on the counter of the sink like she was hypnotized.

When he had the board off, he held out his hand. "Get me the stuff, would you? I just want to see if it fits up here okay." But his sister didn't respond. "Lucinda?"

"Oh, Tyler!" She sounded really upset. "I think I know how that horrible squirrel kept finding you."

"What do you mean?"

"Mrs. Needle. She made me get some hairs from your hairbrush. I just remembered." She shook her head. "It seems kind of like a dream, but I'm sure it's real."

"What are you talking about? Hair?"

She told him a strange, disjointed story about drinking tea and watching sleight-of-hand tricks in Mrs. Needle's room. "I can't remember when it happened. But that's like voodoo, isn't it? They take your hair and make a doll or something? Oh, Tyler, I'm so sorry! She tricked me!"

For about half a moment he remembered that nasty, hissing, yellow-eyed creature chasing after him and was really angry with her. That was Lucinda's big problem—she wanted to pretend like things were okay even when they weren't. Oh, no, Mrs. Needle was a perfectly nice lady! Then Tyler looked at his sister again and really saw the misery on her face, her red, brimming eyes.

"It's okay, Luce. She tricked you. It would have fooled me too. In fact, she probably gave you some kind of drugs or something."

She wiped the tears from her eyes with an angry swipe of her hand. "I hate her! How could anyone be so mean?"

"Hey, she's a witch." He meant it as a joke, but saying it suddenly made it real to him again. Their enemies were not bullies from school or snoopy assistant principals making sure they didn't talk too loud at the lunch tables. No, one of them was a real witch who could do magic. Another was a super-rich guy who wanted the farm and would send crooks and spies to get it for him, people who would probably bump off a couple of nosy kids if they got in the way. Tyler suddenly felt a bit weak in the knees. "Come on," he told Lucinda. "Let's go get the stuff and hide it."

They had just picked up the diary and other papers when something banged against the curtained window and they both jumped. "It's okay," he said. "It's just Zaza." He lifted the curtain, looking around for the squirrel, then opened the window and let the monkey in.

She hop-fluttered onto the bed, then up to Tyler's

shoulder, chattering softly. "I was wondering when you were going to drop by," he said, digging for some pieces of dried apple he had in his pocket. Zaza patted Tyler's hair in excitement, then grabbed for the apple. Tyler scratched her little round head. "I'm gonna miss you. I wish I could take you with me." He laughed. "Man, everybody at school would go nuts!"

"I'd like to bring Alamu to school," said Lucinda. "On a leash. Allison Keltner and those other snooty girls from the swimming club wouldn't be going 'I have one of those, but it's bigger' about *him*, would they?" She chortled. "Then I'd let him burn Allison's hair off."

"Whoa, sis. You're getting pretty hardcore." Talk about the dragons reminded him of something. "Hey, Zaza," he said, scratching her chin, "do you know where that Continuascope thing is? Do you?" He gave her the last piece of apple. "If you know where it is, I'd sure like to know."

Tiny pieces of chewed fruit fell from Zaza's hands into the neck of Tyler's T-shirt. "She doesn't understand you," said Lucinda indulgently.

"Oh no?" said Tyler. "Who'd have thought that the dragon could understand *you*? C'mon." He started gathering up the papers. "Let's finish hiding this. And I never told you my idea, Lucinda."

"Oh yeah. What is it?"

"You know the ghost haunting the mirror in the library? I think it's Grace."

All through dinner Tyler watched the other residents of Ordinary Farm, wondering what they knew and what they might be hiding. Ragnar had told them the histories of most of the other farmhands. Haneb had come from the ancient Middle East. He had been a child when Gideon brought him back, along with the two dragons, who had also been babies. Lucinda had been very interested in Haneb's background. Tyler figured she had a soft spot for the scarred man and was hoping there was some reason that he'd done what the dragon believed he'd done, other than to make a king-sized omelette.

The Three Amigos were Mongolian herdsmen, which was pretty much what they seemed like. The only surprise about them was that they had come from no farther back than the early part of the twentieth century—Tyler would have been equally willing to believe they had been born two thousand years or more in the past. Things hadn't changed much in Mongolia during that time, apparently.

The only one that Ragnar had seemed reluctant to talk about was Caesar, and not because of the old man himself.

"Someone else came with him" was all Ragnar had said. "A very evil man named Kingaree. I have met many fearful men and beasts, but no other has put unease into me as he did. He is the only one of us who has left the farm, and if we never see him again that will go well with me."

If the six-and-a-half-foot Viking was afraid of someone, Tyler didn't really want to meet the guy, either.

Sarah was from medieval Germany, Azinza some kind of disgraced princess from West Africa, Pema from ancient Tibet. Caesar and the mysterious Kingaree had both come from the American south before the Civil War. In fact, every one of the people of Ordinary Farm seemed to have some amazing story, and that was leaving out Mr. Walkwell, a creature as rare as the unicorns and dragons he took care of. It was so frustrating to find this out so soon before leaving.

And what if they weren't invited back? Even if Gideon didn't know all the trouble they'd been into, he didn't exactly seem to be in love with having them. Tyler tried not to think about what Colin had said about Mrs. Needle fixing their memories.

He watched his great-uncle, who was making one of his infrequent appearances at the dinner table. The old man was talking animatedly with Mr. Walkwell but still managing to put away a fair quantity of macaroni casserole, which seemed to be a good sign. From overheard snatches, Tyler could tell that Mr. Walkwell was discussing the intruder he had caught; and Gideon, at least for today, was invigorated by it and seemed to have more purpose to him.

If I tell him I think I found Grace he'll have to bring us back, won't he? And if I tell him that I found my way back out of the

Fault Line he'll want me around to help.

Tyler almost opened his mouth to say something, but a chill ran over him and he turned to catch the barest moment of Mrs. Needle's dark, cold eyes on him before she looked away.

Maybe for once he'd hold off for a little while, Tyler decided. Play it safe. Because he was beginning to understand that more was at stake here than just an old man collecting crazy animals out of a hole in time.

Tyler knew he really should get some sleep—even if tomorrow was their last day on the farm, they still had to get up at the same horribly early hour—but his mind would not rest. He sat in bed with the same questions going through his head over and over, like birds fluttering in a cage that was too small.

Was the spirit in the mirror really Grace, Gideon's lost wife? How serious was the threat to Gideon and the farm from that Stillman guy that Ragnar had told them about? Could dragons really talk, and could his sister understand them? And, perhaps most puzzling of all, had he really fallen into a hole in time then found his own way out again? Could he do it again? Everyone said that only the Continuascope would allow someone to navigate the Fault Line. Was he, Tyler Jenkins, special or had he just been incredibly lucky?

Something flickered at the corner of his eye, drawing

his attention. He looked up to see Zaza's wide-eyed face at the window. Tyler got out of bed and threw open the window, but she only hopped around his window frame in agitation, then threw herself backward into the air before swooping up back up again to the window.

"What's the matter, Zaza?" he asked quietly, in case the black squirrel had returned.

She climbed onto his shoulder and chattered at him, her tail lashing. The fur on it was all puffed out, like she was spooked or something. Tyler peered past her but saw only darkness. He was about to climb back into bed when something glinted below him. Tyler leaned forward and squinted into the night, but couldn't see anything. Then a beam of light hit him in the eyes.

Zaza let out a chirp of fear and leaped off him and out the window. Tyler rubbed his eyes, dazzled. A trio of dark shapes stood on the ground below, swinging flashlights around. For a moment he thought they were Stillman's spies and his heart raced. Then he realized that unless they had been recruited from Munchkinland, they were too small to be grown-ups. There were three of them, and he suddenly realized they seemed more than a bit familiar.

"Tyler?" the stockiest one called up to him. "That you, man? Oh, boy, this house goes on *forever*. We thought we were never going to find you."

"Steve Carrillo!" Tyler said in a loud whisper. "What are

you guys doing here? No, don't answer. Just don't move, *stay quiet*, and I'll be down in a second. And turn off those flashlights!"

Tyler pulled his clothes on right over his pajamas, then hurried across the corridor and woke up Lucinda. She followed him on tiptoes down the stairs. Outside, they found all three Carrillos, Steven and his sisters, Carmen and Alma, wearing dark hooded sweatshirts and dark pants and carrying flashlights.

"You look like you're going to the ninja convention or something," Tyler whispered. He looked back at the house to see if anyone was obviously watching, but the only lights were at the far end, the kitchen and dining room. "Why are you here?"

"Dude, we only came to find out if you were dead or not!" said Steve.

"I told him we shouldn't do this, but Steven thinks he's a spy or something," said Carmen. "He said we could find you guys' rooms easy," she added. "My brother, the genius."

Steve said, "Actually, yeah, we were about to give up when we saw you hanging out the window. How come you two never called us back?"

"What do you mean, called you back?" asked Lucinda.

"We left, like, twenty messages," Steven said. "She always said you were out somewhere, doing chores."

"She?" asked Lucinda. "You mean Mrs. Needle?"

Tyler was getting nervous now. "Lucinda, we have get them out of here before someone hears us."

"We didn't mean to get you in trouble," said Alma. "But Steven kept saying maybe they murdered you or something."

"No, we're fine, but we've got to get you away from the house or we're all definitely in a lot of trouble." Tyler couldn't even guess what Uncle Gideon would do if he knew the Carrillo kids were on the property—go crazy, just for starters.

He was about to lead them around the back of the house toward the Sick Barn when he saw a movement at the corner of his eye, something slinking by above their heads. He looked up, and with a sinking heart saw a dark shape hunkering down along the roofline—the squirrel, that rotten, nasty squirrel.

And it's probably not really happy with me, either, after last time, he thought. *Wonder how long it was stuck in the fruit picker?*

How did the thing communicate with Mrs. Needle? Could it be telling her right now that there were strangers on the property? Was it too late already—was she fetching Gideon?

It didn't matter, Tyler realized. They had to assume she didn't know. He leaned close to Lucinda. "Take 'em to the library—but give me about five minutes first."

"I don't want to go there, Tyler."

"We have to. It's the only place that's far enough from the house that no one's going to know they're here."

"We could just send them back the way they ca—"

"No! They must have been incredibly lucky to get here without Mr. Walkwell or Ragnar spotting them—they wouldn't be that lucky twice."

"Mr. Walkwell wouldn't hurt us," said Alma confidently. "He likes us."

"It's a little more complicated than that," Tyler told her. "Look, Luce, just do it. Give me five minutes. I'll meet you there." And without waiting for any more conversation, he took off at a trot in the opposite direction from the library, across the farm toward the pastures and animal barns.

Tyler had only put a few hundred feet between himself and the house when something ran up his leg from behind and bit him on the back between his shirt and pants. He let out a muffled shriek and tripped, crashing to the ground and rolling, the scratching, nipping thing still trapped against his body by his own clothing.

As he struggled to get away, it was all Tyler could manage not to scream at the top of his lungs, but he knew that if he did that there would be no turning back—the Carrillos would be found, Uncle Gideon would go thermonuclear, and he and Lucinda would be sent away never to return. He managed to pull his shirt up enough to get his hands around the scratching, struggling thing and throw it away from him. It hit the ground and rolled, and by the single dull light above the door of a nearby barn he saw the black squirrel spring back onto its feet, its tail held high behind its back, its yellow eyes almost glowing with malice. It was by far the biggest squirrel he'd ever seen, big as a large house cat. It took a few skittering steps toward him and hissed like a snake.

Tyler turned and ran.

At first he thought the squirrel would only follow him a little ways, then go back to the trees and rooftops where it felt comfortable, but when he looked back the thing was digging along the ground after him like a mad black rabbit. Tyler swore under his breath. He didn't think the creature could actually *kill* him—could it?—but it could sure rip him up with those vicious claws and teeth, and it already had him bleeding in a half dozen places, wounds that were now beginning to sting with every step.

Tyler was headed toward the big stretch of open land where the unicorns lived, trying frantically to think of ways he could escape the creature but not coming up with any. He scrambled over a fence, but had gone only a few more steps before the squirrel caught up and leaped onto him again, scrabbling its way up his side and back and shoulder, straight onto his head.

Now Tyler *did* scream and threw up his arms, managing by pure luck to dislodge the creature before it got its claws sunk into his scalp. It hissed again as it fell, and when it hit the ground it turned and came after him. He could almost swear its chatter was a language, and the words were not friendly ones.

At the last moment he found a fallen branch from one of the live oaks, and just as the black squirrel took a bounding leap toward him again he swung and managed to smack it hard. The squirrel fell but got up, leaping up his arm so quickly that it was halfway through the twigs and dried leaves at the end of the stick before he could throw the branch away with the squirrel in it. This time he did not bother to look back but simply ran across the pasture as fast as he could.

I'm going to be murdered—by a squirrel! He was too frightened even to be embarrassed, but it was certainly going to be the stupidest death of any student in the history of Chavez Middle School.

Tyler was out into open land now, with dry knee-high grass and only an occasional stunted tree. Just before him was the long, low trough where the unicorns came to feed, rushing in like a hurricane when Mr. Walkwell or one of the herdsmen summoned them.

And there, at last, was a gleam of an idea. As he ran through the grass he bent and picked up the first stick he passed, but it was so thin he threw it away. The second one was too heavy to be much use in defending himself from something as small and quick as the squirrel, but Tyler had a different idea.

When he reached the trough he ran around it in a tight

circle, banging on it with the stick as hard as he could, over and over. A dozen yards away the dark, compact shape of the squirrel appeared from a clump of high grass and hopped toward him, little more than a shadow in the light of a partial summer moon.

Tyler put the trough between him and the squirrel and waited. It hopped closer. Now he could hear its hiss, loud as a teakettle. He held the stick up in front of him and the squirrel stopped, waiting to see what he would do. They stared at each other, and Tyler felt as if he was looking at something that was more than a mere animal—there was a nasty, cruel little intelligence behind those slotted eyes.

Then he heard the sound, that rumble like an approaching storm, and his heart seemed to swell in his chest. He hadn't known what they would do at night—if they were even close enough to hear. The rumble grew louder. The squirrel froze, looking around, and the yellow eyes bulged.

"Yeah!" Tyler screamed. "Yeah! How ya like me now?" He turned and sprinted for the nearest tree.

The squirrel hesitated a moment, and that was a moment too long. As it jumped after him the unicorns suddenly burst out of the trees at the top of the nearest rise and came crashing into the meadow like a flood from a ruptured dam, right over the spot where the squirrel was leaping through the low grass. Within moments the entire pasture around Tyler's tree was a seething ocean of pale sides and swinging manes, of kicking hooves and needle-sharp horns.

The unicorns finally galloped off ten minutes later, clearly irritated that they had been summoned for no purpose—that they had found no food in the trough. Tyler climbed down and began limping his way back toward the library, promising them silently that he would make it up to them someday. He owed them. Nothing else seemed to be moving, although there might have been a slow, broken squirming in the trampled grass.

"Hey, Squirrelly—kinda sucks to be you, huh?" he called over his shoulder.

As he pulled the library door open, Lucinda ran to meet him with a flashlight. "Oh, Tyler," she moaned, "it's *terrible*!"

"We'll figure out something to do. They can probably sneak back close to dawn—I don't think Mr. Walkwell's going to be out there all night long, do you?"

"No, it's not that! Steven's . . . gone."

"What? What are you talking about?"

"Come on." She grabbed his arm and hustled him across the darkened library, their footsteps echoing.

Tyler suddenly knew where they were going and his heart sank.

The door to the retiring room across from Octavio's portrait was open. Alma and Carmen were looking in every corner of the small room with their flashlights when Tyler arrived. Carmen, the older girl, shone her light at him.

"Oh, Tyler, what happened to you?"

Lucinda saw his wounds for the first time. "Oh! Are you okay?"

"Never mind me —what happened to Steve?"

"We don't know," Lucinda said. "We were talking, then we looked up and he wasn't there anymore. The door to this room was open, and he . . . he was just *gone*. He's not anywhere else in the library. We've looked for him everywhere. He's disappeared!"

Tyler stared at the mirror above the washbasin. At the moment it was as dark as a piece of volcanic glass. He reached up a finger and tentatively touched the surface.

His finger went straight through.

"Oh, this is bad—real bad." He swallowed and turned to the three girls. They looked terrified. Tyler wasn't too happy about things himself. "Uh . . . I think I know where he's gone."

CHAPTER 25

A MOTHER'S HEART

Lucinda stared at her brother. He was speaking English but she couldn't understand him. "What do you mean you're 'going in after him'? Going in where?"

"Just . . ." He glanced at Carmen and Alma, who both looked frightened. "Never mind. We can't waste any more time—it might be bigger in there than it is in here. In fact, it could lead *anywhere.*"

"Tyler, what are you talking about?" Now Lucinda was beginning to be really scared too. "We have to get Ragnar or somebody."

"No time." To her surprise, Tyler scrambled up onto the washbasin and braced himself on the frame, as if he wanted to take a really, really close look at his own face. She was just about to ask him what he was looking at so carefully when he closed his eyes and then let himself fall forward into the mirror, disappearing through its surface like a man making a perfect dive into still water.

"Tyler!" she shouted, but he was gone. She scrambled forward in time to see him walking away from her—her brother no longer existed on her side of the mirror, only inside the reflected world. The ghost-Tyler disappeared around a corner. Behind her, Lucinda heard little Alma begin to cry.

"What's going *on?*" demanded Carmen, who was close to tears herself. "This is totally crazy!"

Lucinda was fighting her own very strong urge to just run upstairs to her room and put her head under her pillow until the whole problem went away. Her brother had just jumped into a mirror. What next? She squeezed her eyes shut, fighting the urge to scream for help.

I just want to go home now. I really, really want to go home. She wanted to sleep in her own room and see her friends. She wanted to clamp on her headphones and listen to normal music and think about boys and television and what was happening at school. No monsters. No magical mirrors.

But when Lucinda opened her eyes again, Alma and Carmen were staring at her, terrified, waiting for her to do something, and she realized that this was not the time to run away and hide.

"It's okay," she told them. "Tyler knows what he's doing." *One thing at a time, Lucinda,* she told herself. "So you guys came over here in the middle of the night because we never answered our messages?"

Carmen looked at her terrified little sister and made a decision. She took a deep breath, and when she spoke she no longer sounded like she was about to break down. "We . . . we kept calling you. And that English lady kept saying you couldn't come to the phone, or that you were busy, always something. But you never called back, and our grandma was just nodding her head like she knew it all along, and we were wondering if you guys were sick or something. After a while, we were really worried!"

Alma nodded. "And then tonight, that helicopter—Steve said maybe it was one of those ambulance helicopters, and that they might be sneaking you out to a hospital or something."

"I told him that was dumb," Carmen said, "but he was like, 'I'm going! You can't stop me!' So we came with him."

Lucinda grabbed the girl's hand. "Hold on—what helicopter?"

"It was this big one—*really* big, but really quiet. It went right past our house about an hour after dark, and Steve and I saw it," Carmen explained. "For a long time it just hovered by the edge of your property with most of its lights off, but then it went farther in and I think it landed. I don't know—it was hard to see."

Lucinda had a bad feeling. A big helicopter? That had to be the people that Mr. Walkwell and Ragnar were watching out for—like that guy they'd captured out by Junction Road, the one they said was working for that Stillman guy. But a *helicopter*, landing on the farm at night?

She had to do something about this.

"Listen," she told Carmen and Alma. "I have to go tell people what you saw. It's important that you guys don't go anywhere or let anyone see you—really, *really* important. Trust me. Just stay here and wait for Tyler to find Steven. He'll be back—they'll both be back." But even as she said it she felt a cold squeeze in her chest, a dread as deep as the day their dad had told them he was moving out. She stared at the dark mirror, reflecting nothing at this moment but a shadowed wall. Where had her brother gone? What was happening to him right this moment?

"S-stay here?" Carmen said. "By ourselves? Are you psycho?"

"Trust me," Lucinda told her. "It'll be a lot less scary here than anywhere else."

Little Alma looked at her solemnly. The girl's tears had dried now and she seemed to have found her strength. "It's okay, Carmen," she told her sister. "We'll wait here, Lucinda. You go."

Lucinda turned and ran across the library.

336

Only Sarah, Azinza, and Pema were still in the kitchen, leisurely scrubbing out the last of the dishes and preparing for tomorrow's breakfast.

"What are you doing up so late, child?" asked Sarah. "And why do you want Ragnar? He has gone to the Sick Barn, I think. The dragon is very difficult again today."

"She lost her baby," said Azinza in her lordly manner. "Of course she is sad."

Lucinda didn't stay to answer their questions—she was terrified that Mrs. Needle might appear. She thanked the women and headed out toward the Sick Barn. Things were getting more confused every moment. What was she supposed to do if she couldn't find Ragnar? Wake up Gideon so he could learn there were strangers on the property? Including the Carrillo kids, one of whom had apparently fallen through a mirror and into the Fault Line?

She could feel the unhappiness of Meseret in her head while she was still fifty yards away from the Sick Barn. The dragon was making a strange, low groaning that Lucinda had never heard before. The first waves of Meseret's powerful thoughts, just beginning to wash over Lucinda's mind, were almost incoherent—in no recognizable form except anguish and fury.

NO NO NO NO NO NO NO . . . !

Lucinda hesitated at the door of the immense concrete cylinder, suddenly afraid to step inside. It was like walking into a blazing oven of unhappy emotions.

"Ragnar?" she called, but no one answered. "Ragnar? Mr. Walkwell?"

She stepped through the door. She could see the dragon's back as the monster writhed in her pen, the restraints creaking as they stretched. A shape in a white hooded safety suit was standing at the edge of the pen, aiming a rifle at Meseret's vast, shuddering bulk.

"Stop!" Lucinda shrieked. "What are you doing? Don't shoot her!" She ran toward the pen. The figure turned its faceless plastic-shielded head toward her for a moment, waved violently at her to stay back, then turned to the dragon again and pulled the trigger. Lucinda couldn't even hear the sound of the gun firing over the dragon's groaning, and nothing seemed to happen: Meseret still struggled on, her thoughts flooding Lucinda's head in a meaningless roar of upset.

NO NO NO . . . !

Haneb pulled off the hood. His black hair was lank with sweat, his scarred face full of amazement and fear. "Get back! She is dangerous! I give her medicine to sleep!"

"Medicine?" She turned to look at the dragon and saw a clump of feathers wagging on Meseret's near haunch, so red it was almost orange under the bright fluorescent lights. "Is that . . . a dart?" She could feel the chaos of the dragon's thoughts begin to calm a little.

"To make her sleep, yes! But stay back. Half hour until she sleeps, maybe an hour."

The dragon groaned again, this one a sound that was almost human in its misery. Her thoughts, perhaps because of the sedative, were clear enough now for Lucinda to understand.

EGG THIEF RUNS! EGG GOES AWAY . . . GOING NOW . . . FLY, FLY!

Lucinda turned on Haneb. "She's upset about her egg again. What did you *do* to her? Why does she think you stole it?"

Haneb's look of dismay turned to something deeper— an expression of utter panic. "She speaks to you?"

"What did you do? Why does she hate you so much?"

He took a few steps back. If this had been a vampire movie, Lucinda felt sure, he would have been flashing his crucifix at her. Then, to her astonishment, the little man began to weep.

"I did not want!" he cried. "I did not want take the egg! Please do not tell Mr. Gideon! Mr. Colin make me take!"

Meseret groaned and thrashed. Her head snaked around on her long neck as she began to bite at her restraints. If she was about to fall unconscious, Lucinda thought, she was doing a pretty good job of not showing it. She turned back to Haneb, who had fallen to his knees. "What do you mean, Colin made you?"

"He want egg. He made me take it or he tell Gideon I sneak out to the town one day. Just to look! But Colin say Gideon send me back to where I come from if I don't help him. Now the great she-dragon wants to kill me!" He was so upset she could hardly understand him, and the pounding of Meseret's thoughts in her skull wasn't making it any easier, but she was beginning to get the point.

"You mean . . . *Colin* has the egg? It didn't get stolen by the other dragon—by Alamu?"

But Haneb wasn't talking anymore. He had buried his face in his hands and was sobbing.

Now the dragon began to fight even harder. *EGG!* her thoughts bellowed. *TAKING AWAY NOW! STEALING!* And with the ideas a sort of vision came into Lucinda's head— of a hunched, slightly glowing shape moving through the dark, not so much seen as *sensed*, like the night vision option on that combat game of Tyler's. But the object that the glowing figure carried glowed more brightly still—an egg-shaped smear of warmth.

It's happening right now, Lucinda realized. *She can sense someone taking her egg away right now!*

YES! EGG! Meseret was biting ever more frantically against the restraints, not caring if her teeth dug into her own scaled skin. Blood dribbled down her side, purple-black under the fluorescents. *EGG! NOW!* The thoughts were still understandable, but wavery, as though they came from beneath water. The sedative might, at last, be starting to take effect, Lucinda decided with relief.

Then one of the heavy restraints, frayed by Meseret's teeth, snapped with a gunshot noise—*Pow!* Another went, and then another—*Pow! Pow! Pow!*—like fireworks. A moment later the dragon had freed enough of herself to get her midsection up over the edge of the pen, bending back the metal fence at the top like it was no more than a cheap spoon stuck in frozen ice cream. Her head stretched over the edge, one of the restraints still flapping like a scarf around her neck. Her red-gold eyes were wide, rolling, and Lucinda gave up any thought of trying to communicate with this many-ton monstrosity. The idea that her stolen egg was somewhere close by had all but driven the dragon mad, and the sedative wasn't helping much. Lucinda screamed to Haneb, but the little man was crouching, holding his head. He had faced the male dragon bravely, but something about this situation was too much for him. He looked like he was waiting to die.

Still wrapped in torn restraints, Meseret dragged the bulk of her body out of the pen, her long, wing-fringed front legs hunching and stretching as she struggled across the room, knocking over the tables, smashing the equipment. One of the trailing harnesses caught in a set of shelves and the whole thing was yanked off the wall and onto the concrete floor, scattering liquids and broken glass everywhere. The dragon crashed past both Lucinda and Haneb and butted the door of the Sick Barn with her huge head, smashing it off its hinges, but the rest of the door frame and the semicircular wall was concrete and she could not get past it. She roared in desperate frustration—Lucinda could hear it echoing across the farm.

EGG! EGG! The creature's thoughts were so furious and powerful that they burned in Lucinda's head like fire. She bashed at the wall around the broken door like the biggest woodpecker in the universe, but the concrete would not yield even to her great strength. With another bellow of frustration, she turned and headed toward the other end of the Sick Barn.

Lucinda was right in the dragon's way.

Everything around her seemed to ooze into a stately crawl, like a slow-motion video replay. Only her thoughts were moving quickly. The tranquilizer rifle was gone, buried under debris, and Haneb was still down on the floor— he might even be dead already, felled by flying metal.

Lucinda bent and picked up the box by her foot that said TRANQ. DARTS in large, felt-tipped letters. Underneath it had been written BIG ANIMALS—THIAM, PHENC, SCOP MIX, which she hoped meant the drugs were already in the darts.

Meseret was coming toward her, stripping metal shelves

from the wall with her lashing tail, oblivious to anything except the big back door with its metal shutters at the far end of the Sick Barn.

Lucinda reached carefully into the box. There was only one dart left, a cylindrical tube the size of a roll of toilet paper, marked like a hypodermic, with a tail of feathers at one end and a thick needle about four inches long covered with a plastic cap.

Meseret was on top of her, big as a bus and seemingly blind with rage. Lucinda tried hard to keep her eyes open as the monster bore down on her. She held up her trembling hand, ready to try to punch through the ridiculously thick skin with the needle, but at the last moment the dragon swerved around her. Lucinda had only a half second of relief before the remains of Meseret's restraints whipped over her as the dragon thundered past, knocking the needle from Lucinda's hand and tangling her in canvas straps.

It got worse.

Before she even had a chance to scream Lucinda was jerked off her feet and dragged backward across the laboratory floor, through upturned tables and bits of broken glassware, as the dragon crawled swiftly across the barn toward the loading door. She couldn't untangle her foot— her own weight was pulling the knot of straps tight around her ankle. It was all she could do to pull herself double to get her head off the floor.

The dragon smashed hard against the metal loading door where the large animals were brought into the barn on the flatcar. It rattled but did not give, and Lucinda swung in the straps and thumped painfully against the wall and the dragon's immense, scaly hip. Meseret groaned again.

OUT! EGG!

Lucinda banged hard into something else as the dragon twisted and threw herself once more against the unyielding door. Meseret didn't even know she was there and probably wouldn't care. Lucinda struggled to get a chest full of breath.

"Haneb!" she screamed. "Open the door! She's going to kill me if you don't!"

Again and again Lucinda was smacked bruisingly against hard surfaces as the dragon tried to batter down the heavy door. She had hit her head at least twice and she was finding it hard to think. "Please, Haneb!" she shouted, but she had no idea if he was was even conscious.

Then Lucinda heard a deep bass rumble. She thought at first it was the dragon again, groaning in frustration, but then she saw black sky and spotlights where a moment before there had only been the loading gate. The door was rising. Either Haneb had heard her or Meseret had somehow triggered the mechanism.

Lucinda struggled but she was still hopelessly tangled. A moment later they were out into the darkness and cold air. The dragon was running, dragging Lucinda along the ground. *Bump, bump,* then something struck her on the head.

Dizzy. Suddenly there was no ground anywhere, only rushing wind, and Lucinda was swinging free in nothingness, whipped back and forth at the end of a tangle of canvas straps as the ground fell away beneath them and the dragon took to the sky.

CHAPTER 26

THE YRARBIL

Going through the mirror was like crossing half a second's worth of freezing black space. Tyler rolled across the washstand on the far side and hopped down to the floor. As he had guessed, everything in the room was a mirror reverse of the room he had just left except for one thing: the other room had been full of people, the Carrillo girls and his sister, but he was alone in this one.

"Steve!" he shouted, and pushed through the door into what should have been the mirror version of the library. "Steve Carrillo!" It was only then that he realized he might be in more trouble than he had even guessed.

Outside the door, he found himself in an unfamiliar

corridor—something that had nothing to do with what he had left behind on the other side of the mirror. It was dark and covered with dirty, ancient wallpaper like some parts of the house he had seen, but like nothing in the real library. One solitary, flickering oil lamp gave the only light, a weak glow extending a few yards down the corridor on each side. He would have to choose a direction. He listened, but heard nothing.

"Steve?"

When nothing came back to him but a faint, distant scratching, he turned in the direction of the noise and began carefully to make his way forward. It was only as the door he had come through fell away behind him that he wondered, *Why an oil lamp?* Old as they were, the real house and library at least had electricity.

He turned the corridor and found a new oil lamp and a forking of the way. To his right a wide, dark stairway led downward—he could see a few levels into its depths before the light of the lamp would carry no farther. The corridor itself led beside the open space of the stairwell. Two signs hung on the wall below the lamp. One had an arrow pointing down and read *RALLEC.* The other pointed straight ahead and said *YRARBIL.*

CELLAR and LIBRARY—it was easy enough to figure out, and sort of made sense for the far side of the mirror. What he didn't understand was why there was a cellar here when there wasn't one under the real house—at least not that he knew of—and why the library seemed so much farther away than the real library—the one in *his* world.

Maybe it wasn't just a mirror version, everything exactly the same but in reverse. Uncle Gideon had said something about the Fault Line being about time, but Octavio Tinker had written in his journal that alternate realities, alternate worlds, were possible too. So what was behind the washstand mirror at Ordinary Farm might be only another *version* of Ordinary Farm.

Which meant, he suddenly realized, that he had no real idea what might be here at all.

He leaned over the railing, looking down the stairwell into the lightless cellar depths.

"Steve!" he called. "You down there?"

A dry scratching whispered up from the depths, as if someone was dragging dead leaves and discarded snake-skins up the stairs. It didn't sound like Steve Carrillo at all, but it did sound like it was slowly coming closer.

Tyler hurried along the corridor toward the "YRARBIL."

He found it at last, at the end of what seemed like a mile of turning, poorly lit passages. It was at least as big as the real one, maybe bigger, and at least as full of shelves as the other. It wasn't laid out in straight lines, but in haphazard clusters of tables and shelves and other strange furniture. In fact, if there were such things as haunted libraries, this sure looked like one of them. Many of the flickering lights on the walls here weren't even oil lamps but actual candles: their flames jiggled when he passed, which made his shadow seem to dance and jump on the walls.

"Steven? Steve Carrillo? Where are you?"

He thought he heard a noise, not the scratchy hiss and scrape he'd heard on the cellar steps, but a muffled sound like someone calling from another room. He made his way quietly across the big central space, looking without much interest at the backward-lettered spines of the books on the shelves. There were pictures on the wall of this library, too, although he didn't see anything quite like the big portrait of Octavio Tinker. Most of these pictures showed weird-looking old people in even weirder clothing. A few of them were of places—dark, stormy oceans and lonely mountaintops. Glass cases stood in some of the library's open spaces, full of weird objects that looked as though they'd come from the oldest, dustiest attic imaginable. One purple-black ball caught his eye because it looked like a huge gem. He peered into the case to read the label, which said *GGE S'REHTNAP*.

Panther's Egg? What kind of silly crap was that? Not that there might not be some interesting things to explore here some other time. If only the place wasn't so creepy.

Something rustled nearby and Tyler whirled around in time to see a flick of shadow disappearing behind one of the library stacks. "St . . . Steve?" he called. Nobody answered.

Now he went more quickly, trying to keep to the open spaces at the center of the room. Who knew how big it was on this side of the mirror? Maybe it was a whole world! Tyler began to feel quite hopeless about ever finding the boy from the neighboring farm. He raised his voice a little. "Steve?"

"Ssssssssteeeeeeeeeeev . . ." It wasn't an echo that whispered through the room but something stranger and far more disturbing, as though a creature that had never spoken before was trying to imitate his voice. Tyler turned again and saw a cluster of shadows down one of the aisles, something that looked as though it was covered with swinging rags and moved in a hunched-over, sideways motion like a crab. It was visible only for a moment, then scuttled away into the darkness beyond the candle flames again.

"*Sssteeeee . . . ,*" the cracked voice whispered from of the shadows, then the shape appeared again, one row nearer this time. The rags waved like seaweed straining for the surface and the light.

Tyler ran.

He crossed the nearest part of the library in moments, trying to put as many shelves as he could between himself and whatever was following him. He found himself in a gallery of ancient photographs along the back wall, black-and-white pictures of half-built machinery and monuments. A door stood ajar and he ducked through it into a hallway beyond, closing it behind him as quietly as he could. The corridor was lined with more old photos—children wearing ceremonial outfits so strange they looked like Halloween costumes, fantastical combinations of scarves and turbans and long coats. He pushed himself back against the wall between two pictures and tried to be absolutely silent.

When a few minutes had passed without any new noise, and the door between himself and the library still remained shut, he began to breathe a little easier. He was just mopping the sweat off his forehead when a voice spoke quietly beside his ear.

"I think it's gone now."

Tyler squeaked and jumped. He looked up and down the hallway but there was nothing and nobody to be seen.

"I'm here," the voice said—a woman's voice, shaky with age but calm and refined, like something you might hear on television. "Turn around."

Tyler turned, his heart beating so fast he felt weak in the knees. Then he saw something moving and took a step closer to the wall. One of the two rectangles he had stood between was not a photo like the others but some kind of ironwork grille in the wall. On the other side of it, barely visible in the uneven lamplight, was what looked like a woman's face and a suggestion of white hair.

"I didn't mean to frighten you," she said. "Who are you? Why are you out when the Bandersnatch is hunting?"

"Bandersnatch?" The name seemed familiar.

"That's just what I call it. Like in the old story . . . or is it a rhyme?" She laughed a little, and for the first time she didn't sound quite right. "I . . . I can't remember everything I should. In fact, I can't remember much of anything."

It suddenly hit him who he might be talking to. "Grace? Are you Grace?"

She didn't seem to hear him. "You really should find somewhere to hide. There's nothing I can do for you. I'm too frightened of that thing. It's been after me for . . . for years."

"Where are you?" Tyler leaned forward, trying to get a good look at her face, but his sudden movement startled her and she moved back. He was terrified he might lose her. "Don't go away! Where are you? How can I get to where you are?"

"You can't. At least, I don't know how. I'm lost right now myself." She sounded sad about it, but not devastated, as though it happened fairly often.

"You mean you can't get to me, either?"

"No." He thought he saw her shake her head. "But you need to find someplace safer. The Bandersnatch can . . . well, it can find you. And it can be very quiet. It likes the shadows. Look for the light. There's a place at the top of the library where it hardly ever goes. Too bright." She started to move back from the grating. "Be careful. What did the poem say? *Beware the Jubjub bird . . . and shun . . .*

the frumious Bandersnatch!' Something like that."

"Wait! Are you Grace?"

The face hesitated, half gone into the shadows. "Grace?"

"Is that your name? Are you Grace? Gideon's wife? I'm his nephew, Tyler."

"Grace." She sounded as though she was drifting away. "The name . . . is familiar. Gideon? Gideon. I remember . . . I *think* I remember." For a moment she disappeared from the grille entirely, then her face reappeared and her fingers came through the bars dangling something shiny. "Take this. Give it to . . . No, *Gideon*, he gave it to . . ." It slid from her and chinked to the floor, coiling there like a tiny, gleaming snake.

When he stood up again with the gold locket and chain in his hand, she was gone.

The last thing Tyler had wanted to do was go back into the library, but he had to find Steve. The only alternative was to look for him down in the cellar, and Tyler knew it would be a long time before he decided to do that.

Grace, if that was the woman behind the grating, had told him to head for the high part of the library—that he would be safe where it was lightest. He moved as quickly across the library floor as he could, staying out in the open, until he found the main staircase. This led up to a level that ran all the way around the top of the great room, but then a set of stairs rose from there toward the building's pitched ceiling, a floor that seemed to have been used as an attic, with boxes of old books and clothing and other things stacked haphazardly all around. Tyler climbed the steps as quietly as he could. It was indeed brighter than the rest of the library up on the platform below the ceiling: it was flooded with flickering oil light from the central chandelier, but there were also dormer windows in the top of the roof that let in the light from an oily gray sky.

"If you stand on a pile of boxes you can see the rest of the house," someone said.

This time the voice wasn't quite as much of a shock. Tyler managed to stifle his shriek of alarm before he turned and found Steve Carrillo sitting cross-legged on the floor, carving a piece of wood with an antique pocketknife.

"Steve!" said Tyler, relief washing through him.

The black-haired boy looked at him, puzzled. "Do I know you?"

"Do you know me? I'm Tyler! You came to find us, remember? You and your sisters?"

Steve squinted for a moment. "Tyler. Yeah. It's just that I've been here so long. . . ."

"What do you mean? You just came through a little while ago!"

The look of confusion came back to Steve Carrillo's face. "Days. I've been here for days and days."

"Look, never mind. We have to get you back. Come on." Tyler turned and headed for the stairwell, but quickly realized no one was following him. "Steve?"

The other boy looked pale with alarm. "I'm not going down *there*! It'll get me."

"That Sanderbatch thing?" Tyler shook his head. "We'll just stay in the open. Maybe we can find a flashlight or something—I don't think it likes light."

Steve shook his head emphatically. "It's . . . it's made out of dust and paper, I think. I hear it all the time. It's just waiting. Waiting for me to come down."

"Look, don't you want to see your family again? Your sisters? Your mom and dad?"

Steve looked at him doubtfully.

"Trust me. I'll get us back." A thought occurred to Tyler. "You find any matches up here?"

Once they were through the library and into the corridors beyond they lit the bundles of mirror-written book pages Tyler had tied to two halves of a broken broom handle. The paper was so old and damp it burned slowly. Torches in hand, they scurried along the passageways, talking only in whispers, stopping every few minutes when Steven's courage started to fade. He really did act like someone who had been here for months, not minutes, Tyler thought—like a prisoner of war in some movie, his spirit almost crushed. Every echo of their own passage made

Steve jump like a rabbit, and Tyler couldn't imagine what would happen if they actually ran into anything serious. He would probably just fall down and die.

Finally, in an effort to take the other boy's mind off what was happening, Tyler began talking about their escape as if it was a video game. "Okay, we're finally at the end of the first level—we just have to go a little farther. We've earned a lot of rubies."

"Life points . . . pretty low," Steve groaned, but at least he was playing along.

"Look, we're almost through. We beat the boss, so we're pretty much home free."

"We haven't beaten the boss," Steven said. They were nearing the stairway to the cellar now, which to Tyler meant they were almost out, but Steven was walking slower and slower. "The boss lives down there. In the *RALLEC*." He stopped. "Hear that?"

Much to his sorrow, Tyler did. It was the scraping, dragging, rustling noise he had heard before, getting slowly louder as it came up from the depths. "Follow me," he said. "Run!"

The torch flames streamed behind them until Steven had to drop his before it burned his hand. Tyler briefly wondered about setting the corridor on fire behind them— it surely wouldn't burn through to the real-world side of the mirror—but then he remembered the sad, confused eyes of the woman behind the grating. He turned back and stamped out Steven's sparking, sputtering torch, then began to run again.

He didn't know what made him look back just before they got to the room with the mirror—it wasn't a sound. Whatever was following them was as noiseless now as ash blown on the wind. Perhaps it was a feeling, the idea that something was fluttering along behind them like an untethered shadow. But once he looked, he wished he hadn't. All he could see of the indistinct shape was a face made of shadow, and all he could see of that face was hunger and loneliness and madness.

They crashed through the door into the mirror-bedroom. Tyler pushed Steve headfirst into the washstand mirror and then dived after him into the silver-mercury reflection.

Carmen and Alma wouldn't let go of Steve. The girls were crying, but Steve was like someone who'd just woken up from a strange dream.

"Where's Lucinda?" Tyler asked, then felt his stomach grow heavy with dread when they told him.

"I have to go," he said. "I have to go after her. It's that guy your dad was talking to Mr. Walkwell about—Stillman, the rich guy. The helicopter must be his." He sighed. He was exhausted and scared and all he wanted to do now was go to bed. Wasn't this night ever going to end? He didn't want any more answers about Ordinary Farm because all they did was lead to more questions. "You'd better come with me," he said a moment later. "It may be the only chance to sneak you off the property. We might have the police here by morning—especially if your parents find out you're gone."

"It seemed like a good idea when I thought of it," said Steve Carrillo sadly.

"Yeah, I get a lot of those too."

"No more magical mirrors, right?" Steve asked.

"No more mirrors. We're just going to get you off the farm as quietly as possible."

"That sounds good," Steve said, sounding a little more like his old self. "I don't want any more excitement tonight, that's for sure."

CHAPTER 27

NO TRICKS

Colin Needle had to admit he was a little nervous.

It wasn't sneaking across Ordinary Farm by night with a stolen dragon's egg that was worrying him—he'd been preparing to do this part for days, and had been back and forth over the route with an appropriately sized rock in his backpack a half-dozen times, practicing until he knew every potential hazard, with or without a flashlight. No, it was the way the stakes of the game had been raised that worried him.

First off, Colin had never wanted to make a deal with this Stillman fellow. If he had known the true story of Jude Modesto's important client, he felt sure he would have abandoned the whole project. But he had already given Modesto the chip from Meseret's previous egg before he found out, and apparently Stillman had tested it and decided it was very, very interesting, so it was too late to turn back.

Still, Colin had to admit that the half-million dollars would make it easier to deal with his own conscience. He would have asked for more, but he needed to be able to carry it back himself, and this way Stillman would be even more eager to come back for such one-of-a-kind bargains—and Colin would supply them to him.

Second, things would have been much easier if Modesto could have waited just a few days more to set up the meeting. The Jenkins kids would have gone back home and Colin's distraction for Ragnar and Walkwell would have been ready. He had planned to arrange an escape from its pen by the bonnacon, a slow-moving but immensely strong and stubborn bull-like animal that sprayed caustic dung; recapturing it would have taken them most of the night. Modesto's sudden email demanding the sale take place tonight had meant that he had been forced to improvise instead.

Colin had left a glove (part of a pair he had bought but never used) near the barbed-wire fence out on the edge of the property, then made an "innocent" remark at dinner about having seen a surprising number of cars and other activity out on Springs Road near where he had left the telltale glove. He figured that should keep them busy for at least the first couple of hours of darkness, searching for intruders out at the farthest point of the property from his rendezvous with Jude Modesto. Colin certainly hoped so—he didn't want to look up and find himself staring into Walkwell's weird, angry eyes. That man—that goat-horned *thing*—scared Colin Needle almost as much as his mother did, and that was saying something.

Still, it shouldn't have been this way. Everything would have been so much simpler without the Jenkins kids. Sure, it had been occasionally interesting to have people his own age around the farm, and Lucinda was okay, but Colin Needle had big plans and having Gideon's relatives around just made things more difficult.

He stopped to rest on top of a hill beyond an abandoned barn where he could look back toward the house. All good so far, no more than the ordinary number of lights on, Gideon's study and bedroom, the kitchen, a few along the porch and the other outside doors. So much of the house was unlighted at night that most of the time you couldn't even begin to guess at its immense size. Only on bright, moonlit nights like this one could you see the array of roofs, the covered arcades and outbuildings, and the unusual silo and tower rooms that made Ordinary Farm look like some strange Oriental palace.

And it's going to be my *palace someday,* he thought with no little satisfaction. *Because I'm the only one who really cares about it—or at least I'm the only one with any sense. Any guts.*

He heaved up the backpack. The egg was no easy burden, big and lopsided as a partially deflated beach ball, heavy as a sandbag. He got the straps over his shoulders again and made his way down into the shadowy, oak-shrouded valley beside Junction Road, out of the moon's glare.

Colin hadn't really expected a *helicopter*, let alone the biggest helicopter he'd ever seen. Its dark hide gleamed like the shell of a beetle as it crouched on the hilltop half a mile from the road, its rotors lazily turning. It had no markings, but Colin had a feeling that the darker patch on its side was something covering a corporate logo— Stillman's Mission Software, most likely. His stomach tightened. Several men stood waiting outside the copter's open bay door.

Colin wasn't simply going to walk up to them with the treasure in his hands, of course. He wasn't a fool. He'd read plenty of spy novels and seen plenty of movies and he knew all about double crosses. He'd even thought about one of his own, substituting something for the real dragon egg before selling it, so he certainly didn't trust Jude Modesto not to cheat him. While he was still in the shadows he took off the heavy backpack and hung it over the branch of a tree, high enough to be almost impossible to see in the dim light, and counted the trees as he followed the deer path to the edge of the clearing and out into the open.

"You're late," said Jude Modesto. The fat man was trying to sound like an important fellow who'd been kept waiting, but he wasn't very convincing. Stillman and his two bodyguards stood by the copter, the same two huge men who were only a couple of bad haircuts and two pairs of Lycra shorts away from looking like professional wrestlers.

"You changed the meeting time," Colin said flatly. "It wasn't easy for me to rearrange things." Unlike Modesto, Colin knew that the less emotion you put into your voice, the less you had to worry about giving away how you really felt. Which, in his case, was nervous. He'd just noticed that both of the bodyguards were wearing holsters over their dark shirts. Holsters with guns in them.

Well, Needle, he reminded himself, *you wanted to play with the big boys.*

"And this must be . . . your client," Colin said out loud, remembering that he wasn't supposed to know what Ed Stillman looked like. But before Modesto could reply, the silver-haired man in polo shirt, shorts, and hiking boots pushed himself away from the steep side of the helicopter—it looked even bigger from up close, like a flying battleship—and stepped forward. He looked as though he was coming to shake Colin's hand, but his own hands never left his pocket.

"And this must be the enterprising young man you told

me about, Jude," said Stillman. "He reminds me a little bit of myself when I was that age, I must say." He smiled, showing perfect white teeth. "I'm very interested in what you claim to have to offer." Up close, in the light from the chopper, he looked older than on first impression. Colin found himself wondering whether despite his easy, graceful movements, Stillman might be older than Gideon. "And I'm just as interested to know where you got it."

"Uh-uh," Colin said, trying to sound calm but tough. "I don't claim, I don't explain. That was part of the deal—no questions. I know you checked out that sample or you wouldn't be here. Where that sample and the sale item both came from is a secret. Put it this way—it came back from a very special expedition."

"And where is . . . the sale item?" asked Ed Stillman, as if he'd seen all the same movies and read the same books.

"Where's the money?"

The client laughed. "Deuce—the suitcase?"

One of the bodyguards reached into the helicopter and produced a briefcase. He snapped it open and held it out. Colin could see nothing but rows of Ben Franklin's face—one-hundred-dollar bills in bound piles.

"Five hundred thousand, right?" said Stillman.

"Please, Mr. St. . . . I mean, please, sir, let me handle this!" Jude Modesto flapped his hands in frustration. "It's my *job*."

"Your job is done," said Stillman, then he turned to

364

Colin with a wide smile. "So do we have a deal? You can count the money if you want."

Colin reached out and lifted up a bundle at random, fanned it as he'd seen in many films, then put it down and tested another. His heart was beating so fast he thought he might not be able to speak, so at first he just nodded. "Looks fine," he said at last, gruffly.

"Then take it. Where's my . . . sale item?"

"I'll go get it." Colin closed the briefcase, gripped its handle tight, and started toward the trees. "I'm not going to run off with the money," he told Stillman. "I promise."

The man in the polo shirt laughed again, as if this was turning out to be far more entertaining and enjoyable than he'd ever hoped. "No tricks, then? All right, I'm glad to hear it. And if you give me what's promised, you'll get to keep that suitcase and the money in it. After all, that's how men like us do business."

Colin hurried to the trees, trying to remember if he'd done everything right. He'd held back the egg until he'd seen the money. He'd checked the briefcase to make sure it wasn't just a few real bills on top of bundles of cut-up newspaper or something—and here it was in his hands! Half a million bucks! All he had to do now was get the money into the bank. He wasn't sure how he was going to explain it to his mother and Gideon when he suddenly produced enough money to save the farm, but he didn't have to come up with an explanation right away. He could always claim he'd won the lottery. His mother might not believe it, but she'd know better than to start making a fuss about it, and Gideon would be too grateful to ask many questions.

Take that, Jenkins kids! he thought as he counted his way to the tree where the backpack hung. *One in the eye for you, eh!* Maybe he'd even let them come visit sometimes once Gideon was gone and the farm was his. After all, it was better to keep your enemies close—and quiet. Tyler and Lucinda Jenkins were now part of a very elite group, the tiny number of people who knew the important secrets of Ordinary Farm.

Well, knew *some* of the important secrets. Colin grinned.

He almost left the briefcase with the money in it back in the trees, but couldn't bear to think of it being out of his hands that long. Instead he dangled it awkwardly from his fingers as he struggled to carry it and the heavy backpack to the helicopter.

"Here it is," he said as he reached Stillman, who took the egg from him. The helicopter's blades were turning a little less lazily now, as if the great crouching thing were waking up.

Stillman looked inside the backpack. "Good," he said. "Now, get in."

Colin stood waiting for Modesto and the client's body-guards to do as their boss had ordered, then realized that the billionaire in the khaki shorts was looking at him. The smile was still there, but it didn't come close to reaching the man's eyes.

"I said, get in."

"What are you talking about?" Colin took a few steps back, but a huge hand curled around his bicep. One of the bodyguards had moved in behind him. "What's going on?"

"*We're* going on," said the billionaire. "And you're coming with us. I've got lots of questions to ask about your pal Gideon Goldring and what he's been doing here all these years in the middle of nowhere—and *you've* got lots of answers you're going to give me." Stillman chuckled and patted the side of the helicopter. "Besides, wouldn't you like to ride on this baby, Colin? It's a LePage S-99, you know. Top of the line—they make basically the same model for the military. You've heard of a Thunderbird gunship, haven't you?"

"But you said no tricks!"

The billionaire rolled his eyes. "Come now, Colin—you're a big boy. What kind of crap is that, 'no tricks'? Since when do people dealing in illegally smuggled dinosaur eggs—and of an undiscovered saurian, to boot!—since when do people doing things like that trust each other? Give me a break! Haven't you ever heard the old saying, 'There's no honor among thieves'?"

"But you're a businessman!"

"I take back what I said earlier—you don't remind me of myself at all. I don't think I was ever *that* naïve, even when I was in elementary school."

Jude Modesto came forward, his face beaded with sweat that gleamed in the light spilling from the helicopter's interior. "Sir, you never said anything about this. This is . . . this is kidnapping."

"Only if our friend here wants to file charges. But I'm betting that one way or another, he won't. Either he'll like the deal I'm going to offer him—and it's a good deal, one where he'll get to keep at *least* that half a million—or something will happen to him and no one will ever find out where he went. Make sense?" He nodded to the man behind Colin. "Let's go."

The briefcase was taken gently from his hand, then Colin Needle was shoved, stumbling, toward the open door of the helicopter.

CHAPTER 28

HOT WINGS

It might have been an interesting sight in another place and time—the rolling hills at the edge of Standard Valley laid out in blanket folds, glowing gray in the moonlight and rushing away beneath her like the current of a river. As it was, though, she was dangling upside-down, held only by the ankle on the shredded restraint straps of a dragon, and whipped by the speed of their passage like a spider in a gale, so Lucinda was too busy screaming to appreciate the view.

"Go down! Go down! Meseret, *put me down!*"

But all that came back from the dragon was a jumble of heated, dark thoughts, storm clouds full of lightning— anger and fear and something deeper Lucinda could not put a name to, especially not when she was spinning and swinging two hundred feet above certain death.

The dragon banked down, clearing a stand of trees by so little that Lucinda felt the topmost branches whip past her head, then leveled out, following the curve of the land as she headed toward the far side of Standard Valley. If it was Colin she was after—if he actually had Meseret's egg—then the boy was as good as dead. Many thousands of pounds of dragon were going to drop on him like an eagle on a field mouse, if Meseret didn't just burn him to ashes first.

Now that they were flying more steadily, Lucinda finally stopped swinging like a yo-yo. She grabbed the strap around her ankle and tried to pull herself up, but at first she could not even get her head up to the height of her own knee. All those horrible exercises in gym class, knotted ropes and obstacle courses—why hadn't she worked at them harder? All those times she'd run to the wall, clambered up a few feet, then slid down to the ground and walked away, ignoring her gym teacher shouting that she knew Lucinda could do better if she only tried.

But this time she was going to die if she didn't make it. Her foot was going to come loose and she'd fall, or she'd get her head smashed into a tree, or, perhaps worst of all, get dragged a hundred yards across rocks and brambles when the dragon finally landed. And then what? Colin incinerated. Not that he was blameless, but still . . . Tyler and Steven stuck in the mirror, wherever that might lead, and the Carrillo girls helplessly waiting. Their mother, receiving a phone call from someone—probably Mrs. Needle: "So sorry to tell you this, but your children aren't coming back home. . . ."

"No!" She couldn't even hear herself shout against the whistle of wind in her ears, but she felt a tiny twinge of recognition from Meseret, as if despite the fury that filled the she-dragon like a hive of bees, she dimly heard Lucinda's voice. But it wasn't enough to make her slow down or stop.

Lucinda grabbed at her ankle again and began to pull herself upright. It was hard, hard going, and once, terrifyingly, the knot on the strap gave a little and she lost her grip and fell away, banging her back and head against the dragon's rough, leathery hide, but the tangle tightened again and held. Laboriously she pulled herself back up until at last she was able to get her other hand onto the knot of canvas above her ankle. She clung to it, the wind bumping her rapidly against Meseret's side, until she had caught her breath and didn't feel quite so strong a need to scream. Already, though, her muscles were exhausted and burning. But what choice did she have?

"Meseret! Can you hear me—can you *understand* me? Put me down! I'll get killed if you don't put me down!"

But the dragon didn't seem to be listening either to Lucinda's words or her thoughts. Meseret kept flying steadily south, following the slope of the land through every change so that every beat of the batlike wings seemed to carry them higher or lower. Lucinda clenched her teeth until her ears rang and began to pull herself up.

Her gym teacher would never have recognized her. First one hand, then the other on top of it, pull up a few inches, then change hands. Her fingers felt like bony hooks, cramped and agonizing from holding her weight as the wind kept trying to pull her off, to throw her into space, but she knew she didn't have the strength to start over again if she lost her grip. She tasted salt in her mouth: she had bitten her lip until it bled. She couldn't even see because the wind and her own pain had made her eyes fill with blurring tears.

One hand. The other hand. Pull up. Change hands. One hand. The other. Pull.

The wind was full on the back of her head now, her hair whipping the sides of her face and trailing behind her so that at first she could not tell the difference between it and the dragon's long tail, switching from side to side as she banked through the sky.

I'm up! She was all the way above the knot on her ankle, and with one last tug she was able to lift herself upright, clinging tightly to Meseret's broad flank. She was standing in the knot as though it was a stirrup, facing backward toward the dragon's tail end. Lucinda put her free foot on top of the knot and rested there for a long moment, but she knew she wasn't safe yet—as if there was any position that could be called "safe" when she was riding on top of a five-ton dragon gone insane with anger. Nevertheless, she mustered what seemed like the very last of her strength and pulled herself up, using both feet now to keep the restraint rope taut, until she was finally up onto the relative safety of Meseret's broad, scaly back. Lucinda left the knot around her ankle just in case, then clung to the hummock where the top of the dragon's massive hip joint met her pelvis, where the wind was a little less fierce.

Meseret abruptly stooped. Lucinda's heart leaped in fright. Had the creature seen Colin? Was she going to shred him while Lucinda watched helplessly—eat him, maybe? What did the stupid boy want the egg for, anyway? Had he really stolen it, or was it all some kind of misunderstanding between him and Haneb? Did it even matter? Despite the species difference, Lucinda knew that Meseret felt perfectly certain of the boy's guilt and that she would destroy him in an instant to get to her egg.

But that egg isn't even alive! Why was the dragon so angry? Why was she so crazy to protect a failed egg? Lucinda could feel it clearly, though, that mysterious emotion that throbbed behind all the others like a bass note in a complicated song, hard to hear unless you found the trick of separating it out from the other, brighter, showier notes.

Lucinda clung to the dragon's back, hurtling through the air, trying desperately to make sense out of the swirl of alien emotions.

Alien. Maybe that was the problem—she'd been trying to make the dragon's thoughts into human thoughts—

but maybe the only way was to think more like a dragon. But how?

She buried her face against the rough hide and spread her arms and legs wide so that she was touching as much of Meseret as possible. She could feel the massive shoulder muscles pulling back and forth even from several feet behind them. What must it be like to be so strong, to be able to fly, to be able to lift that vast bulk into the air and break through the misty clouds? To dive like a bird and to glide silently? To feel fire in your belly and your throat and know that you could spit it out of your mouth, destroying all before you?

Thinking about the fire, trying her best to think dragon thoughts, Lucinda suddenly felt herself sinking into Meseret's thoughts. She *was* Meseret, although a bit of Lucinda remained.

Fire! She could feel it now—not in her stomach, but waiting in sacs on either side of her throat, although she didn't think of it as anything so foreign as "fire." It was a part of her like her wing tips or her teeth, a bright, hot fan of defense and display she could spread in front of herself with only a thought—defense, display, and one even more important task, one she had not been able to complete and that gnawed at her like a wound. But she was not really thinking of the fire right now, just feeling it, as she could feel her pinions driving, as she could feel her heart beating thunderously in her breast. She was thinking only of her egg.

Her eyes roved over the landscape, looking for anything. She saw figures moving—antlike pale blobs scurrying below, the heat of their existence as plain as the light of the stars overhead. She stooped, anger rushing up inside her again. . . .

Lucinda was startled back into her own thoughts by the steepness of the dive, the finality of the intent.

"No!" she screamed. "No! Don't!"

But Lucinda's objections, her piping human voice meant nothing. It was Meseret herself who realized that the running shapes beneath her had nothing to do with her lost offspring. She could smell their . . . egglessness from hundreds of feet above them. She abruptly lost interest and banked upward. They did not have what she was seeking.

The dragon's thoughts now pulled Lucinda down again.

Her egg. It was not a thought, even, so much as a feeling. Her egg. A glowing ball of light, of . . . possibility. But so many things had gone wrong since she had begun preparing to birth it—it gave her so much pain! First there had been none of the just-right-smelling earth to eat and the shell had not felt right. Because of that she had not been able to quicken it with her breath, and it had lain soundless and warmthless long beyond the time it should have come to life—dead, just like all the others. But unlike all the others, this one had not fully succumbed. Somewhere inside it the spark still lived, although it was growing faint.

Then it had been stolen, and now it was being taken even farther away, and despite the sleepiness and foolishness that made her head so heavy and her thoughts so slow, someone would pay for that.

A joyful fantasy of shredding human flesh like lettuce, tearing and throwing and swallowing, made Lucinda shudder back into her own thoughts.

I felt her—I really felt her! That was Meseret!

The dragon stooped again. Something stood on the ground in the near distance—something bigger than any of the two-legged rat-monkeys, something much bigger. In Meseret's mind's eye, and in Lucinda's now, too, it looked something like a giant dragonfly, glowing near the circling wings with the heat of its building energy. More little blobs of light stood around it like eggs, like lice, like maggots, and one of them had her egg. All the rat-monkeys that held her and restrained her, and now that had stolen from her. Meseret hated them with a bright, white-hot hatred. . . .

The helicopter, Lucinda thought. *It's just like Carmen and Alma said. That must be where Colin's going—but why?*

The death-dealing urge throbbed through Meseret like a single, high-pitched note of song. Her wings creaked as she accelerated, the increased wind almost yanking Lucinda up off the creature's back.

No! Lucinda did her best to find that feeling again, the feeling the dragon herself felt. *Don't—you'll kill them all, and your egg too! Let me help you!*

What? It came to her as an eddy of startled thought, curling and curious. Someone else was in Meseret's thoughts, and even through her storm of fury it caught the dragon by surprise. *Who?*

Lucinda. The . . . rat-monkey. I'm on your back, don't you know that? I got tangled in the straps when you got out of the Sick Barn. Little of this seemed to be getting through, so she tried to summon up the memories as pictures in her mind, like a movie—the struggle, the dragon's escape, herself clinging for dear life.

You . . . talk? Talk dragon?

I don't know—sort of. . . . But you have to stop. I'll help you, but you can't attack that . . . big insect thing. She pictured the helicopter as Meseret saw it and tried to show it to her as *she* saw it, so that for a moment it was both things at the same time, alive and not alive, dragonfly and craft full of passengers. *You'll kill everyone, and we'll never get your egg back.*

No matter. The thought was bleak and ragged, but final. *Egg too long gone. Not quickened. Dead like others.* The thoughts didn't quite make sense, but the refusal was crystal clear. *Egg thief dies. Flying insect house dies. We die. Doesn't matter. No eggs, ever. Nothing matters. Nothing . . .*

The dragon's drugged despair brought tears to Lucinda's eyes but there was no time to sympathize. Meseret was flying more erratically even as she drew closer to the waiting helicopter, the sedative Haneb had given her now becoming a smothering fog across her thoughts.

Please! Lucinda thought, trying to reach her again. *Please let me help! I don't want to die—my mother will miss me! I'm someone's egg too!*

For a moment the remorseless beating of Mesert's wings

slowed. A bit of clear light broke through the cloudiness of her thoughts like a shaft of sun. She banked and began a long descent toward the ground.

She heard me—she understood! Lucinda let out the breath she had been holding so long she couldn't remember when she'd taken it. Then the helicopter engines boomed and roared and it began to rise into the air.

NO! The thought itself was like a jet of Meseret's flame, leaping out, burning everything else to flaking ash. *NO NO NO NO!* The ground heaved up beneath them just as the dragon drove her wings down, caught the wind, and banked upward, rocketing toward the rising copter.

"Don't do it!" Lucinda screamed, but communication was finished. The dragon, muddled and despairing, was no longer listening. Meseret skimmed the pinnacle of a copse of trees, then sped forward. Lucinda could see nothing on her own, but she could still sense something of the dragon's thought, see something of what Meseret saw. The horizon, the growing, glowing shadow of the insectoid helicopter, all tilted as a wave of dizziness went through her, and at the last moment the dragon veered—but too late. She did not hit the helicopter head-on, but still bounced off its side with a crash like a bomb going off. One of the blades struck Meseret's wing in a bolt of red agony that seemed to light up Lucinda's own brain like fire, then dragon and helicopter both teetered in the air, struggling to regain balance, swung apart, and dropped out of the sky.

CHAPTER 29

THE DEVIL'S BARGAIN

"Why are we running?" asked Steve Carrillo, struggling for breath. "I'm tired of running. I've been running and hiding for days."

Tyler stopped to let them all catch their breath. "Because you really need to get off this property. Just . . . trust me on that."

Carmen straightened up and pushed her hair out of her face. "Running and hiding? You spent the whole day yesterday lying on your back playing *Coils of the Man-Serpent.* You fell asleep with the controller in your hands!"

"I'm not talking about *that* yesterday. I was in that mirror for days," Steve said. "It just didn't seem like it to you."

"We're going to be hearing this for years," Carmen said. "'Steve, is your room clean?' 'Couldn't do it, Mom, I fell into a mirror and I was gone for, like, a month.'"

Little Alma patted her brother's arm. "I believe you, Stevie."

Tyler snorted. "Yeah, this is all great, but I really suggest we *get moving again*. Before something a lot worse than the mirror happens to us." Like getting caught by guys with a helicopter, and probably with guns this time. He'd have to get the Carrillos going their own way before they reached the edge of the property where the copter had been. What did that Stillman guy want, anyway? And how had he found out there was anything unusual about Ordinary Farm?

They were out well beyond the last buildings, moving across the open hillsides on the far side of the valley, scuttling in and out among the cottonwoods and the stunted oak trees. Steve was still complaining, but not so often or so loudly—he didn't have the breath. Tyler was just trying to decide if it was time to send the Carrillos off on their own when a massive dark shape loomed up out of the shadows, spreading its arms wide.

Carmen, who was ahead of the others, almost ran right into it. She shrieked and lost her balance, then fell and began to roll down the steep hillside. The thing leaped after her, bulky but quick as a hungry bear, and pinned her to the ground before she'd rolled more than a dozen yards. Tyler was frozen with fear until he saw the shadow bend over the panting, terrified girl. Tyler grabbed the first thing that came to hand, a piece of fallen branch not much bigger than his flashlight, and sprang down the slope.

"Leave her alone!" he shouted.

"Shut your mouth!" the shadowy figure growled at him. "And if you swing that at me, boy, I will beat your skin off."

"Ragnar?" Tyler scrambled down the hill. "Is that you?"

"Yes, me." He lifted Carmen up as though she was no heavier than a rag doll. "The question is, what are the rest of you doing here?"

Back at the top of the hill, Ragnar set Carmen on her feet, not particularly gently, and stared down at them all. "I am not playing a child's game. Tell me quick why you are here. If you are the ones who fooled me with that glove you have bought more than a handful of trouble."

"What glove?" Tyler asked, but when he saw the cold, angry expression on Ragnar's bearded face he decided maybe he would do better answering instead of asking.

"And you swear this is the truth?" Ragnar said when Tyler had finished.

"It's true," said Alma. Her voice was small but surprisingly firm. "We wouldn't lie to you, Ragnar."

He stared at her, then at her sister and brother, and turned at last to Tyler. "I don't think they would lie, but I know you have kept back truth before that you did not want to share. Is that so now?"

Tyler stared at him. He had kept back the story of the woman in the mirror—the one he thought was Grace. He didn't know why, but he still felt there were things going on that he needed to figure out before he could completely trust anyone, even Ragnar. "I've told you all I can," he said at last, and did his best to hold Ragnar's eye. "So now you have to decide whether you're going to trust me."

Ragnar leaned toward him, lowering his voice to a whisper so that the Carrillos couldn't hear. "Do not get above yourself, Tyler Jenkins. You learned much this summer, but the dangers here are greater than you have even guessed." After a moment he straightened up. "A glove was left on the fence to lure Simos and me away from the Junction Road side of the farm. Someone has played a trick on us. If it was not any of you, it was likely one of our enemies. Tyler, take these children back to their house. You three, swear to me you will tell no one—not your parents or other friends, *no one!*—what you've seen and heard here. Swear."

"We promise," said Alma promptly. Her older brother and sister looked at each other, but then agreed.

"Hurry, then. Follow me until we reach the farm road, then Tyler will lead you home."

They ran then. Within only a few hundred yards Ragnar was far in front, lost to sight among the trees despite the bright moonlight. Tyler had just turned back to encourage

Steve, who was lagging behind again, when something huge plummeted out of the sky, blocking the stars and—for one terrifying second—even the moon. Carmen shouted in surprise. Steve tripped and fell. For the first second or two Tyler thought it was the helicopter bearing down on them like something in a war movie, but the thing was almost entirely silent—no helicopter sounds at all.

And then a thin voice, full of panic, floated to him from high above—a voice he thought he recognized.

"No! No! Don't!"

The wind of the monster's passage knocked Tyler back a few steps as its huge shadow swept over him, wings spread wide, tail stretching over him like a knife slash of blackness against the midnight blue sky. Then it was gone.

Steve stumbled to his feet. "Whoa! Do you know what that *was?*"

Even by moonlight Tyler could see the strange, rapt expression on Alma's face as she stared after the departing dragon. "Grandma Paz was right," she said. "It *is* the door to another world."

"That was Lucinda up there," Tyler said. His insides felt like a block of ice. "Lucinda." But what would she be doing up there with that giant creature, unless she was . . . in the dragon's mouth.

He began to run again, even faster.

With the Carrillos behind him, he charged up the last yards to the top of the hill. As they reached the summit

Tyler could suddenly hear the sounds of a real helicopter, the steady, quiet *fwop-fwop-fwop* of its blades as it idled on the grassy valley floor. It was waiting for something—its running lights and the light spilling from its open door showed a last passenger clambering up the stairs, then the door slammed shut and the blades sped into invisibility. The helicopter began to rise.

"That's Ragnar running down the hill," Steve said, pointing at a figure racing toward the scene but still far from the rising helicopter, which was now at least twenty feet off the ground.

"He'll never get . . ." Tyler began, then a huge batlike shape dropped out of the sky. As he watched in horror it smashed into the side of the helicopter just below the rotors with a tremendous *thump* like a clap of thunder. The helicopter pitched to one side, wallowed for a moment in midair, then dropped unsteadily to the ground, but somehow managed to land on its skids. The dragon had fallen into darkness.

"Lucinda!" Tyler shouted, but someone grabbed at his arm. It was Carmen. Sparks began to pop from the doorway of the helicopter where it stood on the ground, its propeller still rotating.

"Don't," she said. "Those are guns!"

And now Tyler heard the cracks, distant but sharp as hammer blows. "What's going on? Why are they shooting?"

"Maybe because they just got knocked out of the sky by

a giant dinosaur with wings?" Carmen said. "You think?"

"But my sister—my sister was on that dragon!"

Steve Carrillo stumbled up and stood, wheezing. "No . . . wonder . . . you guys never . . . call us. Sounds like you've been . . . pretty busy."

Suddenly the field was splashed with light—the helicopter crew had switched the searchlights on, turning the area around the idling chopper bright as day. A shape was running away from the helicopter, toward Ragnar, who waved his arms from the other side of the meadow as if urging the figure on, but more pops and flashes came from the door of the helicopter and Ragnar had to duck down.

"Whoever that is, he'll never make it!" squealed Carmen.

Then a new shape came from somewhere behind the helicopter, moving over the grassy ground in a blur, fast as a rabbit, but bigger—much bigger. Even with the bright helicopter searchlights Tyler could not make sense of it as it snatched up the figure escaping the chopper, threw it over a shoulder, and ran toward them, moving with what seemed like impossible speed. As the figure sped past Ragnar, the Viking turned and followed it.

A last few gunshots cracked from the helicopter, then someone pulled the door closed and the aircraft started to rise once more. This time no dragon dropped out of the sky, and although the engines had a rougher sound than before, the helicopter kept rising until it was a couple of hundred feet off the ground, then it sped away west, its lights rapidly getting smaller until it was lost in the darkness.

The hairy, goat-legged figure slung Colin Needle off its shoulder and dumped the stunned boy to the ground, then put down what looked like Colin's backpack. The goat-man hesitated, then turned to look at the Carrillos, who were staring, wide-eyed. Simos Walkwell looked sad.

"Why are you here, children?" He looked down at himself. "Why? I did not want you to see this."

Steve and Carmen could only stare, but Alma actually smiled at him. "I saw you run, Mr. Walkwell. So fast! You were . . . you were *beautiful*!"

They found Meseret lying in a heap almost a quarter mile from where the helicopter had been forced down. Ragnar bent to hold his hand near her nostrils, which were as big as dessert plates. "She breathes," he said. "She seems to be asleep—perhaps she is not too badly hurt."

"She's drugged," said a voice from the shadows. Lucinda limped into view.

"Luce!" Tyler ran to her and hugged her, folding himself into her warmth. "I thought you were dead!"

"I did, too, especially when she hit the ground and I got thrown." She patted his back and gently pulled away— not because she didn't want to hug him, he realized, but because it hurt. She was staggering a little as she walked toward the others, so Tyler gave her his arm to lean on.

"Haneb gave her a shot just before she broke out," she told Ragnar, then she saw the Carrillos. She smiled a little. Everybody seemed to have given up trying to get them to go home, Tyler thought with wry amusement—there didn't seem much point now. "Hi, guys—you still here? Anyway, Meseret was losing consciousness before she got here, I think. It was just determination. She was after—"

"Her egg." Ragnar lifted up the backpack. "We know—it is here. What we do *not* know is how it got here when we thought it had been destroyed by Alamu."

"Alamu had nothing to do with it. Haneb took it. He says that Colin made him do it." She turned toward Colin. "What were you thinking, Colin? That was so stupid. And now the secret's out."

"I am not certain of that," said a voice. Simos Walkwell was still naked except for the bristly hair that covered his entire lower body. He stood up from examining the dragon and walked back to them. "I heard them arguing when they were on the ground—as Colin was running away. They did not know what had knocked them from the sky. They saw nothing of me, either, I think—I moved fast and kept to the shadows until I was far away from them." He turned to the Carrillos. "If these young ones can be trusted—and I hope that they can—it could be our secret is safe for a little while longer."

Tyler couldn't stand it anymore. "But it's *not* safe. That

Stillman guy is going to be even more certain that something unusual is going on here, and I think it's a pretty safe bet it's all *his* fault." He turned to Colin. "How much were you going to get for selling us out, Needle? What were you going to do with it, anyway? It's not like you ever *do* anything except sneak around and rat on people to your mother."

"That's a lie!" Colin shouted, and his anger surprised even Tyler. "I don't tell my mother *anything*! I want what's best for the farm! I never– I never–!" He broke off, muttering angrily, staring down at his shoes.

"What's best for the farm?" Tyler said. "You liar! You were going to sell a dragon's egg to that creep Stillman!"

"Oh, grow up, Jenkins," Colin snapped. "I was doing it to make the farm some money—we're in debt up to our eyeballs and it's going to get worse. How do you think Gideon's kept this place going for so long? He used to bring all kinds of things back from trips through the Fault Line, old things from the past, and sell them as archaeological treasures—at least, that's what he did till the Continuascope was lost in the lab fire. Now he can't find his way around in the Fault Line anymore. And Stillman was the guy buying them, but he's not going to do it any longer. This was our last chance to get any money out of him."

Ragnar said, "You are a stupid little boy, Colin Needle." His voice was full of contempt. "You have given away everything. You put a dragon's egg in that man's hand."

Colin shook his head. "He thinks it's a dinosaur egg. Just really well preserved."

"I can't believe you'd do that, Colin." Lucinda slumped a little against Tyler. He could feel her trembling with exhaustion. "I can't believe you'd do that to Gideon."

Colin's eyes filled with tears, but his face was angry. "Gideon! Are you joking? He's letting the whole place fall apart! He hardly ever comes out of his room!"

Ragnar called to Mr. Walkwell, who was inspecting the place where the helicopter had landed. "We must take him to Gideon, Simos. He is the thane. He must know what happened here tonight."

"No!" Colin shouted. "If you tell him, we'll all be thrown out! Me and the Jenkins kids, all of us!"

Tyler took a step forward. He had seldom had such a powerful urge to slug somebody. "Shut up, Needle."

"You think I'm wrong?" Colin turned on him. "Look at you! You snuck into the Fault Line. You stole stuff from the library. You brought these kids onto the property!" He pointed a shaking finger at the Carrillos, who were looking pretty nervous. "At least I was trying to help. You were just . . . entertaining yourselves!"

"That's not fair!" Lucinda said.

"Quiet, all of you." Ragnar looked like he'd also like to hit something. "Simos, what will we do?"

Mr. Walkwell was trotting back toward them, hooves

picking gracefully at the uneven ground. He was carrying something.

"Things could be worse," he said as he reached them, dropping his burden on the ground at Ragnar's feet. "Stillman has left something for us. I do not think he meant to."

Ragnar crouched and fumbled open the briefcase. Tyler stared. Steve Carrillo whistled.

"Oh my god," Lucinda said. "That's like a million dollars."

"Half a million," Colin corrected her.

"So for a while at least Ordinary Farm is not . . . broken?" Mr. Walkwell smiled. "Breaked?"

"Broke," Tyler said. "No, definitely not broke. But isn't Stillman going to come back for it?"

Ragnar laughed grimly. "Stillman will be back, but I think he does not care so much about this. For him, it is a little bit of money only. Still, it will make Gideon happy."

"*I* got that money!" Colin said shrilly. "If anyone's going to give it to Gideon . . . "

"Shut your mouth or I will shut it hard." Ragnar glared at him. Colin stopped talking. "So what do we do, Simos?" the big man asked.

"Um, I've got an idea," said little Alma Carrillo. Everyone turned in surprise to look at her. "I mean, if you can't tell Mr. Goldring about how the money really got here, why don't you tell him something else? Tell him those bad guys were trying to buy the farm or something."

"Hey, sis, you're pretty sneaky!" said Steve Carrillo, obviously impressed.

"For half a million?" Tyler shook his head. "They wouldn't believe it."

"A bribe," Lucinda said. She had sat down, and sounded about ready to fall asleep. "Tell Gideon that they tried to bribe you, Mr. Walkwell. That you went along with it to find out what they knew, and then you took the money."

"Gideon will like that," said Ragnar slowly. "He will like the idea that Stillman tried to steal our loyalty and failed—and that we kept the gold for him." He frowned. "But what will we do with the boy?"

Tyler swallowed. He hated himself for what he was about to do, but it made sense. "Don't do anything. We need Colin. If we turn him in he's not going to keep his mouth shut, and then everyone's going to be in trouble—me, Lucinda, the Carrillos, even you guys. We all kept secrets from Gideon."

"Congratulations, Jenkins," Colin said. "You have a brain in that head after all."

"Shut up, Needle. It works both ways. If you tattle on us, then we won't just tell Gideon what you did, we'll tell your mother."

"Wh-what?" Colin Needle looked like he'd been punched in the stomach.

"I know you didn't tell her. You're scared of her, aren't you? So just shut up."

"You don't know about me!"

"I know enough." Tyler said. "Now *shut up* while Ragnar and Mr. Walkwell decide what to do."

For a long moment no one spoke. The Carrillos shuffled their feet. Colin stared sullenly at the ground.

"I think we must keep quiet," Mr. Walkwell said at last. "Otherwise the Needle boy will be sent away. Those on the farm should stay on the farm. If not, they become a different problem—like Kingaree."

There was that name again, Tyler thought, the one even Ragnar was afraid of. What kind of monster was this Kingaree? What had he done?

"So—it seems we make the devil's bargain, as it is called," said Ragnar. "Everybody will stay silent about what they know—but Simos and I will be watching you always from now on, Colin Needle." The big man glared at Colin for a moment, then shook his head. "Still, we have one other problem to solve. The egg. Gideon thinks Alamu took it. Now we have it again."

"We will think of something," Mr. Walkwell said. "But let us think while we are taking these children back to their beds. For them this night has gone on for far too long." He looked at Tyler and Lucinda and his normally gravel-toned voice was almost gentle. "You are leaving us tomorrow, after all."

"But . . . what are you going to do with that . . . that dragon?" Carmen Carrillo asked. "Is it dead?"

"No, just overcome by sleep medicine," Mr. Walkwell told her. "But she does have a deep cut on her wing from that thrice-cursed flying machine. It will need many stitches. Ragnar, can you find a big enough tractor over in Canning to carry her back to the Sick Barn?"

"Carry her back?" Tyler was amazed. "Where can you find anything that big?"

"You would be surprised," Ragnar said. "Meseret is not so heavy as she looks. Her bones are hollow, like a bird's."

"But first, I suppose, you should take the other devil machine and return these children to their own home," Mr. Walkwell told Ragnar. "It will be dawn soon."

The Carrillos walked back to the farmhouse yet again, this time with Tyler, and silent Colin, wiping his eyes on his sleeve. Mr. Walkwell carried exhausted Lucinda on his back, her head nodding. Ragnar had the backpack with the dragon's egg in one hand and the briefcase full of money in the other.

"Seems like you guys must have had a pretty interesting summer," said Steve Carrillo.

"You could say that," Tyler agreed. "Yeah, I guess 'interesting' would sum it up pretty well."

CHAPTER 30

ONE IN THE OVEN

"Well," said Gideon Goldring, wrapped in a clean bath-robe and looking like an ancient king as he stared down the length of the breakfast table, "I knew it was going to be a big morning, what with our guests heading back home today—but I didn't expect things to be quite *this* exciting."

The briefcase full of money was in his lap. Meseret's egg sat in a nest of towels at the center of the table as if it was the main dish. The official story, constructed in haste, was that the she-dragon had sensed where her mate had taken the egg, broken out of the Sick Barn in fury, and recaptured it. The injury to her wing from the helicopter blade was now a battle wound from a scuffle with Alamu.

Lucinda didn't like having to lie, especially about things this big. Unable to look at Uncle Gideon, she turned and looked at Colin Needle, who was also avoiding Gideon's eye. Or perhaps it was the gaze of his mother, sitting at Gideon's right hand, that he was avoiding. Whichever was the case, Colin had a pale, sickly look, and for the first time since Haneb had told her of Colin's role in the theft of Meseret's egg she felt sorry for the older boy. He had been stupid and reckless and arrogant, but she believed him when he said the farm was important to him.

Gideon looked at the briefcase again, then at the egg, and shook his head in disbelief. "My goodness. I can't get over it. A dragon fight, attempted industrial espionage, and I slept through it all." He turned to Ragnar. "How is Meseret?"

The blond-bearded man laughed in a hollow way. He was still wearing the same dirty, sweat-stained clothes from the night before. "She is sleeping. We've given her more medicine. The tractor man should have a loader and a trailer ready this afternoon—I'll bring them back after I take the children to the train station. We'll have her back in the barn by tonight."

"And the damage?"

"We will be able fix everything, I think." Mr. Walkwell was leaning in the doorway, dressed and looking almost normal again. He had not bothered to put his newspaper-stuffed boots back on: his hooves stuck out the bottom of his pant legs. "But it will take time to replace the things for animal medicine and put up new shelves in the Sick Barn. Most are ruined."

Gideon suddenly laughed. "I was going to say it will take money we don't have—but we *do* have it now." He patted the briefcase. "Mercy me. As you can tell, I'm quite surprised by all this!"

"We all are, Gideon," said Mrs. Needle with chilly sweetness. "We all are!"

Another long silence dropped over the table. Lucinda wondered how long it would be until Mrs. Needle squeezed the entire story out of Colin. She had drugged Lucinda and set a vicious, unnatural animal on Tyler—goodness only knew what else she could do. And she was Colin's mother! No wonder he acted like he did. It turned Lucinda's stomach.

"My only sadness," Gideon said at last, "is that we have the egg back so we can study it, but we still we have no baby dragons and no idea of what the problem is."

Something tickled Lucinda's memory but stayed just out of reach.

"I wish you would let me take a hand, Gideon," said Mrs. Needle. Her hand came to rest on Uncle Gideon's arm like an ivory spider. "After all, Walkwell and the Norseman have failed three times now to keep an egg alive. There are charms that I know, herbs I could give her that ensure healthy births in cows and sheep and even poultry. . . ."

"There is nothing wrong with my care of these animals," said Mr. Walkwell in a flat, angry voice.

Suddenly Lucinda remembered. "Wait! Maybe the egg *isn't* dead!"

"What nonsense are you talking, child?" demanded Mrs. Needle. "Leave these things to your elders."

"Just a moment, Patience," Gideon said, shaking his arm loose from her clutch as he turned to Lucinda. "What do you mean?"

She told them how the dragon's thoughts had seemed to stream through her mind as she rode her, most of them quite strange and alien, but some of them so clear that she felt sure she had understood Meseret's meaning. "She was thinking about the egg—she didn't think it was dead, just that it needed . . . something to start it moving."

"Quickening, it is called," said Mrs. Needle with a certain cold authority. "But what does that matter? The conceptus has been lifeless each time. There is no life to quicken."

"It's just . . ." Now Lucinda was embarrassed. What had seemed so clear when she had touched the dragon's thoughts now seemed strange and dubious when she had to explain it, especially with Mrs. Needle staring daggers at her. "It just felt like she thought there was something she was supposed to *do*. She thought about breathing on it—breathing fire. But there was something wrong with the shell. Meseret needs to eat something to make the shell . . . I don't know, *right*. Some kind of dirt, or rocks, or . . . something."

"Some kind of dirt?" Mrs. Needle summoned a tight smile. "Surely you misunderstood, Lucinda. After all, you were terrified—struggling for your life . . ."

"Now, hold on, Patience," said Gideon. "Animals eat all kinds of things to help themselves. Remember when we kept losing the first basilisks until we found out they needed rocks in their stomach to grind up the bones of their prey?" He turned to Lucinda and Tyler. "They eat mice and lizards and whatnot—just gulp 'em down, swallow 'em whole," he informed them with a certain relish, then looked around the room. "Where's Haneb? He's the one that came with the dragons—if anyone'll know, he will."

"He did not want to come in to breakfast," said Ragnar.

Of course he didn't, Lucinda thought. *He's afraid he's in trouble.*

"I will find him," said Mr. Walkwell. It was a pleasure to see him turn and go out the door so swiftly, so gracefully, instead of limping like an accident victim. She hoped he would keep his boots off from now on—around the farm, anyway.

Mr. Walkwell returned in only a few minutes with Haneb beside him, looking as though he was trying to become half his ordinary size.

"Haneb, what are you cowering for, boy?" Gideon

boomed. "We need your help. We want to know about what the dragons ate back in your country." He turned to Lucinda and Tyler. "It's part of Turkey now, but a long time ago Haneb's people, the Hittites, had much of it to themselves."

Haneb still looked startled and fearful. "Ate?"

"Yes, ate, confound it! Did they eat stones? Anything unusual like that?"

He kept his head down as he thought, his hair masking the scars on his face. He had worked hard to avoid Lucinda's gaze. "No stones," he said at last.

"Nothing strange at all?"

Haneb winced. "I am sorry, Master Gideon. I am thinking." He frowned and looked as though he was about to burst into tears. "Sometimes they ate Earth-flax . . . ," he said at last.

"Earth-flax? What is it? Describe it!" Gideon demanded.

Haneb waved his hands. "It is like ordinary flax, but it grows in the rock, not in the ground. You can make cloth of it and the cloth cannot be burned."

"By God, he's got it!" shouted Gideon, making Haneb jump so badly that only Mr. Walkwell's steadying hand kept him from falling over. "*Asbestos!* My goodness, Lucinda, you're right!"

"I am?"

"The mother dragons must eat it to make their eggs fire-resistant. Then they heat the eggs up. Some animals lay eggs and sit on 'em—dragons turn on their internal flamethrowers and quick-roast 'em!" Gideon smacked the table and scowled. "But what are we going to do now? How can we find out whether it can still be hatched? We don't have any asbestos. We ripped it all out a few years ago. Had to, or the inspection boys would have been down on us from the county." He shook his head. "I wish we'd saved some. . . ."

"Meseret won't breathe on anything for a while, anyway," Ragnar pointed out. "The medicine has made her sleep."

"Perhaps we could make a sort of flamethrower from pipes and the blacksmith bellows Mr. Walkwell uses to fix the wagon," Colin said excitedly. He seemed to have forgotten that a short while ago his entire future had hung by a thread. "But we'd have to paint the egg with something that would work as well as asbestos . . ."

A throat was loudly cleared. Everybody turned to see Sarah standing in the doorway with Pema, Azinza, and the cavegirl, Ooola, who had spent the last several days following them like a wide-eyed feral cat. Ooola caught sight of Tyler and smiled a brilliant smile at him.

Sarah's round cheeks were flushed red, but if she was embarrassed to be the center of attention she still spoke strongly and plainly. "If you want something warmed but not burned, why not try talking to the people who do that every day? The girls and I will take some of that very nice

400

paper made of hammered metal . . ."

"Aluminum foil, it is called," said Azinza with queenly condescension.

"Yes, aluminum foil, and we will wrap it around the egg as though it was a plump turkey. Then we will put it in the oven where we can make it just as hot as we choose for as long as we choose." She shrugged. "If it does not offend any of you, that is."

After a moment's startled silence, Gideon laughed and clapped his hands. "Wonderful! Sarah, you are a genius. That is just what we will do. I should say about four hundred degrees . . ."

"Perhaps three hundred," Sarah said kindly. "It will take longer, but be safer."

"As you say, as you say." Gideon struggled up from his chair, waving a piece of waffle on the end of a fork. "To the kitchen!"

Tyler and Lucinda were packed but reluctant to leave, although it was beginning to get close to the time when they'd have to. They hung around the kitchen, as did most of the rest of the farm's inhabitants, all finding excuses to make frequent visits to the scene of the experiment. Even Haneb worked up the courage to come watch. At last, about two hours after they had first put the shiny bundle into the oven, Sarah cracked the door, peered in, and said, "I think something moved!"

She and Ragnar, both wearing oven mitts, wrestled the egg out onto a bed of towels on the floor and began to peel off the aluminum foil. A spiderweb crack had formed on the top. As Lucinda and her brother stared, it bulged in the center, and then a piece of the shell popped loose and fell to the towel. She could just hear the cracking of the shell over everyone's murmuring voices. She wondered if the heat was necessary to make the egg brittle enough for the baby to break it.

Another piece fell off, then another, and a moment later the whole top of the egg cracked loose and swung outward as though hinged. A head snaked out that was no bigger than a small dog's, a tiny version of Meseret with a blunter snout, but with colors that were brighter than hers, horizontal stripes of black and gold. The infant dragon pulled itself awkwardly out of the wreckage of the eggshell and walked a few staggering steps on its wing-pinions before stopping to rest, its throat pulsing in and out, its striped tail coiled around it. The golden eyes looked blearily around, then seemed to focus on Lucinda. For a moment, she could almost feel its simple, wordless thought:

?

No, I'm not your mother, she tried her best to tell the newborn. *You'll meet her soon.*

Someone put a hand on Lucinda's shoulder. It was Gideon, his hair standing up again so that he looked like a scarecrow that had been out in the wind too long. He had his other hand on Tyler and an expression on his face so strange that it gave Lucinda shivers. "I have not treated the two of you as well as I should have," he said. Everyone in the kitchen fell silent. Gideon cleared his throat and continued. "But this . . . the young dragon we thought we'd never see . . . it makes me realize . . ."

As Gideon fell silent again, someone made a noise like a grunt of pain. Lucinda saw Colin Needle standing half in shadow, half in sunlight from one of the big windows, watching. He had his arms wrapped tightly around himself and even from across the kitchen Lucinda could almost *feel* his envy and unhappiness.

Tyler suddenly stood up and said, "Uncle Gideon, I . . . I almost forgot to tell you. I found something in the library. And I wonder if it's anything you recognize." He held out his hand.

Lucinda, as surprised as anyone else, stared at Tyler's fingers as they opened to reveal a bit of sparkle. Gideon said, "What? What is it? In the library, you say?"

"Yes. Near the portrait of Octavio."

Gideon took the shining thing from Tyler's hand and stared at it intently. Everyone in the kitchens craned their necks to see. Gideon held up the golden locket on its slender gold chain. "You found it?" he said, his voice little more than a hoarse whisper. "Was it hidden somewhere?"

Tyler hesitated, looking like he wanted to get something just right. "No, not hidden. It was right out in the open. Like somebody . . . wanted it to be found."

It seemed that all his years had caught up with Gideon at once. His lip trembled and his eyes were wet with tears. "It's . . . it's hers!" he said. "The necklace I gave her. Grace, oh, my beautiful Grace." He lifted the necklace with trembling hands and kissed it. "It's a sign—she sent it to me through the Fault Line somehow. It means she's still alive and she wants me to know it." Tyler was squirming uncomfortably, but Gideon didn't notice. "Bless you, boy. Oh, thank God, you've brought me the greatest treasure of all—my Grace is alive." Gideon Goldring crouched down and took Tyler and Lucinda by the hand. Lucinda couldn't even look at him. She was ashamed of all the lies they were telling him. After a moment she pulled away, and Tyler did too, but Gideon was oblivious.

"I fell in love with her when she was just a girl," the old man said, his voice hoarse. "But I didn't realize it. Only when she had grown up could I finally understand the feelings I had. But her grandfather—old Octavio—fought against us for so long. He didn't want his hired hand marrying his granddaughter." Gideon laughed. "That's all I was to him! Just the young man he'd hired to help him grow crystals. It took years for him to accept me . . . accept us. And then, just when it finally seemed we would be happy, I lost her.

"I still don't know what happened. I had left the farm for the evening and so had Octavio, who had gone off in his own car. The fool was too old to drive—we'd told him that a dozen times but he was too stubborn to listen. So we'd left Grace alone. When I came back late I found my grandfather-in-law's car half off the driveway into the undergrowth, and Octavio himself lying beside it, dead of a heart attack. Grace was gone—I couldn't find her anywhere. I don't know whether she'd found her grandfather and just wandered off in a daze or it was just a terrible coincidence.

"Then Simos found her tracks in the dust of the silo— tracks that disappeared at the Fault Line. Worst of all, the Continuascope was just lying there, as if she had dropped it before she stepped into the Fault. Without it, she was lost with no hope of finding her way back. . . ."

Gideon fell silent again for a long moment, but she could hear his breath hitching. Lucinda, like others in the room, found herself shifting uncomfortably. The poor man!

"But now, thanks to you," Gideon said suddenly, "I know for certain that she is still alive—that she's trying to communicate with me!" He stood up, throwing his arms wide. "And we have a baby dragon! Tyler and Lucinda, bringing you two to Ordinary Farm just might be the best thing I have done in years!" He reached out and captured them again, pulling them into an uncomfortable, bony hug. The ancient bathrobe smelled like talcum powder and sweat. "Bless you both! Please come back to us soon—next summer for certain—and perhaps you could even visit us at the holidays."

Ragnar seemed to take pity on the two of them being squeezed until Lucinda thought she would pass out. "They will miss their train, Gideon," he reminded their host.

The old man loosened his grip. Behind him, Mrs. Needle was smiling, that smile of hers that never reached her eyes. "Oh yes," the dark-haired woman said. "Do take care of yourselves until we see you two again. It is such a very dangerous world out there."

That doesn't sound like a warning, Lucinda thought. *It sounds like a promise.*

Mrs. Needle was making sure she and her brother knew they had an enemy, one who would not give up the farm without a fight.

"Oh, we'll definitely remember to stay safe," Lucinda said, then looked right into the frigid gray eyes and smiled back at Mrs. Needle. It was tentative at first, but after a moment it became much easier. And Lucinda's smile didn't reach as far as her own eyes, either.

CHAPTER 31

THE REAL WORLD

Tyler persuaded Ragnar to take the old truck on a detour to Cresta Sol farm before they went to the station. As they drew up outside, with Ragnar fretting about them missing their train as nervously as their mother had all those weeks ago, Carmen, Steve, and Alma spilled through the white iron gate and ran up the road toward them. Tyler and Lucinda got out of the truck.

"We came to say good-bye," Tyler told them.

Nobody was smiling. Carmen's long hair was blowing in her eyes.

"You have to promise us," Tyler said. "*Us* this time, not just Ragnar and Mr. Walkwell. You have to promise to

407

keep the secrets. Otherwise . . ."

"We know," said Alma.

"We talked about it," said Carmen.

"Yeah, we understand," said Steve. "Because otherwise everything will change. For everyone."

"We swear we won't tell anyone," said Alma, her little face solemn. "Not ever. No matter what."

"Don't forget to write, Lucinda," Carmen said. "And you guys come back soon. So we have someone we *can* talk to about it!"

None of the children could think of much else to say— their hearts were too full. They all hugged, then Tyler and Lucinda climbed back into the truck.

"Did that all really happen?" Lucinda asked. "All of it?"

"You keep saying that." Tyler was looking out the train compartment window at the fields and houses going past and trying to think. There was still so much about the summer he didn't understand. "Of course it happened."

"But look," his sister said. "Look, Tyler!"

"I *am* looking."

"That's not what I mean." She rapped her hand on the window. "Look at what's out there—the real world. That's where we live. Not in a television show, not in a movie, not in a . . . a storybook! Why us?" She leaned in close, lowering her voice so that the man in the baseball cap and the lady with the bag full of knitting materials across the aisle couldn't possibly hear. "Tyler, I *rode* on a *dragon*."

Tyler grinned. "You dangled off a dragon, screaming like a baby, you mean."

"Shut up! You know what I'm saying!" She lowered her voice again. "You jumped into a mirror. You went to the ice age and came back with a cavegirl. She's from, like, a million years ago or something, and she has a *crush* on you, Tyler!"

"That's bull! She does not. Besides, what about Colin the Criminal? Seems like *he* rather fancies *you*, old chap."

Lucinda grabbed his arm so hard it actually hurt. "Don't change the subject—you know what I'm saying. How can we just go back to school like none of it ever happened?"

Tyler was quiet for a long time. "We're astronauts," he said at last. "No, we're *secret* astronauts."

"What are you talking about?"

"Well, astronauts go to the moon, or Mars, or whatever, then they come back and they still have to go to the grocery store, right? They still have to mow the lawn, and, I don't know, eat and go to the bathroom and stuff, right? They can't just say, 'Hey, I walked on the moon, I don't have to eat and drive a car and do normal stuff anymore.' Right?"

"I guess so. But everyone knows about them. They get parades and people interview them on television. They don't have to pretend like everything's normal—because everything *isn't* normal. It isn't!"

To his astonishment, Tyler saw that Lucinda's eyes were full of tears. After a moment's hesitation he grabbed her hand. "No, it's not," he told her. "But that's the secret part. Like spies. They can't come back from a spy mission and say, 'The most interesting thing happened when I was in the underground hideout of Professor Evil Guy . . . ' because it's *secret*, right? Just like the farm. And we have to keep it that way." He squeezed her hand before letting it go. "It's ours, Luce—Ordinary Farm is ours now. We belong there, we earned it, and no one can take it away from us. And we're going back too. But only if nobody finds out."

She took a deep, ragged breath. "But I'll go crazy if I can't talk to anyone about it."

"We're asking the Carrillos to do the same thing, aren't we? But they have each other and you have me. You can talk to me. It's our secret, yours and mine."

Lucinda sat back against the seat. She rubbed her eyes dry with the hem of her shirt. "But what am I going to tell my friends when they ask me what I did this summer? And what are we going to tell Mom?"

Tyler put his knees up on the back of the seat in front of him and pulled a notebook out of his backpack. It was covered with scribbled notes. "We'll make stuff up. Right now, in fact—we've got a couple of hours. We'll write it down and that way we'll always be . . . what's that word?"

"Consistent." His big sister looked at him with something like admiration. "Wow, Tyler, you really thought about this."

"We have to, Luce," he said, finding a blank page. "This is the most important secret in the world." He looked up. "Now, did we go on hayrides?"

Mom was only a couple of minutes late. She was wearing sunglasses and looked very tan—kind of glamorous, Tyler had to admit. She was wearing a skirt, too, which wasn't all that usual.

"There you are!" she squealed, running toward them. She wrapped her arms around them—she was shorter than at the beginning of the summer, Tyler couldn't help noticing, which meant he was taller—and gave them a hard hug. "Oh, I missed you two so much! Did you have a good time? Why didn't you write?"

"We did," Lucinda said. "Well, I did. About four or five times—didn't you get them?"

"I was traveling, remember?" She hugged Tyler. "Look at you! My big man!"

"You look great, Mom," Lucinda said as she got her own individual squeeze. "Really tan."

"Come along, you can tell me all your stories. I'm double-parked so we have to hurry!"

Mom stopped in front of an unfamiliar, shiny car. She lifted the keys and pushed a button and the trunk popped open.

411

"Whoa," Tyler said. "Is this new?"

Mom giggled like a girl and waved her hand. "Oh, it's not ours. I borrowed it from Roger because mine's in the shop."

"Roger?" Lucinda frowned as she got in. "Who's Roger?"

"I met him at the retreat. He didn't even show up until the last week—lucky me I was still there!" She laughed again. "He's so nice. You'll love him!"

Lucinda looked at Tyler. Tyler looked back. He rolled his eyes, and his sister seemed to know just what he meant: Mom was on another one of her "This time everything's going to be great!" freak-outs, which usually happened when she met a new man. Well, it was better than coming home to find her depressed and crying all over the place.

"So tell me about your summer!" Mom said, weaving in and out of traffic in a way that made Tyler wish he had a joystick. "Did you have fun? Did you learn things? What did you do?"

Tyler looked at Lucinda and smiled. She smiled back. "Pretty much what you'd expect on a farm," he said. "Chores. Animals. Early to bed, early to rise. Oh, and hayrides—right, Luce?"

"Oh yeah," Lucinda agreed. "Lots and lots of hayrides."